Finding Alison

D0714882

Finding Alison

Deirdre Eustace

BLACK & WHITE PUBLISHING

First published 2017
by Black & White Publishing Ltd
29 Ocean Drive, Edinburgh EH6 6JL

1 3 5 7 9 10 8 6 4 2   17 18 19 20

ISBN: 978 1 78530 107 0

Copyright © Deirdre Eustace 2017

The right of Deirdre Eustace to be identified as the
author of this work has been asserted by her in accordance with the
Copyright, Designs and Patents Act 1988.

All rights reserved.
No part of this publication may be reproduced, stored
in a retrieval system, or transmitted in any form, or by any means,
electronic, mechanical, photocopying, recording or otherwise,
without permission in writing from the publisher.

This novel is a work of fiction. The names, characters
and incidents portrayed in it are of the author's imagination.
Any resemblance to actual persons, living or dead, events or
localities is entirely coincidental.

A CIP catalogue record for this book is available from the British Library.

Supported by
The National Lottery®
through Creative Scotland

CREATIVE SCOT LAND
ALBA | CHRUTHACHAIL

Typeset by Iolaire, Newtonmore
Printed and bound by CPI Group (UK) Ltd., Croydon, CR0 4YY

For
Tom Walsh
7th July 1962 - 26th October 1997
Your wisdom, courage and humanity continue to inspire

Prologue

And so it began – like all things that shape and pattern our lives – softly, quietly: a faint tap-tapping at the bedroom window hauling her from the depths of an exhausted sleep. She turned on her side, half-conscious now, tugged the pillow down over her ear. Tap, tap, tap – a stray tail of Virginia creeper loosened by last night's storm, dancing on the glass. And then what sounded like her name – 'Alison!' – echoing against the window pane before falling away again. She stretched a heavy arm across to the right-hand side of the bed. Still no Sean. 'Alison! Alison!' again, and the tapping louder now, more urgent. Eyelids fighting the pull of sleep, she hoisted herself up onto her elbows. 'Alison?' A male voice. Sean. She sighed, slowly waking, remembering. Sean. He must have forgotten his key in his hurry to be away last night. Palming her hair from her face, she felt for the bedside lamp, her eyes tightening at its glare. Immediately the tapping ceased, the heavy crunch of feet on gravel disappearing towards the front door. Pushing back the bedclothes, she eased her toes slowly onto the floor. The cold of the bare wooden boards gripped her feet, banishing what remained of sleep. Her eyes found the clock: 6.50 a.m. Another lock-in at Phil's, no doubt. She ran a hand over her eyes, her forehead, the memory of last night's argument heating her temper. Sean would have a skinful now, talk tumbling out of him, incomprehensible, words thick and tripping over each other in their hurry to be heard when he hadn't had a single one for her when it mattered, when it was needed.

Let him wait, she thought, unhooking her dressing gown from the back of the door, buttoning it slowly. The night he'd put her through. She padded barefoot to the hall. The cold of the storm had seeped into the house. She huddled into herself, hugged her arms against it.

Reaching for her key, she glanced out through the porch window. The sensor above the front door threw an arc of pure light into the darkness, its starkness accentuating the pallor of Father Ger's face against the pitch black of his coat collar; the deep knot between his brows, the tight set of his thin lips. It fell too on Kathleen, picking out the gold in her bowed blonde head, the tight clasp of her entwined fingers, shadowing the dent that they made there, pressed to her lips. 'Maryanne!' Her breath caught on the name, her mother-in-law's face flashing before her as she fumbled with the key. Something has happened to Maryanne and of course Sean's not even here when he's needed! She gave the key a second quick turn. On the springing of the lock she took a deep breath, held it as she pressed down on the handle, felt the door yield.

'Father, Kathleen, what's … Kathleen?'

Biting down on her lower lip, her chin trembling, Kathleen, eyes wide with warning, stared straight at her, her head shaking from side to side, as if in slow motion.

2

'Kathleen?' Alison took a step towards her. It wasn't the wind rushing through the open door that chilled her, it was a knowing, deep inside her, an emptying out.

'Alison, Alison,' the priest was holding her by the arm now, urging her backwards. 'Let's step inside, good girl, in out of the cold.'

'Maryanne – is it Maryanne? Has she – has something…'

'Maryanne's fine.' He squeezed her arm in reassurance as they stepped back into the hall.

'But what then? Who…'

Kathleen's arms were around her now, tight, the damp of the rain from her coat causing Alison to shiver.

'Oh, Alison…' Kathleen pulled back slightly, looked up into her friend's wary face. 'Alison, it's Sean.'

'Come on, Alison, we'll take a seat.' The priest took a step towards the sitting-room door, turned on the light.

'Sean?' She looked down at Kathleen, her brow knotted in confusion.

'Please,' Father Ger insisted, and Kathleen, taking her hand, led Alison through the door to the couch.

'But, wait a second, I don't understand.' Alison, smiling now, her thick red curls dancing with the shake of her head. Kathleen sat down beside her, clasped her free hand to Alison's tensed shoulder.

'Sean's down at… What, Kathleen? What? – oh my God!' Her hand flying to her mouth, her green eyes flashing. 'He's driven the car, hasn't he, full and…'

'Sean is missing, Alison.' The priest's words were clear and level, as he squatted down on the rug before her. 'His boat's been found but as yet—' Alison's high laugh cut through his words. He bent his head, took a deep breath. 'Alison, please, listen to me.'

'No, Father, no, you listen to me.' She nodded her head as if to reassure, to encourage her own tentative smile. 'You see, Sean didn't go out yesterday evening. I know.' She squeezed Kathleen's hand. 'I checked.' Her smile widened, her eyes darting from one disbelieving face to the other. 'I went down to the pier – me and Hannah – around seven, when the wind got up. We drove back through the village. Sean's van was parked outside Phil's – he's not missing,' the ghost of a laugh tailing her words. The priest rested his arm on the coffee table, nodded to Kathleen. Kathleen's hand stole to Alison's cheek, turning her face gently to meet her eyes.

'Alison, please. Listen to me now, yeah? Sean—' Her lower lip began its tremble again, she shook her head, straightened her neck and shoulders. 'Sean left Phil's at eleven. The two Careys left with him.' She cleared her throat, began again. 'All three of them left the pub at eleven. The storm was well up.' Alison stared at her eyes, at her lips, moving, forming those words. 'They parted at the mouth of the pier. Sean said he was going down to check on something.'

'Well, of course he was,' Alison interrupted, her head held forward, her hand stroking the length of her neck. 'He'd have been worried that the mooring rope was secure.' Kathleen turned away to hide her fresh tears.

'Shrimp pots, Alison.' Her eyes studied the priest as he spoke, unbuttoning his coat. She was struck by the almost translucent white of his fingers, the neat, blunt fingernails. 'The Careys thought he meant the pots on the quay, not the ones he had out.' He pushed out the words, taking a seat on the couch beside her.

Alison's short laugh was laced with derision. She sat back in her seat, threw out her hands in exasperation. 'Oh, for heaven sake, Father! Out on the sea? Sean? On a night like that?' Eyebrows raised, she threw Kathleen a look of mock vexation. 'Sean's been on the sea since he was a boy, for Christ's sakes! Sorry, Father.' A nod to the priest. 'He'd never risk heading out on a night like that. Never. Not Sean, of all people.'

Another deep breath and the priest tried again, this time steeling his words with a little more conviction and authority. 'Brian Carthy saw him, Alison. Saw the green light on the starboard as he left the harbour. Around midnight.' He paused a moment, allowing his words to settle on her. Alison's lips clamped together as everything inside her tightened, closed. And then the cold of Kathleen's hands, finding hers. 'Young Joe O'Sullivan's mother raised the alarm about an hour ago,' the priest continued, softer now. 'It seems the poor lad saw the boat go down. But we can't make sense – he's too upset, unsure of what time…'

'No, no, it can't…'

'Alison, we'll find him.' Kathleen squeezed her hands tightly. 'The search is already underway, the helicopter and lifeboat have been called…'

'And the local boat is ready to launch at first light, weather permitting,' Father Ger encouraged, his heart sickened. No matter how many times he broke this news, it never got any easier. The false encouragement, the raising of hopes – only to see them shattered again. The anger that he knew would follow, at him, at God, the heart-breaking unanswerable questions. He ran a hand over his bare head, as if to offer it protection. 'The boat hit the rocks just to the left of the pier. He's close, Alison, you've got to have faith – he'll be found and safe by daylight, please God.'

'This is nonsense!' A hot anger roused her from her

stupor, propelling her from her seat. 'Absolute nonsense!' Her voice rose with her. 'Sean would never, do you hear? He would never! I'm, I'm getting dressed, I'm going down there to get him!' Eyes ablaze, she looked into their faces with almost disgust before turning to the voice at the door.

'Mam?' Still sleep-wrapped, Hannah shivered in her nightgown against the door jamb. 'Mam?' Running now, into Alison's open arms.

Fists of foam shivered in the headlights as they rounded the bend on the road above the harbour. Alison strained forward in the passenger seat, eyes trained on the sea. The horizon line was barely distinguishable in the bleak dawn light. Bleached of all colour by the storm's assault, the heavy grey sky stooped to meet a mackerel-backed sea of grey on greener-grey on black, the only break a narrow tear at the rim of the sky to the east, a watery light pouring down, like heaven, bleeding. The sea was falling back into a grudging sleep, lazily licking and frothing the cliffs, its gluttonous appetite almost sated. The wind continued its whip and hurl.

'We'll have to walk from here.' Father Ger eased the car onto the grass verge. 'The road to the pier is flooded. We'll take the cliff path.' Alison had the door open even before the car came to a halt, belting her coat as she ran towards the pier, the wind whipping her hair across her pinched face.

The boats in the harbour heaved and keeled to the dance of the water beneath them, groaning as their flanks collided. The fishermen had already gathered, boots and oilskins sodden and heavy, their urgent shouts flung back on them by the wind as they unknotted ropes and chains, two and three together, winding and fastening and tightening the

6

mooring ropes around the bollards, the boats like wild horses fighting their fettering. And all the time the constant chorus of the yacht masts, like a thousand tiny death knells announcing the inevitable.

Alison ran towards the storm wall, the icy water leaping its foam-littered top, salting and soaking her face, her hair. 'Sean? Sean?' Her shout smacked back in her face. Out beyond the harbour the little punt that the fishermen used to access the pier at low tide tossed and bobbed like a demented toy, the blue and white bow now visible, now gone, its rosary of orange buoys stretched tight in a sinister smile.

'Hey! Careful! Jesus!' The fisherman grabbed her arm, dragged her to safety as a massive white wave leaped the wall, sweeping a stack of empty fish boxes into the water. 'This way!' Her wild green eyes followed the nod of his head to the left, to the tight knot of men and women gathered on the cliff.

Fighting her way through them, breathless, she looked down into the water, her heart straining, heavier, heavier, mouth dry, her teeth finding the corner of her lip, biting down hard, her stomach seeming to heave and fall with the motion of the boat's bow, pitching and tilting against the unforgiving rocks. She felt arms close around her as the weakness spread upwards through her legs, her hips.

Then it burst like thunder over the cliff tops, its giant orange belly and urgent, ear-shattering roar piercing the grey, its mighty blades chopping, defying the wind. Seagulls sheltering in nooks high in the cliffs took to the wing beneath it as the chopper's search beam transformed the cliffs into a magnificent stage set, picking out their browns and golds and reds and the ancient greens of copper streaking the cliff face like giant tears.

7

'Sean!' The wind stole his name from her lips as her body crumbled.

The brandy stung her throat, its fire burning a path down into her darkness. She pulled the blanket tight around her shoulders.

' ... rest in your own bed ... call you when there's news ...' The conversation spun, broken, around her. The tea room in the Sea Safety Centre was crowded, hot, the babble loud and oppressive. She needed to be out, needed to be near him when he returned. She rose on unsteady feet, clasped the blanket tight at her neck.

'Alison, take it easy, you—'

'I'm fine, honestly.' Alison didn't even recognise the woman's face. 'I just need to get some air.'

'Wait then, I'll come out—'

'Thanks,' Alison replied, pressing the blanket into her hands, 'I'm fine on my own.' Holding the hand rail, she descended the stairs to the quay, her stomach threatening to heave with every shaking step.

'Joe?' He palmed his blue cap low on his head, turned back down the stairs. 'Joe! Wait, please!' He stood, head bowed, his foot kicking at the rail.

'What happened, Joe? Where's Sean – did you see him?'

'Gone.' The single word was wet, guttural.

'What?'

'Gone! Seany's gone!' Head dropped to his chest, a wail erupted from him, filling the stairwell.

'Leave him, Alison,' Father Ger, behind, hand on her shoulder. 'Go on, Joe, good lad, get yourself home now.'

'We'll find him, Joe, we'll find him,' Alison called, the tails of his too-long coat disappearing through the door. Poor

Joe. Poor innocent, senseless Joe. Sean's 'right-hand man', his pet since childhood. The absolute devastation in his child-like face ran a shiver right through her. How would he – with the mind and understanding of a ten-year-old – how could he ever even begin to understand all this? Her first tears stung, fell.

'I'll drop you back to the house, you need to—'

'I'm going nowhere.' She shook the priest's hand from her shoulder, continued her unsteady way down the stairs.

Out on the water then, cold hands grasping the bow rail, shouting his name against the roar of the helicopter above, her stomach long since emptied into the water. Exhausted eyes scanning every rock and cove, every inlet and stretch of sand, for a flash of colour, a movement, a sign. Anything. It couldn't end this way. No, Lord Jesus, no, not this way. The angry words she had flung at him in the heat of their passion echoed in her head. A selfish bastard she had called him, yelled at him to be gone, that he was no good to her anyway. Oh Sweet Jesus no, she pleaded to a god she had not believed in since childhood. This couldn't be the end, not after twenty-two years. Not Sean – not her childhood sweetheart, first love; her husband, the father of her child. She closed her eyes, bent her forehead to the cold of the metal rail. Please God, anything, I'll do anything. *Please, please, just give him back to me!*

Alison hardly saw the house that first week. With Hannah safely moved in with Maryanne, she only ever touched home to shower and change before heading back down to the pier. Returning to her bed for a few hours of fitful sleep when the search was called off for the night, then up again before dawn to start all over. The pies and casseroles

9

delivered by concerned neighbours littered the kitchen counters, untouched. Food was the last thing on her mind, a warm mug of soup from the volunteers at the quay enough to keep the cold at bay.

She hated being on the quay, itched all the time to be out on the water. To be nearer him. To be there, out there, in case the others would miss him waving from the safety of a cave, an inlet. She would be the one to find him. He was out there, waiting for her, and every minute spent on land was a precious moment wasted. Besides, she could no longer bear to listen to the hopelessness that had crept into their idle chatter. To watch the agony on the faces of those revisiting what had once been their own reality; their wounds freshly opened, staying close to her, as if she were one of them now. Well, she wasn't! Sean was missing, that's all. Missing. Not drowned.

'That's five now, in under three years,' she heard Ned Fleming announce, calling the death roll on his nicotined fingers, the two fishermen beside him crossing their chests in a silent acknowledgement of luck. And God save her from the likes of Pat Ryan, puffed up with importance in his rescue uniform, pontificating on the number of days it takes a body to sink, decompose, inflate, rise up and, if not spotted then, sink once again, forever. Well, she'd show them. Sean would show them, make them eat their words! And Maryanne. Above all, she could not understand Maryanne. Not once did the woman come to the pier – her only son, her only child, alone, out there. 'Let him rest' was the only answer she would make when Alison probed. 'Let him rest in the one place that he loved.'

* * *

Alison stood at the look-out post in the Sea Safety Centre, a mug of now cold tea cupped in her hands. She stared out at the blues and reds and yellows of the boats circling at a safe distance from the map of underwater rocks. Seagulls swooped and dived, slicing the wrinkled surface of the water. The rescue helicopter hovered above an outcrop to the left, where the sun greened the water. Her eyes watched keenly as two of the larger boats made an about-turn, pointed themselves in her direction. *Today*, she mouthed silently, *please let it be today*. Gulls keened at the mouth of the harbour, where the wind skimmed the sea's surface, making it move, like the twitching hide of a beast, crouching, waiting. The radio crackled to life behind her and she spun round, her heart swelling.

'Anything?' Mike Duggan held the receiver with both hands.

' ... box ... nets ... part of ... bilge keel ... nothing ... ' The words were strung together with static, her heart shrinking with every one.

She hadn't realised that her tears were falling until a hand proffered a tissue. 'Thanks ...' She held it beneath her nose, her eyes scanning across the water, across the exposed rocks and along each tiny inlet from the harbour to Benvoy. Nothing. She carried her mug to the sink, emptied it, watched the water run into and over it.

She turned for one last glance through that too familiar window. There were no boats, no helicopter; they were just a memory now. Only the little blue and white punt stationed outside the harbour wall, still, intact, two seagulls riding its stern.

The search had been scaled down in late November and then called off completely on the 8th of December. Last

11

year. How she had railed at them then – after all their time and effort and support – how she had flung their kindness and their sympathies back in their faces, vowing to prove them wrong.

There was an almost innocence to the bright May sunshine, she thought now, looking out, a certain naivety in the gentle lapping of the water, the clean-washed sand. The storm of that night, eight months ago now, would rage forever, she knew, somewhere deep inside her. But, it was time to accept she had lost. Sean wouldn't be coming back to her. Not today. Not ever. She dug her hands deep into her jacket pockets, turned from the sea.

'Ready?' Kathleen, her smile heavy with sadness, linked her arm, their footfalls on the metal staircase echoing through the emptiness.

Three Years Later

One

Maybe she had consciously decided never to speak again. Maybe she had had enough. Maybe the doctors were wrong when, in the absence of any medical reason, they had put her silence down to 'the trauma'. Maybe, because they hadn't known Maryanne before all this, they weren't taking into consideration the incredible strength and stubbornness of the woman – a woman who could survive all that she had and still find inside herself the courage and determination not only to go on but to find something beautiful about life, something worth living for.

Maybe, maybe, maybe. Head bowed, Alison retraced her steps along the polished parquet floor. If there was one thing she hated, it was waiting. Waiting for anything: traffic lights, a kettle to boil, life. Folding her arms tight at her waist, she stopped just left of the dining-room door and craned her neck to look inside. Still eating. She could see Maryanne's back at the top table. Alison's throat tightened as she took in the slackness in her shoulders, the droop of her white neck, the bow of the paper bib knotted at its nape, a bandage on a wounded swan. She watched a carer spoon-feed the elderly man opposite, her lips mouthing 'good man'. Alison was struck by the notion of an anti-crèche, a veritable pre-school for death, where people slowly unlearned all that life had taught them. Last Steps. No Steps. She turned, as swiftly from the idea as from the vista, her long legs carrying her quickly back to the chair inside the main door, her every step shadowed by a faint mouldering that the home's cheap disinfectant didn't quite mask.

The cane chair creaked in protest at its abrupt occupation. She swung one knee over the other, the uppermost foot continuing to step in the air, with an added circular flourish. She pulled her cardigan tight across her narrow chest, twisted the silver watch face up on her wrist. Ten to six. Hannah would be home from study by seven, she'd need to get back and fix something for tea. Her eyes strayed along the length of yellow corridor, resting on the wooden plaque on the wall opposite.

Sea View Care Home
WELCOME

She twisted a stray red curl around her index finger. God, what was she doing here? Again. This was becoming ridiculous. Okay, she had planned her visit this morning, but to find herself landed outside in the car park again just now – what for? What was it she expected to find here? Peace? Strength? Some kind of forgiveness? Fingers steepled, she cupped her palms over her nose and mouth, the warmth of her heavy outbreath encouraging her eyelids to fall.

'Back again? You'll surely have a bed in heaven!' Kathleen's soft white shoes made hardly a whisper as she approached.

'Kathleen, God, I was nearly…I didn't see you.'

16

Kathleen stepped closer, her smile dimming as she registered the bruise-like shadows under Alison's eyes, the pinched pale skin making her high cheek bones and narrow chin appear more prominent than ever. 'You look exhausted.' She placed a hand lightly on her friend's shoulder. 'Shouldn't you be at home, taking a rest? Mary-anne's not going anywhere.'

'Oh, I just thought I'd stop in and say goodnight.' She allowed her shoulders to relax with her sigh. 'I was worried – she just seemed more removed than ever this morning.'

'I know.' Kathleen nodded her understanding, waves of blonde hair bobbing in consensus around her ears. She touched the tip of her tongue to the groove on her upper lip – a remnant of childhood surgery – a habit Alison had so often seen her employ as she sought for time, for the right words. Bending her knees, Kathleen dropped to a half-squat, her brown eyes meeting Alison's. 'But just think of what she's been through. Imagine at that age – at any age – waking in the dead of night to find some stranger rifling your home. It'd be enough to finish most people off. But you know your mother-in-law better than anyone. Maryanne's a fighter. She'll be fine, just give her some time, Alison, you'll see.'

'But after three months – surely there should be some change. And since she's come here, I don't know, it's as if she's moving further and further away from us.'

'She's adjusting, that's all. You know how fiercely inde-pendent Maryanne's always been. It's one of the hardest things to lose, you know, your independence. I've seen it so often here over the years, patients retreating back into themselves. It's a kind of protection, I suppose, gives them time to come to terms with things.'

'I just feel like I'm losing her, Kathleen. Losing my last

link with Sean and I can't ...' Alison shook back her head, shook back the tears that had gathered, ready to spill.

Kathleen took a deep breath. 'Hey, come on. I'm telling you, that lady is not going anywhere. And while she's in here – and being very well looked after, might I add' – her smile was lit with devilment – 'you need to be looking after yourself. And Hannah.'

'Oh, don't talk to me about Hannah. Honestly, I'm at my wits' end with that girl. She's just constantly angry and sour and ready to jump down my throat and into an argument every time I dare to open my mouth.'

'Hormones! Weren't we all there once?' Kathleen squeezed her friend's shoulder and straightened. 'At nearly fourteen, the poor girl's at the very epicentre of it.'

'She's still hanging with that O'Neill guy.'

'What?' Kathleen's eyebrows shot upwards.

'Oh, she swears blind she's not seeing him, but I'm not a total fool. I see the frantic texting.' Alison hauled her bag from the floor and pushed herself up by the armrests. 'And I've caught her out more than once with her cock-and-bull stories about being "round at Aoife's".'

As Alison stood to her full height, a full head and neck above Kathleen, her friend's nose registered a faint hint of alcohol. They turned and walked in the direction of the dayroom, a mixture of anger and something like pity swelling below Kathleen's chest. *Oh, come on,* she scolded herself, *when hasn't any one of us not sought comfort in a few drinks? Alison was strong, capable – look at what she'd come through so far, for heaven's sake – if anyone was entitled to a few jars, surely it was her?* 'I wouldn't have given that more than a week. What can he want with a fourteen-year-old? Sure, he must be good on twenty!'

18

'I can well imagine exactly what he's after and poor Hannah, you know, maddening and all as she is, there's still a lot of the child in her. She doesn't realise she's so vulnerable. Just the type to be led…Oh God, I dread the thought of the summer, Kathleen, all that hanging around time. I wish I could just get her out of here.'

'A break would do you both good. Have you thought about a holiday?' Kathleen's heart went out to Hannah. That poor girl had been through so much in her short years. She'd been an absolute pet with Sean – his 'little shrimp', as he was fond of calling her. Even now, over three years on, Kathleen could feel her throat tightening when she remembered Hannah in those first months: those big lost eyes – Sean's eyes – staring out into a world that no longer made sense, a world where the carefree magic of childhood had been replaced by loneliness and a terrifying uncertainty. A scrawny little thing for her age, she would follow Alison around like a ghost, constantly watching, wondering, waiting for her mother to come back to her. The poor child might as well have lost them both. Kathleen had done her utmost to distract her with treats and outings, and in time, when Hannah had finally got to a place where she could sleep without the security of knowing her mother was near, she would spend overnights with Kathleen and her son, the child that she had been, slowly, little by little, returning. But no matter Kathleen's efforts, something had changed in Hannah on that night, had put a kink or a knot in her young spirit, and Alison's surrender to her own grief had only served to tighten and fix it like a wall between them. They had lost so much more than Sean; they had lost so much of each other too, and it broke Kathleen's heart to see the distance that continued to grow between them.

'Holiday?' Alison chided, 'it's hard enough trying to live one week to the next.'

'Tell me about it. My hours have been cut back again this week – and they expect us to do twice the work when we're here! Still, I suppose I should be thankful I have a job at all the way things are going. And I firmly believe that if you prioritise—'

'Prioritise? With what?' Alison scoffed. 'Ed Resources informed me last week that they won't be renewing my proofing contract. Apparently schools just don't have the funds to invest in books outside of the must-haves on the curriculum. Their business has completely dried up.'

'And what about Chapters? They've always been pretty dependable, haven't they?'

'They're feeling the pinch, too, taking care of the bulk of the work in-house. The only editing they're outsourcing at the moment is the more technical stuff – not my area, sadly. The bills, I'm afraid, are the only constant these days.' Alison's forced humour only heightened her desperation. 'And now the bloody mortgage rate is set to rise again.'

Kathleen's tongue sought out the groove in her upper lip. She knew only too well the drudgery and constant worry of battling to get by. Her part-time wage as a carer hardly put a dent in her bills. And she still felt the burn of accusation in old Loretta Flynn's eyes every Thursday when she cashed her single parent payment at the post office. God, you'd think the woman was paying it out of her own pocket, the old witch! She often regretted striking out for independence, shackling herself to a thirty-year mortgage so that Jamie could grow up like other kids, in a house his mother owned, so that no one could point the finger, whisper behind her back about all she had 'handed to her'. Of course back then she'd presumed that she'd always have as many hours work as she wanted. There'd be a fat chance of her ever getting a mortgage now! Still, she had her home and she had Jamie – her beautiful, healthy, bouncing boy and now, of course, she had Rob too. Rob. She couldn't keep him out of her mind for more than five minutes! 'What about an interest-only payment? Lots of people are going for that.'

'I'd say I was first in the queue. And first to be refused. Those banks have an awful lot to answer for.' Alison halted mid-step, as if every ounce of her energy was needed to fuel the anger in her voice. 'I called in again about an over-draft last week and it took everything I had in me not to reach across that polished desk and strangle that pompous git of a manager with his own silk tie! He refused, point-blank. Knowing full well that Sean's life insurance and the mortgage protection are set to come in down the line. Money they're guaranteed. And meantime they expect me to carry on paying through the nose with money I just haven't got!'

'That seven-year rule is such a load of nonsense. I mean, what more evidence do they need, for heaven's sake? There must be some way around it – have you ever thought of talking to a TD? Or maybe asking the insurance company for some kind of interim payment? I mean, surely it's all the same to them whether they pay out now or—'

'Kathleen? Can you give me a hand to lift Sadie, please?'

Alison and Kathleen's heads swung in the direction of the brusque call. Standing a little down the corridor, the nurse's smile was duck tight, her impatience evident in the curt swing of her hip back through the bedroom doorway.

'Coming!' Kathleen rolled her eyes. 'Better go. Look, I'm meeting Rob tonight but—'

'Oh, tell him hello from me!' Alison's smile was wide with genuine warmth. Rob, with his big grin and his even bigger heart, was the best thing that had ever happened to Kathleen. She'd been so broken after all that business with Jamie's father, the light had totally gone out of her. And then, after Sean died, the way she had put aside her own heartache and flung herself into taking care of herself and Hannah. Without her, God only knows what would have become of them. Alison had no great recollection of those first weeks, but in the months that followed, when all the other support had dwindled away, Kathleen had been her one constant. Still was. When others crossed the street, avoided asking her how she was because they had tired of hearing it, Kathleen probed and listened and hugged and healed. When Hannah became too much to handle, Kathleen scooped her away, gave her the love and the nourishment that had withered at its root inside Alison. She had saved them. And even now, having her working here in the home, knowing she would keep a special eye out for Maryanne, was another blessing. Alison owed her so much. Bad as things were, she had a good friend in Kathleen, a friend she desperately needed and if she wasn't careful she could lose her too – how often had she postponed their plans lately, on several occasions failing to turn up at all. Plus, Kathleen had a life now, with Rob. They were no longer the two singletons united against the world, against *men*. Alison smiled. It was great to see Kathleen back to her old self. So full of fun and mischief. Rob had brought that spark in her back to life and it literally shone out of her.

'Will do, and listen, give me a shout on your way out and we'll arrange a time for a proper chat.' Heaving her hip, Kathleen mimicked the nurse's smile, turned and was gone.

With one arm folded over her chest and a hand clasped over her mouth to hide her mirth, Alison watched her friend quick-step down the corridor, her miniature, tightly packed frame moving with an energy that always put Alison in mind of a playful pup bursting with life. It mightn't be a bad idea to get Kathleen to have a chat with Hannah, talk some sense into her about that O'Neill creep, Alison thought. Kathleen had always had a way with Hannah, a knack at getting into her space, getting her to open up where Alison would only be met with a stone wall. It'd be worth a try, she sighed to herself as Kathleen paused at the bedroom door, gave one last exaggerated tip of her hip, raised her hand in salute and disappeared inside. Alison took a deep breath, put on her best smile and turned into the dayroom.

* * *

William Hayden sat on the storm wall, coffee Thermos in hand. He watched the incoming tide lick and wash the grey rocks in a lavish, languorous foreplay before swallowing them completely, leaving no evidence that they had ever existed. He ran his fingers through his grey hair, squinted towards the west where the sinking sun split a bank of grey cloud like a freshly sliced salmon, setting the horizon ablaze in its dying glory. Life and death. The coming and the going. Nature acted it out every day in a host of different ways and yet, when it came, people so often greeted death with stupefaction, denial, utter disbelief. As if it were the most unnatural and unheard of abomination. As if it had not been their one certainty, the one companion that had walked with them from the womb. A lone gull skimmed the sea's silver surface, his plaintive call echoing back loudly upon him as he soared to a nook in the high cliff. The night would bring rain.

William threw what remained of his coffee, cold and acrid now, onto the pebbles below, watched them stain, darken. He screwed the cap back on the Thermos and eased himself from the wall. His left calf and foot felt numb. Leaning his weight on the ball of his left foot, he circled the camper. Already the cold of the rain fingered his chest at his open collar. He would drive on. Best to keep moving, to stop only when he was sure that sleep was finally ready to overtake him.

Three weeks now he had been on the road, starting out from Dublin, first on to Donegal and then on down the west coast to Kerry, now west Cork. He still hadn't found that place he was searching for, but something inside him told him he was getting closer. He trusted his inner compass – this guide that he knew nothing of. He had long given up trying to be in control, to influence or change things. He pulled on a jumper and hauled himself into the camper cab.

* * *

Alison was conscious of the time. Conscious of Hannah being left to her own devices at home – if she was at home. She patted the liver-spotted hand in hers.

'Hannah sends her love. She has study this evening, but she'll be in to see you at the weekend.' Alison hoped this wasn't another empty promise. She'd make sure that little madam visited on Saturday whatever it took. She couldn't get her head around Hannah's refusal to visit her gran. To be fair, she had gone regularly to the hospital at the beginning, but in the weeks since Maryanne had moved here she had visited what, two, maybe three times at most. 'The whole village is anxious to know how you're doing, wondering when they'll see you out and about again.'

Maryanne's soft blue eyes stared straight through her, as if she were speaking in a foreign language. As if she didn't have the first notion what Alison was rabbiting on about. No, more than that. As if she absolutely did not care. Her whole face was a blank porcelain mask: no pull on the corners of her mouth, no hint of a set in her chin. But the eyes. God, what Alison wouldn't give to see a flicker of something in them – anger, sorrow, fear – anything that would let her know that Maryanne was still in there, still with her. She bit down hard on her lower lip, squeezed the limp hand.

'Your hair looks nice.' Someone had washed it, made an effort to tame its straggling length into some kind of style. Alison's eyes moved from the two inches of grey at Maryanne's hairline down to the purple zigzag scar above her left eye where she'd struck the door jamb in her fall. She wished the ulcer on Maryanne's leg wound would show some signs of healing. If she could walk unaided again, feel she was getting some of her independence back, perhaps then she might find the will to come back to them.

'The doctors are pleased with your leg.' Alison smiled her encouragement. 'Another week, they say, will see a big difference.' Maryanne turned her head slowly, her gaze drifting past the row of chairs to her left, on out through the rain-spattered window and fixing on the darkening ocean. Alison smiled and nodded to the lady in the next chair, her gaze following Maryanne's. Was she looking for

Sean, willing him back to her? Alison swallowed hard. Was Maryanne trying to say that she wanted to go, to be with him?

Alison let her head drop, closed her eyes, that now familiar heat of resentment bubbling up somewhere deep inside her, a cold overlay of guilt fighting to keep it in check. To his mother, Sean would always be the tragic hero, the handsome young son cut down on the cusp of life. Running a forefinger and thumb over her closed lids she drew a long, slow breath. Sean's face flashed before her in the darkness: the wide smile, the creases that winged his eyes when he laughed. The face that had lit her world. Jesus, she couldn't blame him for dying but another part of her railed that he should be here now, looking after *his* mother, sharing in the rearing of *his* child! And there was that other face too, that closed, sullen face she remembered more often of late as she struggled with Maryanne and Hannah, with money and work. He should be here, with her. He should have to share this mess! She shook her head as if to shake out the anger, the guilt and confusion.

She opened her eyes, lifted her head. Maryanne was staring, not at her but deep inside her, as if she were reading her very thoughts. Alison felt a pink shame ignite at the base of her neck, felt its heated fingers reach upwards to her cheeks and set them alight. She dropped Maryanne's hand back into her lap, cleared her throat as she hoisted her handbag to her shoulder. 'I'd better head home. Tea, for Hannah.' Her voice trembled, each hand massaging the knuckles of the other in quick succession. Leaning forward she placed an awkward peck on Maryanne's forehead 'I'll call in tomorrow, have a good night's sleep.'

Avoiding Maryanne's eyes, she caught the chair she'd

26

been sitting on and placed it back by the table in the centre of the room before rushing to the front door, her trembling fingers pressing in the wrong security code.

'Have you seen any of my people?' Alison knew without looking that it was that tiny little woman with the long grey hair and eyes as blue and as blank as a doll's – was it Gretta they called her? – stealing up slowly on her walking frame behind her, she was looking for a face, an escape, some route back into a world that had long ago disappeared. Alison stabbed her finger at the keypad again then shouldered open the heavy door and bolted out into the rain.

From the office window Kathleen watched her raise her handbag over her head and run through the downpour towards the car park. She looked so wretched, so alone. Whoever was responsible for that break-in had a lot more on their heads than Maryanne's injuries, she sighed. Alison had made such progress in the last year, had begun at last to show signs of the old vitality and passion for life that had marked her out when she had first come to live in this place. These last few months had all but knocked her back to square one, right back to those first raw weeks after Sean had been lost, those weeks when Kathleen herself had been all but broken under the enormity of Alison's grief. Lately, she'd been so preoccupied with Rob that she knew she had let her friendship with Alison slip. If she were honest, it had suited her when Alison cancelled their plans those last couple of times. It got her off the hook without having to feel any guilt. God, she should have known that it was a sign that everything wasn't right with Alison but she had chosen not to give it a second thought, had been only too happy to let her focus shift straight back to Rob. And poor Hannah – and that good-for-nothing O'Neill, he spelt trouble.

She sighed, both hands finding their way to rest on the centre of her chest, right over the spot where a red hot coal of guilt had rekindled. 'Tomorrow,' she promised aloud. She would call tomorrow evening after work, spend some time catching up with Alison and maybe get a chance to have a chat with Hannah; she could take Jamie with her, he adored Hannah and hadn't seen a whole lot of her lately. Maybe she could ask Hannah to babysit for her one night this week – it'd be a bit of pocket money for her, take the strain off Alison a bit. Good, that's settled then, she nodded to herself, flicking off the light and pulling the door shut behind her.

Two

Alison awoke with that same heavy feeling inside and all around her. If only I could stay right here, she thought, eyes still closed. Forget the world, forget everything. A dark sigh rose from the depths of her as she stretched back her neck, arched her body into wakefulness. The dogs pined softly in the back kitchen, somehow sensing her stirring. Turning onto her side, her fingers found the warm dip of her waist, the gentle outward curve of her hip, her thigh, so soft, like a wing, opening. A sharp lick of fire lit her belly, taunting her aloneness. She threw back the covers and padded to the shower. Under its hot stream she scrubbed and scrubbed – at the loneliness, the darkness, that grey hopelessness that seemed to be her constant shadow lately – working the loofah vigorously over and over her body till her skin tingled, tightened, felt some semblance of contact with life.

Dogs fed and watered and let loose to the garden, back in the bedroom she pulled on her jeans and an old shirt. This house needs air, fresh breath, she muttered, pulling open the curtains and unclasping the window. She fixed her damp hair in a knot at her neck. Not bothering with breakfast, she gathered up the empty bottles and jars from the back kitchen. Like so often these days, she felt the need to be away from the house, from its stillness, its deathly quiet. She grabbed her keys, whistled the dogs into the back of the old jeep and bounced down the pot-holed drive to the beach.

The sea cha-cha'd in to meet her, its petticoat held high. Alison noticed the ocean's dark brown under-dress; how it rippled its grey surface, refusing the sun. The 10th of May, first month of summer, Alison thought, and the sea, like me, is refusing to cast off her winter colours and mood.

The two dogs bounding ahead of her, she strolled towards the water's edge, catching herself smiling at their playfulness, their joy for life. Five-year-old Tilly, a beautiful, sleek black Labrador, had been Hannah's tenth birthday present from Sean; Tim was one of the litter of six pups that she had surprised them with last September. Watching them now, she was so glad she had decided to keep little Tim. Tilly had been such a devoted mother that Alison hadn't had the heart to take them all from her and tiny Tim, the runt of the litter, had been the obvious choice to stay. Not such a runt any more, she laughed to herself now, as she watched him dance along the wet sand.

Along the shoreline the sea had spat up a vile yellow-brown froth in its contempt at summer's subtle gestures. Alison lifted her gaze towards the freshly greened cliff tops, the tiny knots of purple heather and sea pinks clinging in all their brilliance to the outcrops. Why do they return, she wondered, year in year out, with their whispers of renewal and rebirth, only to be killed off a few short months later?

Why try again and again, knowing they will perish, knowing death always has the final say?

She turned from the shoreline up towards the dunes, bending to pick a piece of driftwood from the sand. Salt had bleached away its colour and only in its deepest cuts could you see the remnants of life. Its shape was humped and curved, as if by pain, its face eaten away. Sean. Over three years now in his wet, salty grave. What would remain of him?

Holding the driftwood with both hands, she closed her eyes and pressed her nose to its belly. At the rush of salt and tar, the memories fast-gathered. She saw herself again, running, demented to the strand each morning, knowing each day that this was the one, today she would find him. Walking and searching every beach and cove for miles, cursing the tide and then falling to her knees, the sea sweeping in around her as she begged and pleaded for Sean's return; Hannah, cold and tired, little legs trying to keep up yet staying a small distance from the mother with the madness in her eyes. Then returning to the water like a ghost each night when Hannah was safe in her bed, her torch light double-checking every nook and turn in the rocks and caves. In case she had missed him by day. In case he had come on the evening tide and was waiting for her.

She opened her eyes and let the hot tears fall, Maryanne's words echoing in her head: 'Let him rest, can't you! Haven't we seen enough of rosary beads wrapped round the stiffened fingers of young men. Let him rest in the one place he loved!'

Looking out towards the horizon, she drew a defiant hand across her cheek. She was weary of her old grief, of how it had stolen back to reclaim her in the last months, reasserting itself with a vengeance and with a new piercing resentment that, try as she might, she could not shake.

Closure. She hadn't had closure. That's what all the books would tell her. Well, fat chance of that!

She turned her back on the heaving sea, on its mocking hiss and pull. Fixing a windblown curl behind her ear, Alison felt eyes on her, almost looking through her. She turned to face the steep cliff to the left. There, halfway up the old mud track, a man stood watching her. As soon as she looked he turned and moved away, his step slowed by a limp on his left-hand side. He was too far away for Alison to see who he was, but her skin felt the prickle of his deep stare.

Reaching the dunes, she climbed the wooden storm steps and leaned for a moment on the weathered railing at the top. Across the yellow bridge, on the little hill overlooking the river, Mick Farrell was painting the outside of his house in preparation for the summer tourists. She could hardly believe it was over twenty years now since she had first come to this place. Her parents had rented one of those very houses and little did she know that morning as they drove and sang the three-hour journey south to Carniskey that she would be bonded to this village forever. Carniskey, 'Ceathru Uisce' – the Watery Quarter. The very name and the way it could be whispered hinted at the magic it held. There were a dozen little houses, huddled together in a terrace, their tiny windows squinted against the sun and the winter storms. Alison could almost smell that peculiar mixture of must and wet sand that filled every room of that house; see the maroon swivel armchair in the sitting-room window overlooking the bay, and the sea, swelling and sparkling in its splendour and welcome.

That very first year Sean Delaney had asked one of the local girls to 'beg Alison to go out with him'. Just six months older than her, tall and tanned, his dark hazel eyes and shy smile set her legs to jelly. He didn't talk much, seemed more aloof than the others. But just being in his company was enough for Alison. The words and the kisses she could dream.

If she had sung all the way to Carniskey, then she cried all the way home. At fifteen, she'd had her first real taste of loss and heartbreak. She couldn't ring him – he didn't have a telephone. But he had promised to write. He never did. When her father called herself and Claire together to tell them their mother was unwell and needed surgery, Alison flung Sean Delaney, the fisherman's son, to the darkest corner of the back of her mind and poured all her love and attention on to her mother.

And when spring awoke in their tiny suburban garden her father spoke of the sea pinks and how they'd be nodding in expectant gossip now on the cliffs at Carniskey. He put it on the table one evening after supper: the letter from Mrs Phelan confirming their booking of the yellow terraced cottage for the whole month of August. 'Dr Lawlor says it's just the medicine you need – a whole month of sea air and sunshine.' Alison's heart had swelled and then promptly thumped back into place at the thought of Sean Delaney.

'Damn!' she whispered under her breath, her eye catching the hurried step of May Reilly crossing the bridge and turning in the path to the beach. May and her marital woes and endless questions was the last thing she needed. 'Tilly! Tim! Come on!' she called to the dogs, the tips of their tails just visible in the tall marram grass. She started down the steps towards the car park. She'd have to forget going to the bottle bank now – May's telescopic eye would have the bottles counted, their numbers doubled and the whole place informed about 'Alison Delaney's little problem' before lunch. Maybe if May concentrated a little more on her own business she mightn't have found herself in the mess she was in now ... Well, no point in giving them extra fodder, she thought, slipping her mobile from her jeans pocket and pretending to be engrossed in a call as she waved hello to May and hurried towards the jeep.

* * *

Hannah bit down on her pen, her fingers drumming its length. A warm smile spread through her, as she lost herself in the memory of Peter's kiss, the minty taste of his tongue in her mouth. Tonight couldn't come quick enough. She'd say she was studying at Aoife's, concoct some project or other. Mum didn't go in much for detail – much as she thought she was on top of it all, really she didn't have a clue. Besides, she'd be mellowed with a glass of wine or two by the time Hannah got home and would probably be in bed, complaining of tiredness or a headache and blaming it all on the stress of Nan. Closing her eyes, Hannah ignored the hot tightening in her chest, encouraged her mind to wander instead back to last night. She could almost feel the warm, soft leather of the car seat beneath her, the hot pressure of Peter's hand on her thigh, his right hand lightly guiding the steering wheel as the car cut the bends on the Aughtford road; the roar of the exhaust as he shifted gear and that faint smell of mint on his breath when he turned his head to direct the words of the pumping rap song right at her.

'Hannah! Hannah Delaney? Can you grace us with your opinion?' The sharp edge in Ms Fahy's voice jolted her back to the classroom.

* * *

Alison parked at the side of the house and sat for a moment, looking at the lobster and shrimp pots, the salmon nets and bright pink buoys littering the back and side gardens. Sean was still everywhere around her. She hadn't moved or stored the stuff the first year, thinking every day that he'd return, that he'd need them for the next season. As the months wore on and one year gave way to the next, they had become so much a part of the place that she had stopped noticing them. Lately, though, they'd begun to prod at her and sometimes she felt they were looking at her accusingly, making her feel somehow like an impostor. She glared at the sorry, useless collection and rounded the house to the back door.

A sad smile softened her face as she noticed the uncoiled length of rope attached to the post in the garden, the lattice of net falling to the grass below. Joe O'Sullivan. He only ever came now when he knew she was away – she'd given him such a fright that day last October, the day of Sean's anniversary, when she had let her temper and her frustrations loose on him. But since spring, she would see him often, crouched behind the ditch in the adjoining field, watching, waiting. And heading down the drive, she'd keep watch in the rear-view mirror, smile at his awkward scramble over the ditch, the blue cap perched on the side of his bowed blond head, long legs propelling him towards Sean's fishing gear. Poor old Joe, 'Sean's right-hand man' – God, how he used to straighten himself up when he'd call him that! Joe would never give up or give in to reality. 'His Seany', as he called him, would be back any day now, as far as he was concerned, and no amount of convincing would turn him. And he was as determined as ever to make Sean proud, to have everything ready for him on his return.

Poor old soul, Alison thought, turning to the back door. But then again, she sighed, cursing the salt-stiffened, unyielding lock, maybe Joe wasn't the one to feel sorry for. At least he lived his days with hope, with expectation. And even if those hopes were never going to be realised…well, didn't they at least give his days some meaning, some light?

She flicked on the kettle, set the driftwood on the kitchen windowsill to dry and slipped her mobile from her pocket. One new voicemail.

'Alison, this is my third message in two days!' Eugene Dalton's voice boomed at her. 'We need that article, Friday morning at the latest! I'm going out on a limb for you here. Do you want this job, because there's plenty others that would…
' – a pause for emphasis – then, 'give me a ring. Now!'

'Shit!' Her mobile was out of credit, again. Grabbing the house phone, she punched in the number of the local paper and cringed at the Americanised patter of Eugene's receptionist.

'Susie? It's Alison Delaney here. Can you pass a message to Eugene for me?'

'Alison, he's here now if you want to—'

'No, Susie, I haven't time. Tell him that article's ready, but I haven't been able to email it as the broadband's down again. I'll drop it to the office before twelve on Friday. Thanks.' She hung up, not waiting for a reply. 'Right, that gives me today and tomorrow.' She heaped two spoons of coffee into her mug and poured in the scalding water. Sitting at her desk in the window, she punched the computer to life.

* * *

As soon as he saw Tra na Leon, William had known he'd found the perfect spot. Two giant lion rocks guarded the secluded bay and out beyond the glimmering blues and greens, the horizon slept. The cove could only be reached by a mile-long dirt track up off the main beach at Carniskey. Waterlogged and overgrown in places, it wouldn't encourage many visitors. The thick gorse bushes and high rock crops on the left lent ideal shelter to his old camper van. Yes, this was the place.

Without reason or prompt, his mind wandered again to the figure he'd seen on the beach this morning. There was something about her, something around her that, even from a distance, drew him like a magnet. Gazing out towards the horizon, William squinted as the sun suddenly burst from behind a cloud, setting the sea a-dance with a flood of silver lights. He opened the camper door and stepped inside. Clearing a seat beside the small table, he opened his sketch book.

* * *

Kathleen dried her hands on the dishcloth, leaned her elbows on the counter top and gazed out through the kitchen window. She laughed out loud as she watched Jamie thunder towards the goal posts at the foot of the garden and in his enthusiasm fly arse-over-head, missing his goal chance completely. He shook his head, his dark curls dancing as he straightened, his cheeks ablaze with dented pride as he raced to retrieve the ball. That was her Jamie, her little dynamo, bursting with energy and enthusiasm and always ready to have another go.

And that's why his bedwetting really confounded her – at seven years of age and completely out of the blue! Every other morning for two weeks now, and she was no nearer to sorting it. She'd tried several tacks: making little of it; avoiding his room in the morning so that he could at least go to school without the humiliation of her seeing the dreaded dark patch; teasing him out, approaching the subject in a thousand different ways but always with the same result: silence and that sideways head-hang of shame that tore at her.

She watched Joe O'Sullivan now, tramping down the lawn with his two left feet, Jamie corralled in one corner of the goal, crouched and ready. Good old Joe. It was only in the last two weeks that he had begun appearing at the school gate again at day's end. That whole break-in business had really taken its toll on him. What had those guards been thinking to even entertain for one second the notion that Joe could be somehow involved? Sure he'd been seen hanging around outside Maryanne's place, but that had always been his way when Sean was alive and, God help him, he had continued it ever since, probably thinking he was keeping an eye on the old lady, doing it for Sean. Sure what would the guards know anyway, she thought to herself, throwing her eyes up to heaven, and none of them even from the place. Joe wouldn't harm an insect much less the Maryanne he adored! Fools. More in their line to get the finger out and find the real culprit.

Although Joe was now thirty-three, like herself, following a fall at the pier when he was just five years old his mind had not developed beyond childhood. Most people looked on him with pity, or worse still as a source of fun. 'The Trout' they called him, his full, wet mouth always open as if in constant wonder at the world. Rob had had a quiet word with a few of the ringleaders, had taken to accompanying Joe to the local football matches, to the odd pool game at the hall on the quay, and under the wing of his new 'best friend' Joe's confidence had swelled. Typical of kind-hearted Rob, she smiled, no wonder she had fallen so hard for him.

Rob. His name drew a smile as she skipped to the patio door. That was the effect he had on her: he made her skip rather than walk, made everything in her world bigger, brighter, better. They'd been together a year now – give or take a few weeks – and Kathleen had been more than happy with the way things stood. Truth be told she had never dared dream that life could be this good again. So why couldn't Rob just have left good enough alone? Why all of a sudden was he so bent on upping it a notch and insisting on them living together?

And what kind of selfish stupidity had made her broach the whole subject of them moving in together with Jamie? All she was doing was teasing it out for herself, she could see that now. It had been thoughtless and unfair to land something like that on the child when she herself hadn't even known her own mind. Hadn't and still didn't, she sighed, wondering if she was putting the bed-wetting down to her mention of Rob moving in only because it suited her. Because it gave her an excuse, an out-clause, meant she didn't have to be the one to make the decision, at least not yet.

It had been more than a struggle at times, raising Jamie single-handed, securing this home for them; always striving to be upbeat and positive, to prove to the world that she wouldn't be defeated, that she could make it. And she had. She was proud of herself, proud of the young boy Jamie had grown into. And it would be wonderful at this stage, with Jamie growing up so quickly, to have someone to share it all with, all of it, even the everyday humdrum stuff. But it worried her how clingy Jamie had become in the last weeks, going quiet if she said she was going out, not wanting a babysitter – what was all that about? Hannah had been babysitting for the past six months and they'd always got on like a house on fire – she was so good with him, like a real big sister. A tug of guilt pulled at the corners of her mouth – she really *had* intended to call on Alison, but things just seemed to have gotten in the way all day. All day and every day since she'd promised to call last week. She'd give her a buzz, definitely, first thing after dinner.

'Jamie, Joe, dinner's up!' she called, holding the door open for them as they sauntered up the length of the garden, Jamie looking up into Joe's open face, his hands flying and diving in his attempt to explain something. And Joe, his head as always bowed and tilted to the side, that old bleached blue corduroy cap defying gravity and staying put on the side of his small head. Kathleen smiled. Jamie adored Joe. All the children did. She supposed he was their ideal – a grown-up but with a mind like their own who hadn't forgotten the magic of laughter, the wonder of life. Jamie looked up as they neared the door, smiled at her, that big wide smile that never failed to pierce her heart – his father's smile.

'Hungry?' She ruffled his hair as he passed through the door. He would always be her first consideration, her

Number One Man, and it was only natural that he would be a little jealous of Rob – someone else competing for his mother's attention for the first time in his young life. Everything was fine, it seemed, while Rob was on the outside, but she could see how the idea of him moving in with them could be making Jamie anxious. And she could see, too, that despite his tender age, there was wisdom in his thinking. No matter what promises Rob made to her, to them, no relationship came with a guarantee. The past had taught her that. Was she prepared to gamble all she had struggled for? Prepared to hand Rob her trust, her space, her child? And was she prepared for the other option: losing the first real relationship that had mattered to her in over eight years, a relationship she had built so slowly, so tentatively?

* * *

Six o'clock. Alison turned off the computer and stretched her aching back. She glanced guiltily at the laden ashtray. Stuffing the cigarette pack and lighter into the desk drawer, she opened the window and, grabbing the ashtray, headed out the back door to the bin. Soon. She'd quit again soon. She did it before, she could do it again. As soon as Maryanne was out of the woods and she had secured a steadier income, she'd quit then – and for good this time. She opened the bottom press in the kitchen. Her daughter's appetite was growing alarmingly – along with her tongue and opinions. At almost fourteen, her long black curls and fiery brown eyes danced with passion and opinion on everything from meat-eating and religion to sex and the unnaturalness of monogamy. A twin personality to her

41

aunt Claire in London, the two were as close as Alison and Claire had been growing up. Alison cringed at the thought of the next dreaded phone bill. 'I'll ring Claire, she'll know' was Hannah's mantra every time she had one of her many 'crises'.

'What the hell would I know?' Alison muttered, her head stuck in the cupboard searching for pasta. While she appreciated the bond between her sister and daughter, Alison couldn't ignore the little green tickle of envy that feathered her heart every time she thought of them. It was easy for Claire to be all glamour and sophistication, living the high life in her arty circle in London. Hannah didn't have to witness her going through the day to day drudgery of scrimping to get by, having to make do and go without. Putting up with a job she hated and a lecherous boss that scanned her body every time he complimented her on an article – the thought of Eugene Dalton's bulbous nose and that permanent leer on his fat, wet lips made her squirm. But, as Claire was always quick to point out, there was nothing to stop her upping sticks and moving too. But oh no, she had to stick with her girlish heart and tether herself to this no-man's-land where the grey sky stoops to kiss the wet ground in a love affair that lasts eight months out of every twelve.

Claire had moved to London a year before Sean was lost and, though she was loathe to admit it, Alison believed that the loss of her aunt had cut Hannah deeper than that of her father. Two years ago they had both gone to visit Claire in London when Alison's father had moved over there to live with her. Alison would never forget her daughter's tears at the airport. Claire had begged Alison to sell up, move over to London with them, and Hannah could not comprehend why her mother would prefer to return to Carniskey. On the drive home from the airport Alison had tried to explain to her daughter her need to be near Sean and the sea that had been his whole world. Hannah's reaction had stung her to the core and Alison would never forget the fire in her young daughter's eyes when she'd spoken: 'He's dead, Mum! Dead! And you might as well be, too! I hate you – and I hate him!'

'I'm back!' Hannah closed the front door with the force of a north-east gale and dropped her school bag in the hall, dead centre.

'In here!' Alison called. 'Dinner's just about ready.'

'I'm not hungry – I'm goin' to my room for a while.'

Alison followed her down the hall. The bedroom door slammed in her face. Knocking lightly, she opened the door as Hannah set the CD player – and the walls – pounding.

'You okay?' Alison risked, taking in her daughter's puffed eyes.

'Yeah, I'll be up in a minute.'

'I'm just walking down to check the post box.' Alison knew better than to risk asking questions. 'Come and have something to eat then, okay?'

Grunting a reply, Hannah flung herself among the clothes, magazines and childhood teddies that littered her single bed. Lying on her side, she watched her mum stride down the driveway. *Why does she always have to keep her head bowed?* Hannah's sigh was laced with irritation. *It's like she's afraid the whole world is watching her, like she's ashamed or something!* Alison's red ringlets were coiled and pinned tightly at the back of her neck. She could even be pretty, Hannah considered, if she'd just let her hair loose, take that permanent worried look off her face.

43

On the school bus home, Danny Ryan had said her mother was crazy. Said someone had seen her talking to the sea last Friday night and dancing with herself in the beam of the moon. 'Danny Ryan's an asshole,' she spat. Still, it would be nice if Mum were a little more normal and didn't stick out so much. It's like she does it on purpose, she thought, like she hates this place and everyone in it and wants them to hate her right back! She rolled over onto her back. Why would Mum never considering leaving, then? She'd leave in the morning herself if it weren't for Peter O'Neill. Peter O'Neill. Aoife had got it all wrong about him and Pamela Forde. They were probably just talking, there was no law against that. Hot nettles stung the backs of her eyes. She hated Pamela Forde, with her big fat arse. Biting down hard on her bottom lip, she cut the music and rushed to the bathroom to splash her face with cold water.

'Hannah, there's one for you, from Claire!' Alison called from the kitchen. She opened the brown envelope addressed to herself, knowing even before she pulled out the slip of paper accompanying the manuscript what it would say. God, she was losing her touch. This was the third story in a month that had been sent back. So, what had they to say this time?

'…too dark and uncompromising for our publication…'. Jesus, did any of them live in the real world? Life wasn't all pink ribbons and happy-ever-afters. Surely even those duped by the myth of a Celtic tiger had woken up to stark reality by now. Alison balled up the paper, shot it into the bin. She slapped the pasta up on two plates. If this continues, I'll have to start looking for a real job. Sell my soul to some multinational – if there are any of them left.

'Oh, Mum, she wants us to come over!' Hannah, devouring the letter, stuffed her mouth with a forkful of pasta.

'Slow down, Hannah, I thought you weren't hungry.'

'She wants us to visit this summer. Oh, it'd be so cool – can you imagine Grainne White's face: "Are you going on holiday this year, Hannah? Dad's takin' us to Marbella for two weeks."' Hannah imitated the high-pitched boast to a T. '"Yeah, Grainne, me and Mum are off to London – and we don't need a man to fund it, so stick that up your ar—"'

'Hannah, please!' Alison could barely stifle the laugh. 'Anyway, I thought you and Grainne were great friends?'

'Please, Mum, less of the great. She's okay, but she keeps rubbin' it in, you know, about money and stuff.'

'No, I don't know, Hannah. How do you mean?'

'Oh, it's nothin', Mum, keep your hair on. Sooo, come on, are we goin'? Please?'

'Oh, Hannah, you know it's out of the question.'

'We did it before.'

'Yeah, and your grandad footed the bill. Honestly, Hannah, where do you think I'd find the money?'

'It can't be *that* much.' Hannah tsk'd. 'And I'm sure Claire would…'

'Don't even think about asking her.'

'Yeah, but she's loaded. I'm sure she'd be—'

'Hannah, you heard me. I said no, it's not happening.'

'So, this is it then, is it?' Hannah flung the letter down. 'Stuck in this bloody place for the whole summer?'

'Less of the bloody, please, Hannah. This place was good enough for your father all his life.'

'Yeah, and look what it did to him,' Hannah muttered into her plate.

45

Ignore it, Alison warned herself, feeling her heart quicken. The subtle suicide jibes had been an almost constant at Hannah's school until the day an exasperated Alison had burst into the classroom and confronted Hannah's classmates head on. Another fatal mistake that had earned her the moniker 'Alison in Cuckoo-land' and had totally humiliated the child.

'It's only a holiday,' Hannah risked into the silence. 'It's not like we're talking about a world tour. Everyone's entitled to a holiday.'

'Entitled?' Alison gibed, widening her eyes. 'God, this "because you're worth it" generation has an awful lot to learn. Things don't just fall into your lap, Hannah, whether you feel you're "entitled" or not. The world doesn't work that way. Things have to be worked towards, earned.' Conscious of sounding derisive, Alison lightened her tone. 'Besides, happiness isn't something that has to be chased after, you can have it, right here,' she shrugged, attempting a conciliatory smile.

'Yeah? Just like you?' Hannah sat back in her chair, head cocked to one side in defiance. 'Happy, happy, happy,' she jeered, eyeballing her mother across the table.

'You can drop it right now, Hannah.' Keeping her voice even, Alison gathered her plate and moved to the sink. 'I'm not doing this.' If there was one thing she had learned in the last few months, it was to walk away before things escalated between them, before words were spoken that couldn't be unsaid. 'It's your turn to wash up – I'm going down to the beach for a walk.'

'Oh well, surprise, surprise.'

'Oh grow up, Hannah. There are more people in the world than you, you know. People who would love if their

46

only problem was whether or where they were going on holiday! Your nan, for starters. When were you planning on visiting her?' Alison tugged open her desk drawer, grabbed her cigarettes and keys, her temper rising with every thud of her heart. 'And maybe you should stop milking Claire and try earning some money of your own for a change, maybe then you'll understand how far it stretches! You won't even babysit for Kathleen any more – what's that all about?'

Hannah, red-cheeked, made no reply, just scraped back her chair and slouched towards the hall.

'Don't you walk away when I'm talking to you…Hannah!' Her blood boiling, Alison stomped down the hall behind her, checking herself as the bedroom door slammed in her face. Fists clenched, she took a deep breath. 'Stay away from that phone – and get your homework done.' She grabbed her jacket from the back kitchen and immediately the two dogs sprang from their beds. 'Stay!' Alison commanded, her anger ready to spill.

The beach was deserted. A heavy mist draped the horizon and only a few scavenging gulls kept the waves company. She didn't bother with a coat, didn't feel the bite of the wind as she strode to the right of the pathway and onto the sand. Her eyelids felt hot and heavy, like the rock lodged in her chest – a great lump of sadness with a sea of anger and frustration crashing around it, yet unable, in all this time, to remove even the tiniest grain.

The tide was halfway out, the tall rock standing in just a skirt of shallow water. She leaned against it. This was the spot. This was where Sean had first kissed her on that, her second summer in Carniskey. She would never forget the magical mixture of excitement and embarrassment as they had sought each other's lips. She closed her eyes now and tasted again the salt and the sun on his lips. She drew a deep breath, remembering her mother that summer, that anxious look on her face every time Alison went out. 'Remember last autumn, Alison, remember the agony of the postman's visits?' But Alison had explained that Sean had lost her address. Had believed that Alison wouldn't even remember him when she went back to her life in Dublin. Alison knew by her mother's raised eyebrows and the slow shake of her head that she wasn't as easily convinced. But then, Sean hadn't kissed her. Hadn't whispered to her in the dunes how he'd seen her face for months in the water. How the leaves and the rain – and even a part of the cliff at Tra na Baid had fallen when she'd left. And how his heart had tumbled with them.

That was the last summer her mother had enjoyed in Carniskey. Although they came again the following year, her illness had only allowed her short visits to the patio and garden of the terraced house. Their father had hardly left her side. They had both slept in the small downstairs sitting room and Alison and Claire would hear them, talk and laugh, cry and lie in silence into the small hours. When death finally called that following November, Alison found her father's deep peace and acceptance harder to bear than her sister's angry rebellion. She wondered now had her mother known that Sean had come to Dublin for the funeral. Did she know how he'd loved her then and how he'd carried her heart to healing with his letters and visits?

She opened her eyes as the first star winked from the darkening sky. Maybe Hannah and Claire were right. Maybe it was time to put Sean to rest. To move on, move out of this place and start to live again. Make a proper life for Hannah – and for herself. But how could she? With Maryanne, how could she ever be free of the past, of Sean, of this place? She pulled her cardigan tight around her, shivering now from the bite of the evening air, the grip of the cold water around her ankles. She stepped from the rising water and hurried up the beach.

William Hayden watched from the tall grass in the dunes, his pencil moving furiously over the page. Pain and loneliness haunted every stroke.

Three

Alison kicked off her wet sandals and stepped barefoot into the kitchen. Lighting a cigarette, she picked up the note from the table:

'Gone to Aoife's to study – H.'

Alison sighed, dropped the piece of paper back on the table and flopped down into the chair. At least Hannah had somewhere to run. Head bent, she pinched the bridge of her nose between her thumb and index finger – she hoped her sinuses weren't starting up again. God, her head felt like it could burst. And no wonder, she thought, wishing that *she* had somewhere she could offload all the tangled thoughts that swarmed and buzzed constantly, round and round, right behind her eyes; wishing that she could somehow break down the wall she had built around herself and let someone in to share her world. Sure, she had a good friend in Kathleen but Alison knew that she was tired of her jaded repertoire, her endless talk of Sean – knew by the way Kathleen always managed to change the subject lately, to almost physically back away. The other week when Kathleen had suggested that maybe she should see a therapist – that maybe, since Maryanne's break-in, her grief had become 'complicated' and needed a professional ear – Alison had heard her loud and clear. Heard that Kathleen had had enough. And who could blame her? She had listened long and hard enough, and besides, she had Rob now and a whole new life to look forward to – who would want to be dragged away from that to listen to someone else's misery?

Closing her eyes, she clasped a hand at the nape of her neck, arched her head backwards. Had she really turned into one of those energy-sapping, life-sucking people she detested? She was almost thirty-six, life was moving on, everyone it seemed was moving on and yet here she was, stuck in the past and letting it eat away at her. Rolling the worry and resentment – resentment, yes, that's what it was and it was time she admitted it – of one day into the next until it had grown so big it blocked out everything else. But what other choice did she have? How the hell could she change this, all this? Where would she even start? Any time she tried to be positive and look to the future all she saw was Hannah and her increasingly sour moods, the worry of Maryanne's health – and money, always money, or the lack of it! When was her life ever going to be about *her* again? About her dreams, her future? She needed something to jolt her, something to make her feel again. But what?

She plucked the clips from her hair, shook out her curls. They tumbled in a red flame over her shoulders. She pressed her palms to her face, the tips of her fingers massaging her temples. She knew she should get back to the article she'd started for Eugene. Knew too that any attempt at writing would only result in a blank page and even more frustration. God, she felt cold. She'd give herself the night off, she decided, standing, make a fresh start at the article, at life, in the morning. She flicked the oil burner to life, its urgent kick a comfort in the silence. Lifting a bottle of red from the wine rack, she grabbed a glass and her cigarettes. 'C'mon then.' The two still-wary dogs trotted into the sitting room behind her. She pulled the curtains and switched the two lamps to life. Selecting a CD, Alison settled into the armchair by the window, the dogs on the rug at her feet. The warm red liquid caressing her throat, she lay back her head and drank in the lyrics.

* * *

The nurse's soft footfall faded down the night-lit corridor. Maryanne lay back on her pillow in the almost-silence. Her favourite hour of the day, she closed her eyes, the better to savour her memories.

The whole picture was as clear to her as if it had been only yesterday: the infant cot beside her hospital bed, its cream bars flaked a rusty brown where the paint had chipped; the curve and promise of her newborn under the blue blanket, the sweet scent of heaven still clinging to the folds in his flaccid neck. She remembered how the morning sun would slant through the window opposite, lighting a path to his cot, as if heaven was reluctant to abandon his care to this world. Frank's first visit – the bunch of flowers clasped awkwardly to his chest – carrying the ocean in with him on his hair and clothes; the black spot on his thumbnail, his hand dwarfing his infant son's face as it traced his sleeping cheek: 'Sean? Will we name him Sean?'

* * *

Alison poured the last of the bottle into her glass. Almost ten o'clock and still no sign of Hannah. And on a school night. This was so much more than the usual teenage stuff that Kathleen was putting it down to. Herself and Hannah were practically strangers at this stage, most attempts at conversation ending in one or other of them storming from the room. How had she – the adult, the mother – let it come to this? They had been so close before Sean's accident. With him away at sea so often they'd been alone quite a bit, were rarely apart from each other. She smiled now, remembering the jokes they would share and the stories they'd conjure as they lay, late at night, curled up in bed awaiting his return. It was almost as if, when he died, Sean had cheated them of that relationship too. Fire rising in her chest, she drained her glass. She was damned if she was going to let him take her daughter from her too! She stormed into the kitchen, grabbed a fresh bottle from the rack.

Eleven thirty and still no Hannah. She tried her mobile phone again. Then Aoife's. No answer. Damn! She couldn't risk driving now. She'd give her another ten minutes and then she was calling Aoife's mum. This was ridiculous. She set her glass down on the bureau and, using both hands, yanked open its stubborn top drawer. Cards and photographs spilled to her feet. Sean, face tanned and smile wide, stared up at her, his eyes daring hers to meet them as she knelt to the floor.

'Jeez, Mum.'

Alison hadn't heard the key in the front door.

'Hannah? What have you done to your ...'

Hannah stood defiant in the doorway, her former black curls a mass of bright purple streaks.

'I needed a change.' Her voice was low, her eyes taking

in the two wine bottles, the sea of photographs scattered on the rug at her mother's knees: photographs of her, from baby to present, and the face of her father, grinning and weathered deep brown, looking up at her from his boat.

Hauling herself to her feet, Alison moved with an exaggerated erectness towards her. 'You needed a change? Jesus, Hannah, how *far* will you go? Don't you think I have enough on my plate already?'

'This is not about you, Mum. It's about me. I'm here too, remember?'

'Remember?' She fought to still the tremble in her voice, in her whole being. 'I've spent the last fourteen years of my life caring for you. Going without, scraping by, trying to keep this roof over our heads!'

'No one asked you to stay here. We could have left. We could have gone to London, to Claire.' Anger drenched her eyes.

'Is that your answer to everything? Claire? Claire and London?'

'At least she listens to me, she tries to understand ... ' Hannah bit back the tears.

'Oh, it's all me, me, me, isn't it, Hannah? No one else matters as long as you're understood.' She shook her head in exasperation, cursing the words that she knew would follow, even before they had left her mouth. 'Your father will never be dead as long as you're here!'

'Yeah, go on, Mum, blame him.' Hannah could no longer hold back her tears. 'Blame him. I know you do! I know you think he did it on purpose!'

'No, Hannah, please, I didn't mean, I never ... ' She stretched her arms towards her.

Hannah held up her hands to ward off her mother's

approach. Her eyes fixed, her young mouth fighting to bite down her emotion, she turned for her bedroom.

Alison sunk to her knees on the photo-littered rug. If there was one thing she'd always promised herself, it was that she would never put Sean down in Hannah's eyes. Growing up without her father was bad enough, the least she deserved were good memories of him. Her tears warped the image of the carefree, adoring mother smiling up at her from the photo of herself and a newborn Hannah. The dogs edged closer, licking her hands and face.

* * *

The shrill of the telephone hauled Alison from sleep. Her head throbbed as she lifted it from the pillow.

'Hello?'

'Alison?'

'Claire? Oh, hi, how … ' She placed a hand over the mouthpiece, cleared her throat. 'How are you?'

'The best. I tried you last night – were you out?'

'Umm, yeah, just a few drinks with Kathleen – anything wrong? How's Dad?' Her eyes fought to stay closed.

'Dad's wonderful, getting younger by the day. He's even got himself a new friend,' Claire added conspiratorially, her Notting Hill accent causing Alison to hold the phone away from her ear. God, couldn't she dampen it down a notch so early in the morning? 'Her name's Betty Rodgers. A feisty Canadian widow – he met her at the gallery. They are *so* good together. So tell, did Hannah get my letter?'

'Yeah, it arrived yesterday – and the money, thanks, but you know I told you, you shouldn't.' Hannah hadn't told her there was any money enclosed but Alison knew what it meant when a letter arrived in place of the usual email. She threw back the bedcovers, risked swinging her feet onto the floor.

'Nonsense. So, say you two are coming over, please?'

'Not this summer, Claire, I can't. Work and all, I'm far too busy.'

'Hey, everyone deserves a holiday.'

Alison bristled, she could see where Hannah got it from. She eyed the bedside clock. *Shit, past midday! Half the day already wasted!* She didn't have time for this. 'That's okay for you, Claire – you're not on your own, raising a teenager. If I don't work, there's no money.' God, her head hurt.

'You all right, Alison?'

'Yeah, yeah, I'm fine.' She rubbed a hand over her eyes. None of this was Claire's fault. None of it was anyone's fault but her own. 'It's just that, well, with freelance work, if I'm not around the work goes to someone else, you understand. And then there's the worry of Maryanne.'

'How's she doing – any change?'

'Still the same, but the doctors are hopeful. She'll get there.' Alison forced a smile in an effort to lighten her tone. 'So, how's the new gallery going?'

'Fantastic! It's already got some glowing reviews. Hey, but that's not the best news. I sold two of my own works this month – what about that?'

'Oh, well done, you! I told you it was only a matter of time. Dad must be so proud.' Alison was genuinely chuffed for her, for anyone who strived to make their dream happen. Moving to London had been a masterstroke; two small galleries under her belt and now an artist in her own right, her wild-child sister had truly amazed Alison with her focus and determination.

'Yeah, Dad's thrilled. So, how's my best girl?'

'Hannah's fine. Busy with school, the usual stuff, dyeing her hair.' Alison rolled her eyes, predicting the reaction at the other end.

'Cool! Oh Alison, she'd love it here. And Dad would love to spend some time with his only grandchild. If you can't come, why not send Hannah for the summer break? Give you some time on your own and we'd take really good care of her.'

Alison was silent. Maybe this was just what she and Hannah needed. A little time apart, a bit of space from each other.

'Alison?'

'I'll think about it. I'm not sure she'd want to travel on her own.' She'd be off like a bullet – especially without you in tow, a tiny voice reminded her.

'Dad's birthday's on the 28th. Maybe she could make it for that – it'd be such a surprise for him.'

'But her school term doesn't finish till the 31st.'

'Oh, don't be such a bore, Alison. She'll be in school for the next four years – one week's hardly going to make a difference. Please say you'll send her. I can give her a part-time job at the gallery – better education than she'll ever get in a convent!'

'Claire, I said I'll think about it, all right?' Her grip tightened on the receiver.

'I'll foot the airfare, if that's a problem.'

'No. That's not the…' Deep breath, she instructed herself. 'Look, like I said, I'll think about it, okay?' Jesus, could Claire ever finish a conversation without waving her wallet in Alison's face? She was sick to the back teeth of her sister's charity.

'Think of what it would mean to Dad. He's not going to be around forever.'

'Look, I'll buzz you over the weekend when I've had time to think it over. Now I really do have to go, I've an article to finish that's late already. Thanks for calling – oh, and say hello to Dad for me.'

Alison punched off the receiver and tossed it on the bed. She stretched her back and stood. Avoiding the mirror, she padded around the bed to the door, a tight, hot fist squeezing her heart at the memory of last night's drinking, of her fight with Hannah. Stepping gingerly into the hall, she peeped into Hannah's room. She was up and gone. She pictured her, waiting for the school bus, her mother lost in a drunken sleep. She glanced into the sitting room, cringed at the smell of smoke, the piled ashtray and the two empty wine bottles on the hearth. What had possessed her? A glass or two, that was her usual, not this, not two bottles. The photographs were tidied and stacked in a neat bundle on the side table. Poor Hannah! Jesus, what kind of a mother had she turned into? Covering her face with both hands, she closed her eyes and slid down the wall onto the wooden floor, her whole body shaking, releasing her tears.

* * *

Alison dropped two Solpadeine into a glass of water. The keening of the dogs in the back kitchen shot through her head like a hot needle. She crossed the floor to let them out. 'Tim, you little fucker!' The shredded remains of her sandal littered the young dog's bed. Tails tucked, the dogs scarpered through the open door into the garden. Drinking a tumbler of orange juice, she eyed the kitchen clock. Ten to one. Jesus, Eugene's article! She'd have to have it done by this evening if she was to drop it off tomorrow as promised. 'Damn, damn, damn!' She ripped off her night shirt and stepped under the shower.

Alison slipped into a fresh T-shirt and Sean's favourite soft Levi's, belting them tightly at the hips. She flung open the sitting-room windows, emptied the ashtray and put the empty wine bottles in the box out the back. Tried to ignore their clink of accusation.

'C'mon Tilly, Tim!' The shout reverberated in her skull. The two dogs bounded across the lawn and into the back of the jeep. Closing the boot, Alison glanced up at the gable. The earthy brown house martins' nest, neat and new, clung to the eave like a sleeping bat, its tiny opening like a squinting eye at one side. Their arrival each year had always been one of her favourite sights, announcing the summer and Sean's best season. All that work done already and she hadn't even noticed they had come.

She swung away from the main beach and negotiated the steep dirt track to the right. She'd have a bit of peace to write up there. The dogs whined their impatience as she edged the jeep carefully through the water and mud. At ten years old, it didn't take well to rough treatment and if it gave up the ghost she didn't have a bob to replace it.

She parked at the top of Tra na Leon, savouring the heat on her arms and face as she followed the tiny path along the cliff top and out towards the small headland. An old yellow camper van was just visible among the gorse bushes. Is nowhere sacred any more, she sighed. This was her space, the one place she was always guaranteed to be undisturbed. Well, except maybe for Joe O'Sullivan. She'd sometimes see him sitting on the cliff opposite, thinking he couldn't be seen if he kept his head down, taking the odd sneaky look across at her. Poor old Joe. Although wary of her after their few little spats, it was as if he had been keeping an eye on her ever since Sean went, watching out for her in his own sweet way. But Joe never approached her or disturbed her up there, and she'd almost forget he was there as she lost herself in the peace and the solitude that this place alone offered her. When she'd sit on the brink of the headland, her feet hanging over the edge of the high cliff and the tide full in below, she would some- times imagine she was in a boat and sail away in her own thoughts.

The van looked deserted. Maybe someone had dumped it there. Make a nice little writing studio for winter, she thought as she passed it, taking in the vast view of the main beach to the left and Helvic Head, with its arm outstretched, embracing the horizon beyond.

Reaching the outcrop, Alison slipped off her old runners. *Jesus, she could kill that dog, they were the only decent pair of sandals she had*. Sitting on the cliff edge, her bare feet dangling over the ledge, she lit a cigarette, opened her manila wallet and took out her notepad and pen.

Inhaling deeply, Alison drank in the view before her, the gentle lapping of the waves below soothing her heavy head. The tide was going out, the brown and black skirts of the freshly awoken rocks jewelled with glistening barnacles and muscles. All around the horseshoe of cove sea pinks and purple heathers clung like brilliant badges to the lapels of the cliffs. The sand and seaweed on the ocean bed lent the water a mossy green hue, the still submerged rocks and weeds painting a mysterious, undiscovered world.

A scatter-screech of gulls from a rock to the left drew her attention. Alison watched in open-mouthed disbelief as a naked figure emerged from the water. He climbed the rock, shook out his grey hair, stretched his arms above his head and dived. Ducking her head behind the high outcrop, she peeped again. There was no sign of him. Then, like a thunder-burst in the silence, his head and shoulders re-emerged, his face tilted towards the sun, his hair returning a rainbow of droplets to the ocean. She could almost taste his wild pleasure and abandon as he stroked effortlessly to the rock and, hauling his broad shoulders from the glistening green, climbed again. He turned to face the strand. He must have been all of six foot, his whole body a honey brown. Biting her bottom lip, Alison took in the girth of his thighs, the strength and bulge of his hips, his buttocks. A tiny warmth unfurled deep inside her. He stretched again and once more dived to the sandy depths. He surfaced, turned over on his back and floated towards the shore. Shamed by the guilt and embarrassment of her own voyeurism, she turned her head away, her eye catching Tilly and Tim making their awkward way down the grassy slope to the shore. *Shit! They'd give her away!* She looked again. He stood in the shallow water, running his large hands over his face, then squeezing the salt water from his shoulder length hair. The dogs pounced into the water to greet him, Tilly, the braver one, licking the salt from his limbs as he stepped from the lacework of shallow foam. Alison noticed the drag of his left leg as he strode towards the rocks, salt droplets glistening on his shoulders and buttocks. The man, now vigorously towelling his shoulders and back, was the one she'd seen yesterday morning watching her from the cliff top over the beach.

She returned to her notepad and pen, trying desperately to ignore the beginnings of a strange and forgotten excitement stirring inside her. Another thousand words. God, what had possessed her to accept Eugene's offer of a weekly women's column in the local paper? She didn't even feel like a woman most of the time. And as for Career vs Motherhood, well, she didn't have the first and was making a damn bad job of the second. Write about what you know? No wonder she found this article impossible.

When she looked again, the cove was deserted. Her watch read 3.20. Better get home and fix something for dinner – a hot meal for Hannah was the least she could do in her attempt at motherhood. She shoved her feet into her runners, stuffed her notepad and pen into their wallet and whistled for the dogs as she retraced the winding cliff path to the jeep. Passing by the camper van, the rich homely smell of coffee and bacon reminded her stomach that she hadn't eaten all day. Tim's erect tail peeped from behind the van. 'Tilly, Tim, come on!'

Out of nowhere he was standing in front of her, coffee cup in hand. His grey hair was tied in a damp ponytail, his striped grandfather shirt loose over faded jeans. His feet were bare. 'They've joined me for lunch.' The wide grin and deep brown eyes lent him the look of an Indian chief, his dark tanned face a landscape of stories. Alison's memory neon flashed his naked body. 'William Hayden – fancy a coffee?' His voice was deep yet gentle, his outstretched hand standing expectant in Alison's embarrassed silence.

'No. No, thank you – got to get home.' She bent her head and continued with a quickened step along the path. 'Tilly,

Tim!' The dogs didn't budge. Alison hopped into the jeep, dumped her wallet on the passenger seat and turned the key in the ignition. When they'd hear the engine's rev, the dogs would come running. The jeep coughed to life, spat and promptly died again. 'Shit!' She turned the key once more. A faint jump, then nothing. 'Come. On,' she urged, turning the key three times in quick and forceful succession. Not a budge. Alison thumped the steering wheel with her left fist. This was all she needed. She tapped her forehead on the centre of the wheel: 'Shit! Shit! Shit!'

The driver's door opened and she jumped.

'Sorry if I startled you.' The generous smile stole into his eyes, lighting them with more than a hint of amusement. 'Want me to try?'

Embarrassment reddening her temper, she slid from the seat in silence, summoning everything in her to hold her tongue. Where did this old guy get off? And what was with that smirk? William pulled himself up into the seat and coaxed the clutch. He turned the key gently and the jeep slow-shuddered to life. Relief washed through her.

'Just flooded,' William smiled, easing his bulk from the high seat.

'Thanks!' A hint of a smile tickled the corners of her full mouth. She hurried around to open the back door for the dogs.

'Sometimes things run a lot easier if we approach them with gentleness.' His eyes followed her. 'Instead of the full force of our passion.' He seemed to be talking to himself as much as to Alison. 'Sometimes it's easier just to let go.'

She climbed back into the driver's seat.

'See you again, I hope,' he smiled, closing the driver's door and turning back towards the cliff path. Alison pressed the accelerator, dust rising in her wake as she negotiated the track back down to the main road, the dogs bouncing and panting behind. William returned to his canvas chair, took up his pad and studied the sketch before him: the long, slender calves hugging the cliff top; the two narrow feet; the curve and arch of the soles.

* * *

Kathleen flung out her arms, palms up in exasperation. 'For heaven's sake, Alison, what's the big deal? It's only a meal and a few drinks. Hannah'll be perfectly fine, we'll be back before twelve.'

'No, no big deal, it's just that, well, maybe if you'd given me a bit of notice.' Kathleen had been waiting outside the house when she got home and it looked like she wasn't taking no for an answer.

'Notice? Notice? That's good coming from the girl who thought nothing of hopping in a car and driving three hours to Ballymore at the hint of a party!' They both laughed, remembering that night, shortly before Alison had married, the two of them diving into Kathleen's old Renault before sense had a chance to catch up with them, and praying it would last the journey.

'That was then,' Alison smiled, shaking her head and turning back towards the sink.

'Yes, and this is now.' Kathleen reached up, grabbed Alison gently by the shoulders and turned her around. 'You need a break, Alison. Come on, it's all booked, my treat.'

'But you can't afford…'

'What I can't afford is to stand by and watch my friend

turn into some bitter old maid who'd give May Reilly a good run for her money.'

'But last night, Hannah and me, we had a…I really need to…'

'Alison. Stop. The table is booked for eight. I'll meet you here at seven and we'll get a taxi into town. This is "You" time, okay? No Maryanne, no Hannah. And for heaven's sake, please let that hair down, I don't want people thinking I'm reduced to hanging out with an old nun!'

Four

From the kitchen window Alison watched the school bus pull back out onto the road. Hannah slow-stepped up the driveway, the evening breeze skipping playfully through her thick black hair. There was a proud exoticism, a determination beyond her years in her streamlined back and shoulders, the slight upward tilt of her chin. Alison took in the dark eyes, the ripe red lips and wide cheekbones – all her father's. What would he think if he could see his 'little shrimp' now, she smiled sadly, moving away from the window. And what would he think of her mother, a smaller voice inside her quipped. A burning shame heated her chest.

'So, how was school?' Alison placed Hannah's dinner on the table. She would try and establish some sense of normality before broaching the subject of last night.

'Fine.'

'And what had Sister Andrew to say to your hair?'

'Nothin'.'

'Oh? Well, she must be softening in her old age. The least I expected was a stern letter.' Alison pulled out the chair opposite, sat and filled a glass with water. Head bent, Hannah hunched over her plate, absently forking her food.

'Claire called this morning. She's sold two of her paintings.' Alison took a sip of water. 'And Dad's gone and found himself a girlfriend.'

Hannah kept her eyes focused on the meal before her, barely nodding her head in response. Alison knew she wasn't going to make it easy for her. God, she wished Kathleen had picked any other night but tonight to go into town. All she wanted to do – ached to do – was to sit down with Hannah and try to talk things through, put an end to this ugly animosity between them. She rested her elbows on the table, took a deep breath. 'Hannah, about last night – I'm so sorry. I never meant to …'

'Please, Mum, I don't want to talk about it.' Standing abruptly from the table, she placed her barely touched plate by the sink.

Alison stifled a sigh, sat back in her chair. There was no point trying to force it. And it was probably best that they had a bit of space from each other this evening, let things settle. 'Myself and Kathleen were thinking of going into town for a bite to eat later.'

'Whatever,' Hannah shrugged, addressing the floor. 'I'm goin' for a shower. I told Aoife I'd be down by half six.'

'But Hannah, your dinner?'

The kitchen door closed on her words.

* * *

Alison touched the pad of an index finger beneath each eye, dotting the concealer into place. She pressed her lips

67

together, ran her tongue over her top teeth to catch any traces of lipstick. Standing back from the bathroom mirror, she kneaded and tamed her long red curls, tilted her head in self appraisal. The make-up wasn't doing what it said on the tin – the smattering of tiny freckles across her cheeks and the bridge of her nose was still visible. Forcing a smile, she brushed some rouge over the apples of both cheeks, tried to ignore the weariness hooding her eyes.

Hannah had slipped out the door without even so much as a goodbye. What was *going on* with that girl? The hollowness inside Alison's chest seemed to stretch and yawn and she sighed with it. How was she ever going to get through to Hannah, get past this constant bickering and fighting? She'd be first to admit that she hadn't been the most attentive of mothers over the last few years but, damn it, she had tried to do her very best with what she had been handed. And surely at almost fourteen Hannah should have sense enough to see that now. These were the years that she had most looked forward to when Hannah was born: the growing-up years, the turning-into-a-little-woman years. God, all the things she had planned for them to do together. Instead, this, this constant feuding and blaming. Blaming. That's what Hannah did. She blamed her for everything. And much as she was loath to admit it, a part of Alison resented the child for it. Resented that almost coldness that Hannah was capable of, how dismissive she could be – the way a flash of those dark eyes could cut you down to nothing. And that 'whatever' that she was so fond of spouting…She felt the heat of her temper rising again. And she was selfish too, Hannah, just like her…

Stop! She warned herself. Hannah was little more than

a child, for God's sake, a child who needed mothering and guidance, not this. The problem lay squarely with herself, with her own reactions and resentments, not with Hannah. She was just being a teenager, like Kathleen said, and weren't self-obsession and throwing a regular strop all part of that territory? Alison didn't have to think too long or hard to remember the cheek she had given her own mother at that age. How she thought she knew everything back then, she remembered, leaning in closer to the mirror and running a finger over the contour of her upper lip. Those cigarettes are definitely going, she promised, stretching her lip to hide the tiny indentations above.

What maddened her most about Hannah, she supposed, was what a joy she could be with everyone else – with Kathleen, with Maryanne. With little Jamie – she was so good with him, so responsible. Kathleen was forever singing her praises, although she had backed away from them all a little lately too, had gone more into herself. Was there more going on for Hannah than she knew, was something troubling her? Despite Kathleen's assurances, Alison still felt a niggle in her gut, an intuition. But how to get Hannah to open up, that was the problem. Maybe if she started trusting her a bit more, Alison considered, treated her more like a grown up, an equal, would that work? Or would Hannah just go off the rails completely?

'Oh, I just don't *know* any more,' she sighed into the mirror, straightening the neck of her blouse. A tiny button fell to the floor. 'Damn!' She checked her watch. Kathleen was due in ten minutes. Unbuttoning the blouse she hurried towards the bedroom. Kathleen was right, she did need time out. A few hours away from the constant worry of Hannah and Maryanne and the goddamn mortgage.

She'd have a couple of drinks, enjoy a good chat with Kathleen – and a laugh, Kathleen's company always guaranteed you that – and she would put last night behind her. She was finished with drinking at home, alone. It didn't solve anything. She should have learned long before now that drink – that much drink – only deepened her misery, not to mention upsetting Hannah and wasting all the next day on a hangover and guilt. Well, that was it. Finished. From now on, she would make a real effort to spend more time with Hannah – proper quality time – and do all she could to really get to know the beautiful young woman that she had glimpsed walking up the driveway this evening. As she reached for the wardrobe door, the telephone shrilled to life at the bedside.

'Hello?'

'Mrs Delaney? Sister Andrew from St Laurence's – I'm calling to enquire about Hannah's leg. When Aoife told me about the fall this morning, she wasn't sure whether Hannah had broken a bone or not?'

'Oh, Sister Andrew…'

'Is it a bad time?' She could smell Alison's hesitation.

'No, no, not at all. One moment, I'll just turn down the oven.' Alison placed her palm over the mouthpiece. 'Shit!' she mouthed silently, before taking a deep breath to swallow her rising anger.

'I'm so sorry, Sister, I should have called you earlier but between doctors and everything…nothing's broken, thank goodness. Just a bad sprain. I'm sure Hannah'll be back by Monday.'

'Well, thank God for that, Mrs Delaney. Just make sure she has a note to cover her absence.'

'I will, Sister. Thank you. I'll tell Hannah you called.'

That little madam was lucky she'd gone out the door twenty minutes ago. Jesus, she'd hear about this later.

* * *

The restaurant was quieter than Alison had ever seen it, but then, she reasoned, it was a week night after all and people just didn't have the money to socialise like they used to. She wouldn't be here herself if Kathleen hadn't insisted on treating her. Her eyes strayed again to the couple seated at the bar. She watched how his hand stole protectively to the small of the girl's back, the tilt of her head as she smiled up at him, engrossed in his words.

'So, you and Rob?' She returned her attention to Kathleen. 'Should I be ordering my hat?'

'Not likely,' Kathleen smiled, shaking her head. 'Don't get me wrong, Rob's great and we definitely have that *something*...' Her smile widened, her eyes dancing.

Alison nodded, returning her smile. She knew exactly what Kathleen meant. That *something* was one of the things she missed most in life now. That buzz, that fire. That electric connection with someone that sparked some deep part of you that nothing or no one else could touch. Since losing Sean she had slowly grown used to living without it, in much the same way as your eyes grow accustomed to the dark: allowing you to make out shapes, move forward with a certain confidence, but always in the knowledge that the colour has drained from your world.

'But...' Kathleen risked, sighing.

'But?'

71

'Well, Rob wants us to move in together.' She touched her tongue to her lip, her eyes searching Alison's.

'I knew it! I knew you two were made for each other!' She reached across the table and grabbed Kathleen's hand. 'I'm so happy for you both.'

'Oh, I wish it were all that simple.' That sigh again.

'But you two adore each other, what could possibly be simpler?' Alison encouraged, squeezing her hand.

'Well, there is Jamie.'

'And?' Alison smiled, inching back her head. Right from their early days Kathleen had been thrilled at how great Rob was with Jamie. The boy idolised him.

'It's just that, well, Jamie's so stuck on him, you know, too stuck on him. Great while things are going well but, I mean, what if it all went wrong? What if he walks away? Jamie's already been denied his father, how would he cope if Rob were to turn his back on him too?'

'Oh, come on, Kathleen, you know that's never going to happen. Rob loves that boy.'

'Yeah, but that's no guarantee…'

'We all know there's never a guarantee,' Alison cut in, 'but you can't just throw away your future because of what happened in the past. And as for Jamie's dad…' Alison hesitated, knowing to tread carefully. The holiday romance that had resulted in Kathleen's son was the one subject always certain to clamp her shut. She had confided in Alison after the birth: the guy was married, already had a family and apparently just didn't want to know. But people changed, didn't they? People often regretted decisions and spent their lives wishing they had the opportunity to put things right. She knew in her heart that if Sean were still alive things would be so different for Hannah. Nothing Alison could do about that. But Jamie – Jamie's dad was out there some-where and Alison knew that if she were in Kathleen's shoes she'd be doing her damnedest to find the boy his father. 'Well, what's to stop you making contact again?'

Kathleen fingered the stem of her wine glass. 'As you said earlier this evening, that was then.'

'But surely, for Jamie?'

Kathleen lifted her head and met Alison's eyes. 'He knew about Jamie. He had his chance and he made his decision.' Her words were echoed by the old hurt stealing into her eyes.

'I know, but if he could see him now maybe...'

'Jamie is happy as he is.' Kathleen shifted, straightened in her seat. 'The past is the past and there's nothing any of us can do to change it.' Damn, she had never meant to get into all this. Tonight was meant to be about Alison. 'Happiness is in the now,' she smiled, 'in looking forward, not back. And you're right. Rob is my now. My future.' She lifted her wine glass: 'To trusting your heart and taking a chance.'

Alison mirrored her smile. 'To the happy couple,' she toasted, clinking her glass.

* * *

Fingers trembling, Hannah struggled with the clasp of her bra, the smell of weed in the fogged-up car threatening to make her gag. Though Peter's words were disjointed and seemed to come from far away, like an echo, they still carried the force of his anger and spite: ' ... fucking tease ... waste of ... crazy as ... mother ...' The white of her bare thighs flashed in the glare of the dashboard lights, her words struggling to negotiate her heavy tongue.

Peter O'Neill pressed down the window, flicked the reefer out onto the ground and gunned the engine. He'd had enough of this shit, Peter cursed, swinging out of the lay-by and onto the main Carniskey road. He couldn't believe Hannah was only fourteen when he'd first spotted her: that wet suit moulded to her body, those wild dark eyes. She might have been young but boy did that body shout she was up for it! He dropped a gear, paced for the hill. Well, he'd been wasting his time – and his stash! – and by the looks of her now, he thought, flashing a sidelong glance at her sheet-white face, if he didn't get her out of this car soon, he'd be scraping her dinner off the floor too. He drummed his fingers on the steering wheel. Pamela Forde. The corner of his mouth stretched towards his ear. Now, there was a girl worth getting to know.

* * *

'Jesus, Rob!' Kathleen fought to keep her voice down, conscious of Jamie asleep upstairs. She steadied herself with one hand on the kitchen table, the other making a tight fist over her heart. 'What gave you the right?' A deep breath to contain her anger. 'Don't you think you should have at least discussed it with me first? You knew how sensitive he was about the whole bedwetting thing!' Her eyes shone with temper.

'Come on, Kath.' Rob pushed himself away from the counter and walked towards her. 'It's not like I interrogated him or anything, it just came up…'

'Just came up? All I've had is silence, no matter what I tried, but oh, with you, it just "comes up"?' She jerked away

74

as he reached a hand towards her shoulder. 'He didn't even know that I'd told you! What's he to think now? That he can't even trust his own mother?' She pulled out a chair, flopped into it.

'Hey, he's cool with it. Glad to have got it out of the way, if anything. Anyway, aren't you firing off in the wrong direction here? Shouldn't it be that babysitter and that O'Neill guy your tongue should be targeting! Imagine, at her age, bringing him in here – and drinking…'

'You're missing the whole point.' Kathleen rubbed a hand to her temple, the fire in her words waning. 'It wasn't your place, you had no right.'

'But you're glad he trusts me, right?' Rob leaned back against the counter, fingering the coins in his trouser pocket. 'That he had that confidence? Man to man and all that. The boy's growing up, Kath.'

'Oh, yeah? And you're the expert all of a sudden? I've done this alone, remember, for seven years.'

'Easy.' Rob raised both his hands in defence. 'I'm only saying, maybe it's time to cut the strings a bit, you know, give the guy some space to breathe.'

Kathleen's head shot up, her eyes flashing. 'Space?' Her short laugh was loaded. 'That's what all this is really about, isn't it? Making space. Here. For you. You just couldn't allow me the time to sort it out for myself, could you? You had to go playing your stupid games.'

Shaking his head slowly, he moved towards the door, rested a hand on the door jamb and turned, his steel blue eyes searching her face. 'Who's the one playing games here, Kath? Maybe you should ask yourself that.'

She heard the front door click softly behind him, his car cough to life in the driveway. She stared straight ahead, seeing nothing. This wasn't what she'd envisaged twenty minutes ago, coming home in the taxi. Coming home to tell Rob that she was ready to give living together a shot. Her heart felt as if it were pulling downwards, like a large leaden drop, tugging, trembling, falling.

* * *

Rob parked his old Volvo under a street lamp on the pier and strolled to the slipway, the night wind combing his dark hair. Disgruntled bedfellows, the boats in the harbour heaved and sighed in protest at their tight mooring. He jumped down onto the wet sand. All was quiet, the peace of the night seeming to wrap its arms around him, attempting to still him. 'Damn it,' he cursed, throwing back his head and closing his eyes. He'd gone and blown it! Why couldn't he just have left things as they were? At least then he'd still have her – well, part of her.

But that was the whole problem. Part of her wasn't enough. He wanted all of her. He bent and picked a flat stone from the sand, skimmed it over the orange-tinged water. This dating like teenagers was killing him. He was staring down the barrel of forty, for Christ's sake! He was tired of fooling around, always playing the clown, no ties, no responsibilities. He wanted roots, a home. Family.

All his life he'd been in a hurry: moving on to the next job, the next country, the next big thing. Even when he'd come here eighteen months ago he had only signed a six-month contract with the company, had every intention of moving on. Until Kathleen happened. It was like this rush of energy had exploded into his life. He had marvelled that such a small body could contain such force, such zest. It was all centred there in those huge brown eyes: the strength, the determination, that 'can do' fire. And then that dent on her upper lip, lending her whole face a childlike vulnerability that wrung his heart.

His dark sigh haunted the silence. For the first time in his life a woman had succeeded in anchoring him to one spot and he would have been more than happy to stay here for the rest of his days. He zipped up his jacket, shoved his hands deep in his pockets and, head bent, followed the curve of the tide. He'd walk on a little, see if the place couldn't work its magic on him. Since moving to Carniskey, this little pier, at night, was where he would always come when he needed to think, to clear out his head, to decide. It was on this very sand that he had decided it was time to put some roots down; on this very sand not a week ago that he had mustered the courage to suggest to Kathleen that they give living together a shot. And now he'd gone and...

'Come on, help me out here!' he muttered, sidestepping the lick of the tide.

* * *

Eight o'clock. Alison marched into Hannah's room and flung back the curtains. 'How's the leg, Hannah?' She pulled the bedclothes from her sleeping daughter. 'Sister Andrew called – *very* concerned. Now, UP! You're coming to town with me to sort that hair out!'

A low moan escaping her lips, Hannah curled herself into a ball, the memory of last night burning the fog from the edges of her mind.

'And you can make a start on this mess when we get

back!' Alison straddled the mound of clothes on the carpet, jiggled and forced the window clasp. With Hannah already sleeping when she got home last night, she had decided not to confront her, had decided to wait until morning – a new day, a new beginning. And this time she wasn't going to fall into the trap of wrestling with her daughter, of shrinking under her sullen, dismissive tone. She was taking control. The girl needed guidance and this time Alison was determined to provide it. There would be no row about yesterday's truancy – what was done was done – but neither would there be any doubt that a turning point had been reached and that things would be done very differently from here on. 'Up, Hannah. Now. I'm taking the dogs for a run and I want you ready to be out that door by nine.'

* * *

The tide was full in, a brisk wind fashioning white wings from the wave caps. Alison sat on the grass verge above the dunes and watched the dogs gallop towards the water. Tilly plunged into the breaking foam, little Tim halting in mid gallop at the water's edge, his calf-like hind legs almost somersaulting over his neck. His yelping was a mixture of excitement and fear: witnessing his mother's delight, straining to join her but locked in by his own apprehension. Alison thought of the Tim inside her, that part of her that secretly strained towards life and adventure, a force deep inside her bursting to break free but always held back by the stranglehold of fear – fear of failure, of disappointment, of loss – locking her into the safety of the known. The water sparkled and danced its invitation, every glisten of the sun, every pound of the surf echoing seductively to the hollowness inside her.

Tilly swam with the strength and vigour of her Icelandic ancestors, Tim running excitedly back and forth along a few feet of water line, crouching and jumping, all the time yelping his hunger to break past that line of white fear, to be free.

Knees tucked beneath her chin Alison watched on, deep in thought. Just what kind of an example was she showing Hannah, she wondered. Right from the first moment she had held her, Alison had promised to raise her daughter to be confident, courageous, to go out into the world with purpose and passion, with a strong sense of worth and belonging. And Hannah was a strong girl – determined, intelligent, passionate. But how was she ever going to learn to throw herself into life, to express that passion, that determination? No wonder the girl was in such a knot. She pictured Hannah as a grown woman, digging and sifting back through these precious years, trying to make some sense out of what she had become and finding, at the root of that search, a broken mother. Alison knew that she alone had the power to prevent that happening. A new determination cementing inside her, she stood to make her way home.

* * *

Eyes downcast, Hannah swivelled in the hairdresser's chair, not hearing a word of her mother's instructions to the stylist. They could shave the whole lot off, for all she cared, it didn't matter any more. Nothing mattered.

'And I'll meet you at three, then, Hannah, at the nursing home? You can take the bus out.' The touch of Alison's fingers on her shoulder made Hannah want to jump up and scream – at her mother, the stylist, at the whole bloody world!

Alison paid the receptionist, stepped out of the salon and turned down left past the library, head bent in thought. Hannah hadn't as much as opened her mouth all morning. No words of protest, no exaggerated sighs or shrugs or 'whatevers'. Perhaps a firm hand and a stronger belief in her own capabilities were all that Alison had needed all along. Could it really be that simple? She had noticed that look in Hannah's eyes, in her whole face: that shrinking shame and embarrassment that Alison was all too familiar with herself. Hannah was obviously taking the whole Sister Andrew business to heart – surely that alone was a good sign. She slipped the envelope containing Eugene's article from her bag and crossed the street. Underneath her frustration and annoyance, a huge part of her went out to Hannah. From her own experience, Alison knew that there was no punishment, no retribution to match the solitary knife of self-loathing. When they met up later, she decided, she wouldn't rake over old ground with Hannah. Instead they would start from this moment: clean slate, new beginning.

'Alison?' Kathleen waved from the footpath opposite and weaved through the traffic stopped at the lights. 'I'm glad I caught you.'

'Hey, you're out bright and early. So, how did it go with Rob last night?'

'Disaster,' Kathleen sighed, her whole body seeming somehow slackened, starved of its usual animation.

'What? But you did tell him you'd…'

'That's a whole other story.' Kathleen waved a hand in dismissal. 'There's something I really need to talk to you about. Look, this is kind of awkward, I…'

Alison inclined her head towards her, her brow knotting. It certainly wasn't like Kathleen to be stuck for words.

'It's Hannah,' she managed.

'Hannah?' Alison rolled her eyes in mock exasperation. 'The mitching?' she nodded. 'I know all about it and believe me it won't…'

'No, no. No, it's Jamie.'

Alison pulled back her head, puzzlement re-establishing itself between her brows.

'Remember the problem I was telling you about, the bedwetting? Turns out he told Rob last night.' Kathleen took a deep breath. She had wrestled with this all night long: her burning anger with Hannah, with that O'Neill bastard! And her guilt at landing another load on Alison, yet knowing she had no other choice. 'I'm not blaming Hannah and I think she did the right thing deciding not to…'

'Hang on, slow down.' Alison touched her on the sleeve, as if to stem the flow of words, the confusion. 'Not blaming Hannah for what, for heaven's sake?'

'She had him round when she was babysitting. Peter O'Neill.' Kathleen spat out the name. 'Drinking. Jamie woke with the racket and came downstairs.' She looked into Alison's wide eyes. 'O'Neill shouted at him, threatened to come back and get him if he opened his mouth.'

Alison drew back her hand, folded her arms across her chest. She swallowed. 'When was this?' Her voice was dark with temper.

'About three weeks ago.'

Alison shook her head, her teeth working her lower lip. 'I am so sorry, Kathleen...'

'No. Please, it's not your fault. I just thought ... well, I knew you'd want to know, for Hannah's sake.'

'Listen, I'm late with this' – Alison held up the brown envelope – 'but rest assured I'll deal with this. Can I call you later?' Not waiting for Kathleen's response she turned on her heel, her quick, heavy step voicing her fury.

Kathleen stood on and watched her – head bowed, shoulders hunched – disappear into the crowd. How different everything had been just last night. Over their meal and a couple of drinks they had put the world to rights, both of them looking to the future, making plans. Kathleen had hardly been able to contain herself in her race home to Rob to...

She stood to her full height, raised her chin. Just who the hell did he think he was, walking out like that and accusing *her* of playing games? And to top it all off no call this morning – not even a text! She re-crossed the street, a hot fist squeezing her heart. Let him walk! She had managed perfectly fine before he came along and she would manage again. Games! She'd show Rob Tyrrell she was well above his schoolyard tactics!

* * *

Alison stubbed out her cigarette, drained her coffee. Standing from the street-side table, she yanked the engagement ring from her finger and stuffed it deep in her jeans pocket. She cut through the cobbled side street and down towards the Apple Market. The sky had darkened, the first swollen raindrops beginning to fall.

A tinny bell announced her entry to the empty shop. She stood at the counter in the semi-darkness, her teeth almost cutting through her lower lip. A door groaned on weary hinges and a ruddy face set with keen, close-set eyes materialised before her. 'Mornin', love. Rain's not far off.' His two remaining teeth, chipped and stained, hung from his gums like badges of victory.

'Is it ever?' Alison smiled shyly. She fished in her pocket and proffered the ring across the counter. 'What can you give me for this?' She held her head high, cursing herself for sounding like a child in a sweetshop.

'Let's see then. Umm, pretty.' He rolled the delicate ring between his thumb and forefinger before moving to a counter at the rear of the shop to study it further under glass and lamp, his tuneless whistle filling the room.

'Say, six-fifty, love?' He shot the words out of the corner of his mouth, his head still bent to his task.

'Six hundred and fifty euro?'

'Six. Five. O.' He removed the tiny magnifying glass from his eye.

'But it cost over twelve hundred – and that was pounds.' Alison had reckoned on at least a thousand.

'Sorry, love, best I can do.' He stole a glance at her, weighing up the desperation in her tone, the determined set of her jaw.

'Surely you can make it eight – isn't the price of gold…? I will be back for it, it's my…I'll be back before summer is out.'

'Sorry, love. No can do. Six seven five, tops. That's it.' He moved back towards her, the tiny diamonds sparkling in his outstretched palm.

'Okay. Yes, I'll take it.' Alison knew she would change her

mind if she hesitated one second longer. She had signed the paperwork, taken the cash and returned to the street before she allowed herself to listen to the questions shouting in her head. What would Sean think? Remember the day he'd bought it in Appelbys? Remember his words as he slipped it on her finger? Maybe she would never get it back…

She stuffed the money into the inside pocket of her leather bag. It's my ring and my call, she told herself, a warm bud of confidence causing her to straighten her shoulders. She could do without a diamond on her finger for a couple of months if it meant being able to get Hannah away from here. She zipped up her coat, pulled the collar up round her neck and ran through the downpour towards the travel agents.

* * *

William Hayden eyed Dr Fogarty across the desk. 'How long?' His voice was steady, his eyes inviting the doctor's to meet them.

'Four, five months at the outside. The chemo and radiation would buy you another two.'

'We've already been there, Doc. I'm not interested in drawing it out.'

'But there are so many advances now, it would be—'

'No, thanks all the same.' He dropped his eyes, unrolled and buttoned his shirt sleeve. 'I've had fifty-four good years. Been blessed with a strong mind and body. I'm not going backwards at this stage.' William paused, shook his head. 'Not when the final result's already in.'

'I understand. And I do appreciate it is your decision.'

Fogarty had seen it so many times. The desperate grasping at treatments, alternative cures, faith healings. And the added misery and disappointment that went with them. He knew that were he in William's shoes he'd be doing the very same.

'So, the hip, how's that been?'

'Bit more troublesome than before, but the swimming seems to help.' William didn't mention the nights, frequent now, when he'd have to leave his bed, the burning pain in his hip and upper thigh not allowing him to lie or sit.

'Any headaches, dizziness, loss of vision?'

'No. None.' Neither did he mention the bouts of melancholy, the chilling loneliness he could sometimes feel surrounding him, seeping into him, or his confusion at the tears that caught him, so often now, completely out of the blue.

'Okay then,' Fogarty sighed, rising. 'We'll up the painkillers for the secondary on the hip. I'll need to schedule another scan for the brain tumour – say, four weeks from today? Maybe keep you in for a few days at that stage, decide on the best course of pain relief. And if you change your mind about the other treatment in the meantime, feel free to …'

'Thanks, Doc.' William stood to leave, shaking the doctor's hand. Fogarty held it warmly.

'I should say that the high risk of blackouts puts driving out of the question from here on. Perhaps a family member could … you know you will need support as time goes on.'

'No family, I'm afraid. The curse of the roving bachelor.' William smiled, regret colouring his humour.

'We'll talk more when I see you in four weeks.' Fogarty held the door open, his other hand finding William's shoulder. 'Take care of yourself.'

He studied William's face as he leaned on the reception desk to fix his next appointment: the healthy tan, that wide grin, the hint of the rogue that lit his eyes. Incredible how someone so near the end could still possess such light, such good humour. He closed the door, moved to the window and stared down on the roofs of the sprawling city. He was a wealthy man, successful, renowned and respected in his field – all the boxes ticked on what he had spent his best years striving for. And yet the dying man who had just walked from his rooms had more life and energy in him still than Joseph Fogarty had ever had the pleasure of knowing. At only fifty-three he was already burnt out, but the lifestyle that he had been seduced into insisted that he carry on for at least another ten, fifteen years: all that time dealing out death, breaking the same news to the same pained and pleading eyes in so many different faces. He lowered himself into his chair with a sigh and buzzed through the next patient.

Five

Alison let her eyes wander over the stack of CDs on the sun-faded carpet, the electric guitar, the straw sun hat perched on the bed post, the knapsack and school bag bulging from the space between the wardrobe and wall. Well, at least she had made an effort to tidy before she left, she smiled. Sitting on the bed she smoothed a palm across the pillow and inhaled deeply, chasing Hannah's smell. Eight days now since Hannah had left for London and not an hour went by that Alison didn't agonise whether, in her haste, she had made the right decision. It had all happened so quickly: Hannah was in the air before Alison had fully realised she had let her go. She hadn't even wholly made up her mind that day when she had called to the travel agents. It was seeing Hannah in the nursing home that evening that had finally sealed it. She had watched from the door of the dayroom, her hand clutched to her throat as if fighting the lump there that threatened to choke her. Hannah standing behind Maryanne's chair, her head resting on her shoulder, arms clasped tightly round her grandmother's neck, and the two pairs of eyes, one more lost, more pained than the other.

Alison's mind shot to that moment at Departures, Hannah gripping her in a childlike hug – their first real physical contact in what seemed like forever. Alison had wanted to melt into her, to cancel all plans and turn back for home. Hannah then, gently pulling away, her excitement and frantic prattle failing to hide her trepidation.

She straightened the two teddy bears against the pillow. Hannah was safe and well settled in – and so happy, if her voice on the telephone last night was anything to go by. She had a truly wonderful summer ahead of her and Alison had no doubt that Claire would spare nothing to make it a holiday that Hannah would remember for the rest of her life. And Kathleen was right. Alison had given her that opportunity and she should be proud of herself, proud of her strength as a mother. And she would make Hannah proud of her, too. When she returned, Alison would be different, stronger. She would use this time to sort out her life, get rid of that gnawing resentment, the dark negativity that had come to stalk her every step. She rose from the bed, closed the bedroom door softly behind her, refusing to entertain the gaping emptiness inside her.

Back in her own room, she unclasped her hair and the fiery curls danced below her shoulders, framing her cheeks. The blue shirt accentuated her full bosom when she tucked its tails inside the waistband of her jeans. Bit too 'woman on the make', she decided, pulling the shirt free and letting it hang loose. She wasn't particularly in the mood for the scene in the local pub – and why did Kathleen have to invite May, of all people! Alison could picture it: Kathleen would have met her in the street or somewhere, mentioned they were going out, listened to May's troubles, felt sorry for her and asked her to come along. Typical Kathleen – and typical May, to wheedle her way in when it suited her! Now they'd have to watch every word they uttered – that's if they got a chance to utter anything over May's incessant gabble about Paul's affair and the woes of being a newly separated thirty-something.

'Come on, that house will close in around you,' Kathleen had urged when she'd rung to ask how Hannah was settling in. Alison had declined, but Kathleen persisted, adding how she was missing Rob and could really do with some company. 'Come on, Alison, do me a favour, please?' Kathleen had been so good about the whole Hannah incident, how could she refuse her? But now May? She sighed, strapped on her watch. Quarter to nine. She topped up the dogs' water bowl and locked them into the back kitchen. She'd walk the ten minutes to Phil's. It was still bright and the fresh air would help to lift her tiredness. She could grab a lift home with Kathleen.

The small thatched pub was already full. The dance of the banjo and the heat hit Alison like a burst of life when she opened the door. Kathleen and May waved from their table under the window. Maybe it's not so bad to get out after all, she smiled to herself, ignoring the heads that turned to look at her as she made her way through the crowd to join them.

'Alison, you're looking wonderful! What's your tipple?' May, her blonde bob waxed and teased to within an inch of its life, stood and kissed the air either side of Alison's face. That perfume could strip walls, Alison thought, catching her breath.

'We're in for a long one, girl, so what's it to be?'

God, how long's she been here, Alison wondered. Kathleen, reading her mind, threw her eyes to heaven and patted the stool beside her.

89

'Budweiser, please – a bottle.'

May tottered to the counter on her high red heels.

'She had an early start,' Kathleen confided. 'Paul called to see the children this evening and they had a massive row. Poor May – she'd secretly hoped the whole thing would've fizzled out by now, that he'd have come back, tail between his legs.'

'I can't believe she'd even consider having him back.'

'Well, I suppose everyone deserves a second chance.'

'Including Rob?' Alison smiled. 'Don't tell me you're still giving the poor guy the cold shoulder.'

'Rob's not…ssh, here she comes, I don't want her knowing any of this. So, how's Hannah doing?'

They chatted and laughed over the music. It seemed an age to Alison since she'd done this. There's still life in the old place, she thought, finishing her second bottle and moving to the bar to order a round. The music stopped and the guitar player called on Bill Fleming for a song. The old man turned from his pint at the counter, palmed his cap and began:

> *From pigtails to wedding veils*
> *From petticoats to lace…*

A lump lodged itself in Alison's throat. She leaned her elbows on the counter and rested her chin on the heels of her hands. This was her father's song. The one he would sing to herself and Claire all those years ago when he'd tuck them into bed at night.

> *So slow up*
> *Don't rush to grow up*
> *Stay awhile*
> *In the special years.*

Hannah, Hannah, Hannah. Her smiling face at the airport, the anxiety in the set of her mouth at Departures, the smell of her lingering on Alison's shirt sleeve on the journey back home, alone in the car. The room burst into applause, saving her, calling her back. She took a deep breath and, turning her head to attract the barmaid's attention, Alison half jumped at the sight of William Hayden sitting at the end of the bar, his eyes smiling through her as if reading her soul. He lifted his glass and nodded his head in greeting. Alison returned a tight smile and looked away in embarrassment.

'Who's your man at the bar?' Kathleen couldn't wait till Alison was seated.

'Oh, he's some old guy, I don't know, camping out up at Tra na Leon. Thinks he owns the place!'

* * *

Hannah sat cross-legged on the white bedcover, fingering the iPhone, its purple metallic case dancing under the lamplight. A 'welcome' present from Claire, it was the very latest model, the most expensive. Grainne White would turn green when she saw it!

She stretched out on the bed. It had been nice of Claire to turn it around so that it faced the same way as her bed at home. It did help her sleep better. She hadn't slept through a full night yet, but at least now she wasn't waking with a start in the dead of night, her heart pounding as she fought to figure out where she was, another version of that awful dream of Peter O'Neill fading as she came to.

She left the bed and padded to the window. Down below Claire and Grandad were sitting at the table on the small patio – an exact replica of the empty one next door. Claire was explaining something, her hands working in backwards circles, Grandad throwing his head back, laughing.

She picked up the whelk shell from the window sill, felt its rough curves. She had carried it all the way from the beach at Carniskey – a kind of link to home, to Mum. She brought it to her ear now, the thunder of the sea pulling her lips to a smile; then to her nose, its neutral smell causing her to lick it, searching its salt, before placing it back on the windowsill and returning her attention to the patio below. Claire did look like Mum: the hair, the eyes. A plumper, happier, more-alive Mum.

Mum would be visiting Nan again today, at least that's what she had said on the phone last night. Hannah had asked her to give Nan her love, knowing while she said it that it was useless, stupid. She pictured her mum, sitting there in the nursing home, holding Nan's hand and talking on and on as if some big tide of words would somehow lift Nan back from wherever she had gone. Hannah just couldn't understand how her mum did it. Day in, day out, sitting in that place. She knew she couldn't. She knew too that she would never be able to put into words how she felt, seeing Nan there but not there. How that stare in Nan's eyes made her shiver with fear, with loneliness – just like after Dad died.

Mum didn't seem to mind, though. Sometimes she even thought that Mum liked it, that she was attracted in some weird way to sad things. Maybe, Hannah thought, it made her feel closer to Dad, maybe it was her way of holding on to him.

Hannah couldn't understand anyone thinking like that. As far as she was concerned, once someone was gone they were gone. You just shut it out, shut the whole thing out. That's why she had decided not to use Claire's laptop today to check her Facebook account. She was tired of Aoife's messages about Peter O'Neill and Pamela. They could go to hell, the two of them. What did she care? She waved down to Claire who was beckoning her from the patio.

* * *

The musicians were packing away their gear, a few of the locals conducting their own singsong – a mixture of comeallyas and rebel rousers – when May returned from the Ladies, her eyes puffed and red. 'One for the road?' she slurred to the barman, cleaning the tables.

'Sorry, love, it's well gone time.' He hurried on to the next table.

'Come on, May, best be getting home,' a sober Kathleen urged. 'The babysitter'll be getting itchy to go.'

'Home?' May's pitch was high and hostile. 'I haven't got a home, Kathleen! Not any more, and that Purcell slut cosying up with my Paul somewhere…'

'C'mon, May, it's not so bad, we'll talk in the car,' Alison soothed. She could feel the eyes on them, could sense the gossips smelling out a little late-night entertainment.

'Not so BAD? And what would you know about it? It's all right for you, at least your fella's dead. He's gone. Safe from the clutches of the likes of that Purcell vulture and her—'

'May, please—'

'You're a widow. There's some dignity in that. You don't have to lie in bed wondering where he is, what he's up to.' She grasped the side of the table with both hands, her narrowed

93

eyes piercing Alison. 'You can strut around the place like a half lunatic but no one's pointing the finger at you saying, "Oh, there she is, so washed up she couldn't even keep her own man!"'

Alison squirmed under the spotlight of the silence and the forty pairs of eyes she imagined boring through the back of her head. She reached for her cardigan and handbag, a hot fire burning behind her eyes.

'I'll give you a lift.' Kathleen's gentle voice threatened to unplug the dam in her heart.

'Thanks, Kathleen. I'd prefer to walk.' She almost knocked over a stool in her rush to the door. It had been a mistake to come out. She should have known better. Nothing ever changed in this place.

She crossed the road and negotiated the dark passageway to the beach. Her eyes accustomed to the blackness, she walked along the dry sand to the clutter of rocks on the right. She knew every inch of this place. Knew it and loved it even more in the dark than in the glare of daylight. And it knew her – and every secret and longing stored at the root of her.

Her heart swelled and fell with the rhythm of the waves, swelling and crashing, swelling and calling, her dry eyes locked on the dark horizon. Slipping off her shoes, she soft-stepped towards the water. The wet yielding sand gripped at her bare feet – childlike, impatient in its wanting, its yearning to claim her. She stood at the water's edge, at the tail of silver ribbon the moon had spun out across the still sea. She imagined it was a spotlight, a search light, and Sean was holding it, out there at the other end, searching, calling for her. The waves were his whisper, the tide all the time drawing back, making room, tempting her on. And in its retreat, revealing what lay beneath. Rocks emerged, and they became people – her mother, her grandfather, calling to her. Oh, the sea knew her well. Slowly, slowly, drawing back, revealing its own and her own depths.

Her loose jeans rolled easily over her knees. She stepped slowly from them. A few paces forward, she closed her eyes and concentrated on the sound, that mighty, hypnotic echo-sound of the sea. She imagined a huge cavern out beyond the horizon from where the tide sprung and to where it returned every night at dark, offering up the treasures it had seduced into joining it. She could picture its vast blue-green interior, an Aladdin's cave of old ships and bounty. And Sean there, waiting for her.

The wet sand clung tighter now, a more adult desperation in its grip. Alison paced forward, her heels sinking deeper, deeper, the breaking waves caressing and licking her bare thighs.

The strong hand on her shoulder broke her reverie. She turned her head slowly and stared into his dark eyes. He didn't speak but, holding her gaze, turned her towards him. His arm gently around her shoulders he took her cold hand in his and led her from the water. William took off his jacket and draped it around her. 'Come on, you're cold – I'll take you home.' Her whole body trembling, he helped her step into her jeans and shoes and then led her silently up the beach and through the black passageway. 'Which way?' he coaxed, his arm firmly fixed around her shaking frame. He followed her lead, past the pub, up the hill from the village and in around to the back door, neither of them uttering a word.

* * *

'Don't mollycoddle the lad!' Frank's words echoed back to Maryanne, as sharp in memory as they had been in life, and with them came the picture of one particular September evening. Sean would have been, what, eight, maybe nine? School was just back after summer and Sean was fighting to keep his eyes open over his homework at the kitchen table. He had been out with Frank since five that morning, shifting pots ahead of the oncoming storm – had got in barely with time for breakfast before heading to school. 'We need to get down and tighten that mooring.' Frank grabbed his hat from the hook on the back door, Sean almost tripping over his chair in his rush to join him. '*We* need to get down ...' He could never address the child by his name, had seldom uttered it since that first night at the hospital – God forbid he'd show any bit of a feeling, or 'weakness', as he'd class it himself! Sean, struggling into his coat then, his arms stretched and tightened beyond their years from hauling pots, pulling nets. Sometimes Maryanne felt that Frank didn't see a boy at all but a man the age and strength of himself. And why wouldn't he, the way that poor Sean would master every task he set him, completing it quicker and better than someone twice his age. She would often notice the way the child would stand back then, dark eyes stealing sideways from the work to his father, a hand in his soft curls hiding his face, his whole being straining for those few words of praise that never came. 'That'll do,' was the closest Frank was ever able to come to it.

'But Frank, his homework – and can't you see the boy needs his bed, he's fit to drop,' she'd protested that evening.

'Don't mollycoddle the lad!'

* * *

'Go and put on something dry,' William urged as they stood in the moonlit kitchen. 'I'll fill the kettle, you'll need something to warm you up.' Like a lost child she moved down the darkness of the hallway and into the bedroom. William felt for a switch and turned on the kitchen light. He found the kettle, filled it with water and plugged it in. Leaning back against the counter, he took in the room. The sea occupied the whole of its length. The blue walls were stencilled with shells and fish. Stones, shells and driftwood occupied every window ledge, shelf and press top. The centre light over the kitchen table could have come straight from a captain's cabin. Old glass buoys, green and blue, hung in their netting from the thick wooden beams supporting the ceiling. A four-foot lighthouse, crafted from driftwood, occupied the centre of the front bay window. The window to the side housed a large desk and computer, a sea of papers and clippings littering the surrounding floor space. Although the room was warm William sensed a familiar cold, an emptiness around him as he stood looking out at the moon lighting the sea beyond. He studied the photographs framing the window. The same face, at varying ages, looked back at him from every one. A handsome face, tanned and healthy, the eyes alive with youth and energy. In most of the photos he wore his fishing gear, yellow oilskins and a navy cap. The tilt of his head, the lopsided smile and the way his strong hands held a salmon, a mooring rope, a lobster, all shouted of his pride and abandon in his work.

'That's Sean.' Her quiet words startled William and he spun around to find her in the doorway. Her hair hung loose over her shoulders, its rich red accentuated by the white oversized dressing gown.

'Sean?' He stepped towards her, his brow creased. 'I don't even know your name.'

'Alison, but not to be confused with the wonderland variety.' She stepped past him to the front window and flicked a switch setting the huge lighthouse aglow, its soft red light casting a warm beam across the room.

'Nice to meet you, Alison. To finally know your name.' William watched her. Trance-like, she gazed out the window.

'You can see this light, you know, all the way from Helvic Head, over there.' He followed her finger out into the darkness. 'I've lit this every night of every year since Sean was lost. Out there. Hannah and I, we put it together that November.'

'Hannah?'

'My daughter. She's in London. And I need a drink.' She turned swiftly from the window.

'I've boiled the kettle...'

'No tea and sympathy, thanks. There's only one cure for the sea's salty bite.' She bent at the sink and opened the cupboard below. A bottle of Jameson's in hand, she took two glasses from the overhead press and switched off the kitchen light, bathing the whole room in the soft, warm glow of the lighthouse. She sat at the table. 'You'll join me?' She motioned to a chair opposite and poured two generous measures. William took the seat offered, raised his glass.

'To Alison,' he smiled. 'Are you warming up?'

'How did you know where to find me?' Her head was bent, her two hands hugging the glass.

'I left the pub just after you, was making my way up the track when I noticed you.'

'The sea, sometimes it calls me.' She took a fast gulp of the burning liquid.

'You really love it, don't you, the sea?' Not one day had

gone by since he'd come here that he hadn't seen her on the beach.

'I should hate it. It's taken everything from me. And it still roars for more.' She emptied the glass in two short bursts and promptly refilled it. 'It's like it had claimed me.'

'Have you lived here always?'

'The love affair with this place began when I was just fifteen years old. I moved here at twenty. Packed in college, my degree, the lot, to answer its call.' She lit a cigarette, moved her gaze to William.

'You've not been here before. Will you stay long?'

'Just a couple of months, but yeah, I can see the attraction.'

'It's much more than that.' A dark passion lit her eyes. 'It's an obsession. And the loneliness and longing it stirs in you binds you to it, like it owns you.' The melancholic resignation in her young voice drew him like a magnet. He wanted to know her more, to know and share the secrets of that sadness haunting her green eyes. And in their haunting, he glimpsed Helene.

'Where are you from?' The passion had deserted her voice.

'Dublin, originally. Then Paris, Montpellier, parts of Italy, Spain. I've moved about a lot.'

'And I have walked the same stretch of sand for the last seventeen years.'

'Must get lonely here in winter.' He sought out her darkness.

'Winter's my favourite time. Grey and wet. Wild and deserted. You can hide in the greyness, you know. And it soothes the longing. Makes you feel at home in yourself.' She looked away into the distance before continuing. 'No pressure in winter to be part of a busy world. Winter is the soul's season. It can shine in the quiet, the anonymous darkness.'

'Why can't it shine in the sunlight?' William urged her on.

'Because then you're certified. Crazy. It's under the spotlight and everyone's picking at it. No, mine lives in the greys and the blacks.'

'You're a writer?'

She raised her eyebrows.

'I've seen you, on the beach.'

'A writer? I wish! No, it's taken that from me too.' Her face grew hard.

'And Sean. How long...'

'Do you always ask so many bloody questions?' Her sudden hostility startled him.

'Forgive me...maybe it's time I left. I...'

'No! Please, stay a while.' Her fingers were on his arm, her eyes filled with childlike pleading. She topped up his glass, drained her own and then coloured it again with the golden liquid. Her step was unsteady as she rose from the table.

'Do you like music?'

'Some.'

She flicked on the stereo. *The Marriage of Figaro* haunted the room. She turned up the volume and, eyes closed, moved like an ethereal spirit across the floor, her arms and hips slowly undulating to the music's melancholy strains. Her head, slightly back, was tilted to one side like a ghost of Venus, the full lips slightly parted in longing and promise, her long red curls a flame licking her shoulders and back. William looked on open-mouthed, entranced.

100

'Dance with me, William.' Arms stretched towards him, she twirled and giggled, almost landing in his lap.

'Thanks,' he smiled. 'I'll sit this one out.'

'Come on!' She tugged at his hands, twirled under the bow of his outstretched arm.

'Oh God...' She rushed from the kitchen. He hesitated a moment before following her out into the hall. He heard the retch from behind the bathroom door.

'Alison?' He knocked gently, pushed back the door. 'Alison?'

She was on her knees at the toilet bowl, the long robe trailing behind her.

'Alison, you okay?'

She retched again. He moved gingerly towards her and taking her hair in his hands held it behind her neck.

'Please, just leave me alone.'

He passed her some tissue and flushed the bowl. 'I'll get you a drink.' When he returned from the kitchen, she was sitting on the floor, her back to the radiator, knees bunched up under her chin.

'Drink this.' He handed her the glass, wet a flannel under the cold tap and folding it, pressed it to her forehead. He hadn't noticed the silent tears slow-winding down her cheeks.

'Alison, it's okay, maybe you should lie down...'

'It's not okay! It'll never again be okay. Just leave me, please.'

'But I don't...'

'Just get out of my house! Go. Get out and leave me alone!' She hurled the glass at the wall, threw down the flannel and fled to the bedroom, slamming the door behind her.

William bent and gathered the shards of glass, the tiny

slivers of anger and hurt glittering on the bathroom floor. With a heaviness in his heart and step, he closed the back door and disappeared into the velvet night.

* * *

Lilies or sunflowers? Rob fingered the coins in his pockets. He was already late for work. Lilies or sunflowers? If you were to give him a thousand, he couldn't remember which were her favourite. But he was certain of one thing: his big mistake had been leaving it three days before making contact. He had thought he would give her some time to cool down, put the whole thing into perspective, miss him. He had been stubborn, yes, but by God he had found out to his cost that she beat him hands down in that department, too.

If he had that time back over again, he would have camped out on her doorstep that night, would have refused point-blank to leave until she had taken him in – if only out of embarrassment. He had seen it played out in a movie once, it had worked for that guy.

He scraped his fingers through his hair. It was almost two weeks since he had seen her now – if you didn't count that evening he'd bumped into her in the shop. She had seen him come in, he knew it. Knew it by the way she had suddenly leaned into Jamie's football coach, all pals and laughs over the deli counter. Kathleen couldn't stand that guy! He remembered her saying once that the reason he drove a soft top was because no car with a roof could house that ego. The swing of her hips then as she sashayed up to the counter, all the time pretending she hadn't seen him in the frozen food aisle.

'Wonderful,' she'd answered when he had caught her at the door and asked how herself and Jamie were doing. But her eyes weren't as quick as her tongue and something in them, something missing from them, gave him his first flutter of hope in over a week.

'Well, have you decided?' The florist's impatience, impeded by her fixed smile, found its way out in the flick of her wrist as she ran the blade of her scissors along the length of red ribbon, curling it like the peel of an apple.

'Can you mix lilies and sunflowers?'

Six

William had fallen into a deep sleep in the late afternoon, his hip and his racing thoughts having kept him awake through most of the previous night. He didn't hear the soft knock on the camper door. It was the dogs barking excitedly around the gorse that eventually roused him.

'Alison?'

'Oh, I thought you were out.' She turned around, retraced her steps. She had been relieved when she'd received no answer. Deciding to come here and face her embarrassment was one thing, going through with it was another. She lifted her head, her eyes for a second meeting his as she thrust the bunch of wild daises into his hand. 'An apology – for last night?'

'I was sleeping, sorry. Really, there's no need.' His eyes were shadowed, making him look older, wearied.

'Will you come in?'

'No, thanks. I'm taking the dogs to Sliabh Carraig, they've been cooped up all morning.'

'Right. How are you feeling?' he risked.

'Miserable.' She lowered her head. 'Tired, sick, foolish,

confused – all of the above.' She grinned her despair, her shoulders rising then falling with her sigh. An awkward silence and she turned to leave.

'Is it far – the mountain?'

'About five miles. I'll go, sorry to have woken you. Catch you again and, well, sorry.'

'Alison!' He called to her back. 'Fancy some company?' Facing him after last night couldn't have been easy – the way she had herself hidden away in that big man's jacket screamed her discomfort. She hesitated a moment before turning again to face him.

'If you don't mind the incessant yelping on the way, sure.' Her smile was uncertain, timid almost.

'I'll just get a jacket.' He disappeared into the van. The pregnant sky stooped in conspiratorial whisper to the rising sea. 'Bring a hat,' she called after him through the open door. 'Rain's not far off.'

'Is it your hip?' Alison motioned to the walking stick in William's hand.

'Yeah. I didn't figure you as a mountain person,' he remarked, steering the conversation away from the pain that knifed his hip as he raised himself into the passenger seat.

'I'm not usually.' She started up the jeep. 'Just felt I needed to get away from the sea for a bit. Plus, it's a change for the dogs.'

'I've never been up there – hope you don't mind me tagging along.'

'Of course not,' Alison smiled. 'You can help me keep these two under control.' She was grateful to this stranger who had cared enough to see her safely home last night. And the way she had treated him after … That familiar burn of humiliation heated her chest.

'They're beauties – have you had them long?' He had learned from last night to keep the conversation light, was wary of upsetting her or causing offence with his curiosity.

'Tilly five years – she was a birthday present for Hannah. And she presented us with Tim and five others last July.'

Driving slowly towards the mountain, Alison enjoyed the easy small talk, the light silences. She felt strangely at home with this almost stranger.

'We'll leave the jeep here, maybe walk as far as the waterfall?' Alison pointed towards the long white fingers of water massaging the mountain face in the distance. She eased into a neat parking space. There weren't many cars for a Sunday, the sky's threatening greys probably keeping many indoors.

'Wow, what a beautiful spot.' William tugged on his jacket and joined her as she released the straining dogs from the boot. Carpets of purple and blue heathers softened the craggy ground, long haired elders and tight curled lambs dotting the hills and dips. Pulled back on themselves by the wind, the whitethorn bushes in the distance put him in mind of reluctant brides.

'You should see it on a bright day.' Alison zipped her jacket, shoving her hands into its generous pockets.

'Won't they bother them?' William worried as the dogs raced ahead in the direction of the disinterested sheep.

'No, I think they're afraid of them. They'll investigate nothing bigger than a rabbit. Cowards, the two of them.' They laughed companionably as they slow-strolled the path to the waterfall.

'This old man's going to have to sit down.' William sighed as they neared the frantic foam fall. He eased himself onto a large, flat rock, the walking stick held in both hands between his legs. Alison turned off the path and, squatting down, began to pluck at the blue and purple blooms.

'You like flowers?'

'Wild ones, yes. I admire their stamina, their independence. There's a spirit and beauty in them that the greenhouse variety don't have. A real survivor's life force, I suppose.'

'You could be describing yourself.' William voiced his impression as he took in the wild red curls tumbling over her shoulders. There was a wildness and vulnerability about her, a strength and a kind of sad delicacy in the wiry frame lost in the bulky wax jacket. Her face reddened and she bent her head in fake concentration. Neither spoke, each enjoying the quiet solitude, the easy togetherness, the company of their own thoughts.

'Just listen to the power in the roar of that water.' Alison joined him on the rock, a bunch of wild heathers held lightly in her hand. The rush and urgency of the water's fall filled the still air.

'You came here to get away from the sea.' William turned to face her. 'But the water seems to move with you.'

'She moves with me.' Alison's green eyes locked on his. 'And in me.' That look was in her eyes again. That haunting.

'Why refer to the sea as "she"?' William held her gaze.

'I know what she is.' Her words were hushed, as though confiding a secret. 'I've witnessed her gentle seductions, her flirting and teasing. That hypnotic allure. And her manic and desperate hold. She's the ultimate mistress, William.' She nodded her head slowly, her gaze shifting back in the direction of the ocean. 'With her gentle comforts, her whispers of adventure, freedom and danger.' She broke off, as if reluctant, afraid of being overheard. When she spoke again her voice was barely more than a whisper. 'Her kiss-smack on a stern is really a lick of his soul; her undulating beneath the boat, an erotic promise and teasing. The way she will spurn him in winter and laugh, thrusting herself at the cliffs. And he'll watch from the shoreline, straining to touch her, to feel her yielding curves beneath him. Then he'll shut down his heart to all around him. And wait. Wait and hope through the darkness of winter for spring and her opening and invitation.' Her words tapered off, her gaze moving to the waterfall. 'That's the Carraig fall,' she offered, pointing. 'It rushes all the way from here to Carniskey and empties itself into the ocean at the left-hand side of the bay.'

'Seems urgent in its journey.' William studied her profile. 'Under her seductive spell as well?' He was entranced by her personalisation of the sea and its wanton appetite.

* * *

Having separated the bouquet, Kathleen set the sunflowers on the kitchen window and carried the vase of lilies to the hall table, where their scent would greet her every time she walked in the front door. She could never decide which were her favourite: the sunflowers with their burst of colour, their promise of hope, or the pure white lilies her mother had always adored. She had to hand it to Rob for remembering that she had settled on both.

She crossed back into the sitting room, smiling in spite of herself as she remembered the florist's early morning delivery of the bulky, awkward bouquet and the silly 'I'm Sorry' card with the big sad face on it that would melt the devil himself. Big child! She'd had to work for a minute to recover her anger after she'd read it.

Rob could never be serious for more than five minutes. It was what most niggled her and what she most loved about him all at the same time. That slight gap between his two front teeth, the way his eyes danced with a mixture of mirth and mischief. Rob could turn any situation into a pantomime – no wonder Jamie adored him. She bent and straightened the magazines on the coffee table. She really hadn't realised how much she had come to depend on him, on his wit, his charm, his presence. It was as if he had stolen into her while she wasn't looking and that part of her he had occupied creaked now in the cold wind of his absence.

Only yesterday she'd had to check herself again at work. She had always vowed that if she ever found herself being impatient or short with the patients, or giving them less than the hundred per cent care and kindness they deserved, she would quit her job at Sea View and let someone more suitable take her place. These last weeks she had found it a real struggle, putting on a smile and a heartiness that was a million miles away from how she was feeling. She had swapped shifts today to give herself a break, some time on her own just to be able to breathe, feel, recharge.

She glanced at the clock on the mantelpiece. Another two hours before Jamie was due back from his friend's. Was this what life was going to be like from now on? Jamie, growing up, busy with his own stuff and her sitting at home, waiting. Much as it pained her to admit it, Rob had been right. She did need to cut those apron strings, stand back a little and give Jamie room to grow. And meantime she would do what exactly? Today was the one day she had to herself this week and she was having difficulty filling it. She grabbed a cushion from the sofa, patted and plumped its feathers, then threw it back down on the couch. What was she doing? She had cleaned and straightened the whole downstairs already this morning. She hated feeling like this, wallowing.

She'd call on Alison. The one sure cure for self-pity was to get out and visit someone who had a genuine problem. She grabbed her keys from the kitchen table, the sunflowers smiling at her from the window.

Her heart dropped. Just remember, a tiny voice whispered, he was the one who walked out. He was, Kathleen answered, and he won't get a chance to do it again. Tilting her chin she shook out her keys, slung her bag over her shoulder and pulled the door behind her.

* * *

The dogs danced back as the first heavy drops bled from the sky. 'Come on, old man,' Alison teased, standing up from the rock, 'we don't want you getting arthritis.' William rose, flexed the fingers of his right hand, silently cursing their prickling numbness, a side effect of the stronger medication. He'd had no choice in the end but to go with it, aware that the consequences would be a lot worse if he didn't. The rain fell heavier now. He pulled a cap from his pocket, placed it on his head as he walked on to join her. She turned around to wait for him. The rain had darkened and tamed the curls framing her face. There's a beautiful life and energy clamped behind that sadness, he thought, her soft smile whispering a forgotten girlish joy.

Alison watched him walk towards her. She hardly knew him but she liked him, trusted him for some reason. She sensed some kind of a strange understanding between them, something that loosened the lid on the darkness she carried.

Most of the journey back to Carniskey was passed in silence. Both were lost in their own thoughts, each appreciating the other's quiet reflection. The rain fell hard and Alison concentrated on the road through the fogged-up windows.

'Tired?' she asked as they neared the village.

'Hey, don't write me off just yet,' William laughed. 'Fifty-four's not quite slippers and pension book. Fancy a pint to round off the day?'

'I'll pass this time, thanks. I have a job to finish for Eugene and I promised Hannah I'd phone this evening, see she's behaving herself.'

'Eugene, your boss?'

'Eugene Dalton, he's the editor of the local paper. I do a women's column every week.'

'Ah! So you *are* a writer.'

'Not in the sense I'd like to be. I hate it – a women's column, of all things! No, in my heart and my dreams I'm a poet.' Alison smiled. 'And a best-selling novelist,' she added with a laugh.

'So, what's stopping you?' William was excited at the hint of passion behind her cynical laugh.

'It won't put bread on the table,' she sighed, 'or keep Hannah in pocket money. No, dreams are a luxury I just can't afford.'

'But everyone's got to have one. They're the threads that keep us connected to the magic beyond this world.'

'What's yours, then?'

'At the moment? A pint. I'll hop out here, grab one before I head back up.'

Alison pulled in at the entrance to the strand, opposite

111

the pub. The sea, high and dark, crashed to the shore, littering the beach with froth. 'It's like a massive pint of the black stuff – my dream is out!' William laughed, pushing the door open against the wind. 'Thanks, I really enjoyed the trip.'

'Thanks for the company.' Alison returned a relaxed smile. 'Mind yourself.'

'See you soon.' And he was gone, the wind wrestling with his unbuttoned coat.

Alison drove in nearer the beach. The sea rushed in, in a galloping frenzy, urged on by a strong wind from the horizon. Each wave stood higher than the one before, crashing head-long in their race to the shore. There was an anger in it and in the sickly brown froth that shrouded the sand. Alison had never before seen such a wide and continuous line of froth; it must have been two metres wide and stretched almost half the length of the bay. It pulsated under the fingers of the wind, like something living, warning, threatening. She shivered. The sea was angry with her. She had refused its call last night. At the last second William had urged her back. And she had gone with him today, away into the mountains, ignoring its call, its rising temper. She stepped from the jeep and its salty perfume rushed at her nose. The wind almost lifted her, the cold spray stinging her cheek with an angry slap. She hopped back into the jeep and banged the door on its temper. As she backed up to leave, it hurled its filthy froth at the windscreen.

* * *

Warmed by a hot shower, Alison slipped into a soft cotton shirt and pants, towelled her damp hair and clipped it up.

Microwave dinner before her, she sat at the computer and worked straight through on Eugene's article. She worked with an energy she had almost forgotten and by eight thirty the article was complete. A great sense of satisfaction lifted her. Maybe later, after her call to Hannah, she'd set some time aside for a little private writing. She had more or less quit since those last rejections, but she really missed it. She lit the fire in the sitting room and drew the curtains, locking out the wind and the rain. Back in the kitchen she flicked on the kettle and then, changing her mind, took a bottle of red wine from the press. She would treat herself to a glass – a reward for a good evening's work. Maybe she should visit the mountain more often! She moved to the window and flicked on the lighthouse. There was company in its warm glow. She found herself wondering if William could see it from his camper and immediately snapped him from her mind. Passing the computer, she twiddled the mouse, her face breaking into a huge smile. An email from Hannah!

Hi Mum, just to let you know I'm okay. Grandad's party was a bit of a bore but he liked the clock you sent him. I started my job at the gallery and people keep asking me things I know nothing about but Claire says just to keep on smiling and that I'll get to know it all in no time. How are Tilly and Tim? Give them a kiss for me. And Nan. I won't be able to talk to you tonight 'cos Claire's taking me to the London Eye and then for something to eat, she says it's best not to do it the other way round. Talk soon, H x

Alison re-read the email, twice. Although her face was fixed in a smile, she couldn't ignore the slight sting and the sense of something shrinking in her chest. Claire. So it was just

'Claire' now, was it, no 'Aunt'? She sat back in her chair. For God's sake, why was she being so petty, so childish? Hannah was busy, she was happy – isn't that what she wanted? Wasn't that the whole point of sending her over there? And so what if they didn't get to talk tonight, there was always tomorrow. She leaned her head back on the chair, loneliness settling around her like a cloak.

* * *

William shaded in the damp curls and then, cursing under his breath, threw down his pencil, opened and closed his fist, hard, shook his hand out from the wrist. He studied the smile and the eyes on the page, anxious to have captured that faint promise of light behind them. He grabbed the pill bottle from the shelf behind, shook three painkillers out into his hand. He popped them in his mouth, took some water and flicked his head back to swallow. Moving cautiously, he lay down on the narrow bed and closed his eyes, listened to the rain and the wind knocking outside. Helene's face floated up from the darkness.

* * *

Stirred by the birdsong and the sun squinting through the bedroom drapes, Alison stretched, turned on her side and tugged a pillow down under her chin. Monday morning. She thought of all the people leaving their beds, swallowing a quick breakfast and racing to another week at the office, the shop, wherever. That would be her soon if she didn't start earning some real money. With the pressure of Eugene's job off her already, maybe this week she could try a new story, maybe fiddle around with some of the old ones, make them more sellable.

The London Eye, followed by a meal. How could she compete with that? How would Hannah settle back into just getting by after three months of Claire's extravagance? Maybe it had been a mistake, sending her. Maybe a taste of what life could be like would drive an even bigger wedge between them, make Hannah more restless. She pushed the pillow away and rose from the bed. The next ten weeks, she reminded herself, pulling back the curtains and flooding the room with light, were a chance she had been given to sort herself out, make life better for the two of them. She would use every minute.

The sea had worked out its temper from the previous day. The sky, too, had spent its grey and the sun peacocked in its unsmudged blue. Alison unfolded her canvas chair at the foot of the cliff. The dogs, delighted with their early call, shot off up the grassy slope. Lighting a cigarette, she flicked through the thick brown folder of handwritten pages and, choosing a story, read through the opening lines:

Are you out there in the darkness? I thought it was your step I heard below the window. In bustling, living daylight you are not in evidence, but when the night enshrouds your home in still, black velvet, you step from the shadows to taste again the life you once savoured...

Having swam and raced and investigated every dune and crop, the dogs lay sleeping at her bare feet, so exhausted by their efforts that they didn't even raise their heads when William walked over to join her. 'You're an early bird,' he called, resting his back against the cliff.

'It'd be a sin to miss this.' Alison looked up at him, her

hand shading her eyes. 'What a change from yesterday.'

'Doing your article?' He tipped his head towards the writing pad on her knee.

'No, actually. I got it finished last night – a first for me. It's usually a last-minute panic.'

'So, this is the dream stuff then?' He looked down at the neat handwritten page.

'An attempt at a poem.' She covered the page with her hand.

'May I?' he ventured, eyebrows raised.

'No, it's stupid. It's only…'

'Don't dismiss it.' William cut her off. 'Let it speak for itself.' He held out his hand.

Alison hesitated, half of her embarrassed, the other half straining to know his opinion. She thrust the pad towards him. 'I'm going to test the water.' She sprung from the seat, hurried to the water's edge. William sat into the canvas chair, eyes fixed on the page.

The Fisherman.

Her hand was light and curved, the words hurrying across the page at a slant.

> *A man of the sea*
> *You became it*
>
> *Summers, I remember*
> *When you lapped and teased*
> *the slipway of a sheltered strand*
> *And stirred by your stillness*
> *I stripped and dived*
> *Into your glistening depths*

October, and changes
Huddled down into a winter coat
I watched you from the cliff top
as waves of torment spewed
your frothy fury round my head
I sometimes crouched to become
the rock that broke your anger
But never dared to delve
Into your squally depths

Your tide gone out
I lie on the strand
Coarsely crafted
By your touch.

William's eyes rose from the page and settled on Alison. Head bent, she threaded the shallow water, hands thrust into the pockets of her rolled-up jeans. His arms strained to reach her. To touch that wounded place in her, brush away the pain that bowed her head. She strolled back up the sand towards him, sat cross-legged at his feet.

'Well?' She nodded her head shyly towards the page.

'It's beautiful,' he answered. 'Thank you for sharing it with me.'

She still couldn't figure out why she had shown it to him. She'd never shared her poems with anyone before, not even Kathleen. They made her feel foolish, weak and vulnerable – especially the stuff about Sean. She drew a piece of stick through the sand. 'Did you ever lose someone you loved?' She spoke without raising her head.

'Yeah, but that was a long time ago.' He looked down at her, her eyes stealing a look into his.

'Sean's gone over three years now.' She sighed as she stood. 'But I'd lost him long before that.' She brushed the sand from her feet, slipped on her shoes. 'I'm heading for town – did you want anything?'

William closed the pad and handed it to her. She was so terrified of opening up, had this knack of physically removing herself every time she teetered at the edge of her pain.

'Or if you'd like to come along …' It was out before she'd thought about it.

'Why not?' William needed no persuasion. The more time they spent together, doing ordinary things, the more she would open herself to him, he hoped.

'I won't be going for about an hour – will I collect you at the van?'

'No, no, I'll walk down. Meet you outside Phil's?' He folded the canvas chair and tucked it under his arm. They walked slowly back towards the slipway.

'Oh no,' Alison whispered through her teeth. May, togged head to toe in black designer Lycra, was power-walking the sand. Her eyes were trained on William and Alison. 'Lovely morning, May.' Alison forced a smile.

'Exquisite!' She nodded towards William, her small eyes squinting. 'Morning.'

'And a very good morning to you, May.' His voice was deep and confident, his grin full width.

'You're a bad one,' Alison laughed, as they reached the jeep. 'Still, that'll keep her off someone else's back for the morning. See you in an hour.'

She was still smiling as she rolled out onto the main road, but as she reached home the doubts began to surface. What had possessed her, asking him to join her like that? She

118

really didn't know the first thing about him. He could be anyone – and he could completely get the wrong idea. She pulled up outside the front door. Was it that she was just missing Hannah? Reacting to the isolation, to the exclusion she had felt when she'd read the email last night? Oh, quit analyzing, she told herself, hopping down onto the gravel. It was just a bit of company, for heaven's sake, a trip into town. It was what people did. Normal people. Where was the harm?

Seven

Alison pulled on a fresh pair of jeans and a pale green T-shirt. People always told her green was her colour – brought out her eyes or some such nonsense, she scoffed, pushing her toes into her ancient flip-flops. In the bathroom she scrubbed and moisturised her face, smiled when she caught herself humming as she fixed her hair into a loose loop at the base of her neck. She hesitated a moment before spraying a tiny burst of perfume on her neck and wrists – no harm in taking a little pride in yourself, she instructed silently, pushing William's approving gaze out of her mind. Eugene's article tucked into her leather bag, she smiled into the hall mirror before hurrying out the door.

'I'll park down by the quay, that's fairly central to everything.' And it's got the cheapest hourly rate, Alison added silently. 'Anywhere in particular you want to go?'

'I'd love a prowl around in the Book Centre,' William answered over his shoulder, keeping an eye out for a vacant space.

'Coffee?' Alison suggested as they entered the bookshop.

'Yes, thanks. Black, no sugar. I'll be with you in a tick.'

William moved to the 'Health and Psychology' section, while Alison chose a table in the small coffee bar, sunken a few steps below the shelved areas. She placed their order and took out Eugene's article to give it a quick, final scan.

'This is for you.' Sitting down opposite, William pushed a slim Gary Larson volume across the table towards her.

'How did you know I liked him?' The surprised smile lit and lifted her whole face, just as William had always supposed it might.

'An inspired guess, check out page seventy-nine.'

Alison flicked to the nominated page and threw back her head in a throaty laugh. The man at the next table cast a disapproving glance over his glasses. She cupped her hand over her mouth, her eyes wet with mirth. She flicked to a random page, passed the book back across the table. William's raucous laughter was infectious. The man with the glasses shook out his paper and turned his back slightly. Eyes widened, William drew a finger across his upper lip, his nod directed towards Alison's mouth. Licking the cappuccino froth from her top lip, Alison felt something fall from her shoulders, felt a light-heartedness, a freedom rise like a forgotten tide inside her.

Weakened with wet-faced laughter, they left the bookshop and ambled companionably down Michael Street, stopping here and there to listen to the buskers, sample some treats from the stall holders at the French Market. Later, sipping coffee at a street-side table they wild guessed at the outrageous items the shoppers might have in their bags, diagnosed the varied causes of the hurried, anxious looks on their faces.

Eugene Dalton's jaw dropped when he saw a radiant Alison arrive with the article. Early. It almost hit the brown carpet of his outdated office when he took in the unlikely companion waiting for her outside the door – and the way she smiled into the older man's face.

'Let me treat you to dinner.' William's hip was feeling the strain of the day's walking. 'Anywhere you'd recommend?'

'It's ages since I've eaten out in town. An Beal Bocht, that used to be one of my favourites. Let's go there. It's just down here, under the arch,' she added, aware of William's limp and the tiredness in his face.

'Lead the way.'

They headed down the narrow cobbled street, passed under the archway and into the dimly lit restaurant.

'Table for two, please,' Alison smiled to the young waiter. 'By the window, if possible.'

'This way, please.'

The formal black trousers and crisp white shirt looked completely out of place on his young, snake-thin body. His skin was the colour of honey, his long black hair tied in a sleek pony tail. A foreigner, Alison guessed, so young and so far away from home. Like Hannah. A tiny blade of loneliness nicked her chest as she followed the waiter to the window alcove.

'Perfect,' William grinned.

'I'll leave you to choose.' Handing them their menus, the waiter lit the soft red candle in the centre of the table before disappearing behind the bar.

'I haven't been here in – it must be five years!' Alison looked around her as she spoke. 'And the place hasn't changed one bit,' she smiled. The wooden floors, old and worn, were patterned by cigarette burns from the pre-smoking-ban era. Old oil lamps, jugs and earthenware hot water jars jostled for space on the picture high shelves along each wall. The intimate, confessional-like booths whispered decades of secrets and sharing, the half-light through the narrow, sharp-peaked windows soothing the bleached table wood.

'It's beautiful,' William replied. 'So peaceful. There's a gothic, almost a spiritual feel about it.'

Alison smiled inside. He could feel it too.

'I'm starving.' She opened her menu.

'And what does the lady recommend?'

They debated the menu, the aroma from the kitchen urging them on.

'Wine?' William asked, as the waiter took their order.

'I'm driving,' Alison sighed. 'But maybe one glass? Red, please.'

'A bottle of your house red, then.'

'I'm exhausted.' Alison sat back in her seat.

'I've really enjoyed today. Your company's a tonic.'

'You weren't thinking that last Saturday night.' She bent her head slightly, her cheeks colouring.

'We all have our bad days. And nights,' he reassured. 'That's what makes us human.'

Lifting her head, she folded her arms, looked around her again. 'Me and Sean used to come here a lot when we were first married.'

'You married young?' William sat forward, tasted the wine and nodded his approval to the waiter before resting his elbows on the table, his arms folded before him.

'I was almost eighteen when Mum died. I'd just started college.'

'What did you study?'

'English literature, I was going to be a famous journalist.' Her smile held a hint of regret.

'And what happened?'

'When Mum died, a lot of my ambition died with her. And a lot of other stuff too. It was the death of our family in a way.' She bowed her head, traced her forehead with her middle finger, then, looking up, met his eyes. 'Claire, my sister – the one in London – she couldn't handle it. I suppose she felt that when all her love, all her efforts at keeping Mum alive failed, then she had somehow failed too. She blamed herself in some bizarre way. God, was she angry. I don't think I'd ever seen anyone quite so angry. So hurt. It was as if she felt betrayed by everything she believed in. She threw herself into wild parties, drink, sex, anything that helped her forget.' She stared into her glass for a moment before lifting it to her lips.

'And your dad, was he still alive?' William prompted.

'Dad was still with us – in a way. He accepted it really well. Quietly. I suppose he had gotten used to the idea long before Mum died. He hadn't fooled himself like we had. Then he got so caught up in Claire's problems. I suppose it gave him a focus,' she shrugged.

'And where did that leave you?'

'Alone, and I suppose kind of unmoored in a way. I couldn't do the student thing any more. The lectures that I'd devoured before just floated over my head. I began to spend more and more time down here with Sean. Before eighteen months were out, I'd packed in college and moved down for good.'

The food arrived and Alison seemed glad of the distraction. 'Looks delicious,' she commented and, as if by some wordless agreement, they left the conversation and concentrated on their food, their silence punctuated by small talk and laughter.

* * *

Sean must have been almost seventeen, Maryanne supposed, by the time the darkness had come to inhabit his whole face. Right from his early teens she had watched it establishing itself, almost imperceptibly at first, in the tightening line of his mouth and then gradually, year by year, inching its way forward, upwards, until it simmered in his eyes like a threatening storm, the weight of that darkness causing him always, in those years, to hold his head at a downward tilt.

That consuming desire to please his father long folded and stored away, at six foot two Sean now stood head and shoulders above his childhood idol. Tides were turning. Maryanne could almost hear again that brittle cautiousness that had crept into Frank's words, could see him again now, standing half stooped on the back of the lorry, stacking the lobster pots that Sean hauled up to him with a strength and vigour that could only ever be a memory now for Frank.

How vividly she could picture Sean's hands. Their solid span, the dip between thumb and index finger scarred and cracked and hardened by years of salt water and heavy, wet rope; the roughened, reddened knuckles; the deep gouge in the pad of his left index finger where a hook had once embedded itself – those same strong hands that could still rest on Maryanne's shoulders with the gentleness of an angel's wings.

It hadn't frightened her, Sean's darkness. What it had done – and she realised this one evening as she looked away from Frank, sitting by the fire, holding the wrist of his right hand in a vice grip in an effort to stem its tremor – what it had done was to somehow transfer itself into the small corner of her heart that still had room for Frank and to cut the light there, turning that space into something resembling one of those old travelling trunks she remembered from childhood: battered, locked, forgotten.

* * *

'Did you marry straight away after moving?' They had almost finished their meal and William was anxious to steer the conversation back to Alison and her bond with Carniskey.

'Oh no, I lived here in town for a couple of years. Worked in the college, on their magazine. They were good years,' she smiled. 'We married just after my twenty-first birthday – and yes, Hannah was already on the way.' She beckoned the waiter. 'D'you fancy a coffee?'

'No. I'll stick with this. The advantage of having a reliable chauffeur.' William grinned, refilling his wine glass.

'I moved to Carniskey then.' Alison rested back in her seat. 'We bought that little fisherman's cottage I'm living in now. It was late spring and so beautiful. The whitethorn and the gorse and the sea pinks put on their finest colours to welcome me.' The memory glowed on her face. 'Sean was like the king of the place, with the long season stretched out before him. His mood, every move he made mimicked the awakening, the hope all around him. It was all I could have wished for.' She inched her head forward. 'Just about the same time that you arrived this year, actually. Did you feel it? The celebration, that sense of hope?'

'That was what made me decide to stop off here,' William nodded, smiling. 'Just like you've described. Like it's calling you to join it. Like you're being drawn here, have a part to play in it all.'

'What do you think your part is?' Alison sat forward, excited to find someone who voiced what she so often felt – a sense of something bigger at play, something beyond us, moving us.

'I don't know yet. And I don't question it. I've learned just to go along with it. To follow my instincts. Everything reveals itself in time.'

'Is that why you move about so much?'

'Partly. And partly because I don't want to attach myself to any place, to any person in particular.'

'Why not?'

'Because there is nothing permanent in this life.' Elbows on the table, he joined his hands, prayer-like, his fingertips touching his lips. 'Nothing we can hold on to or take with us. Everything is constantly moving, that same cycle of birth and death moving through every life, every relationship, everything.' He paused, his eyes holding hers. 'Nothing is ours to keep. Or to own. And I suppose I've learned that through the heartache of attaching myself too much, centring my life on someone. Then they're gone. Heartbreak is a cruel but thorough teacher. It's taught me just to live each day. No expectations, no regrets. Just each moment.' He smiled at Alison, at the frown of concentration rippling her brow.

'But is that not very lonely?'

'I spend most of my days alone. But no, I can't say I'm lonely. And look at the company I have this evening,' he joked, in an effort to move the conversation away from himself, back to her. 'So, did you keep your job at the college after you married?'

'I quit shortly after. Sean was my whole world then. Sean and Carniskey. And anyway, Hannah was on the way.' That smile again, lifting her whole face. 'We were so excited that autumn, preparing for her.' And then just as quickly that familiar shadow, beginning in her eyes, stealing her light. 'I think that was what kept Sean going. Kept him up.'

'Up?' William raised his brows.

'Yeah, or maybe because of my own preoccupation with Hannah's arrival I didn't really notice any change in him that winter. But the following one …' She fell silent for a moment, busied herself sugaring her coffee. 'You could read him, you know.' She stirred the coffee slowly, thoughtfully. 'Sean. Read him by the sky. By the colours and height of the sea, the length of the day …'

'His mood?' William prompted.

'Even more than that. His whole being. On the days that the sun shone it was like it shone through him. From him. A calm and open sea and Sean would be up before the birds, moving through the house like a life force.' Her smile was wistful now, her gaze somewhere far away. 'October always heralded the changes.' Her eyes returned to William. 'The gradual withdrawal. The long solitary walks on the cliff tops. Hours in the shed, mending nets, making pots. Sullen and sulking like a teenager rejected by his first love.' She looked down, folded and unfolded the paper napkin in her lap. 'As the weeks and months went on he'd retreat further and further from myself and Hannah, stalking from the room every time she'd cry or look for his attention. Usually before Christmas the long silence would have descended and would last till his lover accepted him back.'

'His lover?'

'That's how it felt. He couldn't go out on the sea and

he tortured himself watching it. Watching her. Every day either out on the cliffs or along the road between home and Tra na Baid. Driving slowly, stopping, watching, yearning. Then home to us like a dead man – no talk, no emotion. Complete shutdown.'

'How did you cope?' William hadn't been prepared for her honesty and openness.

'It's amazing what you learn to live with,' she half-smiled. 'What you get used to. I learned to live around it. Around him. I had Hannah and my writing. I threw myself into them and waited out my time for spring.' She sighed, her thoughts and her eyes straying away again. William didn't speak, waited for her to return to him.

'In a lot of ways it was like being back in the days when we'd first met and I'd return to Dublin at the end of the holidays. The heartache and the longing every year. The promise of the following summer. It was as if those teenage years had been a preparation, you know, for what lay ahead?' William nodded his understanding.

'But nothing could have prepared me to lie beside someone at night, sit down to meals with them, loving them, wanting them, seeing them, but they're not there.' Aware of the new, sharper edge that had entered her voice Alison paused and, biting down on her lip, glanced out into the half-light under the archway where a gentle rain polished the patterned stones.

'Did you talk to him about it?'

She looked again towards William and it was as if the same soft rain had brushed her eyes. 'It didn't matter what I said or thought. It was like he was in his world and there was no place there for me. I made the mistake one day of suggesting I go back to work. Things were tight, you know,

129

no money coming in. He spoke then, all right. Ranted and roared about how no one would question his providing and caring for his family. Hannah must have been eight, maybe nine at the time. I remember her crying, running from the room…'

'Did he hurt you?' William's voice was soft, echoing her pain.

'No, no, never. Not in any physical way. And that outburst was an isolated one. It was the silence that hurt most, the withholding of all communication, all emotion. That hurts in a far deeper way, I think. It was like he was punishing me for the way he felt the sea was punishing him.'

'And you stayed? Didn't you talk to anyone?'

'What was the point? To the outside world, Sean was his usual self. If somebody called to the house, he'd chat away as normal. Then, as soon as they left, he'd clamp up again. The same in the pub – he'd go quite often, stay late. It was as if he was blaming me, me and Hannah, at least that's what it felt like. And I suppose I just got used to it over the years.' Her sigh was heavy. 'Reasoned that it was a kind of depression, that he had no control over it. That you only hurt those you love, all that kind of stuff. That was my way of making sense of it. And I just lived and hoped for an early and long season when I knew I'd have him back.' Her right hand had found its way to her wedding ring, twisting it round and round in circles towards her heart. It was a habit she had developed in the early days after Sean was lost, touching it every time she thought of him, spoke of him. It was a habit that had angered her lately and it angered her even more now when she saw William watching her.

'I know what you're thinking.' She folded her arms across

her chest, challenge lighting her eyes. 'You think I was stupid, don't you, that I was weak?'

'Alison, I wouldn't for a second—' He sat forward, eyes wide, meeting hers.

'Why wouldn't you? You didn't know him. You could never understand the— '

'I understand how much you loved him.'

'And he loved me.' Her words weighed with something much deeper than sadness, she turned her head slowly towards the window. 'Loved me with a fierceness I know I'll never find again.'

William sat back in his seat, fingered the stem of his glass. He knew that fierceness that she talked about, knew the gaping, unfillable emptiness of its loss. 'And he's gone three years now?' His voice, gentle, inviting her back to him.

'Missing three years since October.' Her hand twisting the wedding ring again as she turned to meet his eyes. 'His body has never been recovered. And it's like a continuation of the same theme,' she sighed, sitting forward as she rubbed the tips of her fingers along the arch of her brows, then rested her chin in her hands. 'He's gone but he's not gone. Just like he was with me but he wasn't with me. And it just wears me down. Sometimes I feel like I never had him, like I'd always lost him. Yet somehow he's still there. Oh, I'm making a complete mess of this – it's hard to explain, sorry, I've gone on too long I'm …'

'No, you haven't.' William touched a hand to hers. 'I feel privileged that you could share your thoughts with me. It takes a lot of courage.'

'That's something I certainly haven't got.' She drew her hand away. 'Just look at me, for heaven's sake! If I had courage I would have left Carniskey long ago. Got out and

131

got on with making a life for myself and Hannah. But I can't. I'm stuck. I've stuck myself to it. And for what? I can't even tell myself never mind trying to explain …' Her eyes burned with frustration. 'And I can see what it's doing to me. I know people are right when they say I'm half mad, but I feel powerless to change and…and look at you sitting there! I haven't the first clue who you are or why I'm telling you all this.' Slow tears fell, almost timidly, from her eyes. She scrunched the napkin tight in her fist. 'I'm going to the Ladies.'

William sat back, stared at the slow trickle of rain down the windowpane, the street light tracing its meander with a soft orange glow. He smiled at the beauty of tears, their liberation, their healing. He had never seen Helene cry. But he had seen the dark depths of her tears, dammed behind her eyes. Maybe, if he had understood pain then, he could have helped her release them. Maybe if he hadn't been so selfish, so wrapped up in his own smug ambition…

'Can I get you anything else, sir?' The waiter's voice was soft, as if acknowledging the sacred space surrounding the small window table.

'No, thanks, just the bill.' William looked into the young man's eyes and for one brief second wished he was there again. There at that wonderful launch into life where anything, everything was possible, the whole world and all its adventures out there for the taking. A small fist of fear tightened around his heart at the thought of the little time left to him, the uncertainty, the unknown that followed. He was relieved to see Alison return to the table.

'Time to head on?' She gathered up her bag and jacket. 'I hope I haven't bored you.' The lightness of her tone failed to mask the sadness in her wearied face.

'I've enjoyed every moment.'

They left the city behind and followed the dark, winding road to Carniskey. 'That was one thing that took me a while to get used to,' Alison remarked, 'when I moved out here first. The darkness. That absolute blackness at night. In Dublin we had a street light outside our bedroom window. Same when I lived in town. That pitch black at night was quite a shock, but I soon grew to love it. Isn't there something about the dark that allows you to be yourself?'

'I think it encourages the parts of us that are too timid for daylight.'

'And it heightens the senses,' Alison jumped in, enthused. 'You know, like when you try to find your way in the dark, you're much more aware of sounds and smells, the presence of objects – even the energy around them.'

'Maybe it's more our natural state,' William offered. 'I mean, when you think of our nine months in the darkness of the womb. And who knows, maybe we came from darkness before that. Maybe all this electricity and neon we've invented is killing off parts of our soul.'

* * *

'Yes!' Rob spun on his heel and punched the air. He flopped down on the couch, swung his feet up on the cushions and laying his head on the arm rest, closed his eyes. Thank God she had said yes because at this stage the girl had just about exhausted him.

He had never imagined that winning a woman could be such hard work – especially a woman who had already declared her love for you. They were a strange species, women, and none stranger and harder to crack – he was willing to bet – than the one he had chosen.

And that wasn't the only thing he had learned about women. That line you often heard about them thinking they had a monopoly on feelings, well it was *actually* true. All this talk on the phone about how hurt her feelings were, how confused she felt. Almost four weeks now since she had given him the door – well, she had really, given that she had left him with no choice but to walk out – and not a word about how *he* might have felt. Did she think he was made of wood? Didn't the flowers and the calls and the texts and those big balloons he'd had delivered to her work tell her anything?

She had literally laughed out loud when she had admitted that yes, she had seen him that evening in the frozen food aisle at Whites. 'Lurking,' she called it, before laughing and likening him to a stalker. He could have taken offence, claimed his 'feelings were hurt'. But oh, he knew better. Practically a whole month now he had waited to hear that laugh, the full, deep uncensored thrill of it. He knew as soon as it reached his ear that she was melting and that a yes would surely follow. What did his pride matter when risked with losing that?

He stretched to his full length, luxuriating in his plans. Saturday night – all going well – would lay the foundations and within two weeks, he reckoned, he'd have the whole thing cemented. He smiled to himself. Rob, the humble construction worker, building a whole new world!

* * *

Alison snuggled down under the bedclothes, pulled the pillows beneath her shoulders and relived the day in her head: the morning on the beach, the book shop, wandering around town, the meal and the chat, the laughter on the way home. She sighed, her whole body seeming to join in her smile. Something inside her felt different, like a stone had been lifted, shifted somehow, and the light was finally getting in. She didn't allow herself one moment's guilt about missing today's visit to Maryanne or Hannah's telephone call. This had been the first day in an age that she had taken completely for herself and she reckoned she well deserved it. Maryanne wouldn't miss her for the one day and Hannah was barely fitting in her five-minute calls as it was. Anyway, she reasoned, she'd be better for both of them if she learned to take some time for herself.

She liked William. Loved his sense of fun – it had been so long since she'd laughed like that. At nothing. At stupid, childish things. And the way she could talk to him. About things she had never dared voice before. Things that she'd hardly admitted to herself, let alone spoken out loud. But something about him drew her out, encouraged her, made her trust him completely. There was a gentleness in him, a genuine acceptance, something in his eyes, in his whole face that let you know he already understood what you were struggling to get across. He could make a really good friend. There was something totally safe about him. *He won't be around much longer*, a niggling voice in her head pushed to the front to be heard. *He'll be leaving as well.* She switched the voice off with the light, turned on her side and, smiling, closed her eyes, allowing the day to replay behind them.

* * *

William sat on the edge of the cliff at Tra na Leon. He closed his eyes to block out the light of the stars. Darkness. Darkness and silence and emptiness surrounded him. He could hear his heart beat. Feel the warmth of his exhaled breath on his upper lip. The sound of the waves embracing the rocks below rushed to meet him, the giggle of the shingle as it danced with the tide.

And he could feel it again. That cold metallic hand squeezing his heart, making it shrink and pound harder, like a tiny creature, cornered. He sat with it and listened.

When his cancer had first been diagnosed six years earlier, William's doctor hadn't held out much hope. But the brain tumour had been removed and the chemotherapy and radiation had eradicated the invader from his body. He shivered now, remembering that time. The fear, the anger, the denial. And above all the unbearable loneliness. He had brushed death's cheek in the quiet of that sterile ward, had watched it lead Joe, a frightened thirty-three year old, slowly, bed by bed, down the ward, and then across the corridor to the single room, death's waiting room, and finally away to its own world. William had waited, resigned, ready to follow, ever watchful, even in sleep. But death chose to pass his bed and William had walked from the hospital. Walked into a world that he had never really been aware of before. His intimacy with death had opened his eyes and his heart and his mind to a life he had so long endured but had not lived. He walked back into that world as if he was entering it for the first time. Death had stripped him of all but his name. Layer by layer, it had peeled away who or what he was, or thought he had been. It had shown him how what little control he imagined he possessed could so easily be thieved – from his mind, his feelings, everything, right down to his bowels. Dignity, pride, independence, talent – all that he had for so long defined as self, stripped like garments, one by one, to reveal a naked, frightened child. And he looked at the world again from that child's place: enthusiastic, liberated, open. He knew at that moment, when he turned at the door and took one last look down the hushed ward, that he would never again take one single day for granted. And he would never again fear death.

When the cancer returned before Christmas, this time positioning itself under the brain from where it could not be lifted, William had not panicked. Like an army invading and claiming new territory, it had travelled to his hip by February. William did not fight back. Any attempt at surgery, Fogarty advised, carried almost certain loss of motor and nervous function. Loss of mobility, loss of speech. William had decided to go with loss of life in its entirety. He was aware that radical drug treatment would prolong the time left to him. But he had been there before. Had endured their harrowing effects. No, not this time. This time death would take him. And he would go sooner in relative health, rather than later, ravaged by the battle the drugs would fight, and eventually lose.

This evening in the restaurant was the first time he had felt that pinch of fear, felt that pull towards life, and he couldn't understand what had prompted it. Was it that it was getting closer now? Was it the raw life in Alison's throaty laugh? Or was it the huge sense of birth and reawakening, the almost magic of this place? It seemed such a contradiction to die at this time of year. He sat on, eyes closed in the darkness, till all the voices stilled in his head and peace returned with the dawn.

Eight

Straightening the pot of pansies at the front door Alison sat on the step and opened her post: a telephone bill – double its usual amount from all the calls to Hannah; a final reminder for her last oil fill; a motor tax renewal form. Great, she sighed, pushing back her hair. How on earth am I going to pay even one of them? She had gone out with William for a drink a couple of evenings last week and had treated herself to a new shirt in town on Thursday, hardly extravagance. And of course there was no sign of Eugene's eighty euro for her article – delivered early again this week. Was it always going to be the same, this barely scraping by, counting out every cent?

She had always hated taking money from Maryanne. Felt useless and awkward every time the woman would slip a note into her bag or pocket with a stern, 'Not a word now. It's how Sean would have wanted it.' And you didn't argue with Maryanne. At the beginning Alison had decided to treat Maryanne's 'gifts' as a loan. Vowing to pay back every cent once Sean's body was found and the life assurance came through had helped her to hold on to some small bit of pride. One blue wellington: that had been the sea's great compromise. One blue wellington thrown up on a beach six miles west.

She'd be glad of one of Maryanne's handouts now, she sighed, pushing herself up off the step and walking around the house to the back door. She'd have to drive into town to collect her money from Eugene. *Damn!* She bumped her toe on the corner of the path. *Damn!*

She banged the back door shut behind her, switched on the kettle and opened the fridge. *No milk!* She grabbed a glass and, filling it with water at the sink, stared out the kitchen window. The piled pots and nets seemed to glare back at her. That was all Sean left her: a useless collection of pots and nets that most of their money had been sunk into. Their last conversation flashed into her mind. She had followed him out to the back kitchen, pleading with him at first as he pulled on his boots and fishing jumper. 'Are you out of your mind, Sean? Look at the sky, for Christ's sake! Look at the stripes on the water!' He hadn't answered, just zipped up his coat, tugged on his cap and walked out the door. Alison had followed him out to the van, her voice and her temper rising against the wind. 'Will you listen to me, Sean? Think of us for a change, think of Hannah. Sean, SEAN!' The thin, tight line of his mouth had reminded her of a fault line, the pressure behind it mounting. He sat into the driver's seat, closed the door on her words. 'Go on, then, you selfish bastard,' she had shouted in desperate defiance. 'Go on! You're not with us anyway, you might as well be gone!' He had looked at her from somewhere far deeper than his eyes, then turned the key and was gone. Arms hugging her trembling body, Alison had caught Hannah's eye as the child turned her face from the back bedroom window. In that tiny moment something inside Alison had known that her life was about to change forever.

She turned now from the window, grabbed a pen and paper from her desk and sat at the kitchen table. Her hand moved in a frenzy:

For Quick Sale
Lobster & Shrimp Pots / Salmon Nets
Contact: Alison Delaney, Carniskey. Tel: (051) 785330

She grabbed her keys and drove to the village.

'Alison, how are you keeping?' Joan, Carniskey's shrewd and only shopkeeper, smiled from behind the counter, scanning Alison from head to toe.

'Fine, thanks. Can you put this in the window, please?' Alison thrust the note across the counter and looked straight into Joan's pinched face as she read it.

'No problem, Alison. There's a small charge of two euro.' She reached for the sticky tape. 'Will that be all?'

'Yes, thanks.' Alison's smile was tight. In her rush out the door she almost knocked Theresa Doyle sideways. 'Oh, Theresa. Hi! Sorry.' She smiled widely into Theresa's disapproving face. Turning the jeep, she headed back out of the village. 'Damn!' She had meant to pick up some milk.

Leaving the engine running, she swept back into the shop. As she reached the fridge, she could hear the whispered conversation at the counter. Hand grasping the fridge door, Alison listened.

'Sure, who'd buy them?' Theresa was pontificating. 'A drowned man's gear? Anyone'd know they'd bring bad luck.'

'And to think of all the hard work and money poor Sean

put into getting them. And there he is now, gone, God rest him, and she selling off the lot.' Even in a whisper, Joan's voice had an edge that could cut through stone.

'I wonder has it anythin' to do with that new fella she's been seen with – that hippy type up over the strand?'

'Don't you know it has, Tess. May told me she saw them early one morning. Right cosy the two of them were below on the strand.'

'What is she thinkin' of, throwin' herself at an ould fella like that without tuppence to his name?'

'That's the way it's gone nowadays, I'm afraid, no respect for themselves – or anyone else. Poor Sean, isn't he the lucky man that he's not around to see it?'

'And she's the young one packed off to England, I believe. Still, at least she's not around to witness it, though the same one can be a right little pup too, you know. I heard—'

Joan tapped Theresa on the arm and silenced her mid-sentence. Theresa followed her friend's slack-jawed stare to where Alison stood, arms folded, before them.

'Oh, Alison we were just … ' Joan began, her mouth opening and closing like a landed fish.

Alison glared at them, shook her head and snapped the note from Joan's hand before walking slowly towards the door and out of the explosive silence.

She sat in the jeep, taking deep breaths to cool the heat of her threatening tears. She was damned if they were going to make her cry. She jerked the jeep out onto the road. Oh, Hannah was right, she seethed as she tore out of the village, past her own house and on towards town. They're nothing but an insensitive bunch of good-for-nothing dried-up old gossips. What the hell was she still doing in this place? She passed the football pitch and swung onto the main road.

She'd go into town, collect her money from Eugene and use the computer in the library next door to place her ad in one of the fishing papers. She turned up the music, drove on at speed and wished from the bottom of her heart that she'd never again have to set foot in Carniskey.

* * *

Hands on her hips, Kathleen turned from the boiling kettle and looked into Alison's pale, sleep-deprived face. Her blood had boiled in tandem with the kettle as Alison recounted what had passed in the shop the previous day. 'Alison Delaney, are you telling me that you'd actually take heed of anything they'd have to say? That you'd let them do this to you? Honestly, I thought you had more spunk in you that that!'

'I don't mind them having a go at me, blast them, but when they started on Hannah!' Alison stubbed out her cigarette, her temper rising.

'I'm sure Hannah could care less! The girl has more sense.' Kathleen grabbed two mugs from the press. 'God, if we were all to listen to everything that was said about us we'd never put our heads outside the door.' She resented that even now she could still feel a slight stab of that old pain of falling prey to the village vultures. She spooned in the coffee, lifted the kettle. And she knew that survival meant forever thickening your skin and holding fast to your own strength, your own worth. 'Why do you let them get to you? You're just feeding them, you know.' She placed the mugs on the table, pulled out a chair to sit.

'Maybe it gets to me because they're right,' Alison sighed, drawing the steaming mug into both hands. 'Sean worked so hard to get all that stuff, and selling it off, well, maybe it is wrong.'

'No, Alison. It's what Sean would have wanted. You know he'd want to provide for you. The best for you and Hannah, that's all he ever wanted, you know that.'

'Yeah?' Her eyes searched Kathleen's face. 'Then maybe I asked too much, maybe he'd still be alive if…'

'Don't even go there,' Kathleen cut in, anger sharpening her words. 'Sean is gone. It was an accident. A horrible, tragic accident. But it happened and there's nothing you could have done or can do about it. Except kick it in the teeth and get on with your life.' She grabbed her friend's hand. 'You've got to leave the past where it belongs, Alison. Believe me, torturing yourself isn't going to change things. It's not going to bring him back.'

'It was the look in his eyes that day.' She took a deep breath, pushed out the words that had always refused to be voiced. 'I can't help thinking sometimes that it wasn't an – that he knew what he was doing. Knew where he was going…I, I really don't believe it was an accident.'

'Alison, you don't know that. You'll never know. And even if that was the case, then it was Sean's decision. His decision. For his own reasons. You had no part in it. You've got to let it go. Let him go. It's you and Hannah now, and that has to be your focus if you're ever going to get past this and get your life back.' Kathleen felt that old knot of discomfort twist and tighten her insides. Her tongue sought out the groove in her lip. Sean's death had been no accident. At sea since childhood, he would have known full well that night when he left the harbour at Tra na Baid that he wouldn't be returning. The great unspoken truth about the mighty Sean Delaney!

She squeezed Alison's hand and, rising from the table,

searched out a tissue from her bag. 'Come on, dry those eyes before that pretty face turns into a sponge,' she encouraged, smiling, as she draped an arm around Alison's shoulder. 'Life goes on, Alison, hard as it might be. It really is up to you to decide what to make of it.'

'Oh, I'm sorry.' Alison half-smiled, cursing her weakness as she sensed Kathleen's withdrawal, her frustration. 'And you're right' – her words caught on an involuntary in-breath. She dried her cheeks with the backs of her hands, patted her nose with the tissue. 'It is up to me and I can't let every bit of senseless gossip I hear drag me back there. I won't.' She shook her head. Kathleen was right. Sean was gone. Gone. Nothing that Alison or any loose tongue in a shop could say or do would bring him back. She straightened her back and, while everything inside her was grasping at the tail of that new determination she had almost let slip, another truth slipped forward, startling her: she no longer really wanted him back.

'And promise you'll learn to listen to no one but yourself.' Kathleen's voice was soft with understanding. 'You're the only expert on your life, Alison, on what you want it to be. Nobody else.'

'I know, I know. And I really do want to have myself sorted when Hannah gets home. I do. And I will.' The conviction in her own words told Alison she was already part way there.

'Good for you. So, how is our little London bird?'

'She's loving it, absolutely loving it and really, I have you to thank for—'

'Stop!' Kathleen held up both hands in protest. 'The first thing you have to do is learn to take a little bit of credit. You're doing a wonderful job with Hannah. I know how tough the going can be when you're doing it all on your own.'

'How's Jamie?'

'Jamie is busy – with summer camps and fishing and friends. Honestly, I hardly see him these days and when I do he's exhausted.'

'No more wet beds, then?'

'All over, thank God, but you know…' Kathleen paused, widening her eyes in emphasis. 'I can't understand this. You know how he adored Rob, right?'

Alison nodded.

'Thing is, he never even asks about him.' Her head shook in incredulity. 'I mean, never. Like it was the most natural thing in the world for him to disappear out of our lives. Strange, yeah?'

'Kids have a great way of just getting on with their own thing, don't they? Sometimes I think we make problems for them, worrying about things that they're completely oblivious to.'

'Well, isn't Jamie a case in point? I mean, it's quite obvious now that he couldn't care less whether Rob moves into my bed or up to the moon, and all that worrying I did!'

'So, are things back on track with Rob then?'

'We'll see. This last month's been a real roller coaster. But being with him again on Saturday night, well, it just felt so natural, so…just so right.' Kathleen's whole face lit up with the memory.

'There's your answer then. Go for it!' Alison was glad she'd at last seen sense. Poor old Rob was patient, but Kathleen's will could test a saint.

'As I said, we'll see.'

Saturday night had been fantastic, but Kathleen had been gob-smacked when Rob had kissed her goodnight at the door, mumbling some excuse or other about an early start the next morning. Sunday? In all the time she had known him Rob had never left the bed till after twelve on a Sunday. All those flowers and balloons and texts and can't-wait-to-see-yous and then running off like a frightened schoolboy. Exasperated, Kathleen had nursed a bottle of wine herself that night, Jamie away at a sleep-over and the empty house folding in around her. And with each glass came a new question: had Rob gone off her? Had she left him waiting too long? And then of course the biggie: had he found someone else?

'What is it?'

'Men!' Kathleen put on a wide smile. 'They must be the strangest species.' Alison has enough on her plate, Kathleen decided, the chat and advice she had come for could wait. 'Listen, I'd better go collect Jamie from camp. So, you okay?'

'I'm fine, honest,' Alison smiled, and she meant it. 'Thanks again, you're the best.' She linked her arm in Kathleen's as they walked to the door.

'So, what exactly is the story with your man up on the cliff?' Kathleen had a glint in her eye as she opened the front door. 'May Reilly'll kill me if I leave her without any gossip.'

'You're the secret spy in their camp, aren't you? You're a weasel, Kathleen Carroll, a fake!'

'My cover's blown!' Kathleen threw her arms in the air. 'C'mon, who is he? Give me the sordid details.'

'There aren't any, honestly,' Alison laughed. 'He's fifty-four, for Christ's sake, Kathleen, and hardly an Adonis.'

'Where's he from?'

'Dublin, but he's been wandering around Europe for years.'

'Oh. Doing what?'

'You know, I don't know. I never thought to ask him. He's just a nice guy, you know, easy to talk to …'

'Probably a dirty old man who goes around the country seducing vulnerable widows!' Kathleen's eyes were wide with mischief.

'Stop it, Kathleen, he's not anything like that,' Alison laughed. 'Anyway, I haven't seen him in days. He could have moved on, for all I know. Now, come here,' she threw her arms around Kathleen, 'thanks again, you've been great.'

'Anytime, and remember, keep them fuelled with talk – I'm enjoying the break from the spotlight.' She stepped out through the door. 'Aha! Speak of an ass!' Kathleen nodded towards the mouth of the drive and the two dogs bounding down to the gate to welcome William. Alison felt a tiny jump inside her chest.

'Great guard dogs,' Kathleen smiled. 'I'll go.' She kissed Alison on the cheek. 'Don't want word going out of a three-some!'

'How are you?' Alison smiled, standing back from the open door.

'Good. You not on terms with the beach? Haven't seen you there for days.' William stepped into the sunlit hall. He hadn't been in this part of the house before and his eyes widened in amazement. Not a sign of the sea anywhere. The wooden floors reflected the rich yellow walls. And what walls. All along them was a most beautifully scripted calligraphy in a deep plum ink.

'Wow, yours?' William asked, moving past her to read the inscriptions.

'Yeah, I took a night class, years ago.'

'And the writings?'

'Mine too.' Alison, embarrassed, was glad of the telephone's ring. 'I'll just get that, come on in.' She hurried past him into the kitchen.

'Hello?'

'Mum?'

'Hannah? Oh, it's great to hear you. Everything all right?' She pulled a chair over under the phone.

'Fantastic, Mum – and you?'

'Good, I'm good. What are you up to? Are you enjoying it?'

'Oh, Mum, I love it! Everything's so fast and alive and so *not* Carniskey! Claire was so right, you wouldn't believe all the stuff I've learned about the gallery, I love it there!'

'That's brilliant, Hannah.' Alison smiled at the rush in her daughter's voice, at the hint of London already in her accent. What that girl wouldn't do to be like her aunt Claire.

'And you should see the clothes Claire's bought me, Mum, they're bang on trend and—'

'Hannah, you have your own money. Make sure you're paying your way.' Alison picked up on the old defensiveness creeping into her voice. She didn't want to argue with Hannah or lecture her. 'I'm so glad you're enjoying it, sweetheart. I miss you so much – so do Tilly and Tim. They sniff around your bedroom door every morning to check if you're back.'

'Aw, give them a hug for me. You should see the gear on the dogs over here, Mum – jumpers, jackets, jewels in their collars, the lot! So, what are you up to?'

'Busy, actually. I get my women's column stuff out of the way early every week and I'm working on a couple of stories, I'm really enjoying it.'

'Looks like you'll have to send me away more often then.' Hannah smiled. Mum sounded good. Lighter, more alive or something. Aoife might have been right after all.

'I didn't send you away— '

'Relax, Mum, just kidding. So, isn't there something you've forgotten to tell me?' Hannah pressed her lips together to stifle her laughter.

'What? How do you mean something to— '

'I had an email from Aoife, she told me your news.'

'News? What news are you talking about?'

'I hear you have a new friend. Male? C'mon, Mum, spill the beans!'

'That's utter nonsense! Has Aoife nothing better— '

'Come on, Mum, tell me – is he cute?'

'Hannah, there's no such thing.' Alison kept her voice low, aware of William just down the hall. 'Unless she's talking about a visitor that I've chatted to a few times. Honestly, you can't breathe around this place!'

'What's his name? What's he like?'

'William. And he's over fifty and I have absolutely no interest— '

'Why are you whispering, Mum?' Hannah cut in. 'Oh, he's there, isn't he? I knew it!'

'No!'

'Okay, Claire. Coming!' Hannah called. 'Gotta go, Mum, I'll let you get back to your friend. Oh, and remember to smile and take that cross look off your face.'

'Hannah!'

'And let your hair loose. It suits you much better. Oh, wait till I tell Claire— '

'Hannah, don't you dare…'

But she was gone. Alison was left holding the phone

in her hand, a mixture of puzzlement and amusement playing on her face. Who would have thought that the local grapevine could reach all the way to London! There was nothing like that between her and William. She knew that. He knew that. What they had was more ... Oh, she couldn't find a word for it, but it certainly wasn't romance. But she had to smile at Hannah's girlish excitement – and her new-found confidence. At the huge contradictions in the little girl who seemed to be turning into a woman overnight. How she missed her. She took a deep breath, replaced the phone and rose from the chair, a great sense of liberation rising with her. It didn't matter what anyone around here thought. She'd had enough of pretending, of hiding out and hurting. The time had come to start being herself again, to start living.

'I'm just about to put something on for tea, will you join me?' Alison called down the hall to William.

'Thanks, I'd love to.' William stood engrossed in the words before him. Some were just single words, shouting their own message. Others strung together and whispered sentences. Others still stretched to form verses, poems. He was taken aback by their rawness, their questioning, the life that pulsated behind them.

'Looks great,' William smiled, taking a seat, 'I hope I'm not intruding.'

'Not at all. It's nice to have some company for a change. That was Hannah on the phone.' Alison poured two glasses of wine.

'How's London treating her? Mmm, this is good,' he nodded, tasting the scampi.

'Sounds like she's having the time of her life,' Alison nodded. 'But she's still managing to keep an eye on me.' She stole a shy smile across the table. 'Seems she had an email from a friend in the village – telling her that her mum had a new man!' Her cheeks pinked.

'Well,' William's smile was slow, disconcerted. 'Has she? Is that where you've been these past few days, entertaining the new mystery man?' William teased. The little niggle of jealousy caught him by surprise.

'No,' Alison laughed. 'They're talking about you!'

'Me? Well, I hope you set the record straight and told her you were just doing your bit for the community, care of the aged and all that?'

'I tried, but Hannah seems quite taken with the idea. Probably thinks it would be a nice distraction, keep me off her back. And if you want to know, I've been holed up here, shielding myself from the speculations of the masses.' She told William about the shop and the conversation she'd overheard between Theresa and Joan.

'Looks like we're causing quite a stir about the place.' His eyes smiled right through her. 'But why let it bother you? Why hide away? We enjoy each other's company. Should it matter what anyone else thinks?'

'I know, I know, but it's just that, well, I suppose I've lived here so long. Came here as Sean's girlfriend, then his wife. That's how I'm seen by everyone. Like I'm not a person in my own right. And I suppose over the years I've come to see myself as they see me. As they judge me.'

'Do any of them try to know you, as yourself?'

'Kathleen, the girl that was just leaving as you arrived, she's great. The best. Other than her, I suppose I've never really given anyone else a chance. I think I've always been afraid that they wouldn't approve, find I didn't fit in or something.'

'That's a bit unfair on them – and on you. Anyway, why do you feel you need to fit in? Surely there's room for a little difference, even in a place this size?' William's eyes followed her as she lifted the plates to the sink, lit a cigarette and sat again.

'I suppose it's the need to belong, isn't it? When Sean was here, I felt I was part of the place. Being his wife, I belonged here. Now, a lot of the time I feel like an outsider, you know, like the place is not really my home, that I have no right to be here. It's stupid, I know. But I feel if I act the way they'd like me to, if I'm the person they expect me to be, then I'll be accepted. And there's this huge pull inside me. This longing to belong and, at the same time, this fight to be myself. To be true to me. Do you know what I'm talking about?'

'Only too well,' William nodded. 'I think this hunger that we feel – to fit in, to be approved of, to belong to somebody or some place – it's what causes most of the pain and confusion in our lives.' He sipped his wine, his eyes and his thoughts for a moment far away. 'I wasted a lot of years searching for that.' He looked into Alison's eyes. 'The end of that search is what allows me the freedom that I have now. You see, I don't believe we belong – not to this world, not to anyone or anywhere in it. And that hunger, that longing we feel, is the cry of the soul. A cry for the home it came from. And the more we try to soothe it with attachments to people, places, cars, houses, money – all the jewels this world offers – then the louder it howls.'

'So, how do you stop it?' Alison sat forward, elbows on the table, that same frown of concentration rippling her brow.

'That's it, you see. We don't. At least, that's my belief. You let yourself feel the hunger, see where it draws you. In that stillness, it loses its shyness and it speaks to you.' He paused, then asked, 'What is it that you do, Alison, that allows time and the whole world and all those questions to slip away? When do you lose yourself?'

Alison didn't have to think about it: 'When I write.' Her answer was almost a whisper. 'Then there's nothing in the world but me and the page. And a beautiful, comforting quiet. I don't mean when I do Eugene's stuff, but when I just write, not knowing what's going to come out on the page. It's like … it's like I'm a different person. Like the world and all the stuff that goes on in my head stops and I can just …'

'Be?' William offered, nodding. 'And that, I think, is the closest that we'll ever get to belonging in this world.' They sat in silence for a moment, each digesting the conversation.

'So, do you write much?'

'That's just it. I never seem to find the time. There's always something else that needs to be done. And I get so frustrated!'

'The cry of the soul,' William smiled. 'What you've written in the hall. They're beautiful. Raw and real. They have soul.'

'They're my frustration walls,' she laughed. 'I write there when I'm angry. Or hurt, or lonely. Or just confused. By the time I'm finished I've usually worked out whatever it was that was bothering me.'

'Why don't you send your work out? You have a real talent.'

'Oh, don't think I haven't tried. Poems, short stories. But they come back time and again with the same old few lines. "Sorry, not successful on this occasion", or something about it being too dark.'

'You're just hitting the wrong market. Ever thought of concentrating on something bigger?'

'Like a novel?' she smiled.

'Ever considered it?'

'In my dreams.' Her smile was wistful now. 'The one dream that has held fast since childhood was having my very own book on the shelf, with my name on the cover. Something that I had given to the world. Something that I could pass on to Hannah.'

'So?' William quizzed, 'what's holding you up?'

'Oh, I'm afraid I'll start and won't finish. Or worse, that I'll finish and I'll fail, that no one will want it.'

'There you go again! Pre-judging your audience before you've even written the first word. Don't think of the audience. Write what's in your heart. A dream that has lasted all those years surely deserves a chance, yeah?'

Alison nodded. She felt a warmth stir inside her, as if her dream was smiling, having been voiced. 'Come on,' she smiled. Rising from the table, she reached and took a picnic basket from the top cupboard.

'Where are we going?' He eased himself up from the table.

'Grab some wine!' She packed cheese and crackers from the fridge, a fat candle in a round, storm globe. 'The beach. I'll just get us some towels to sit on.' Her words trailed behind her down the hall. William laughed out loud. He loved that almost wildness in her, that spontaneity – the spur of the moment change, those little bursts she could make at life.

They sat at the base of the dunes, the picnic basket between then. 'To dreams,' Alison smiled, clinking her glass to his before raising it to her lips. She turned and lay on her stomach, her bare calves and feet in the air. 'Now, William Hayden, stranger, I want to know about you.'

'What would you like to know?' He shifted down on his side, watched the soft glow of the candlelight play on her face.

'Why you left Dublin? Where you went next. How you survive. Why you're here – that'll do for starters.'

'Okay.' William's gaze moved from her face, out across the whispering tide and on out to the horizon. 'I was twenty,' he began, 'an architecture student in Dublin. Bored, hungry for change. I took a summer job in Paris teaching English and at night I indulged my passion. Art. I took an evening class in a little centre near the school. They thought I had talent' – he smiled at her, his eyes and his voice hinting his humility – 'encouraged and fostered it. By the end of the summer William Hayden, Architect was dead, replaced by a lover of Art and the French. And I just never went back.' He sipped his wine, his eyes moving back to the ocean.

'How long did you stay in Paris?'

'Five years. Then the rambling began. I'd move from place to place, country to country. I'd get by painting sceneries, private commissions of houses, yachts. Summers I'd do portraits for the tourists.'

'So, where was home?'

'Wherever I'd land. Dublin didn't hold the same meaning as it had. My mother had died in the meantime and my father, well, he was never in the picture.'

'But Paris – surely after five years…'

'Paris was nothing to me any more.' There was a slight harshness to his words that she had never heard before. 'Not without Helene.' His sigh was heavy, loaded.

'Helene?' Alison prodded, intrigued at the almost-reverence in how he whispered the name.

'I met her that first summer. She was the model in my life drawing class. And the inspiration for all that followed.'

He paused, sipped his drink, his eyes fixed on the horizon. He could see her now, as clearly as on that first night. Dark hair, cut close to her head, those carved cheeks, the taut golden skin. Full red lips, arched and slightly parted. And the eyes: huge and black and staring, filled with an innocence and vulnerability that gave her a lost, almost endangered look. Apart from the red voile draped across her upper thighs, her long boyish body was uncovered. His hands strained to touch again the satin-soft hollows between her neck and shoulders, the small round breasts. But on that first night his eyes could not be drawn from the haunting in hers, from the secrets he imagined might lie behind them.

'Tell me about her,' Alison hesitated. 'Helene.' She tried out the name again, tasting its sacredness.

'She knew little of her birth.' He shifted his weight from his hip. 'She'd been raised in a home, fostered out when she was five. By age ten she had been with three different families and at sixteen she struck out on her own and moved to Paris. She'd been there three years when I met her, surviving on what she'd make from modelling at different art classes.' He paused again. Alison didn't speak, anxious to know more, anxious not to break the magic in his eyes and his words. 'I was captivated by her … by everything about her. Within a month I'd persuaded her to move in with me and for the first time in my life I knew what it felt like to be complete. To be home.'

'So what happened – what made you leave Paris?'

'I went to a gallery opening in London the following September. They'd accepted some of my paintings and it looked like this was going to be my big break. I flew to Dublin for a couple of days when the exhibition finished. I was on a high. My work had been really well received. She must have thought I wasn't coming back.'

'She left?' Alison prompted, after a few moments' silence.

'I searched for her for six solid months, eventually tracked her down – or what was left of her—' He broke off, his voice trembling. Alison took his hand. He cleared his throat, continued. 'In Montpellier. She was using again, she was destroyed…'

'I'm so sorry, William, I shouldn't have…'

'No. No, it's okay.' He squeezed her hand tight, held it fast in his. 'It's good to remember. It's like what you were talking about earlier tonight, about this belonging. Helene had spent her life drifting, surviving, trying to figure out who she was, where she had come from. She thought she'd found some kind of belonging in me. With me. And when she thought I'd left her, she just didn't want to feel any more.'

'And you?'

'I felt I'd failed her. I had. I should have seen – I should have known. I tried everything, arranged rehab. She quit after five days, refused point-blank to see or speak to me after that.' He shifted, rested his back against a rock, all the time keeping hold of Alison's hand. His sigh was long and deep. 'I stuck around for eighteen months, cursing myself, my stupidity. I'd fallen victim to my ego. Thought I was going to be the next big guy. It was all I had talked about and to her it must have seemed all I cared about. It had taken me over. No wonder she felt she'd lost me. Do you mind?' William reached for Alison's cigarettes.

'Oh, I didn't know you…of course, go ahead.'

'There was never again going to be anyone for me after that. I was never going to cause that pain, suffer that pain again.' He drew deeply on the cigarette. 'After eighteen

157

months I bound up my wounds and moved on.' He exhaled slowly into the still night air, the sound of the surf washing the silence.

Alison took both his hands in hers. 'Let's swim,' she whispered, pulling him upwards. She unbuttoned her shirt and let it fall from her shoulders, stepped out of her jeans and pants and unclasped her bra. She stood before him, her wild red curls lit by the moonlight, tumbling over her breasts. His eyes held hers as he freed himself slowly from his clothes. Hand in hand, they walked slowly towards the water.

The soft wet sand yielded beneath their feet, the bite of the water tensing their naked skin as they followed the moon's trail, the water rising to their waists. Alison dived into the silent depths, surfaced breathless and smiling a few feet away. He stood watching, mesmerised by the darkened curls clinging to her head, the light of the moon bathing the pale, raw beauty of her face, her neck, her shoulders.

Seeing his chance, Joe O'Sullivan stole from the high dune grass, helped himself to two cigarettes, a lump of cheese and some crackers. He put the wine bottle to his head and drained it before returning again to his watch post.

* * *

Just after midday the following Wednesday, Alison saw the blue lorry negotiating the mouth of the drive. She tapped the screen saver and rose from the computer, her eyes strained and itchy. The clock read ten past twelve. She had worked straight through since returning from the beach at eight thirty that morning. Just one week since she'd started and already she had written almost eighteen thousand words. Something just seemed to have clicked inside her that Tuesday. A belief in herself, in the worth and beauty of the story she would write. The last week had gone by in a flash. She'd hardly stepped outside the house, except to walk the dogs at seven each morning and make a half-hour visit to Maryanne in the afternoons. There had been one frantic evening visit to William to tell him she had started, how alive and full of drive and passion she felt. He had been almost as excited as she was, as she tried to explain how she felt like she was back in those early years again with a real life, with real possibilities, how she had finally broken free of Carniskey without even stepping outside it.

She went out through the back door and around the house just as the lorry pulled to a halt at the top of the drive. A tall man with wiry black curls hopped down from the cab, lifting a small boy down to the ground behind him. He took a few long strides towards Alison, the little blond child keeping up behind. He wiped his big hand on the seat of his jeans and offered it to Alison.

'Tom O'Donnell, I rang about yer ad in *The Skipper*?' The Donegal lilt lent him a real gentleness. 'This is wee Daniel.' He motioned with his head to the child behind.

'Oh, Tom, hi. I wasn't expecting you till Friday.' Alison took his hand.

'Och, with the weather so broken we thought we'd make use of the day. Mind, ye have it good down here,' he remarked, looking out towards the bay.

'This has been our best week.' Alison couldn't understand why she felt so awkward in his presence. Was it his size? The black curls and familiar fishing gait reminding her of Sean? 'The stuff's round here, if you'd like to take a look.' She led him around the side of the house. The little boy screamed as the two dogs rushed towards him, knocking him onto the ground.

'Tilly! Tim! Oh, I am sorry. It's okay, Daniel. They won't hurt you, they're just excited to see you.'

'See, Dan, they're just lookin' to play with ye.' Tom straightened the little boy. 'He's well used to it,' he smiled. 'He's got two of his own at home.'

'I'll leave you to look at this lot, come inside when you're ready and I'll put on some tea, ye must be hungry after the journey.' She disappeared in the back door.

Ten minutes later Tom knocked on the open back door. Alison turned to find him leaning against the jamb.

'I'll give ye five grand for the lot.'

'But— '

'I can give ye cash, shift the lot today?'

'I didn't, well— '

'It's a fair deal, and the most I'm prepared to offer,' Tom cut in. 'As I said, cash in hand.'

Alison nodded, open-mouthed.

'Have we a deal, then?' Tom stuck out his big hand again.

'A deal,' she managed to mutter, shaking his hand.

'Great, I'll start shifting it then, we've a long drive home.' He was gone before she could say any more. She sat down slowly on the chair. Five thousand? Had she heard him right? If he'd said three, she'd have been more than thrilled. Would have settled for two and a half, with the bind she was in. A huge smile creased her face. Five thousand euro! She'd never dreamed of having that amount of money. She could paint the house outside, fix the leak in the back kitchen roof – maybe even have a holiday with Hannah! Best of all, now she would have the time and peace of mind to write without the constant panic of where the next bob was coming from. Life was turning. At last things were on the up. She could feel it in every cell of her body. Joe O'Sullivan, she thought, rising up frantically. Some of Sean's gear would have to be left for Joe. She rushed outside. 'I'll give you a hand,' she called to Tom's back. She moved to where he was sorting the pots. Tom smiled to himself.

By three o'clock they had shifted the lot, had eaten their fill of sandwiches and cake, and Alison stood at the top of the drive waving them off. She wondered why she'd had such an odd feeling around him at first; he was such a lovely man, gentle, shy and yet chatty, and so interested in herself and Hannah, their life in Carniskey. She hadn't mentioned that the nets and pots had belonged to a man lost at sea, mindful of Joan and Theresa's 'bad luck' theory and fearful it might make him change his mind. Five thousand euro? She still couldn't believe it.

She walked back around the side of the house. The garden seemed huge without Sean's gear strewn all over it. Huge and empty. She sat down on the grass. So this was it then, Sean was finally gone. The uncovered grass was dead and yellowed from its years in the darkness. But here and there, she noticed, a green tuft peeped its head. There's still life, still hope, it seemed to whisper to a tearful Alison. And she knew it was right. She would make a rockery, she decided. Here, just outside the kitchen window. She would use the stones and shells from the kitchen and fill it in with wild plants to remember Sean, to remember their love.

* * *

Tom O'Donnell pressed the call button on his mobile phone. It was answered on the first ring.

'Well?'

'It's done.' Tom spoke quietly. 'I've got the gear, paid over the five like ye said.'

'And Alison? How was she?'

Tom sighed at the loneliness and desperation in Sean Delaney's voice. 'She's fine, Sean, she's happy. I'll talk to ye when I get back.'

He replaced the phone in its holder.

'It's a queer old world, Dan,' he sighed, stroking the sleeping child's hair.

Nine

Just shy of his twenty-first birthday, Sean had been. The sun that day – the whole of heaven – had seemed to shine on and through him.

Maryanne felt the heat of her pride well up again now, just as it had that clear May day, and spill from her eyes, her body unable to contain it. At thirty-two feet, with its dark blue hull and the solid red stripe at its base where it met the water, *The Maryanne* dwarfed every other fishing boat in the harbour.

A knot of well-wishers had gathered at the end of the pier for the priest's blessing, young Alison to the front, her red curls dancing as she angled her head and aimed the champagne bottle at the bow. Frank looked on from beneath the peak of his cap, his pride evidenced in the outward thrust of his chest, his hands remaining stubbornly in his pockets while neighbours and fishing colleagues clapped Sean on the back and shook his hand.

His own man now, Sean hadn't seemed to notice, his whole attention fixed on the boat: the pristine wheelhouse, the high pot hauler, every part of him aching, itching, she knew, to feel her yielding on the water beneath him.

Alison had wanted it raised after, hauled from the depths. But Maryanne had been fixed in her opposition, knowing that had the wreck been recovered then this memory, this day, would have sunk in its place to the sea bed. No, she would remember her son and *The Maryanne* exactly as she saw them that day: strong, pioneering, invincible.

* * *

She would lodge the money, Alison decided, collect her ring and then take William for a celebratory meal. She parked at the top of the dirt track and half-ran the short path to his camper. 'William?' She knocked on the door. 'William?' She looked out over the slumbering sea while she waited. 'William?' No answer. She tried the handle. Locked. Maybe he's swimming, she thought, following the cliff path to the outcrop and looking down into the cove below. It was deserted. She drove down to the main beach, but couldn't see him anywhere. He wasn't in the shop. She tried Phil's, bought some cigarettes. No William. Climbing back into the jeep, she turned for town. She had been looking forward to sharing the evening with him, telling him about her great windfall and the book and how well it was going, about the optimism she felt when she woke each morning – hurrying breakfast, rushing to the beach with the dogs, hungry, like a young lover, to get everything out of the way so that she could indulge in the dream that had finally been given light.

His body weeping a cold sweat, William lay on the bed, pain burning his hip and lower back. His mouth, dry and open, begged a drink. Blankets tight around him, he couldn't control the shivers that rippled through his body.

Neither could he chase the image of Helene, naked on that crack house bed, her eyes, dark and staring and pained with loss.

* * *

The evening sun blushing the sky at her back, Alison sat in the kitchen window and twirled the newly polished engagement ring around on her finger. It winked up at her, happy to be back where it belonged. She felt restless, felt an urgency to share her good fortune, to speak it out loud and make it more than the dream she feared she'd awake from. She looked out towards the sea, her eyes straying in the direction of Tra na Leon. Surely William would be back by now.

Ten minutes later she was at his door, knocking and calling his name. She tried the handle. Still locked. She sighed and turned for home.

* * *

When Tom O'Donnell reached his home in Killybegs just before ten that night, Sean was waiting for him at the kitchen table. He passed a sleeping Daniel to his mother Ella, who took him upstairs to bed. Tom drew a bottle of Paddy's from the side dresser and placed two tumblers on the table.

'Hannah? Is she tall? Is she like me?'

'I didn't see her, she's away for the summer – in London, with her aunt.'

'London? Jesus, she's hardly old enough to—'

'I don't think it's for ye to judge, Sean.' Weary from the journey, Tom hadn't the energy to disguise the impatience in his voice. 'Ye haven't been there. Ye don't know how things have been. Alison seems a strong and capable woman, I'm sure she knows what she's doing.' Tom sighed, dropping into the chair.

'Did she mention me?' Sean's dark eyes searched every inch of Tom's face, his whole body straining towards him across the table.

'No. No, she just spoke a wee bit about the place, about the sea. She seems proud of Hannah. A real beauty, according to her mother, and wilful with it.' Tom held the whiskey a moment on his tongue, relishing its burn.

'She always was,' Sean smiled, fingering his beard. 'Right from the day we brought her home she made herself heard. She demanded a lot from Alison. How did she look, Alison? How would you say she's doing?'

'I can't understand how ye left a woman like that behind.' He shook his head, remembering the shy dip of her head, the rich red hair. 'She was shy, didn't give much away. But ye'd know she was strong, ye know. No fool.' Tom laughed then. 'She'd be no great shakes at poker, though! Ye'd want to have seen her face when I offered the five grand – the two big eyes nearly jumped out of her head!'

'There was always a lot of the girl in Alison. Well, in the early years anyway, before I wore it out of her.' He swirled the whiskey glass in his hand, looked into its golden depths as if searching the past.

'She looked really well, Sean. Healthy. Happy with life, I'd say.'

'And the place?'

'A bit neglected from the outside. Could do with a painting up. But the kitchen had a homely feel – even though I'd say she had half the stones from the beach inside it. She had a lot of pictures of ye on the walls.' Tom sat back in his chair, drew a hand across his eyes before fixing them again on Sean. 'She hasn't forgotten ye.'

When he had first met Sean at the tail end of December, Tom had been struck by his quiet manner and aloofness. He knew instinctively there was some other story behind this lad who had arrived in Killybegs – off a Spanish vessel, he'd said, that he had worked aboard for the past few years. There was something in the bend of his head at the bar, the habit he had of staring silently into his pint, oblivious to the singing, the dart playing, the general Saturday night commotion around him. And the depth in those eyes, like they were always looking back, searching for something.

Sean had found work on one of the shrimp boats that operated from the quay and had taken a room with Tom and his wife and young son. It had been a tough winter and they were glad of the few extra bob from his lodgings. Sean was an awkward house guest at first, eating his meals in silence before disappearing again to his room under the eves. Little Daniel had taken an instant liking to him. At just five years old he seemed to sense the loneliness in the stranger. He would stare at him across the table and when Sean would raise his head, Daniel would bestow on him the full width of his gappy grin. He would take books and place them by Sean's bedroom door. And on the occasions when Sean would sit silently, smoking beside the fire, Daniel would sit on the mat at his feet, quietly leafing through a fishing magazine and pointing out a fish or a boat – 'She's a nice one, Sean.' Or maybe colouring or drawing a picture and offering it to him for his room – 'This one's for you, Sean, it's a big Spanish boat like yours.' Sean would nod or smile at the child, offer him the odd word. And as the weeks passed Tom watched the child gently tease him from his inner prison. Before January was out the boy had taken to leading Sean down to the pier or up along the cliff tops and, sometimes, craftily, down past the little sweet shop in the village.

Following a week's unexplained absence in early February, Sean had returned to the house with a bad viral infection that had confined him to bed for the best part of three weeks. Tom would lay awake at nights and listen to him call out for Alison in his drugged, fitful sleep. Daniel heard it too.

'Will she come soon, Alison?' The child, eyes wide with curiosity, had looked up at Sean, who sat by the fire, a blanket over his legs. It was Sean's first week to rise from the bed and Daniel could not get close enough to him. A fitful cough seized Sean and tears ran down his cheeks.

'Time for your bed.' Ella had gathered the child to take him to his room. 'Don't tire Sean out with your questions. He's not better yet, Daniel. Now, say goodnight.'

Tom had filled two glasses of whiskey, handed one to Sean and then sat into the armchair on the other side of the open fire. 'Was she yer wife?' he had prompted gently. And something had snapped in Sean, causing the walls he had built around him to crumble.

Through the night, Sean talked and Tom listened, rising only to refuel their glasses or the fire. Sean painted a picture of the beautiful young girl who had given up her family, her home, her whole future to be with him, of the love she had poured on him. He spoke of the black emptiness that would descend on him like a cloud at the end of each summer, wrapping him inside himself. A self he despised for what he was doing to the beautiful young woman he would hear crying quietly to herself at night, beside him in the bed and he not even able to put out an arm in comfort, despite an overwhelming longing to do so. And the child: the little girl with the eyes and smile that mirrored his own. The way she would withdraw sometimes behind her mother when he entered the house. He could see what it was doing to Alison, see how the weight of it bent her head, hunched her shoulders. He'd retreat to the pub, play at being normal and let the drink dull the self-hatred that scalded him.

He recalled how slowly, ritually, the cloud would lift with each spring, as if the extra light in the long evenings somehow melted it away from him. Then, he would come back to her. And year in, year out, she would welcome him and she would blossom under his light and his love, like the trees and the flowers and the cliff tops all around her.

Come September, he would see her again, watching for changes in him. Notice how she would keep Hannah out of his way and how Alison herself would soft-step around him, the light being slowly thieved from her face as the evenings shortened.

'So ye left?' The dawning sunlight stole through the kitchen window, brushing the contours of Sean's bowed face.

'That evening I'd thought to end it. I could see the years had begun to break her. I had destroyed her and I couldn't live to see the child cursed in the same way. But I couldn't even do that right!' His head rose with his voice. 'I'm nothing but a coward – a cruel, selfish coward – and I clung to the life I despised as much as myself.' He looked into

169

Tom's eyes and then into the dying fire, a heavy sigh dragging the words from the very vaults of him. 'When the boat went down and the water gripped me, I fought. I fought and I struggled till the sea saw me for the pathetic fool that I was and flung me in disgust to the rocks.' Shaking his head, he drew his lips into a thin, tight line, clamped a fist over his mouth, his eyes fixed on the glass in his lap. 'Two days later,' he continued, 'I'd made my way to Fernelagh. Got a job on a Spanish boat that had sheltered there overnight. I stayed with them six months and then put down two years in Scotland, different seasons in different ports. When I couldn't stand the loneliness any more, I signed up with another Spanish boat and then, well, you know the rest.' He fell silent then, remembering the look on Alison's face that evening when he left. Remembering Joe O'Sullivan's bewilderment as he followed Sean from the rocks across miles of fields. He had told him to go home, to forget Sean Delaney. And when Joe refused and kept following, Sean had flung at him every name and insult that he had guarded him from in their childhood. Roared at him till Joe finally turned and ran back through the fields in the darkness.

'So Alison believes ye're dead?'

'I am. That night on the rocks, I died to all that I was. There's no life for me, I know that now. Not without Carniskey, without Alison.' He lifted his gaze from the fire, looked straight into Tom's eyes. 'I'm a dead man, Tom, but even death refuses me.' He paused, drained his glass. 'And I can never go back, though every drop of blood that flows through me howls for that place, and for her.'

After that night Sean never spoke of Alison again. Neither did Tom share with his wife the dark secrets that had been passed to him, though day and night he tossed the story over and over again in his mind, unable to fathom the depths of pain it must have taken to drive a man to cast himself away from all that he knew, all that he loved. The dark torment he had seen in Sean haunted him, fought with another part of him that almost despised this man that could leave his wife, his own child – leave them to struggle with their grief and their lives, down there on their own and him, all that time, alive and so near; it had to take a certain amount of callousness to manage that.

Every time it threw itself up in his mind, Tom tried to tell himself that it wasn't his affair, it had nothing to do with him. But it was useless. The fact that it had been spoken, that he had heard it, he couldn't help feeling a certain guilt, a kind of responsibility, as if he were somehow an accomplice in it all.

He had seen the advertisement in the June issue of *The Skipper*. Had passed it to Sean one night after supper while Ella was busy putting the boy to bed. Sean had grabbed it like a gift from the gods. Seen it as a chance to make up to Alison in some small way for the suffering he had stamped into her. Tom didn't hesitate to assist, eager to lift some of the darkness from the man he had come to know and to like so well, to help him atone to the young widow and child. And to rid himself of their terrible burden.

* * *

You wouldn't have to be a mind reader to know that Kathleen's patience was just about worn to its last thread. Rob sighed. Kathleen laid it all out there like a great big picture book – with sound.

He sat back from the table, his hands resting across his middle. What a meal she had cooked for him last night – she had really pulled out all the stops: candlelight, soft music – and that dress! Red was definitely her colour. Red for passion, heat, fire. He closed his eyes, called up the tight band hugging her tiny waist, the shimmering material spilling from her hips in an avalanche of temptation. He had wanted Jamie to call out from upstairs a second time just so he could watch her, hand lightly touching the banister as she swung up the stairs, the tiny mole on the exposed V of flesh on her back only momentarily managing to draw his attention upwards.

She had produced the tickets with dessert: *A Midsummer Night's Dream* in the grounds of the old Protestant church, Saturday night at dusk.

'Could you get anything more romantic?' she had gushed, cheeks flushed, her hands finding his across the candle-lit table.

Her darkening eyes registered his hesitation. She drew her hands back slowly, folding them over the tiny diamante that danced at her cleavage. 'What is it?'

'No can do, I'm afraid.' He shifted his gaze from the confusion on her face, straightened his place mat, twirled the stem of the wine glass. 'I've a job to check out in Cork on Saturday evening. I won't get back here till ten at the earliest.'

'On a Saturday? But you can change it, surely?'

''Fraid not, Kath. You know how lean things are at the moment. If I'm not there, ten more will jump in ahead of me.'

'But you're the boss, Rob. Surely you can send someone else.' There was no disguising her impatience now.

'I can't, it's a big job and I don't want to risk losing it. I know the guy and he'll expect me to turn up in person. I'm sorry, if it was any other night.'

That was when the clattering began, the stacking of dishes, cutlery.

'But I can pick you up after,' he offered, rising to help.

'Oh, for heaven's sake, Rob, I can't go on my own! It'll be all couples and I'd look like a right spare – leave that, please!'

The dishwasher door seemed to require an extra hard bang. 'Listen, I'm tired,' she turned, hands gripping the worktop behind her. And she did look tired, worn out, deflated. The whoosh of water into the dishwasher filled the silence.

'I'll call you.' He kissed the cheek her turned face offered, kneaded her bare shoulder. 'Say goodnight to Jamie for me.'

He sat up to the table now, sighed. He hoped the text he had sent her when he got home, and the two today, would be enough to hold her to her promise to meet him later on Saturday night. He picked up his pen, drew a line through the last item on his list.

* * *

'William!' Alison's heart swelled when she saw his legs stretched on the camper doorstep. A niggling disquiet had bothered her since she'd returned again yesterday to find the camper still locked and empty. She had walked on out to the cliff top and sat in the evening sun, a sense of another ending, another stone of loss dropping inside her. She had known that he wouldn't be around forever, he had made that more than clear when he had spoken about not attaching himself to any one place, any one person. Maybe she had called on him too often, had become too close for his liking. But surely he wouldn't have left without at least saying goodbye. She had gone home then and thrown herself into her writing, only permitting him to enter her head again when she fell in to bed, exhausted. And he had refused to leave. Even when she had finally managed to fall asleep he had walked towards her on the wet sand, calling her name over the roar of the waves. She had woken with his voice still in her head and an uneasiness that gnawed at her until she grabbed her keys and swept down the drive and on up towards Tra na Leon. A huge smile wreathed her face as she hurried along the path towards him.

'William? Oh Jesus, William, what's happened?' She was on her knees beside him. He sat on the step, his back against the jamb of the door. His face was grey, the lips tinged blue, his eyes sunken in their black sockets. Dried blood caked his nose and lip and streaked his shirt.

'Alison…good. I tried to get up, fell…' His breathing was laboured, his words weak and heavy with effort.

'Right, the doctor – can you stand?' His damp forehead burned under her trembling touch. 'Come on, put your arm around my shoulder. Good. That's it.' She prayed that the hint of authority would mask the panic in her voice. Rising slowly to his feet, William howled in pain as his left leg took his weight.

'Okay, William, put your weight on me, that's it. Easy, easy.' She sat him into the jeep, fastened the seatbelt around him and eased down the dirt track, conscious of every bump. She picked up speed on the main road to town and in a record fifteen minutes mounted the footpath outside the doctor's surgery.

* * *

'I know I can't insist,' the doctor sighed, 'but a hospital environment would be best.' Removing the blood pressure cuff from William's arm, he moved around behind him to listen to his chest. 'Your immune system will be very low at this stage, you're extremely susceptible to all that's out there. Take a deep breath.' He listened in silence. 'And out. And again.' He draped the stethoscope around his neck, passed William his shirt. 'You've got a particularly nasty chest infection. I'll prescribe an antibiotic and a steroid for the next ten days, then you'll need to see your consultant in Dublin. In the meantime we'll need to increase your pain medication—'

'No, honestly, what I'm on is fine. I just haven't been able to take it the last couple of days, it'll settle again once I get back on course.'

'Well, I'll write you the script, you'll have it if you feel you need it. I really do think you should consider a bed at the hospital, just for the next few days till the worst of this is over.'

'No, doctor, thanks. If I go in there, I know it will be the start of the end. And I'm not ready. Not just yet.'

* * *

Kathleen eased the brush through Maryanne's hair, folding the curls at the base of her neck around its soft bristles. 'Bet you wouldn't put up with that nonsense, Maryanne.' She half-smiled, reaching for the hair clip on the bedside locker, 'And neither will I for too much longer. Him and his texts. Talk is cheap, that's what I say. Words are easy, it's actions that count. Am I right?' She fixed the clip above Maryanne's right ear and moved to her left side. 'And I was so looking forward to it,' she sighed. 'I could see it all: the stage lit by the stars…and there'll be a full moon too on Saturday night. A nice bottle of wine and the feel of the grass cooling between my bare toes.' She halted the brush in mid stroke. 'Would you believe him, Maryanne – about Cork, I mean?' Something had niggled Kathleen about the way Rob had avoided her eye when he came up with the whole Cork excuse. Why would he be meeting someone late on a Saturday evening of all times? No, something wasn't right. It just didn't fit. And the way he had hightailed it out of the place – no such thing as even staying overnight, never mind the whole moving-in business that had started all this nonsense.

Rob had had a change of heart, she was almost certain of it, and the sooner she admitted it to herself the better. 'He wants to go somewhere quiet on Saturday night, somewhere we can talk.' She continued the brush strokes, slow and gentle. 'That can only mean one thing, right. But Rob being Rob, he just can't come out with it.' She opened the second hair clip with her teeth before settling it in the soft curls behind Maryanne's left ear. 'Well, I'll make it easy for him, won't I, Maryanne? No point in dragging it out any longer. If he wants out, then best let him go. And I'll survive, sure don't us women always?' She reached for the hand mirror. 'There. All done, take a look.' She smiled, squeezing Maryanne's shoulder as she fought to hold back her tears.

* * *

William sat in the passenger seat and watched Alison skip across the road and into the chemist. Her movement was much more fluid, so much lighter than that of the girl he had seen on the beach that first morning at Carniskey. He closed his eyes. The jab the doctor had given him was beginning to take effect and he could feel a comfortable heaviness settling into his whole body. The sun through the window warmed his face. Within minutes, he was sleeping soundly.

'You okay?' Alison opened the door and slipped the shopping bags onto the back seat. William was in a deep sleep, his face relaxed, mouth slightly open. She drove towards home, the barking of the dogs stirring him when they reached the house.

'Alison, I'm sorry, must have dozed off. Sorry for all the trouble...'

'Nonsense, no trouble at all. Now, you wait there while I take in the shopping and then I'll help you in.'

'I'd rather go straight on, if that's all right with you.'

'Straight on?' Alison began pulling the bags from the back seat. 'I'll have the spare room ready in five minutes. You're staying here for the weekend at least, I don't want another fright like this morning.'

'But...'

'No buts. I'm not listening to nonsense. You're sick. You need a proper bed. Proper food. And don't worry, I'll leave you to yourself. Now, sit tight while I take this lot into the hall. Get down, Tim!' And she was gone. William sighed a smile.

He sank into the cool cotton sheets and stretched his full length in the double bed. It was one of the few luxuries he missed, especially when the pain caused his leg to cramp and his movement was so restricted on the narrow camper bed. Alison had pulled the curtains and ordered him to sleep. He was glad of her kindness, of her insistence. And the way she had of making nothing of his imposition. He would really miss her, he thought, drifting into a deep sleep.

* * *

Alison rushed to answer the telephone before it disturbed William.

'Hello?' She smiled, breathless, into the receiver, knowing it would be Hannah.

'Alison? Hello, Tom O'Donnell here ... I bought that gear from you on Wednesday?'

'Oh, Tom, how are you?' Alison's heart skipped and fell. She knew it had been too good to be true. He had thought it over and changed his mind, realised he'd overpaid.

'Just ringin' to let ye know we got back safe and sound and to thank ye again. Delighted with the buy.'

'Good. Great!' she beamed, relief flooding through her. 'And Daniel got over the journey okay?'

'Slept for the most of it,' Tom laughed. 'Still talkin' about yer dogs.'

'Aw,' Alison felt awkward, couldn't think what else she might say.

'Well, I'll go now and thanks again. We might call on ye sometime if ever we're passin' that way.'

'That'd be nice, sure. Anytime. Goodbye then.'

Sean replaced the extension phone in the hall and walked into the kitchen.

'Well, there ye have it.' Tom looked at the young man, at the emotions that tensed and shadowed his blanched face. Sean didn't answer, didn't even look in Tom's direction as he took his jacket from the back of the chair and shrugging into it, walked out the back door in silence.

Ten

Early the following morning Alison unlocked the camper door, running through a mental list of William's medication, clothes and whatever other bits and pieces he might need. The stifling heat hit her as she stepped inside. The place was like a hothouse, the air stale and oppressive. Leaving the door ajar she threw open the tiny windows. So, this is William's world, she thought, surveying the cramped interior and feeling a little awkward at entering his private space when he wasn't there. A narrow bed ran along one side, the covers discarded on the floor. It doubled as a seat, a small table fixed to the floor in front of it. Some overhead presses, a sink, a portable breakfast cooker and a tiny fridge occupied the other side. A miniature wardrobe and shower closet made up the rear. An open pill bottle lay on the floor, its contents scattered beneath the table, a plastic tumbler nearby. Bending to retrieve them, Alison's eyes were drawn to the loose pages on the table top. She lifted the top page and from beneath two huge eyes stared pleadingly at her from the most delicate, most beautiful face Alison had ever seen. The thickly shaded hair clung to the sharp contours of the elfin face. 'Helene,' Alison's lips mouthed the name, breathing in the love that had gone into every stroke. A shiver rippled through her. The eyes were almost lifelike and seemed to stare deep into Alison's, as if questioning her presence in William's intimate space. She placed the blank sheet back on top of the drawing and moved swiftly to collect William's things. She didn't belong here. Didn't want to be here. Could feel the hurt and loneliness expanding, groaning in the tiny space. And yet William always seemed so contented, she thought, locking the door behind her, so easy-going, so accepting of life. It was as if his home had let her steal a look inside the hidden places of the man she presumed to know so well.

She pulled in at the beach and set the dogs loose for a run. The sea was an angry grey, the high wave tops like diving mermaids. So much for today's sunshine and heat; the rain and wind were on their way again, the sea never lied. Better for William, she thought, remembering the stifling heat in the camper. She shuffled out of her shoes and walked barefoot along the water's edge. It was hard to believe that a chest infection could knock so much out of someone so quickly, and it seemed to have worsened his hip as well. A few weeks ago he could walk without a stick, but yesterday his left leg could bear no weight at all. Poor old William, she smiled. It hadn't suited him at all to be taken in charge by her. She could see how it hurt his male pride. But she couldn't have left him back to the camper on his own, not in that state. He needed some comfort and what if he were to fall again? Imagine if he'd knocked himself unconscious and she hadn't known he was in there. She shivered and cast the thought out of her mind. She had become so fond of him and there was a real and deep trust between them. She knew he'd be leaving soon for some new place and part of her envied his freedom. But she also knew that no matter how far away he'd travel, they would always have that bond, that friendship. She'd make sure that they kept in touch. She sat on the sand, buried her toes in its warmth. If only she and Sean could have parted like that. It would have been so much easier to accept. To get over. She would never forget her parting words to him. Would always feel the chill of his silent response.

She watched two surfers battle to conquer the rising waves, their long yellow boards like magic carpets shooting the tunnels before the waves upended them and then burst in frothy laughter to the shore. Then they'd rise again, the two young men, their wetsuits glistening like sealskin, their laughter rising with the roar of the tide.

'Hi, Alison.'

Alison jerked her head sideways, shaded her eyes with her hand. 'Oh, May, hello.' Alison didn't bother with the polite smile. She still hadn't forgiven May for her outburst in the pub that night – what was it she'd called her, a half lunatic? And *lucky* to be a widow?

'Suppose you've heard the news on O'Neill?' May hunkered down beside her.

'Sorry?'

'That young O'Neill. Hannah's good friend, I believe? Caught red-handed breaking into Phil's last night.'

'That's terrible.' Alison held May's stare while her hand searched out her shoes. She pushed herself up from the sand. 'But at least they caught him, that's something.' Head bent, she shoved her feet into her shoes, all the time feeling May's eyes drilling through her.

May's smile was tight, her narrowed eyes registering every tiny movement on Alison's face. 'How *is* Hannah these days? And poor Maryanne – any improvement?'

Alison lifted her head again, a wide smile planted across her face. 'Hannah is wonderful, May, she's loving London. And Maryanne's doing well, she's strong.' She held May's eye, daring her, almost wishing her to go one step further. 'Now' – Alison fought to keep the shake from her voice – 'I must be getting home, William will be wondering where I've got to. Give my love to the girls.' She whistled for the dogs, then turned her head back towards May, an extra sweetness to her smile: 'Oh, and Paul of course.' Head high, she marched back across the beach, her anger rising with every step.

She closed the hall door behind her, leaned against it and took three deep breaths. Hannah could never. She wouldn't. A cold finger walked her spine. Jesus! She had told Hannah about the money Maryanne kept, wrapped in newspaper and hidden in the freezer. The two of them had laughed at it! Maryanne had referred to it as her insurance against burglars – when they'd see that sum, she said, they'd be quick to run. Oh Hannah, she sighed, closing her eyes and drawing a hand down over her face. No wonder she had refused to visit Maryanne at the home. It was all so obvious now: the mood swings, the anger. Hannah's guilt.

She grabbed the phone from the bedroom and stepped across the hall to check on William. He lay curled on his side, facing the door, his hair spread like a silver mist on the pillow. He was sleeping soundly.

Back in the garden, Alison tapped the phone to her chin. Maybe she should leave it for an hour, give herself time to cool down, to think straight. She paced the garden, her heart pounding, the heat of her temper making her itch. She'd explode if she waited one more minute. She pressed in the number.

'Hannah?'

'Mum, hi, I was ju—'

'Now you listen to me, lady. I want the truth or so help— '

'Mum?'

'I said listen, Hannah!' She bit down on her lip, took a deep breath. 'Peter O'Neill was caught breaking and entering last night.' She kept her voice calm, level. 'Now, I want you to tell me— '

'But Mum, I have nothing to do with Pe—'

'Your nan, Hannah. Was it him? Did you know all along?'

'Mum, please, I— '

'The truth, Hannah!' Alison closed her eyes, gripped her hair in her fist.

'No.' Hannah's voice was almost a whisper.

'No what?'

'No, it wasn't him.'

'Don't be such a bloody fool, Hannah! Why are you shielding that—'

'I'm not.' Alison could hear the tremble of tears in her daughter's voice. 'I know he didn't do it. He was with me, remember?'

'Remember? Remember what?'

'Remember I'd told you that I was in Aoife's, but you rang and I was— '

'At the bonfire, oh Jesus, oh yes!' Alison words tumbled out on a tide of relief.

'And you thought,' Hannah paused, 'you thought I…you thought me and him? My own nan?'

'Oh, Hannah, I just panicked. I…' But Hannah was gone.

'Shit!' She punched in the number again, waited. 'Come on, Hannah.' But it went straight to answer phone.

Alison slumped down on the yellowed grass. She didn't

know where the tears came from, had thought she had cried herself dry. But she let them come, let them wash through her. And when they stopped she rose to her feet, collected a pen and pad from her desk in the kitchen and settled herself at the table under the hawthorn tree in the garden. Just like her tears, the words came slowly at first, then faster, faster, pouring out onto the page before she had even thought them. It was as if something, someone else inside or beyond her had taken control and she was just the vessel through which the words tumbled. It was almost four o'clock when she stepped back into the house.

'William?' She knocked and opened the door, a tray of tea, scrambled egg and toast balanced in her other hand. She turned on the bedside light. 'William?'

'Alison, what time is it?' He turned towards her, squinted at the light.

'Just after six – I've fixed you something light to eat.'

'Six? I've slept all day?'

'Pretty much,' she smiled. 'How are you feeling? Any better?' His face had lost some of its grey, but his eyes were still heavy and dark.

'Tired. That jab yesterday really knocked me for six. I'm sorry to be such a nuisance.'

'And I'm not listening to any more of that. Now, do you think you can sit up a little?' She fixed the pillows behind his head and helped him sit up against them. 'I'll leave you to eat, I need to make a few calls.' She stepped from the room, conscious of his embarrassment at needing her assistance.

* * *

Alison wound the cord of the kitchen phone round her finger. With Hannah still refusing to answer her mobile phone, she had decided to try Claire on the landline. She sighed again. 'It was the way May said it, Claire, the look in her eyes, you know, she was clearly hinting that Hannah'd been involved.'

'Oh, for heaven's sake, Alison, surely you know your own daughter better than that.' Claire threw her eyes to heaven. She could do without this. First Hannah in a state of high hysterics all evening and now Alison. Honestly, she was exhausted and had planned a nice relaxing evening: a few glasses of wine and her feet up in front of the television.

'I just panicked. I mean, with all that stuff that went on before she left, well, what else was I to think?'

'Mmm.' Claire held her hand up to the light, studied her nails. She could do with a fresh manicure.

'Maybe if you asked her again?' Alison felt suddenly tired. And she felt such a fool. Why did she have to jump in every time with her two big feet? No wonder Hannah wouldn't speak to her. In Alison's book there was nothing worse than finding yourself accused of something you had absolutely no part in.

'She's in her room, Alison, she's upset, there's really no point.' Claire looked at her watch. Her programme was about to start in five minutes. 'Leave it for tonight, I'll have a good chat with her tomorrow, things will look different then.'

'You think?'

'Come on, don't make this bigger than it is.' Alison's dramatics could drive you to drink, Claire often thought, but there was always that niggle of sisterly guilt when she thought of all that Alison had been through. 'It'll all be fine, you'll see. Talk tomorrow then?'

'Okay,' Alison sighed. 'And thanks again, Claire, for everything.'

'No worries, take care.'

Alison replaced the receiver. Of course Claire was right. Why make this into another big production and ruin all the headway that herself and Hannah had made over the summer. She tried to picture her daughter, alone in her strange bedroom. 'I love you,' she whispered.

* * *

William had eaten little and sat against the pillows, his eyes half closed. Alison removed the tray, helped him to the bathroom and back into bed. 'Call me in the night if you need anything.' She stroked his cheek and felt his forehead. At least his temperature seemed to have gone.

'Alison?'

'Yes?'

'Will you read to me, something of your own?'

She hesitated, her old awkwardness returning. Then she thought of Claire, of her determination, her self-belief. She took a deep breath, smiled. 'Sure. Just a minute.'

She returned to the room, a small notebook in her hand. She sat on the side of the bed and began to read, her voice low and soothing:

To the Sea

Will you miss me, rock and sea
And purple grey and yellow stone
Will you remember how you lifted

And dropped your white lace petticoat
And teased me to your depths
Will you keep the secrets
Your lonely love-roar drew from me
And mourn my morning visits
With my notebook and my wishes
And all those frantic moonlights
When I smuggled stones of sorrow
And hid them round your bed
Will you smile when you remember
The water-spirit child
Shaped in your womb-sand
Roar in your recalling
How I left you all those years
Returning with the heavy foot
Of life upon your bed
Your salt and mine
Together
Washing out my wounds
Will the sea pinks bloom
And wonder am I coming
Will this rock pray the sun
To warm my seat
Will you stretch your frothy fingers
Up the beach to reach me
And throw yourself upon the wind to follow
Will you miss me, friend
When I am gone forever.

William listened, the melancholy music of her words washing over him, the last two lines replaying in his head.

'Promise me, Alison.' His voice was a whisper as he

reached out and caught her hand. 'Promise me you'll get your work out there.'

'I promise I'll try,' she smiled, bending to kiss his cheek. His eyes were closed, sleep seducing him once more.

'Goodnight, Will,' she whispered and felt his hand squeeze hers. She lingered a moment in the doorway and caught herself talking to someone she had long ago sworn did not exist: 'Please God, let him be well.'

* * *

A suit and tie! Kathleen nearly fell down where she was when Jamie led Rob into the kitchen. She straightened her T-shirt, wiped her hands on the seat of her jeans.

'Rob? I thought we were just going somewhere casual?'

'Cork,' Rob grinned, patting the lapels of his jacket. 'No time to change.' He swivelled on his heel to face Jamie. 'So, all set?' He winked and Jamie almost ate his lips in his attempt at seriousness.

'Rob, it's almost ten o'clock – the babysitter's here, he was just going to bed.'

'I promised you a spin, didn't I, Monster?' He took Jamie's hand and moved to the door, calling, 'You might need a jacket,' over his shoulder.

'But Rob, hold on a sec—'

'We'll wait in the car.'

'Rob, wait!' He was going to do it in front of the child! That man was a bigger fool than she had given him credit for. He was banking on poor Jamie's presence to dampen down her hysterics. Well, he wasn't getting away with this one!

'Rebecca,' she called to the babysitter as she grabbed a jacket from the cloakroom, 'can you hold on for half an hour?' She could feel her face positively beam with temper.

Jamie sat forward in the back of the car, his head between the two front seats and his full attention focused on Rob. Kathleen swore under her breath as she tugged open the passenger door. Wasn't one heart enough for him to break?

Jamie's eyes widened. He threw off his seat belt and stuck his head forward, his hands grasping the headrests of the seats each side of him. A bright orange glow filled the sky above the harbour. The car rounded the last bend and there it was, right in front of them, like something straight out of a story book. 'WOW!' His eyes stole up and over the storm wall, right up the whole height of the red and blue balloon, then down again, slowly, to the mighty lash of the bright orange flame hissing hot air into its belly. The basket sat on the pier, weighted by sandbags and two men dressed in the same reds and blues as the balloon. 'WOW!'

'What the ... ' Kathleen's mouth stood open, ready for more words to follow, but none came.

'I told you I'd promised to take him for a spin.' Rob's whole face hung on his grin, his hand stealing across to cover Kathleen's. 'You going to join us then?'

Kathleen turned her face, looked at him through watery eyes, her tongue touching the groove on her lip. It seemed so long ago now, that very first date, when she had told him how she had always dreamed of taking a hot air balloon flight – by moonlight. Rob had remembered.

'Come on, Mum, hurry!' Jamie was out of the car, opening her door.

The whole of Carniskey below was like a magical toy village, the house and street lights glowing like tiny searching

190

eyes. The cars, mere ants, lit head and tail, moved in slow motion along the roads while the moon silvered the sea where it broke in absolute silence along the curve of the cliff.

'Sorry I was late.' Rob's hand stole around her waist. 'I wanted it to be perfect, dark enough for the moon's magic.'

'Oh, Rob.' She raised her face to him, the light from the flame catching her smile.

'And while I'm at it,' he cleared his throat, 'Cork. I'm afraid it was a bit of a…'

'Lie?' Kathleen smiled, standing on her toes to reach his lips. 'I knew it!' She kissed him again, her lips lingering. 'Thank you, it's perfect.'

'Sorry it had to be on the night of your play, but I'd been planning this for weeks and if I had to wait for another full moon, well…'

'But how did you keep it to yourself?' Something that had always amused Kathleen was Rob's almost childlike enthusiasm, that excitement he had about life that seemed to have him constantly talking, blurting.

'By keeping away from you as much as I could – it was the only safe bet. I let Jamie in on it, though,' he winked.

They both turned to look at him then. Jamie was gripping the lip of the basket with one hand, the other frantically pointing out landmarks to the two attendants.

'He's in absolute heaven.' She turned back to Rob. 'He missed you, you know. He never said much but that look on his face when he walked in to the kitchen with you tonight, no one could find words for that.'

'I made a right mess of that, didn't I, the moving in thing? It was so stupid. I was so stupid. I should never have asked you, put pressure on you. It wasn't right,' he sighed. 'I won't be making that mistake again.'

The hiss of the flame grew louder in her silence. She gripped the top of the basket with both hands, her heart dropping with her eyes to the water below. Rob moved behind her, bent to his knee. 'Kathleen,' he slipped the tiny box from his pocket. She turned slowly towards him, the moon lighting her tears.

'Will you marry this old fool?'

* * *

Alison sat at the kitchen table and opened her writing at where she had left off earlier in the evening. She re-read the last paragraph and within minutes her pen resumed its furious race over the page. She wrote on with a passion and drive, stopping only now and then to light a cigarette or to gaze momentarily out into the light of the full moon. The lighthouse remained unlit in the window. At two o'clock, exhausted and conscious of an early rise to tend William, she headed for bed, peering into William's room as she passed. He was sleeping heavily. She set her alarm for seven and switched off her bedside light.

The ring of the telephone made her jump. Hannah! She groped for the receiver.

'Hello?'

Nobody.

'Hello? Hello, can you hear me?'

The line went dead. 'And goodnight to you too.' She replaced the receiver, pulled the duvet over her shoulders and buried her head in the pillows. The first heavy drops of rain that the sea had promised threw themselves at her window, the wind gathering itself to drive them on.

Sean lifted the receiver again and pressed in the first three digits of Alison's number. He hesitated, then dropped the receiver back into its cradle. He drained the whiskey glass and stumbled to the dresser for a refill.

Eleven

William was woken by the hum of the electric shower, the sound of a woman singing just audible above it. His eyes accustomed themselves to the strange room: the dark green walls, the golden drapes, the floral hatboxes on top of the old mahogany wardrobe. His momentary confusion lifting, he smiled as he stretched in the bed, remembering Alison and her kindness. A dull ache and heaviness restricted his left side. He remembered her reading to him last night, her warm kiss on his cheek, the softness of her hand in his. He wasn't being fair to her, not telling her everything. Lying here in her house, surrounded by her comfort. What would it do to her if she knew the truth?

It was better that he left today, contact Fogarty on Monday and maybe move to Dublin, closer to the hospital. It was pointless putting off the inevitable, fooling himself – especially if it was going to be at Alison's expense. No, he would leave as soon as possible and she need never know. Alison knew he was a rambler, would think nothing of him upping sticks and moving on again. He threw back the bedclothes, eased his feet out onto the floor. A faint dizziness threatened his balance. He stood up gingerly, knocking the lamp to the floor as he grabbed the bedside table to break his fall.

'William? William, what are you—'

'It's okay, I just moved too quickly. I … I need the bathroom.' His words were weighed with frustration.

When she had settled him back into bed, Alison carried a tray of breakfast to the room. 'Mind if I join you?' She smiled, laying the tray on the bed and opening the drapes. William watched the light rain slow-cry down the window pane, the sky beyond low and grey, as if counting down his days. His eyes returned to Alison. She wore that same oversized dressing gown, her damp hair loose over her shoulders. He thought back to the last time he'd seen her wearing it, when she had swayed to Mozart and, later, her brokenness in the bathroom.

'What are you thinking?' She placed the tray between them as she sat on the bed.

'I was thinking of the change in you since the first time we met – the first morning I saw you on the beach.'

'Oh, that miserable one,' she laughed, pulling back her hair. 'I think I've finally dumped her.' She piled marmalade on her toast and took a hungry bite.

'I sold all the stuff, you know, the nets and pots. Wait till you see the garden – its HUGE!' She chewed hungrily, swallowed. 'But wait till I tell you the big news.' She raised a finger to hold his attention while she took a sip of her coffee. William smiled, warmed by her enthusiasm, by the way her energy charged the whole room. 'Kathleen was on the phone before seven. She's getting married, William! Rob proposed last night – and get this: in a hot air balloon, over the harbour, by *moonlight*! Can't you just picture it?' Her eyes danced as she detailed the scene, the champagne, the fireworks that Rob had arranged on the pier when they landed.

William swallowed back the lump that had gathered in his throat, his heart swelling and straining against his chest, as if to free itself from the cage his illness had condemned it to and to soar into the light and the life that Alison painted. She must have seen the change in him then, caught the shadow that dimmed his eyes. She stopped mid-flow, her eyes questioning, fixing on his.

'You feeling all right? How's the hip?'

'Good,' he nodded, smiling. 'That doctor of yours is a real healer. I'm really much better. In fact, I was thinking of heading home today. I've taken enough of your time.'

'We had a deal, remember,' she cut in. 'You're here 'til Monday at least and it's not up for discussion. As for taking my time, I've hardly seen you for five minutes.'

'Yeah, but…'

'William, the room's here. It's empty. Your sleeping in it isn't bothering me in any way.'

'But I'm fine, Alison, honest. I…'

'It's just one more day. God, anyone would think I was torturing you. Anyway, you weren't so fine when you tried to stand up earlier on. Now eat. And try to have a little patience?'

They chatted on, Alison telling in excited gushes of Kathleen's wedding plans, her own progress with the book.

'For the first time in years I feel passionate about something, driven, you know. I can't wait to get started in the mornings and toss it around in my head at night. Life has a purpose. I feel alive again, satisfied.'

'And you look it.' William smiled at the fire in her green eyes, the animation in her whole face.

'Thanks for the push,' she smiled, gathering the tray as she stood. 'I wouldn't have started without your words of encouragement.'

'No, you did it yourself. This is yours, Alison. Your dream. Your passion.' His eyes held hers, that same feeling rippling through her again, that sense that his eyes were licking her soul.

'I'll just take these back to the kitchen.' She bowed her head to hide the colour rising in her cheeks.

Dressed now, she returned to the room with books and a radio. She handed him a small whistle. 'Call if you need me – I won't be far away, so don't think of trying to escape,' she smiled, leaving the room.

When the rain lifted in the afternoon, Alison left her writing and went out into the garden to make a start on her rockery. She mapped out a space running across to the hawthorn tree from where you could see the rocks at the curve of the bay. At the tree's base she dug a small, deep hole. Back in the house she selected her favourite wedding photograph and another of herself and Sean with a newborn Hannah. Hannah still hadn't retuned her call. The temptation to ring her had been so strong this morning but she had stuck with Claire's advice and held back, giving Hannah the space she knew she deserved.

She wrote their names and the dates on the backs of the photographs, placed them in an old tin moneybox of Hannah's and sealed the lid with tape before wrapping the tin in a double layer of cling film. Returning to the garden, she placed it in the hole beneath the hawthorn and pressed the moist earth tight above it. She carried the stones from the kitchen: grey, mottled, pink, striped, black – each with its own story and love of the sea – and placed them on the newly turned earth, leaving space for plants that she would choose for their colour, their wildness and strength.

The rain returned now, big, heavy drops like the tears of a god. Alison looked out towards the sea and as she did she caught a movement at the other side of the ditch. She recognised the blue corduroy cap. Joe. How long had he been there, watching? A finger of red anger uncurled inside her. This was her private space. A special, sacred time. 'Joe!' He sprang from behind the ditch and took off like a hare towards the road, one hand gluing the cap to his head. She smiled after him, her anger softening. Joe had been one of the constants in her and Sean's life together and maybe it was fitting that he was here to share today as well. She remembered the stories Sean had told her of their child-hood. Denied a place at the local school, Joe would follow the others there each morning – a bag filled with old news-papers and two prized books on his shoulder – and every morning the door would be shut against him. The laughter when he'd appear at the window, knocking until the master would lose his temper and chase him away. Joe would sit patiently on the wall at the gate, waiting. Waiting until they would pour out at three o'clock and he could follow them home, never tiring of the teasing and the bullying that bought him a place in the crowd.

Sean had always had a soft spot for him – and for the elderly mother who lived with him in the old coastguard's cottage. God, how Joe had idolised Sean! She smiled, remembering the way Joe would pull himself up to his full height when Sean would praise the way he'd gutted a mackerel or salted the bait. How his eyes would twinkle when Sean gave him his 'wages' at the end of the week. She had loved that in Sean: that gentle, almost fatherly love, that kindness that, no matter what his own mood, Sean never failed to shower on Joe. She brushed the rain and the tears from her face. Poor Joe, he'd probably felt Sean's loss more than anyone else. All those mornings she had opened the back door to find him sitting there, waiting: 'Is Seany back yet?' His eyes would never meet hers and she had always felt that he knew something more, felt that he blamed her in some way. And she had turned on him for it. Roared and ranted at him one morning, pinning him to the wall and forcing his eyes to meet hers as she screamed in his face that he would never see Sean again.

The wet earth cloying at her boots mimicked the tug at the root of her heart. She knew she had wronged him. Vented her own anger, her own suffering and guilt on the poor lad. He had never come close to her after that, no matter how she tried to entice him, and as time moved on she had given up trying. As the rain drove her indoors she vowed to try again, try harder to put things right with the child-man that Sean had always watched over.

* * *

After supper William showered and for the first time in days felt something like his old self again. Later that night as he lay on the couch, candles bathing the sitting room in their half-light, he felt a keen awareness, a heavy regret for all he had missed out on these last years through his fear of attachment, his resolve to never again suffer the loss of someone he'd given his heart to. Soft shadows danced the walls, mimicking the lick and curve of the flames in the open fire. Alison, cross-legged on the rug before him, her head bent in a mixture of concentration and shyness, read from her poems. Her hair curtained her face, the soft curls tumbling to kiss the page in her hands. He smiled to himself at the way she would half look at him to gauge his response, at her girlish lack of confidence. She was beautiful. Beautiful. Not just the face, the long, slender body, but the whole of her: that whole contradiction of vulnerability and strength, pain and passion.

For the first time since losing Helene, William felt a connection, a deep longing stirring inside him. A yearning that he hadn't been ready to allow himself to feel, to offer himself to. Until now. Now, when it was too late. His whole being ached to reach for her, to hold her, to love and shelter her delicate beauty. He knew he didn't have the strength to resist her much longer. When he left in the morning, he would make arrangements for the move to Dublin as soon as possible. She had had more pain in her life than many could bear and he couldn't – he wouldn't – be the cause of another hurt that would tear open the wounds that had only so recently begun to heal.

'Will? What did you think?' She smiled up at him, her brow furrowed.

'Can you read it again?' Lost in the torment of his own feelings, he had hardly heard a word.

She began again, her soft lilt knifing his soul.

Back to the sea

You feel it wash over your weathered soul
Its hypnotic roar drawing from your heart
whispered memories of a little girl
who was part of this place

200

Part of summer evenings
when shoals of silver sprats
danced round the root of Gully's rock
to kiss your jiggling toes
Part of the spray and the foam
that winter-dashed the high slip walls
and sent seagulls sideways gliding
towards nooks in the copper stained cliffs

It played with you too
leaving its salty kiss on your lips
that you could savour it, late at night
in your high mahogany bed
safe under blankets and coats
the wind wrestling with the thatch above
stirring moss-stained mice
from the thick memory walls of your home
while your dreams bore you off
out on the cradle waves
your spray tightened cheeks spattered
with the blood and the scale
and the smell of the catch

Today again, the foamy fall
and the spray washing back like banshee hair
The wind mimics her death cry and knives
the surface of a mackerel backed sea
of grey on greyer grey on black
The cliffs and the stacks stand stern
never turning their heads
from the sting-slapping sea
with her belly of secrets

They scan the horizon
dream the return of the man
who was king of this place.

'You know, for someone who curses the sea, you seem to have a great affinity…no, a great love of it.'

'The great love-hate relationship,' she smiled, and sipped her wine. 'I suppose you can't live beside it for so long, share so much with it, without coming to know it, to respect it.'

'Well, it's certainly inspires your work.' He sat up on the couch. 'You have a wonderful talent, Alison, never forget that.'

Her eyes smiled into his and he locked on them as if his very sustenance could only be drunk from their depths. He cleared his throat. 'Now, this old man needs his bed.' He stood to go to his room, to be alone with his thoughts and his longings. With the fears that lay waiting in the darkness.

* * *

Next morning, the rocks and clay that Alison had so carefully arranged the previous day lay scattered and thrown about outside the kitchen window. Fury weighing her step, she silently cursed the dogs as she strode towards the garden. The hole beneath the tree was freshly dug out, and empty. Would Tim have managed that? Then she saw the footprints in the wet clay. Prints of a man's large shoe. Cold fingers of fear brushed the back of her neck. Someone, some man had been out here in the dark last night while she lay sleeping. And the dogs hadn't even alerted her. She hadn't slept that heavily, conscious that William might call her during the night.

'Problem, Alison?'

She swung around at William's call from the kitchen window. He could see her confusion, the tension tightening her mouth.

'Oh, it's just Tim!' She walked towards the window. 'He's gone and undone all the work I put in yesterday.' From the side of her eye she saw the little tin box, opened and empty, lying on the yellowed grass nearby. 'It's nothing, just a wasted day's work,' she smiled. 'How are you feeling this morning?'

William was dressed and shaved and looking a lot brighter. She stood under the open window looking up at him, the morning sun playing in her hair.

'Much better, thanks. I'll be off and out of your way in an hour. Fancy a coffee?'

'Sure.' She rounded the house to the back door. He was going home. 'Would you not think of spending one more night?' she called, kicking off her boots in the back kitchen. What if whoever it was that messed up the garden came back again tonight? 'There's nowhere in particular you've got to be, right?' She ignored the part of her that jeered, contesting that being on her own wasn't the real reason she wanted him to stay.

'Thanks, Alison, but honestly, I'm fine. I can rest at home today, plus there's some stuff I need to get on with.' His face was still drawn, his weight loss showing in the way his shirt hung at the shoulders.

'Anyway, I can't get too accustomed to these comforts. You're spoiling me.' He poured the scalding water into the mugs and turned to bring them to the table. The limp was more pronounced than ever and Alison could see the wince in his face when his left side bore his weight.

'You're tired of my company already?' she teased.

'Alison, never!' He sat the mugs on the table and, taking her in his arms, hugged her tightly. She closed her eyes and drank in his closeness, his freshness and warmth, the feeling of absolute comfort and security that washed right through her. He buried his face in the thickness of her hair, a deep sigh laced with longing escaping from the depths of him: a longing for all he had never had with her and yet could still feel its loss. He pulled away gently, his hands still resting on her shoulders, eyes searching hers, his lips burning to touch the bow that arched and parted hers.

'Alison,' his voice was heavy and hoarse, 'dear, sweet Alison. What would I have done these past few days without you?'

She didn't speak, reading more in his eyes than his words or his thanks could ever say.

'I'll miss you,' he sighed, giving her shoulders a tight squeeze before turning to sit, not trusting his heart or his tongue to hold their silence.

'Then you'll at least wait till this afternoon?' She busied herself sugaring her coffee. 'I want to go up there first, check that everything's okay for you.' The determination and authority that had driven her words in the past few days was replaced by a dull resignation.

* * *

Alison's jaw dropped and she stopped mid-stride. Along the side of the camper, bright red paint trickled like blood from the thick, ugly scrawl above. She moved nearer, her step hesitant. 'Git Out Git Out' repeated itself again and again along the length of its side, on the door and windows, the paint splashed about on the steps and grass. It must have been done last night, the rain clawing red tears from each letter. She stepped around the back. The generator was upturned and thrown near the gorse. Alison hauled it back into place. Along the back of the camper 'SEANY' screamed at her in a large, childish scrawl. She shook her head in a mixture of temper and understanding. Joe. This was his work. It had to be. He was the only one who ever called Sean by that name. If she caught him, she'd have his tonsils! She touched the paint. It hadn't quite dried but she would have to make a start on it soon before the sun made it stick. She drove back to the house, where she'd left William reading in the sitting room.

'Just popped back to get a few bits and pieces,' she called from the hall. She filled a basin with cloths, sponges and a bottle of turps. In the bedroom she threw on an old T-shirt and her gardening jeans. On her way back out she popped her head round the sitting-room door. 'Just going to …' He lay on the couch sleeping, the open book resting on his chest. Alison tiptoed in and covered him with a throw before scribbling a quick note to say she'd be back for him at four.

Two hours later she sat on the scrubbed step of the camper door and lit a cigarette. Her arms and her neck ached, her hands raw and tight from the water. She would kill Joe when she caught him. What if he comes back and does it again tonight, she thought. That would be all William would need to run him out of the place. Not that he seemed to need any more prompting, she sighed, drawing heavily on her cigarette. Her mind returned for the umpteenth time to their embrace this morning. Had she imagined the desperation in his sigh – in the way he'd held her so tightly? How his eyes had misted over when he'd whispered how he'd miss her? A niggling voice whispered at the back of her mind. *He's going away. Away from here. Away from you.* She stamped out her cigarette and began to scrub at the remaining paint with a renewed energy. *He's leaving here, he's leaving you.* The little voice sang with every stroke of her arm, the waves crashing in contempt to the shore below. Alison clenched her jaw. She scrubbed and scrubbed till the camper shone like new in the afternoon sun. She would come back again later, she decided. She'd make some excuse to William and she would catch that little bastard if he came back again and march him straight home to his mother.

Happy that the generator was working and that the windows and door were secure, she whistled for the dogs and headed for home.

* * *

Claire was right. Again. She couldn't really blame Mum, could she? Hannah sat on the steps of Claire's gallery and scanned the crowd for her aunt's red jacket. She tucked her knees under her chin, folded her arms round her calves. She wouldn't dare treat Claire like that: slamming doors, the 'whatever' treatment, filling her with lies and then making her feel guilty when she caught you out. It was easy to make Mum feel guilty, Hannah knew. Knew that she had worked on it too. Claire would send her packing if she tried any of that on her. But Mum had put up with it. Put up with Nan and the hospital and everything – imagine Claire doing that every day. Fat chance!

She lowered her head, her thick black curls screening her face. She swallowed back the burn that heated her chest and closed her eyes to block out the memory of that night, of P O'N – she could no longer even think his full name, never mind say it! Why had she ever bothered with that loser? And what else was Mum to think after all that stuff with Kathleen and Jamie and everything. Poor little Jamie, she had always considered him her little brother. Some big sister she'd turned out to be, standing behind that eejit, letting him roar like that. She pictured Jamie's face, the tears springing from his eyes. She hugged herself tighter. She would make it up to him, bring him back one of those dinosaurs she had seen at the market on Little Lane. Funny, she had thought of Jamie the moment she saw them that day.

And she would ring Mum tonight, she sighed, lifting her head. Like Claire said, Mum had enough on her plate with Nan and all without her adding to it. She glanced at her watch. Five forty-five. Claire had arranged to pick her up after work, but she was late. Again. She looked up the street, pictured Claire tottering towards her on her five-inch heels, shopping bags swinging – though she was supposed to be uptown at a meeting all afternoon – all flushed and breathless with apologies.

Her eyes wandered over the crowds milling along the footpaths, each with a face like they were setting off on some mission to save the world. A young couple, hand in hand, jerked backwards out of the horn blast of a black taxi. A gaggle of Spanish students, like ducks in their yellow T-shirts, marched behind their guide up the steps beside her. She touched her hand to the spot where the sun scorched the base of her neck, pictured the beach at Carniskey, the surfers skimming the waves.

'Hey, Hannah!' Harry, a college student who also had a summer job at Claire's gallery, loped down the steps towards her, his blond fringe dancing.

* * *

William waved her off just after seven and returned to the sitting room to lie down on the couch. He felt weak, exhausted *all* the time, but while Alison was about he had done his best to pretend he was back to some kind of normality. He shifted on his back till the pain eased in his hip. Alison's spirits seemed to have lifted after her chat on the phone with Hannah but she had seemed a little distant with him all evening. The edge was missing from her humour and whenever she spoke it was as if she was preoccupied, bothered by something else entirely. She was probably exhausted, and who could blame her, all the extra work he had put on her and then that damned generator kicking up and Alison having to haul it to the garage for repair. No wonder she seemed a bit out of sorts; she'd probably be glad to see the back of him in the morning when the generator was fixed.

He closed his eyes and allowed his mind to wander back again to this morning. He hoped he hadn't offended her, that she hadn't felt hurt or rejected. He could almost swear that she burned for that closeness as much as he did. It was there in her eyes, in the full and open invitation of her lips. It had killed him to turn away, to snap the magic, the unspoken yearning between them. But it wasn't him that she needed. Alison needed to know, to recognise, that she was coming alive herself, and not to confuse that feeling with loving him.

Besides, it would have hurt her more if he hadn't pulled away. Their absolute separation in a couple of months' time would surely destroy her. And he could never die in peace were he to leave behind that legacy of pain.

He had done his best to hide his disappointment when she told him she was going out tonight. He had barely seen her since this morning and when she told him that he had either to spend another night with her or sit in darkness in the camper, his heart had lifted at the chance of one more evening alone with her. But another part of him was glad that she was spending a few hours with Kathleen, getting involved in her plans for the wedding, looking forward. It was just what Alison needed. She had spent long enough in the past.

* * *

Alison had parked at the beach and walked the steep track to Tra na Leon so Joe wouldn't know she was there. She sat now on the narrow bed in the camper, staring into the eyes on the drawing in her hand. She felt a strange affinity with the charcoal image, recognised the pain, the isolation, the deep searching that William had captured so brilliantly in Helene's eyes.

A low muttering outside startled her. She sat upright, holding her breath. She could barely make out the low singsong words:

'We'll have a good one this year, Seany

Back with us this year, Seany...'

Joe. She knew it! She rose softly, flicked on the light and burst out through the door.

'Joe O'Sullivan!' she screamed. He made to run but tripped on the grass, the can of red paint spilling like fresh blood round his head. Alison grabbed him and pulling him up by the shoulders of his coat, sat him on the step of the camper.

'What are you playing at, Joe? Do you realise the work you gave me today?' She bent to his bowed face. 'Joe!' She shook his shoulders and he began to keen like a trapped and frightened animal.

'Look at me, Joe.' Her voice was high with temper. He shook his head quickly from side to side, muttering. She grabbed his chin and forced his eyes to meet hers. His eyelids fluttered nervously over his bead-like eyes.

'Why did you do it?'

He stuttered, then howled at her, 'Seany's comin', Seany's comin'!'

'Oh, for Christ's sake, Joe, Sean is gone! He's gone, understand? He's not coming back. Sean is DEAD! HE'S DEAD!' Alison could see her words strike his face like blows and, realising the strength and venom in her words and her hold, she let go her grip on his chin and shoulder. She hadn't wanted to hurt him, just to frighten him off.

'Get out of here, Joe. And if you come back again, I'll march you down to your mother and she'll get the guards. They came for you before and they'll lock you up this time. Mark my words, if I catch you up here again, you've had it!' He sat on, the head, still bowed, dancing from side to side.

'Go on, Joe, get home. I'll tell no one this time.'

Still half-sitting, he made a sudden lurch from the

step and ran for the track. Safely out of reach, he turned and shouted: 'You mark my words. He's comin'! Seany's comin!' He threw something from his pocket and ran into the gathering darkness. Alison stepped forward and picked up the wedding photo of herself and Sean. She smiled her sadness at Joe's determination. At his lasting insistence, his genuine belief that Sean would return. And at how the years had never worn or thwarted his love for him.

* * *

The ring of the telephone released William from a hellish dream of burning fields and naked, emaciated bodies piled high along the scorched ditches. He reached for the phone on the coffee table.

'Hello?' His voice was hoarse, still wrapped in sleep. 'Hello?'

The line went dead. He dropped the phone in his lap and ran his hands over his face, wiping the perspiration from his forehead. It rang again.

'Hello?'

'Hello,' a male voice, hesitant. 'Is…is Alison there?'

'I'm sorry, she's out at the moment. Can I take a mess—'

The caller hung up again. At least he had chased the nightmare, William sighed, checking his watch: eleven fifteen. Easing himself into a sitting position, he stood and made his way to the window, to the blackness outside that seemed to beckon him.

Sean felt the bile rise and burn inside him. 'She's out,' he whispered, and then, his voice rising, 'and some bastard is sitting there in my home!' He punched his fist into the table, sending the glass smashing to the floor.

Tom O'Donnell threw back the bedclothes, swung his legs out onto the floor and sat on the edge of the bed, his head in his hands. His heart hammered, beads of sweat gathering on his forehead as the image, clearer than a painting, formed again in the darkness, as it had every night since: the tiny body spread out on the shingle at the foot of the cliff, the torchlight lending the pale skin the luminosity of an angel.

He cursed the day that Sean had come to stay with them, cursed the night he had spilled his past. But most of all he cursed his own stupidity and foolish judgement for showing him that ad in *The Skipper*. Had he not a whit of sense? He had seen the depth and the darkness of Sean's pain, should have known to stand well clear and mind his own family.

Sean hadn't worked in over two weeks and the whiskey bottle had become his almost constant companion. He hardly slept beyond the times his head would hit the table in a drunken slumber in the small hours. Days he'd spend alone on the cliff, looking out beyond the ocean, out to the past and how he might change it. The atmosphere in the house was dark and charged and little Daniel had withdrawn into himself with the confusion and hurt of Sean's rejection.

Sean had roared at him late one evening when Daniel followed him along the cliff top. Roared at him to go home, that he was a nuisance and he was sick of him following him everywhere like a dumb pup. When Sean returned later with the dark and no Daniel, panic shook the house and within an hour the whole community could be seen combing the cliffs and the strands, torches winking and dancing in the blackness. Just after midnight his mother, who had sat silent and trancelike by the fire for hours, rose without speaking and opened the door, her steps all the time quickening, quickening, till she ran to the small shed at the top of the pier. She tore open the door and the harbour light shone into the cramped interior. And it shone on the small golden head asleep on a mound of salmon nets under the window. Still she didn't speak, but lifted the sleeping child in her arms, her silent tears unleashed as she carried him home to the warmth and safety of his bed.

If they had lost Daniel that night, he would have finished Sean off with his own hands. Instead, drunk on relief, he had welcomed Sean back into the house, a house now divided and heavy. Ella made it clear by her silence that she wished Sean gone, while Sean tempted the child with sweets, coloured pens, stories, but a wedge of hurt was planted firmly between them, strangling the spontaneity and trust that had once propelled the child towards his 'uncle Sean'.

Sean's drinking had worsened after that. Tom could see how it fuelled his torment when the child would pull away from him or answer him without looking in his direction. With Sean drinking later and later into the night, something inside Tom refused to let him rest. He was constantly alert, constantly on watch for something. He could feel what he could only describe as a heavy darkness gathering, approaching, in the same way a storm darkens and looms, pulling the sky and the horizon tighter, shrinking the light. That night with Daniel had been a warning. The whole bloody thing needed sorting, needed ending now, and Tom knew he had no option but to ask Sean to leave.

He heard the crash in the kitchen, groped for his shirt and trousers in the dark, his bare feet light and uncertain on the stairs. He entered the kitchen and switched on the overhead light. Sean squinted in its glare, replaced the telephone receiver with a hurried thump, guilt and confusion thundering his face.

'Don't ye think ye've hurt her enough?' Tom's whisper was laced with anger.

'I just wanted to hear her …'

'Ye gave up that pleasure a long time ago when ye left her alone with that wee child.' He shook his head at the splinters of glass, the pool of golden liquid at his feet.

'I never stopped loving her, never …'

'It's not about ye, Sean!' Tom caught him roughly by the shoulders. 'What would it do to her? Have ye thought about that? If she knew that all those years she mourned and searched, ye were ALIVE? Think, man. Think beyond yer own selfishness!'

They talked and argued till Tom's anger was spent and Sean was sober. They reached a deal. Tom would travel one more time to see Alison, would ask the questions that tormented Sean. And then Sean would leave. Go back on the Spanish boats, go wherever. And forget.

* * *

'You went to your bed early last night.' Alison turned from the sink as William stepped into the kitchen. 'I got back just before twelve – no sign of life.'

'Well, I figured that once you girls got together you'd be at it till the small hours.' William, lying awake in the darkness, had heard her come in and go straight to her room. Had half-risen from the bed to knock on her door with the excuse of telling her that she'd had a missed call. Old

214

fool, his head had mocked, leaning back down against the pillows.

'So, you ready for home?' she smiled, a forced breeziness in her voice. She was anxious to steer the conversation away from last night. Away from the awful foreboding that had crept into her after Joe had run off. Away from the panicked feeling that something terrible was about to crash in around her, a feeling so real that it chased her down the steep track in the darkness and home to the safe familiarity of her own bed.

'All set. By the way, some guy phoned last night, just after eleven.' He scanned her face.

'Guy?'

'Yeah. Didn't get a name or a message, I'm afraid – I told him you were out.' Her puzzlement looked genuine.

'Probably some kids messing.' She dried her hands, folded the towel. 'There's been a few of those lately. Anyway, better get going. I checked with the garage, the generator's fixed and they've left it back up.' She grabbed her keys, the dogs' heads rising with their rattle.

William turned the key in his door. Since he had come to know Alison, the short drive to the camper had been the first time he had felt any awkwardness, any uneasiness between them.

'Alison, you shouldn't have.' William beamed at the neatness of the camper: the folded clothes, the scrubbed cabinets, the beautiful wild flowers on the table.

'Welcome home,' she smiled.

'What's this?' He motioned to the neatly wrapped package on the table.

'I know you always swore you wouldn't have one,' Alison apologised as William unwrapped the mobile phone, 'but I don't ever want you to find yourself in a fix like you were last week … Show me … ' She held out her hand. 'I'll set it up for you before I go, I'll put in my number and the doctor's, to start with – you can add others yourself.' She explained pin codes and puk codes, glad to be in control of something. Glad of the mask for her loneliness.

'I'll ring you later, check that it's working.' She moved towards the door.

'Aren't you going to stay a while?' He needed to be near her. To see her, to hear her. But there was a restlessness about her, an almost impatience to be gone.

'Can't, I'm sorry. The house painters are due in the morning and I need to get the place sorted beforehand. Anyway, you need to rest. I'll talk to you later? Bye, then.' Her eyes never meeting his, she fastened the door behind her.

William sat on the bed and sighed out some of the heaviness from around his heart. He studied the tiny phone in his palm. Bit late in the day to be getting techno friendly, he chided, placing the charging phone back down on the table. He sat on, allowing the emptiness to settle around him. There he was, such a short time ago, talking to Alison about attachment, thinking he had it all figured out. But what he wouldn't give at this moment to be back in her home. To watch her move around the kitchen, to hear her singing to herself – completely out of tune – when she forgot that she wasn't alone. Even just to be in his room alone and know that she was about the place. He lifted the lid from the box of charcoal, opened his sketchpad.

* * *

216

Alison sat in front of the blank computer screen. She'd type up some of the pages she had written over the last few days. She wasn't in the mood to write anything new and maybe going back over the work she had done would spark her again. God, she missed him. Funny how easily, how quickly she could get used to having someone around the place again. William had just fitted in so seamlessly. There was never any awkwardness between them, no need to fill their silences with small talk. It was almost like he had always belonged there.

William hadn't felt so, obviously, with the hurry he'd been in to leave, even pretending to be better than he was. And he had seemed so tense and distant on the drive up to the camper, as if he was already away, somewhere else. She sighed into the silence, feeling as if the life had somehow drained from the house. 'Oh, come on!' she scolded, flicking the computer to life. Hadn't she felt the same when Hannah had gone to London? She was lonely, that was all, just missing the presence of another body about the place. And what was it William had said to her, about not attaching yourself, not trusting your fulfilment to somebody else? Her fingers moved swiftly across the keyboard.

The telephone rang and Alison glanced at her watch. Just after ten. Where had the last three hours disappeared to? She took a deep breath. 'Hello?' She closed her eyes, willed it to be his voice.

'Hey, just thought I'd let you know I've figured out how to use this thing.'

'William, how are you feeling? Settled back in okay?' It felt as if someone had turned on a light inside her.

'I'm just going to hit the hay. Just wanted to thank you

again, Alison, for everything. If there's anything I can ever do for you…'

She missed him so much, and it wouldn't be long now before he was moving on, moving out of her life altogether, so why not go for it, she argued, covering the mouthpiece and taking a long, slow breath. 'Actually, there is something.' She pulled the newspaper cutting from the noticeboard beside the phone. 'The Maritime Festival's on in town at the moment and there's an open poetry reading on the quay on Saturday night. And fireworks. I'd love to go but I'd never brave it on my own – fancy coming with me? That's, of course, if you feel you're up to it.' She closed her eyes and stretched down the corner of her mouth, trying to ignore the hesitation on the other end of the line, the voice screaming *fool!* in her head. William bit down on his lip. He had already telephoned Fogarty and arranged to return to Dublin the day after tomorrow.

'Saturday night?' he repeated, stalling. Leaving her today had only proved to him how desperately he wanted her, needed her. It had taken every last ounce of resolve to pass the night without seeing her, without hearing her voice. He knew he couldn't trust himself to be close to her again without…

'Yeah, eight o'clock, but I understand completely if you've got…'

'I'd love to, Alison, I never miss fireworks.' It was the way she tried to mask the disappointment in her voice that broke him. He'd ring Fogarty's secretary again tomorrow, arrange to go up on Monday. One last night together, just to say goodbye, and the fireworks would make a perfect parting. 'But there's one condition.'

'Yeah, what's that?'

'You have to promise to read a poem.'

'In front of that crowd? You must be joking!'

'That's the deal.'

'Go on, we'll talk tomorrow,' she laughed. 'Goodnight, Will. Sleep well.'

'You, too. Goodnight.'

Twelve

Although almost a week had passed since Rob's proposal, every time Kathleen thought about it her right hand immediately sought out her ring finger, the feel of the narrow band and the bump of the diamond flooding her chest with a golden warmth. It was real.

She kicked off her shoes, tucked her legs beneath her on the couch and selected a bridal magazine from the stack on the coffee table. A Christmas wedding – that gave her less than six months! She wasn't going to have one spare minute, she smiled, flicking leisurely through the pages. There was the dress, the venue, flowers, invites, cake, music, the honeymoon and God knows what else. She had half-suggested that they wait until next summer, give themselves time to breathe, to save, but Rob was having none of it. He wanted to start the brand new year as her husband and, besides, he'd added, he didn't want to give her one extra minute to mull it over and risk her changing her mind. As if!

Right from the moment she had found herself pregnant

with Jamie, Kathleen had banished all thoughts, all hopes of marriage from her mind. Already married, she knew before she even broke the news to Jamie's father what his reaction would be: he would pull down the shutters and lock her out. Through the nine months of her pregnancy Kathleen harnessed every ounce of strength and determination that was in her and, concentrating on the tiny life growing inside her, pushed all feelings of loss and rejection to a place where her mind or her heart couldn't reach.

Even when her tiny son was first placed in her arms, her tears weren't for the man she had lost, for the father her child would never know; they were the tears of a survivor, a warrior who had battled alone and had emerged still standing.

It was later, years later, when she had proved herself a competent mother, had won back the respect of family and others, years later when Jamie had grown into a healthy, confident, pleasure of a boy, when she had begun to relax, to stop proving herself, that the first chinks began to appear in her armour. It was hardly noticeable at first – vague sadness, tears appearing from nowhere, something hot and heavy pulling downwards at her heart as she watched other fathers, mothers with their children at the beach, outside school, shouting their pride at the playing pitch. Jamie rarely questioned who or where his father was. Always accepting, loving and happy, he threw himself into life just as she had taught him to. Shouldn't that have been enough for her? Shouldn't that have been her one solid reason for celebrating what she had, cherishing it? The very one reason not to run, like she had, back to the child's father and demand – no matter what the cost to herself – that he acknowledge Jamie, that he get to know him and play a

221

part in his life. The outcome of her efforts had only ensured that Jamie would never have the opportunity of meeting or knowing his father.

Guilt cemented the walls that she built around herself and Jamie that winter. Guilt and a steely determination to never again risk anyone rejecting them or making them feel they were second best.

She hadn't bargained on Rob. Hadn't even noticed as brick by slow brick he dismantled her defences. It was only when she thought she had lost him that she realised he had stripped away every last stone, realised there was room in her life for the light he had created.

Well, maybe not every last stone, she grimaced now as she flicked through the magazine, her eyes dancing from one unimaginably tiny bridal gown to the next. She opened the page she had marked last night. She had just about one stone to lose, she smiled, her finger tracing the tiny button detail on the back of the ivory gown.

* * *

They rounded the bend and Carniskey bay languished before them in the afternoon sun. 'Almost there,' Tom smiled into the rear-view mirror. Daniel sat up and wiped his eyes with his fists, then remembering the little parcel on his lap he grasped it tightly. The previous evening before bedtime he had carefully placed his gifts inside the plastic bag: a biscuit each for Tilly and Tim, a small rubber ball between them and a shell from the beach for Alison. Tom smiled, taking in his tight grip on the bag.

They swung into the mouth of the drive, the beautiful

warm yellow of the cottage beaming its welcome. The front door was now a rich red and Alison was putting the finishing touches to the matching window boxes, planting them with bunches of red and white carnations and white lobelias that swept like bridal trains from their bases. The place looked so vibrant, so alive, so different to the neglected greys Tom remembered from their last visit.

Her curls tamed in a high ponytail, Alison wore a loose blue shirt, bunched and knotted at her waist over red thigh-skimming shorts. Removing her gardening gloves, she walked towards them, her frown giving way to a broad smile as she recognised the car's occupants.

'Tom!' Her eyes were bright and wide with surprise. 'Daniel, lovely to see you again.' Alison laughed as the child raced past her, calling the dogs, the plastic bag hopping off his knees.

'Hope ye don't mind us stopping off – we had a bit of business in Passage.' Tom walked towards her shyly, his big hand thrust forward, 'How are ye keepin'?'

'Great. It's so nice of you to call.' She smiled, taking his hand. 'What do you think?' She gestured with the other hand towards the house.

'It looks really well. Some change! Did you do all this yerself?'

'I can only take credit for the door and window boxes, a few lads from the village took care of the rest. But yeah, I've really enjoyed it. I want it to look good for Hannah when she gets back. I'm sure she'll be feeling grey enough after the colour and excitement of London.'

'She due home soon?'

'About six weeks, but all this takes so much time. Coffee? Come on, we'll find Daniel.'

223

Daniel was sitting on the back lawn, a dog at either side of him.

'There's a picture,' Tom smiled. 'Couldn't get him to sleep last night with the excitement of comin'.'

'Stick on the kettle,' Alison called as she went through to the bathroom to wash her hands. What a lovely surprise, she smiled to herself. Besides Kathleen, it wasn't often that she had unexpected callers and every day had always been so predictable. But between the painters and William and Kathleen and now Tom and Daniel the place seemed to have a real buzz about it again, a new life. It was nice of Tom to remember her. She liked that kind of shy awkwardness he had about him, his pride in the child. A real honest-to-goodness gentleman, she nodded, drying her hands.

Tom looked about the kitchen. The changes were inside as well as out. The cold blue walls were gone, replaced by a warm terracotta and most of the stones and shells had disappeared from the window ledges and press tops. Two pictures of Sean remained: one on the wall near the lighthouse, the other, a smaller one of him and the child, sat on the mantle over the fireplace.

'You've been busy inside too,' he remarked when Alison returned to the kitchen.

'Yeah, there was no stopping me once I got going. It's given me a great rush of energy. Will we take this outside?' She piled a tray with mugs, biscuits, juice and the coffee pot.

'Let me carry that.' He followed her out the back door and over to the little circular table under the hawthorn tree.

'It's a beautiful spot ye have here – plenty of tourists in the summer?'

They ate and drank and talked easily, little Daniel coming and going for bits for the dogs.

224

'Is he your youngest?' Alison smiled towards the child tumbling on the lawn.

'My one and only – and lucky to have him. I was a bit late settling down. A life on the sea doesn't allow much time for making a family. But it's great to have himself and Ella to come home to,' he smiled, and Alison could see the pride and contentment shine from his eyes.

'That was the problem with me and Sean – my husband? The sea always came first.'

At least she had brought up the subject, Tom thought, relieved. He hadn't known how he could broach it, felt bad enough sitting there with her, knowing that he would relay every word she uttered right back to Sean. 'It must have been tough on ye, alone with the child.'

Hesitant at first and embarrassed at not having previously alluded to Sean's tragic death, Alison found herself slowly relaxing in his gentle company. Found herself speaking aloud her pain and her anger when Sean had first gone missing. The months of waiting and searching. The no-man's-land she had wandered in: no body, no hope, no evidence of whether he was dead or alive. The years of waking with a start in the dead of night in case some dream had allowed her to forget.

'It's only really in the last few months that I've finally let go. Putting that ad in the paper was a real turning point. A final owning-up to the fact that he wasn't coming back. It's funny.' She paused. 'It was as if doing that, doing something real and decisive instead of just tossing it over again and again in my head, gave me back some control, you know, some power over my life.' When she paused again, Tom didn't speak, instead he watched the emotions and thoughts play on her face.

'I've started to live again. For me. For me and for Hannah. It's hard to explain, it's like I've turned a corner and life is waiting for me again.' She unfolded her arms as she sat forward. 'When I wake in the mornings now, I haven't that weight on me like before; instead there's a kind of excitement about the day, about what might come next.' She laughed, a beautiful, life-filled laugh. 'God knows when I last felt like that! I'd completely forgotten what it was like.' She was silent again for a moment, her eyes moving towards the rockery.

'And I know I'll never forget Sean – our time together will always be a huge part of me. It's just…' Her brow creased as she sought out the words. 'I suppose I've remembered me. I have a life to live too, a part to play – not least as a mother to Hannah. And I suppose, well, it's time to get on with it. Time to let go.' She took a deep breath, her smile a mixture of sorrow and relief.

'Could ye ever imagine a life with him again, with Sean, now?' The words stuck in Tom's throat. He knew now what it felt like to be a traitor, he thought, loathing himself for his promise to Sean. But if this is what it took to get Sean out of their lives – and out of Alison's life – then he could live with his own discomfort.

'What would be the point?' Her eyes turned on him sharply. 'Isn't that what I've wasted the last three years doing?' She held his eyes and Tom could feel the burn of his shame flare under her gaze.

'Sean's dead. He's never coming back.' Her eyes drifted off out towards the horizon. 'That part of my life is closed. As I said, it's time to move on, to live again. And no imagining, nothing is bringing me back to that darkness again.' There was a finality, even a hint of harshness both in the words and in the closing of her face that left Tom in no doubt as to what he would carry back to Sean.

'I'm sorry.' He lowered his head, focused on the welt at the heel of his thumb. 'I shouldn't have ...'

'Please, there's no need.' Alison smiled at his bowed head. 'It's been good to talk about it. It makes me realise all the time I've wasted, makes the future more precious.'

'Well, I wish ye all the best, ye deserve it.' Tom lifted his head, met her eyes, the honesty and vulnerability in them threatening to strangle the truth from him. 'It's time myself and Daniel hit the road,' he coughed. 'Let ye get back to your work.'

'I suppose you'll want to get some of the road behind you,' she smiled, rising. 'Thanks for calling, Tom. It was really lovely to see you both again.' She gathered the tea things onto the tray and he carried them back into the house.

'Dad, Dad! There's a rabbit over the ditch!' Daniel burst into the kitchen, the dogs at his heels. 'Wow!' He ran towards the lighthouse, the rabbit forgotten.

'Easy son, take your time.'

'Wow!' He looked up in awe.

'Alison made it, with her little girl.' Tom took him in his arms, lifting him up so that he could see the light inside it. 'Maybe we might try one, what do ye think?'

'Look, Dad, look! It's Uncle Sean!' His eyes came level with the photograph on the wall.

'What?' Alison's heart lurched.

'Is that yer husband?' Tom's words tumbled out like a waterfall. 'Well God, that's a good one. He's the very image of my cousin – a Sean too! Well, what do ye know, the very image – och, it's a queer old world.' He turned away from the photograph. 'Now sir, say so long to Alison, it's time for

227

the road.' Avoiding Alison's eye, he strode towards the door, the child's head straining to take in the picture again.

'Uncle Sean has an Alison too,' Daniel piped up, but his words were drowned in Tom's sudden burst of song:

'Oh, show me the way to go home

I'm tired and I wanna go to bed...'

Alison followed them out to the car. 'Safe home,' she waved as they backed up to face the road. William waved to her from halfway up the drive and she skipped down to meet him.

'Wait till I show you the place!' She looped her arm into his. Tom watched in the rear-view mirror. The two walked slowly up the drive, her head leaning in towards his shoulder. I wonder did he arrive around the same time as the new enthusiasm, he smiled, pulling out on to the road.

* * *

Alison doubled back along the crowded quayside, searching for a parking space. 'This is pointless,' she sighed. 'What if I drop you here and head back up Barrack Hill, I'll surely find a space there. Meet you in the Moorings in about ten minutes?'

'Suits me,' William smiled, opening the door. 'I'll order you a brandy to steady the nerves!'

'Make it a double,' she laughed, as she pulled away.

The pub was jammed with people shouting conversations above the music and Alison could feel the festival atmosphere seep right into her bones as she pushed through the crowd to join William at the bar.

'There's not a hope of a seat. Will we move outside to

a table?' Holding the glasses high, he motioned with his head to the door. Alison wove her way back through the crowd and out onto the quayside. What an evening! It was just after seven and an almost midday heat was still in the sun. Everyone peacocked in their brightest colours: reds, yellows, blues and whites dotting the length of the quay. Children pleaded with mums and dads to dig deeper into never-ending pockets for rides on the carousel, the ghost train, the helter-skelter. Young girls like Hannah queued and giggled at the roller coaster, nudging and whispering as the boys passed by with their awkward glances and smiles. Along the footpaths buskers and street painters, fortune tellers and mime artists all hawked their trades.

'I could have made a tidy little sum here tonight.' William nodded towards a young man sitting on an orange crate, a little girl in plaits and summer dress on a canvas chair opposite. A small crowd stood around as he captured her smile, the dimple on her left cheek, the strand of stray hair falling across her forehead.

'Do you miss it?'

'Sometimes, yeah. I miss this atmosphere, the holiday buzz. It gets inside you, doesn't it?'

'I'm going to get another one of these inside me before I read,' Alison laughed, knocking back her drink. 'You like another?'

William looked at his watch. 'Still almost an hour to go, why not.'

He watched her walk towards the bar: her flowing white skirt skimming her ankles, the khaki linen shirt nipped in to hug her narrow waist. There was an elegance and pride in her walk, her head slightly tilted back, the sunglasses holding the flaming red curls away from her face. He could see the heads turn to look at her and felt a pride swell inside him that he was the one sitting with her. She walked back towards him, laughing at what the man in the white shirt had whispered to her at the door. Her whole body radiated a carefree confidence, a joy, flooding him with a contradiction of rapture and despair.

Alison linked her arm in his as they walked along the riverside and down towards the new plaza where the readings were scheduled to take place.

'Oh William, the brandy's not working, I'm as nervous as hell!'

'You'll be great, just take your time. Remember, good deep breaths and look straight at me. Pretend I'm the only one in the audience.'

William sat in the front row, looking up at her as she prepared to take her place in the centre of the stage. He smiled, wondering was it the breeze or her own apprehension that fluttered the pages gripped so tightly in her hand. There was still a beautiful vulnerability about her, her nervousness showing in the way she shifted her weight from one foot to the other, her near fear of the microphone. The first line was almost a whisper. Then she looked straight at William, began again and read with a strength and passion that seemed to transform her.

The applause was fantastic. William rose to his feet, his face beaming with pride as he held his hands high and clapped louder and longer than anyone else.

'You were brilliant, Alison, absolutely super!' He hugged her to him, planted a kiss on each of her flushed cheeks. 'They loved you, I told you – who wouldn't?'

'That book that I started?' Her eyes danced with excitement.

'Yeah?'

'I sent the first chapters off to three agents during the week.' She gripped his hands tightly in hers.

'That's brilliant, you finally— '

'I'll probably never hear from any— '

'Stop, right there. You've got to start taking yourself seriously, start believing in yourself or no one else will. You've taken the first step, now, just forget that they're gone and keep on writing. Leave some space for a little magic.' He folded her in his arms again, wishing for her the success and fulfilment she so truly deserved.

The readings finished, they strolled to the end of the pier. The streetlights had come on and the magic of the balmy half-light drew lovers, young and old, to the watery playground. A warm breeze swept in from the Atlantic, fingering the sail ropes of the moored yachts, drawing from them a symphony of a thousand tiny bells. Hearing in them the lonesome echo of his own death knell, William reached for her hand, his arms aching to hold her, to clasp her to him, to draw in her love and her light and banish the fear, the gathering darkness. But he couldn't, he wouldn't steal that from her. He would have to tell her tonight. Tell her he was leaving on Monday – for a week to begin with, and then for good. He squeezed her hand tightly and she moved in closer, resting her head on his shoulder.

The crowds gathered together on the pier at midnight to watch the fireworks blaze their dance over the ocean. They awed and clapped as the fireworks popped and spirited upwards, sending fountains of dazzling silvers, blues and reds showering back down to the ocean. Alison stood in front of William, her head tilted towards the sky. His strong arms stole around her waist and she leaned back into him, clasping his hands in hers. He held her tight, the delicate smell of her stirring his every sense. He closed his eyes and breathed her deep, deep inside him. Laying back into the warm comfort of him Alison felt a rush of pure contentedness and peace flooding right through her, a homecoming, and she wished she could stay in that glorious moment forever. William felt the pressure of the warm tears behind his eyes. He loved her. He loved her and wanted her with a passion and a longing he never thought he would experience again. A solitary tear escaped his closed eyelid, trembled a moment before beginning its slow meander down his cheek. The world had redeemed him, had gifted him this one final taste of how it felt to be truly and wholly alive. He held her tighter, savouring the weight of her slight frame on his chest, her heart almost melting into his. He would cling to this moment in the weeks ahead. This moment would carry him through.

The last firework danced down the sky and disappeared into nothingness, stealing the awe and the magic from the crowd. The applause ebbed away and parents shuffled children towards home. Couples, huddled closer against the night air, ambled back up the quay. William and Alison stood long and silent, neither wishing to break the spell that encircled them with words or movement. Still in the circle of his arms she turned towards him, her hands reaching for his shoulders, then stealing around his neck. Their eyes locked in silent conversation, each reading in the other's the echo of the yearning and hunger inside them. She felt herself rise up onto her toes, her lips seeking his. She closed her eyes, her teeth gently biting back her bottom lip in protest at her boldness. But it could not be held, its wet plumpness reaching, searching till it burned with the fire of his touch. Their tongues sought each other, gently, shyly at first and then with the hunger and force of a desperate wanting. He pulled her tighter to him, the firm fullness of her breast pressing to his chest, the touch of her fingers on the skin inside his collar sending an urgent, electric longing coarsing through him. His hands moved down the curve of her long back, to the slender hollow at its base, out onto her hips. She yielded under his touch, swayed and pressed herself to him, whispering her hunger to join him. Alison felt as if the fireworks had somehow seeped into her and were exploding now inside her, their magic showering those deep, forgotten places, shattering their darkness, her lifeblood rushing, swelling, in celebration.

William pulled away gently, his hands moving to cup her face. She looked up into his eyes, her full and parted lips whispering her desire. Neither spoke. He brushed a stray curl from her forehead, placed a gentle kiss on its centre. Then on her eyes, her cheeks, her lips. He held her face to his chest, a deep sigh escaping him. They turned and walked back along the pier in silence.

'No, I'll go straight on,' William replied as they neared Alison's house and she invited him in for a nightcap.

'You okay?' She looked across at him. 'You've been very quiet.'

What was usually an easy silence between them had turned into an awkward quiet on the drive home. Neither had mentioned what had happened on the pier: the magic of their lips' first meeting, the strength of the passion and longing unleashed by the silent manoeuvers of their tongues and bodies.

'Tired, that's all. The hip's playing up. I need to lie down, it's been a long evening.'

She pulled to a stop near the camper.

'It was a wonderful night, Alison. One I'll always carry with me. Thank you.'

'Yeah, it was the best,' she smiled, straining to touch him, aching for his arms to reach for her. William opened the door, silently cursing his selfishness, his weakness.

'I'll see you tomorrow?'

He turned away and swung out of the seat, unable to bear the hurt in her eyes, the confusion on her whole face.

'Maybe. I'm heading for Dublin on Monday for the week, so I'll have to pack, clean the place up a bit.'

Monday? Her heart, her voice, her head, everything shut down in an instant.

'Goodnight, Alison.' He closed the door and walked away before she could utter any of the hundred questions gathering in her tight throat.

Alison sat for a moment in the darkness. She threw her head back against the headrest, her heavy sigh filling the silence. What on God's earth had possessed her to kiss him? She loved him. Yes, she knew she loved him. As a friend. Someone to share her thoughts, her ideas; someone she could count on, who could make her laugh and feel alive and who understood and accepted the depths of her. And with one kiss she had managed to catch all that, ball it up and throw it away. What kind of fool was she? Ignoring all he had said about not wanting a relationship – he couldn't have made it plainer – and launching herself at him, driving him away!

Maybe she should go after him, explain to him that it was a friend she wanted, not a lover; explain how she had allowed the atmosphere on the quay to confuse the two. Why hadn't he mentioned before that he was going away on Monday? Because he wasn't – but now he was. Now he couldn't wait to get fast enough and far enough away from her.

But hold on a second, she reasoned, ignoring the hot impatience of the tears stinging the back of her eyes, he had kissed her too, hadn't he? Had held her so tightly her breath had almost left her body. And then that silence, his coldness. Her eyes locked and fixed straight ahead. She turned the key in the ignition and started down the track.

William stood inside the camper door and waited to hear her drive away. He would never forgive himself for that look on her face when he'd said he was leaving. It was like he had reached in and torn the very life out of her. He felt every bit the heartless bastard she must think he was. Once before he had loved someone the way he loved Alison and once before he had seen the results of that love. He wouldn't wait until Monday. He would leave tomorrow. Leave before the fire of his passion had a chance to burn through his resolve and drive him back to her. To destroy her. Hearing the chug of the jeep down the pathway he opened the door and stepped out into the starlight. His howls echoed in the thunder of the waves as he sat on the edge of the cliff, a man condemned, and waited for the dawn and the beginning of his final journey.

Alison tossed and turned in her bed, begging sleep to release her. At 4 a.m. she padded to the kitchen, stood at the window and stared out at the moon's silver runway across the sea. She switched on the lighthouse lamp for the first time in weeks. And for the first time in weeks she felt that old loneliness pressing down on her. She wished that summer was over, that Hannah was back. That William had never set foot in her life. It was senseless trying to fool herself, she sighed. She did have feelings for William. Maybe her loneliness had contributed to it, maybe the fact that he had been so instrumental in helping her make that final push to let go of the past, but, whatever the reason, her feelings of friendship had developed into something much deeper and it was pointless trying to deny it.

She sat on the window seat and, closing her eyes, savoured again the burn of his lips on hers, the thrust and hunger of his tongue. He felt it too. It was there in his eyes, his sigh, the fire in his fingers as they traced her back. But he was running from it, choosing, for his own reasons, to leave it behind. She knew she had no option but to let him go, just as he had helped her to let go of the past. She called the dogs from their sleep and led them down the hallway to her room. She lay on the bed, one dog flanking each side, her tears finally inducing sleep.

* * *

It hadn't been a big wedding. But that was what they had wanted. Well, in truth what they'd had to have, Maryanne supposed. What with the baby coming, the loan on the boat and trying to get the deposit together for the house, things were tight. She was glad to have been able to help them out with the compensation she had received from Frank's accident, feeling that if not in life then in death Frank had finally been able to give something back to his son.

Alison had looked every inch the radiant bride in her

own mother's wedding gown, and Sean tall, tanned and so, so handsome – if not a little awkward and confined – in his three-piece.

Maryanne hadn't allowed herself any tears that day. It was Sean's day, Sean and Alison's. She had instructed herself a thousand times as she battled the lump in her throat that she would have to save her own feelings for when she returned home that night; home to a house that she knew would ache with his absence for the rest of her days.

They hadn't taken a honeymoon. Alison, God help her, insisted she had all she could ever have wished for, so why on earth would she want to move away from it? Maryanne had pressed them to take a small holiday, offering to pay for it herself if money was tight. But Alison had stuck to her guns and her man. It was the height of the season, she had quoted her husband, and who knew what winter would bring?

Maryanne knew. Over the years she had watched Sean curl in on himself at the tail of every season, saw how he measured his worth on the length of his day on the water, the size of his catch.

Alison was proud. Proud and determined. She had to hand the girl that and there was no denying that she worshipped the very earth under Sean's feet. But would that be enough, Maryanne had wondered, as they turned from the altar, hand in hand, Alison fresh and fragile as a newly-bloomed lily, her long, slender body leaning slightly towards Sean, as if to shelter herself from the storm of applause that echoed back down on them from the rafters? Maryanne had kept her hands joined in prayer.

* * *

7.30 a.m. William sat at the bus stop, his eyes as heavy as his heart. The first bus, due at eight, would get him to Dublin before midday. He would book in somewhere overnight, see his solicitor in the morning and make his final arrangements from there. The village was shrouded in Sunday morning silence, the blinds and curtains in the houses opposite still closed against the light. It was a fitting time to leave, he thought, while the place was sleeping. In an hour or so they'd be up, heading for mass, walking the beach, gathered in twos and threes outside the shop, the Sunday papers under their arms. They'd talk of the week, the weather, the forecast for fishing and silage. And life would go on just as it did before he came. No one would notice he had left or wonder where he had gone. And that was life. The sea would keep turning, the swallows would teach their young to fly. And Alison … Alison would survive. She had come through a lot worse. She was strong. Strong and young and determined. And beautiful. He would miss her. And he would treasure last night for every minute that was left to him.

As if his thoughts had somehow made her materialise, William looked up just as she drove past with the two dogs and swung in onto the beach. She had seen him, he knew, but she had kept her eyes fixed straight ahead. He checked his watch, another twenty minutes before the bus was due. He tucked his rucksack under the seat, crossed the street and slipped through the passageway to the beach. The dogs were already in the water.

Alison was sitting on a rock at the base of the dunes, head bent, her hair curtaining her face.

'Alison?'

She lifted her head, tucked her hair behind her ears. Her

face was pale, her eyes, hooded and lifeless, pulled away from him.

'Alison?' He hunkered down to where she sat, ignoring the stab of pain in his hip.

'I'm leaving today, Alison. I thought it was best to—'

'Sneak away? To steal off?' She rose from her seat, her voice rising with her. 'Without even as much as goodbye?' Her eyes were alight now, their anger and pain searing through him. 'What did I mean to you, William? Was I just someone to play with? To pass a few weeks with 'til something more exciting came along?'

'Alison, I never thought of you— '

'You've made that more than clear,' she cut in, not wanting to hear his excuses. 'You never considered anyone but yourself. With all your questions, your pretence at caring – I should have seen you for what you were.'

'Alison, I do care!' He caught her arm as she turned to walk away.

'Let go of me, William Hayden.' Her voice matched the steel in her eyes. 'Go on to the next one with your free spirit, no attachment bullshit!' She took a few paces, then turned. 'You should have learned with Helene. You can't just take what you want and walk away.' She shook her head, bit down hard on her lip to stop her chin from trembling.

'I'm going to hospital, Alison.' Arms outstretched, he stepped towards her, his eyes pleading. She folded her arms around her middle, her head tilted in question.

'With my hip? I'll be back in a week to collect the van – we'll talk then?' He looked at his watch and her anger bubbled anew.

'Why? What's the point?' She threw her hands in the air. 'You're leaving anyway. You left last night, after you kissed me.' Her deep breath fuelled her anger. 'You got what you wanted and, like all selfish bastards, you're off on your way.' Unable to hold her tears any longer, she turned and ran towards the shore.

'I love you, Ali—' The wind caught his words and flung them back up over the dunes, away from her hearing.

He checked his watch. The bus would be leaving in under five minutes. He looked after her as she walked away along the water's edge, everything inside him straining to follow, to catch her, to turn her round, to fold her in his arms and promise never to leave her. And that would really make him the selfish bastard that she'd called him. He couldn't promise her anything. Except a few months of misery and then he'd be gone and never coming back. He turned and walked back up towards the street. This way was for the best; it would hurt her least in the long run. It didn't matter what he felt, what she thought of him now. It would all be over soon and he could never hurt her or anyone ever again. She turned to run back to him as he disappeared into the passageway.

Alison unleashed the dogs from the boot and rounded the house. The sky had greyed over and rain gathered behind the mountains. She jumped with fright when the figure crouched at the back door hopped to his feet.

'Jesus, Joe! What are you at?'

'Is Se…Seany back yet?' Recognising the fire in Alison's eyes, he took a few steps backwards.

'Sean is dead! Dead! Dead! Dead!' Alison emphasised every word at the top of her voice. 'He's dead, Joe! Gone! Can't you get that into your thick head?' she shouted, advancing at him like a madwoman.

'He's not!' His defiance fuelled her anger.

'He's gone, Joe. That's what they do! They make you love them and then they leave.' Her voice softening, she turned to open the door. 'Just go home, Joe. Just go home and leave me alone.'

Head bent, he stood his ground, his foot rolling the gravel under his boot.

'NOW, Joe! Get out of here NOW or I'll call the guards. GO ON! And don't ever ask about him again!' She slammed the door behind her.

Joe hopped the ditch into the neighbouring field and sheltered in under the bushes as the first drops of rain began to fall. 'I'll wait for ya, Seany,' he muttered, pulling the black anorak tight around him.

Thirteen

High on the cliff top above Killybegs harbour Sean Delaney sat chewing over the news that Tom had brought back to him: the warmth of Alison's welcome, how happy she appeared, the new life she had given the place and the new life she had created for herself. She was still at that writing she had always been so bent on. Sean had never seen the point of it himself, had laughed out loud that time when she had tried to explain to him that she fished for words deep inside herself in the same way that he trawled the sea for his catch. She had packed it away after that. Well, away from him anyway. Always willing to please, he smiled, that was Alison. Always bending and shifting to suit him 'til in the end there was hardly a bit of the girl he had fallen in love with left.

The child was still in London, happy, it seemed, and Alison spent part of every day down at the home with Maryanne, according to Tom. His mother had always had a soft spot for Alison, constantly reminding him of how lucky he was to have such a loving and supportive wife. And there was always that something in the way she would say it, almost like a warning, as if she was fishing, knew more than she was letting on.

Maryanne hadn't spoken since the accident, Alison had told Tom. His mother, who was never short on advice or opinion – Sean couldn't credit that she could hold her counsel for so long. But then some things aren't easy to speak out. There are some things in life that there are no words for, no matter how deep or how long you trawl. Sean knew that, knew it better than anyone. Still, he felt, if he could only get to Maryanne, explain things to her, they could work it out. She could always see his side, always.

His brow creased, a darkness crowding his eyes as his thoughts turned again to Alison's reply when Tom had asked how she would feel if Sean were back in her life. There was absolutely no question, Tom had said, but she wouldn't want him. He lay back in the long grass and pulled deeply on his cigarette. Tom had described how she had searched and waited, desperately clinging to the hope that, dead or alive, he would be returned to her. He could see how someone like Tom might think there was no going back, no mending that. But Tom didn't know the old Alison. He didn't understand how she'd given up everything for him, had made him her whole world. All those years together had to count for something. It was all right saying that she wouldn't have him back, but Tom didn't think it out. She believed he was dead and what she had said to Tom wasn't how she would *really* feel. Not if there was a chance he was still alive. No, he knew Alison. He knew what he meant to her. Tom had never known that kind of love. How could he understand?

He sat up again and looked down into the harbour. Tom was in his boat below, mending nets, the child sitting on the stern beside him. He watched as Tom reached out a hand and ruffled the child's hair. His mouth tightened. What would Tom know about loss or wanting, things that had never touched his world? Himself and that boy were never out of each other's shadow, Ella always back at the house. What gave him the right to talk about moving on and letting go? Forgetting. Move him away from his family and he'd soon see there was no forgetting! Tom was a good man, to be fair to him, but simple with it and he hadn't the first clue what he was talking about. He had told Sean that, as far as he could tell, there was no new man in Alison's life. Jesus, wasn't that proof enough for him? Sean had always been the only one for her and she was still waiting for him. She wasn't lost yet. Much as Tom had tried to drive home to him that he should forget and move on, Sean knew better. He wouldn't be moving just yet. At least not in the direction Tom thought.

* * *

'Can I ring her, Dad? Tell her where I left it.'

'Och, Daniel, the dogs'll have it well broken up by now. Can't ye bring her another, the next time we call? I might find a big scallop shell for ye in the pots some mornin', bet she'd like that.' The child had him tormented about the shell for Alison that he had left in the plastic bag in the field. You'd swear it was gold, Tom laughed to himself, taking in the child's solemn face.

Sean had been up and off early again this morning. That had been his pattern since Tom had come back with the news from Carniskey. It had really knifed him hearing what

244

Alison had said, and the way Sean had taken to avoiding him since, Tom felt as if he almost blamed him for not bringing back the response he wanted.

Though he had only met her twice, Tom had a great fondness for Alison. She was a sweet wee thing, and honest, and God knows she had been through more than her share of sorrow. He could see how shaky her happiness was and so he had laced her words with more anger and bitterness in the retelling – his own anger, he knew. He couldn't get out of his head the torment the girl had come through and now Sean wanted to go back and turn all that heartache into nothing, into a joke! No one, not even the strongest could cope with that. It would be the finish of her. Whether Sean liked it or not, he had involved Tom in the whole mess and he would do all in his power to make sure that Sean never looked on her face again. And he would never feel guilty about embellishing Alison's words: she had done her suffering and now Sean had to carry his.

He had spared Sean the bit about the man who'd arrived just as they left. Hadn't told him how she half-ran to meet him, linked his arm, allowed her head to lean towards his shoulder. The man had enough to carry, there was no point in twisting the knife.

Sean had packed in the job with Matt Holland and would be leaving by the end of the week, he'd promised. Where he would end up God only knew, but the whole fiasco was of his own making and every man, Tom believed, had to learn to live with the consequences of his own actions, no matter what the cost. Though he wished him well, he wouldn't be sad to see Sean go. It would be good to have the place back to themselves again, would give Ella and himself a chance to sort out the distance that all this business had carved between them. There was no future here for Sean and the sooner he left, Tom reasoned, the sooner he could put this whole episode out of his head and get on with the business of living.

* * *

Alison cried through the whole of Sunday. She didn't eat. When darkness fell, she pulled the curtains and went to bed, where she tossed and turned until morning. Monday and Tuesday passed in slow motion: solitary beach walks in the drizzling rain; afternoon visits to Maryanne that she could barely endure; long telephone conversations in the evening with Hannah and Kathleen. She told neither what troubled her. Wednesday night found her in her favourite chair in the sitting room, music playing, a bottle of wine by her side.

When does anything change, she sighed. She'd been in this spot before summer began. Almost mid-July now and here she was again: same music, same wine, same goddamn tears. Had the pain of losing Sean not taught her anything?

She had never expected to fall for William, had never even considered that things might go that way. He was a friend, someone she understood and who understood her. They shared similar interests, ideas, were both outsiders in a way, who empathised with one another's loss. But there was never any question of romance. Never. Then all of a sudden, without warning or sign, it had just consumed her. And now he was gone and she was right back to where she had been before she had met him.

Nonsense! She sat up defiantly in her chair. She was no

longer mourning Sean, no longer waking each day with a dread of filling it. She had brought the house back to life, had given Hannah the holiday and space she was crying out for. Not only had she paid off the bulk of her bills but she still had some savings left over, and to top all that she had written over thirty thousand words of a novel. But above all else her time with William had proved something she thought impossible: she was capable of loving again.

She sat back, smiling. William would laugh if he could see her now, pep talking herself like some kind of half lunatic. They'd had some good times together, times she would treasure. His company and support had helped her through that really tough time when Hannah had first gone, had inspired her to look inside herself for fulfilment. Now he had decided it was time to move on, and why shouldn't he? He had never promised her anything; in fact, he had made it clear from day one that he wouldn't be around forever. So what reason had she to be angry with him? She wanted more, he didn't. It was as simple as that. William had moved on, and now so would she.

Back in the kitchen she flicked on the computer. She sat and typed 'til tiredness defeated her and she tumbled into bed exhausted, satisfied with her night's work.

* * *

William despised the white nothingness of the ward, its hushed stillness and sterility fevering his longing for Alison and the wildness of Carniskey. He closed his eyes and called up the greens, blues and greys of the sea; the golden browns and fiery reds of the mountains as the rising sun roused them from sleep. The heathers, the sea pinks and whitethorn had begun to die away before he left but wreaths of horse daisies and the red tears of fuscia had softened their passing. He chased the roar of the ocean, the dance of the shingle that had lulled him to sleep in the camper. And Alison. Everywhere Alison. In her rolled-up jeans paddling the foam; on her knees among the heather in the mountains; in her shorts digging the rockery; her smile stealing the light from the moon that night they had swum together; the way she stood on the podium reading, her nervous bow, that girlish smile. And her kiss…

'I'm taking a walk,' he muttered, passing the nurses' station for the third time that morning.

'But Mr Hayden…'

William didn't turn from the lift, just held up his hand, his frustration finding expression in the sharp clench and release of his raised palm.

'Leave him, Kathy,' the older nurse advised, 'give him some time.'

The hospital foyer was bright and welcoming, masking the misery in the wards upstairs. Stuffed toys, chocolates, 'Get Well' balloons – the place was like a shopping centre. Even in these places commercialism thrives: William spat out the thought as he pushed his way through the smokers at the door and sat on a bench in the sunshine. He wondered if the sun was shining in Carniskey too, as he settled the drip-trolley beside him. He had seen Fogarty twice since Monday and he had recommended this stuff to build him up. For what, William had asked, a healthier, heartier death? They would do a scan this afternoon, see what new territory had been claimed, get a better idea of what time was left to him. William prayed it would be short. He felt like a caged lion. He knew the nurses were only doing their job – and a good one, too – but Jesus, the way they soft-stepped around him! Their smiles of pity, the way they called him 'love' and 'dear' – some even speaking loud and slow, as if he were either deaf or foreign, or both. He felt the mobile phone in his pocket and his fingers ached to press her number. Just to hear her. To tell her how he missed her. To tell her why he had to hurt her.

* * *

Rob crunched the car to a halt on the gravel outside the black iron gates. 'I can see you back then, all right,' he smiled. 'Fat little face squashed between those bars.'

'Oh no,' Kathleen turned to him, 'we didn't bother with gates. See that old stone wall over there' – she pointed towards the rear of the property – 'whoever built that factored in our sort. Perfect little footholds between the stones, and not too high to throw the apples back over.' Her smile was wistful, remembering those long ago September days: the crunch of dry leaves under their feet as they jumped silently from the wall, stifling their giggles so as not to alert old Mr Warner. She could almost taste the soft sweetness of the windfalls, feel the sticky dribble of juice down her chin.

'Such a pity,' she sighed, squinting through the gates at the gnarled rhododendron and hydrangea bushes battling to smother the gravel path. Two of the upper floor windows were completely obscured by creeper and the glass in the fan light over the front door had been smashed. Broken roof tiles littered the ground.

'I know my memory is probably coloured by nostalgia,

but you should have seen the place back then, Rob – the soft green lawns and the rose gardens, the sun always seemed to be shining up here.'

'How long has it been empty?'

'Oh, years. Ten, maybe more. Old Warner left it to a nephew in England. He came occasionally in the summer the first few years but he was an odd old sort. It had started to fall apart even before he put it up for sale.' She laughed then, remembering. 'When I think of how often I used to come this way after school. I'd look in the windows, imagine what I would do with each of the rooms.'

'Fancied yourself as a bit of a Lady of the Manor, then?'

'Oh, shut up, Rob!' She elbowed him in the side. 'It was a silly childish dream, don't tell me you never had any.'

'No, I was never the dreaming kind.' He leaned across and opened the glove compartment. 'Well, not until I met you, at least.' He handed her the red envelope.

'What's this?'

'Only one way to find out.'

Her thumb stole under the seal, lifting it, and a big silver plastic key hanging from a red ribbon fell into her lap.

'A plastic key?' Brow furrowed, she held it up by the ribbon between them.

'It was the biggest one they had in the card shop. They don't seem to go in for the whole twenty-first thing any more, not like they used to.'

'Huh?'

'They can't hand over the keys until Monday, but I just couldn't wait…'

'Keys? What are you on about, Rob, what keys?'

He motioned with his head towards the house and her brow knotted even deeper.

'Maybe your dream wasn't so silly after all.' His smile widened into a full grin.

'What, you mean…no, you can't.' Her head moved slowly from side to side, her eyes almost popping from their beds.

'Yep. I know there's lots to be done, but I got it for a song and I can do most of the work myself. Just think…'

Her squeal filled the car as she threw herself towards him and smothered his words with her kiss.

* * *

Hannah's email arrived the following Tuesday and Alison couldn't believe what she was reading:

London's great, Mum, but I don't know how anyone actually lives here. The heat is awful and everywhere's crowded ALL the time, everyone rushing round like they're running from a fire or something! The first thing I'll do when I get home is get into my wetsuit and catch some waves. I miss surfing so much and Aoife and the girls – even Grainne! I can't wait to lie in my own bed and listen to the wind and rain. I can't wait to see you again, Mum…

Alison printed off the email and put it in the folder, along with the others Hannah had sent. She would show them all to her one day in years to come, show her all the growing up she had done in one short summer. She hugged the folder to her, a huge smile creasing her face. Her little girl was coming home *and* she was looking forward to it!

She turned and looked out the window. It was just after

nine and already the sky was darkening. Her eyes strayed in the direction of Tra na Leon. She had arranged to go and look around the old Warner place with Kathleen tonight but had changed her mind at the last moment, something telling her that William might be home, that she'd get a chance to talk to him, to explain her reaction to his leaving. To apologise for her anger. But when she had walked along the cliff an hour ago the camper was still locked and empty. Maybe he would come tomorrow.

She had passed the weekend watching the camper like a child waiting for Christmas. She didn't go into town, never strayed from the house for more than an hour for fear she would miss him, afraid that the next time she went up to Tra na Leon the camper would be gone and she'd never see him again. By ten o'clock on Monday night she'd begun to give up hope. What if he didn't come back? Surely there was stuff in the camper that he needed. He wouldn't just leave it there, would he? Now Tuesday had come and gone and there was still no sign of him. He had definitely said he was only going for a week. She paced the kitchen, no longer able to ignore her growing restlessness. Dropping the folder back on the desk, she picked up her mobile and tried his number for the fourth time that day. It was still switched off.

She bit down on her lip. *Something* was wrong, she had sensed it all evening. Seized by a feeling of urgency she switched on her computer. She made a list of all the Dublin hospitals and began ringing round them in alphabetical order. Her search was short and in less than half an hour she had located him in Beaumont.

The following morning, after a hurried arrangement with Kathleen to care for the dogs and a garbled excuse about a sick aunt in Dublin, she was on the road, without a thought of where she might stay, what she would say to him. She only knew that she needed to see him. And that was enough. She'd had her fill of sudden partings, with no goodbyes, no discussions. Days and nights and years of wondering, wishing. She was damned if she was going to let that happen again. She drove on over the bridge, out onto the main Dublin road and whatever awaited her at the end of it.

Alison walked the length of the narrow ward, searching each bed in turn for his face. Some of the patients were sleeping, others lay staring ahead of them into nothingness. Only two caught her eye and she smiled apologetically. She felt like a voyeur, like she was invading their most intimate space. She tried to move without making her presence heard or seen, tried not to encroach with her eyes or body movements. But the momentary eye contact she had made with those two patients told more of their story, of William's story, than a thousand questions could answer. The emaciated frames, the hollowed cheeks, the prominent eyes filled with a kind of innocence and trepidation. Alison was taken back to a similar, smaller ward in another Dublin hospital, to that familiar stare of child-like fear and questioning on her mother's dying face. Her throat tightened. She swallowed hard, closing her ears and her mind and her heart to the unbearable truth screaming inside her.

She stepped quietly to the bed by the window at the far end of the ward. William lay sleeping in a T-shirt and shorts, his hands clasped across his chest. His face looked grey and long, the closed eyes sunken. Her heart swelled, gathering every drop of blood in her body to itself. Her head swam, her legs threatening to buckle as she lowered herself onto the plastic chair by the window. Her hand stole to her lips as if to prevent the anguish that howled inside her escaping them. Her eyes moved to the bedside locker, bare except for a jug of water, a glass, and a grey and white stone from the beach. No books, no magazines, no get-well cards. Fighting the swelling in her throat, she looked away towards the car park below the window. Through her misted eyes a sea of cars glinted in the evening sun. A constant dribble of visitors and staff criss-crossed the narrow walkway to the hospital entrance, their path lit by a blaze of colour from the flowers and shrubs that lined each side. Just one wall separating two wholly different worlds, Alison sighed, her eyes returning to the white hush of the sleeping ward.

Later, when the patient opposite protested loudly to the nurse's ministrations, William's eyes fluttered open, momentarily fixing on Alison before closing again. She didn't speak but moved closer and covered his hands with hers. His eyes remained closed as he lifted his fingers and laced them between hers.

'William?' She smiled her whisper and his eyes opened slowly. Afraid. Afraid to lose the dream. He gently turned his head to the side to face her, his cheeks lifting in a slow, incredulous smile.

'Alison? I thought I was dreaming…'

The disbelief and delight in his slow, low whisper tempted her tears but she held on to her smile, defying them. She squeezed his hands, not daring to speak.

'How long have you been there – why didn't you wake me?'

'Not long. I didn't want to disturb you, you looked so

peaceful. Plus, you're easier company when you're sleeping,' she added, a forced jollity in her low laugh. 'How are you feeling?'

'A million dollars for seeing you,' he smiled, his eyes holding hers as he moved to sit up.

'No, don't move.' She shifted from her chair and sat on the bed beside him. 'So, this is where you've been hanging out?'

'You can't imagine how good it feels to see you.' His eyes drank in her face, her hair, the loose green shirt, the tiny freckles on the exposed V of her chest. When she bent and kissed his cheek, the subtle smell of honeysuckle, the tickle of her tumbling curls on his skin sent a surge of hot life burning through him. He reached out a hand to stroke her cheek, his eyes looking in through hers. 'Let's get out of here for a bit.' He eased himself into a sitting position.

They sat on a wooden bench to the right of the hospital door. Other patients in nightgowns and slippers were gathered round on benches and wheelchairs. Some chatted and laughed with visitors, others sat deep in thought, their faces held to the sun. The breeze played with Alison's hair and she tied it in a loose knot behind her neck. She took a deep breath before turning to face him.

'How long have you known?' She lifted her sunglasses and looked into his eyes.

'Six months or so.'

She nodded, slowly. 'And the prognosis?' Her questions were straight, matter of fact.

'Two months, maybe less.'

A hard slap stung her heart.

'And there's nothing…'

255

'No.' He knew what her questions would be. The same ones he had had the first time round. 'It's over this time. I've been very lucky. Last time I beat it – won myself six years. This time it has the winning hand.'

They sat a moment in silence, Alison digesting the full and final impact of his words. Her mind raced, searching back for the clues she had missed. That time he was sick, of course she should have seen that it was a whole lot more than a chest infection, would have seen if she hadn't been so wrapped up in her own stuff. That day when he'd held her in the kitchen – the desperation in his sigh, in his kiss that night on the pier.

'You okay?' William broke in on her thoughts. 'I'm sorry, I didn't mean to land any of this on you,' he sighed. 'But you understand now why I had to leave the way I did.' At least now she would know that he hadn't just abandoned her, hadn't just taken what he wanted and walked away as she had believed. He remembered her anger on the beach that last morning they parted, her hurt and confusion. But time would have taken care of that, would have allowed her, one day, to look back in fondness at their time together. Whereas this, he could see in the white-knuckled clench of her fingers, in the pain piercing her eyes, in her silence, this was wounding her in a far deeper place. 'You should have just left it, Alison, you shouldn't have come.'

'I couldn't just leave it.' She raised her eyes, tilted her head back slightly to hold the tears that threatened. 'Not the way we parted. There were things I needed to say to you, to explain.'

'You can't imagine the number of times I almost called you, to ask you to come. But I didn't want you to see or know this. I wanted you to think of me out there somewhere, to remember me as the person you shared those great times with, not wasting away in some hospital bed.'

'And I wanted you to remember me laughing,' Alison smiled, her tongue catching the tear that had escaped down her cheek. 'The way you had taught me to laugh again. Laughing and alive, not that person you met when you first arrived. That last day on the beach – it was like I'd turned back into her. I wanted you to know that I hadn't.'

He eased his arm around her shoulder and drew her to him. 'I've replayed that morning a million times. I never meant to hurt you, I wanted to ...' He leaned her head into his chest, stroked her hair. 'You'll never know how much that night at the festival meant to me. Your kiss...'

'I thought it had driven you away.'

'What drove me away was how much I wanted you. Oh, Alison.' He sighed, kissing the top of her head. 'I honestly thought that by leaving I could protect you.'

'Don't talk any more, William, just hold me.' She lay back in the crook of his arms, the sun warming her face, his closeness warming the very core of her.

The clatter of the tea trolleys scattered the visitors towards home. 'I'll go,' Alison whispered, seeing the tiredness in his face. They were back in the ward and he lay on the bed, Alison beside him on the chair. 'I'll call again in the morning, sleep well.' She kissed his lips and, head bent, walked back down the ward. Reaching the door, she turned to look back at him. He lay turned towards the window, the setting sun stretching its fingers up the bed. She couldn't see the tears pool in his eyes, slowly trickle to the pillow.

Alison half-ran to the jeep and, safely inside, she unleashed the hot tears that had bulged and burned in her throat all evening, her whole body shaking with their release. She must have sat there for over an hour, her mind wandering frantically back and forth: back to her mother in her last weeks of life, to the guilt she had felt as she prayed to God or whoever or whatever was out there to take her, to release her and end her misery. Back to her lamplight searches for Sean, willing the beam of the torch to touch him and at the same time dreading what she might find. And back to the pier and how even the magic of the fireworks had been dimmed by William's kiss.

Fourteen

Alison sat in the hotel car park above Dun Laoghaire pier. It was almost 11 p.m. Not much hope of finding a bed anywhere at this hour, she thought, locking the jeep and walking towards the water. The air hummed with the chat and laughter of the crowds gathered around tables outside the hotels and bars. Hard to believe that less than two weeks ago William and herself had been just like them – carefree and happy, relaxed in the buzz and seduction of midsummer. How had he hidden it so well? She turned off the main street towards the harbour. A wolf whistle followed her from three men at the corner. Ignoring their beer-fuelled courage, Alison carried on, head bent, towards the pier.

She climbed over the storm wall and down onto the rocks. The incoming tide whispered its welcome, its hypnotic pull and fall drawing her like a magnet. She unknotted the cardigan from her waist and, pulling it tight over her shoulders, huddled down into the darkness.

She wondered if he were sleeping now, pictured him alone in his bed under the window. He had looked so out of place, so totally alone when she'd looked back down the ward as she was leaving. He didn't belong there. The image of him swimming naked in the cove at Tra na Leon returned to her. He had seemed such a natural part of the place, the water and the sun caressing him, making him their own. There had been an energy about him that morning, an air of celebration, a total abandonment to life that had triggered something forgotten in her.

She lit a cigarette and, inhaling deeply, tried to concentrate on the hiss and lick of the tide in an effort to calm and untangle the questions that circled endlessly in her head. Would it have been better for both of them if she had left things as they were, accepted their parting and not gone in search of him? Could she cope with another death, with reliving her mother's last weeks, Sean's disappearance? Had she the strength, the courage to stay? To walk away? Would she have come if she'd known what she was going to find? Honestly?

The following morning, after a quick wash in the hotel foyer bathroom, Alison sat down to a light breakfast in the dining room. Despite just a few hours' sleep reclined on the passenger seat of the jeep, she felt strangely energised. She secured a room at the hotel for the next two nights and took a brisk walk along the pier before driving straight on to the hospital.

William was sleeping. Alison moved to the window as the sound of an aeroplane taking off from nearby Dublin Airport shattered the silence. She tried to imagine what it must be like for William, lying here day in day out, watching those planes, filled with expectant holidaymakers, crossing his patch of blue. Did he wonder about the journey that he was embarking on: where he was going, what, if anything, awaited him? A shiver of cold fear rippled right through her at the thought of entering the absolute unknown. Alone. With no map, no language, nothing to …

'Good morning, dear. William? William, you have a visitor.' The nurse's chirpy call broke into Alison's thoughts and she turned from the window as William stirred, his eyes and his smile fixing on her.

'Look at that day,' she smiled, moving to his side. 'Do you think you could come out for a couple of hours?' Her eyes entreated the nurse, who was still hovering.

'What are the chances, Mary?' William winked at the nurse and she caught a glint in his eye that hadn't been there before.

'I don't know, William. Are you seeing Mr Fogarty this morning?'

'Don't think so.'

'I don't see any reason … I'll just have to check with his team. Leave it with me a moment.' She returned William's wink and soft-stepped back to the nurses' station.

'What do you fancy doing, if you can come?' Alison sat on the bed beside him.

'Okay, William, three hours max,' the nurse smiled, checking the watch at her breast. 'It's almost twelve now, so we'll expect you back by three.' She disconnected the drip and secured the cannula in his arm with a plaster. 'Lunch before you go?'

'No, thank you, Mary. I'm sure she'll feed me.'

'I'll leave you to get dressed.' Alison moved away from the bed as the nurse drew round the curtain. 'I'll just pop downstairs for a moment, I want to make a phone call.'

Alison stepped out of the lift and crossed the foyer to the main door, searching her mobile from her bag.

'Hi, Kathleen?'

'Alison, how's it goin'?'

'Good, are the dogs all right?'

'I had them out for a run this morning and I'll tell you, a bit more of that and I'll be fitting into that dress in no time! How's your aunt?'

'Good, thanks. Listen, Kathleen, I'm going to be another day or two, do you mind watching them for me?'

'No problem.' Alison's voice seemed heavy, forced. 'Is everything all right?' Kathleen asked, concerned.

'Yeah, yeah, I just want to spend a little more time. Will you tell Maryanne I'll be back by the weekend? Thanks, Kathleen, I'll talk to you tomorrow.'

And just like that she was gone. Kathleen tossed the phone in her hand. Typical Alison, she sighed, rushing up there at the first call. Didn't she have enough on her plate already with Maryanne? Surely there must be some other relative closer who could be called on. The only aunt Kathleen ever remembered Alison mentioning was that half-cracked spinster in Terenure – and she hadn't been running down here when Alison was in trouble.

She had been so disappointed when Alison had cancelled their plans to go and look around the house on Tuesday evening. Work, she'd said, but surely she could have taken a break for an hour? While Alison did congratulate her on the house and seemed genuinely pleased for her, Kathleen remembered having felt at the time that Alison showed no great excitement about it, no real interest. And why should she, she asked herself now, filling another pint glass with hot water and a slice of lemon. She couldn't expect others, not even her best friend, to be as over the moon as she was. This was her stuff, her life, the whole rest of the world wasn't bursting with celebration just because she was. And she had to start being mindful of that. Her world had changed, had been transformed, but Alison's hadn't and maybe she was shoving that fact in Alison's face by constantly talking of the wedding and the honeymoon and the house. But it was hard not to, there was so much going on inside her and it just kept bursting out, she couldn't contain it! And she didn't want to. This was once-in-a-lifetime stuff and these would be the memories she would look back on in years to come. But she would be more mindful, she promised, of Alison and of her world.

Alison was missing that guy William more than she was letting on; Kathleen knew by the way she always changed the subject – quite snappily at times – whenever Kathleen brought up his name. Right from the start she had copped that Alison fancied him but just wasn't giving in to it – just as well, Kathleen supposed now, the way he'd just upped and left like that. Maybe the break away from the place would do her good, could be exactly what she needed. She tipped back her head, emptied the glass and stood it on the sink. Only six more to go to reach the day's quota.

* * *

Approaching Killiney, William rolled down the window and took a deep breath through his nose. 'Now, that's what I call medicine,' he smiled, the salt air filling his lungs. Parking close to the beach, Alison busied herself taking a fold-up chair from the boot while he eased himself slowly from his seat. Already the crowds were about, the afternoon sun peacocking in a cloudless sky. They found a quiet spot over to the right of the walkway. Alison kicked off her shoes and unfolded the chair for William. She bent down and slipped off his sandals, the hot sand hugging his feet.

'Fancy a paddle?' They ambled to the water's edge and stood a while in silence, the sea licking their feet and ankles.

'I thought I'd never see you again.' Her hand stole into his as they walked slowly along the shoreline, the sun warm on their backs. 'When you hadn't come back at the weekend, it was like Sean all over again – the angry parting, the not knowing.'

'I'm sorry.' He gripped her hand tightly. 'I never meant to put you through that. I should have been honest with you, but I thought I was protecting you,' he sighed. 'And if I'm honest, I suppose I was protecting myself too. From seeing the pain in your eyes, knowing I caused it.' His arm encircled her waist and he drew her close. 'Months ago, I thought I had this all figured out. Thought I was ready for it, you know, resigned to it. But this last while with you has given me a new love for life, for this world. And I don't want to go, Alison.' His voice had dropped to a whisper. 'I was running from that as well.'

Three little girls in bright bathing suits ran giggling past them into the water. They both watched them a moment, smiling.

'What happens next?' Alison ventured as they turned to walk back up the beach. 'Is there more treatment?'

'Palliative care,' William sighed with a mock grin. 'Whatever that means! They'll move me to the hospice in Raheny in the next day or two, as soon as a bed comes up.'

'What's it like, the hospice?' She sat on the hot sand at his feet.

'I haven't a clue. Quiet and peaceful, I suppose. A prelude

of what's to come. They're specially trained to make you comfortable, to help you die – as if anyone could …' His voice trailed away with his gaze, off up over the cliff tops.

'Are you frightened?' She looked up, waited for his eyes to meet hers.

'I feel …' He swallowed back, looked again towards the children playing at the water's edge. 'I feel like a child, without a mother's hand to hold, crossing the street.' His smile was stitched with pain. 'If that makes any sense.' Alison could almost feel her heart physically tearing. Unable to bear the lonely resignation in his eyes, she bent her head slowly to the sand.

'One more favour?' William asked as they drove out of the village.

'Sure.'

'Could we take a little detour? I'd love to take a spin by my old home, see how it looks.'

'Just show me the way.' To hell with the hospital's three-hour deadline, she thought, she'd make some excuse about traffic or losing her way. She knew all too well the impor-tance of saying goodbye.

'Turn left at the top of this street, then straight on through the lights.' William shifted in his seat and stretched out his leg to ease the fire in his hip. 'Just down the end of this street, then right.' They had been driving for about twenty minutes when they turned into the narrow, tree-lined street. 'That's it!' He pointed to a small terraced house on the right. 'The cream one. Can you pull over for a minute?'

The garden of the neat two-storey house was newly mown, a row of red rose bushes lining each side of the narrow pathway to the blue front door. A little girl sat on a tartan blanket under the window, her dolls and tea set spread out before her. She looked up from the doll on her lap and lowered the tiny teacup from her mouth. Tight blonde curls framed her face. William rolled down the window and smiled at her. She returned a slow, shy smile before turning her attention back to her charges.

'Has it changed much?'

'The door and the windows are new.' He stared at the house, as if looking in through it. 'The roses, they were my mother's. Her pride and joy. I can see her now, pruning and weeding.'

'What was she like?' Alison prompted.

'Quiet. I remember her always as being quiet, thoughtful. And fiercely independent. She ran a dressmaker's from the front room there.' He pointed to the window where the child sat. 'When I'd come home from school, I'd always find her in there surrounded by materials for wedding dresses, jackets, trousers for alterations. She'd work away into the night. That little room was her whole world.'

'Did she like it?'

'I don't think it was a case of liking it or not. It was what got us by. We never went without, she made sure of that. And she never asked anyone for help, always drumming into me the importance of being able to get by on your own.' He smiled. 'I can hear her now: *Love many, trust few, always paddle your own canoe.* That was her mantra.'

'And your father?'

'He was a medical student, American. He went home for a holiday shortly after she became pregnant and he never came back. That's all she ever told me about him.'

'And she never met anyone else?'

'No one was going to hurt her again.' He shook his head slowly. 'She never really got involved in anything outside of the house. Except for those roses, she minded them like they were children.'

'It must have been lonely for her after you left?' Alison realised how little she knew of him.

'She pushed me, you know, to grow up, to live on my own. To leave and not feel the pull to come running back.'

'She obviously loved you very much,' Alison sighed, knowing how hard it had been to let Hannah go just for the few months of summer.

'Yeah, I'm only understanding that now.' He wound up the window. 'Suppose we'd better head back.' He looked ahead as if to turn and look at the place once more would break him.

Back on the ward William silenced the nurse's recriminations by placing a swift kiss on each of her cheeks and telling her that that was the perfect end to a perfect day.

'Well, you'll have to speak to staff nurse in the morning.' Her young face burned with embarrassment.

'Leave her to me,' William smiled, sinking back onto the bed.

Alison placed the menu back on the table. She had neither the appetite for food nor for the raucous laughter from the table to her left. She slipped from the dining room and called the lift. She needed space, quiet. Back in her room she showered, changed into a T-shirt and shorts, and ordered a salad and a bottle of wine from reception.

Glass in hand, she sat out on her room balcony. She could see the pier below and the Sea Cat making its way out into the darkening night. She lit a cigarette, put her feet up on the chair opposite.

William had been exhausted by the time they got back

to the hospital and she had watched the light and life drain from him as he lay down on his bed. She tried to picture him as a boy in that little house in Drimnagh, growing up alone with a mother who did her best to rear him so that he would never experience the kind of hurt that had been hers. It hadn't worked. Funny, the similarity she could see between this woman she had never known of until today and the person she herself had been when William first met her. Was it just a coincidence that William had come into her life at the start of summer? Perhaps. But inside she felt there was something much bigger at play.

She sipped her wine, her mind wandering back over their time together. It was hard to believe he had only been in her life such a short time. With his gentle persistence, William had helped her give voice to the thoughts and feelings that had screamed silently inside her for years. He had encouraged her to examine them and to let them go. She had let Sean go. Along with the guilt, and all the questions that she had finally accepted had no answers. And to fill their place she had released the passion buried behind them. Being with William had helped her to recognise all the strength and energy she had wasted on the past, on nursing her hurt and battling things she could never change. It wasn't anything in particular that he had said or done. It was just something, everything about him.

She pictured him again in his hospital bed, the loneliness in his eyes when he spoke of the hospice where he would wait for death. A shiver raced down her spine. How could she leave him tomorrow? Even the next day? How could she return to a world that he had brought back to life for her while he lay dying among strangers?

Her first instinct had been right. The moment she stepped

onto that ward yesterday she knew immediately what lay ahead and though she didn't honestly believe she had the strength to endure it, she knew even then what she would do. With the memory of her mother's dying so fresh again in her mind, she had been afraid, terrified, and had buried the whole question until she was alone on the pier last night. Hours she had sat, trying to think it out, but it was all too much, too raw, too immediate. She needed time. Time to think it through honestly, coldly. To let it sit. But in that one crystal moment, outside William's old house, she knew for certain that her gut, as usual, had been right. *'Without a mother's hand to hold…'* Alison felt as if William's mother had spoken to her then, had given her the permission and the strength to go with what the deepest part of her had already decided.

Above all, William had taught her to love again. She could love and let go – and this time, she believed, without losing herself in the parting. She opened the patio doors and stepped back into the warmth of her room. Tomorrow could not come quick enough. Tomorrow she would ask him to return with her to Carniskey.

* * *

It was only when you gave yourself time to look back on these things, Maryanne thought, only when you were separated from them by the grace of years, that you could start to make sense of it all.

She would never forget Alison's face that morning when she'd arrived at the door, shivering in that thin coat, the hair wild around her head and that poor bit of a child clinging to her hand, shaking, the priest, white-faced, behind them.

'He's gone,' she'd whispered through her sobs as Mary-anne steered them towards the kitchen, grabbed some warm towels from over the range.

'Hush now, girl, come on, warm yourself,' she'd soothed. 'Give me that child.' She had released the child from Alison's death grip, folded her in her lap, her blood fired with temper, but not with surprise. No, Maryanne had seen this coming a long time and she knew the madam that was behind it too. Nothing went unnoticed in these small places.

'I begged him not to go ...'

'Easy, Alison, easy pet.' The girl was hysterical, her tears putting the fear of God into the shivering child.

'He could see the weather, he knew that boat ...'

'Boat?' Maryanne's heart had stopped.

It was then that the neighbours began to arrive, with their heads bowed, their sidelong glances of sympathy; their hurried whispers about rescue teams, forecasts, searches that had come good after days. It wasn't too late yet, one echoed the other, frantically stamping down the truth that shone from their eyes.

Someone had called the doctor. Maryanne brushed aside his concerns for her, instead leading him, straight-backed, to the bedroom where Alison was settling Hannah, away from the roars of Joe O'Sullivan in the kitchen, away from his stuttering insistence that he had seen Sean crossing the fields at Mount Airy in the darkness.

She had put it down to shock in the first few days, that numb, calm feeling, that quietness inside her. Had put it down to knowing that it would spell the end for her if she gave the reality of his being gone even one moment's acknowledgement.

Days turned into weeks, and still no body. By day, Maryanne busied herself with the child, poor mite, her mother now all but lost to her too. Nights she lay in her bed, searching within herself for the first hint of a mother's knowing, a mother's grief. She found neither.

Months crawled by and Maryanne watched on from somewhere outside herself. Watched her heart harden towards Alison, envying, almost despising the raw grief that drained and closed her face, that caused her young body to bend in upon itself as if to protect itself from crumbling. She listened to herself whip the girl with her anger, urging her to call off the searches, forbidding the raising of the boat, everything inside her screaming, straining to feel something, something.

'Maryanne, sweetheart, what's the matter?' The nurse's hand was cool on her forehead, the tissue soft on her wet cheeks.

'Are you coming back to us, pet?'

* * *

'What was all that about?' William asked as Alison sat on the bed and planted a good morning kiss full on his lips. He had been watching her talking to the staff nurse just outside the ward, noticed the body language, the heightened expressions.

'She thinks she owns you,' Alison began, her colour heightened. She had already spent an hour with the oncologist, at least he'd had the humanity to hear her out, to see reason.

'Oh, yesterday? Don't sweat, Fogarty'll be around in a while, he'll put her right.'

'What time's he due in?' Alison was bent by the bed, rummaging in the locker. 'God, you travel light.'

'I won't be needing much,' he smiled. 'He should be up before ten, why?'

'I'd like to meet him before I head home.'

'You're going today? Oh, right.' The disappointment in his voice, the way he tried to mask it. Alison turned her head to hide her smile.

'Good morning, William, Alison.' Joseph Fogarty smiled, took her hand. William looked from one to the other. How did he know her name?

'So, how are you today, William?'

'Good, thanks. Yesterday did wonders for me.'

'Yes, I heard you were on the missing list for a while.' He shook his head in mock disapproval. 'Please, take a seat,' Fogarty motioned Alison to the chair as he pulled the curtain around the bed. Alison bit down on her lip.

'So, Alison here tells me you're considering homecare?'

A confused William glanced from the doctor to Alison and back again. She took his hand. 'Yes,' she jumped in, 'we've talked it through and William feels he'd be more comfortable at home with me. I've discussed it with the GP and he can arrange all the help we need from our local Hospice Homecare Team.'

'Good. Well, it seems both of you have worked this through and William, well, you are the boss here. I'll get the GP's details from you, Alison, and send him on all the information he'll need.' He turned again to William. 'I won't say goodbye just yet, William – we'll have a chat after lunch before you leave.' He patted a silent William on the arm and rose to draw back the curtain.

'Alison, if you'd like to come with me I'll get that information from you.'

She stood to follow and winked at a stunned William, a huge smile lighting her whole face.

Alison returned twenty minutes later to find William sitting on the side of the bed, deep in thought.

'Ali, I can't let you ...'

'Please, William, don't.' She sat on the bed and took both his hands in hers. 'I'm not rushing into this with my eyes closed. I know what's ahead – for both of us. I've thought really hard about it and it's what I want. Not just for you, for me too. For both of us.' She smiled through her tears. 'Please, say you'll come.'

His eyes, brimming with tears, fixed on hers, his mouth clamped tight to steady the shake in his chin. He shook his head, nodded slowly and they wrapped their arms around each other in silence.

'I'm going to head back to the hotel.' Alison drew away after a long moment and wiped her palms across her wet cheeks. 'I need to collect my stuff, make a few calls.' She stood to leave, her hands finding his again. 'And Fogarty wants to have a chat with you, go over your meds and stuff. I'll collect you, say, about four?'

William nodded, his hands squeezing hers, words still deserting him.

I hope I can count on Dr Clarke, Alison prayed, as she swung out the hospital gate. She hadn't spoken to the GP yet and she knew nothing of the hospice service in Waterford. What she did know was that her doctor wouldn't let her down. She would ring him first, she decided, before Fogarty had a chance to get in touch. She'd liked him, Fogarty. He understood William, the spirit of him, knew that a hospital or hospice wasn't the place for him to end his days. She'd felt bad telling those white lies about her training in cancer care. But they weren't really lies. Her last few months with her mother had taught her more about cancer in a real and raw way than any course could match. She had better give Kathleen a ring too, she nodded, she was going to need the support of a true and strong friend.

* * *

'It's not that ye're not welcome here.' Tom tried again, explaining to Sean, 'It's just, well, the house is small, and me and Ella, we need our space. Things haven't been good with us lately and ye being here, well ... ' Ella had taken the boy to a concert in the local hall and Tom had seized the opportunity to talk to Sean about his leaving. He had hoped it wouldn't come to this. Despite everything, he liked Sean, felt responsible for him in a way. He should never have shown him that advert in the paper, he knew that now. But at the time he had thought that maybe, in some way, it might help to ease the man's torment. But it had only worked to deepen his pain, and Tom cursed his own well-intentioned yet ill-guided interference.

'I know how you're fixed, Tom, and I know I've stayed longer than I should.' Sean could see how awkward Tom felt, having to bring up the subject. He knew Ella was behind it. He had heard them arguing, noticed how their conversations would dry up when he'd come in the back door unexpectedly. Through her silence Ella had made no secret of her wanting Sean gone from the house and he couldn't blame her after what he'd put her through that night young Daniel had gone missing. 'I'll be gone out from under ye before the week is out,' he continued, 'and I'll never forget all that you've done for me, Tom.'

'Will ye go back on the boats?'

'Where else,' Sean sighed. 'There's no other place for me. Not the place I want anyway.' He held his head in his hands, bent it low to the table.

'Come on,' Tom urged, taking his coat from the hook behind the door. 'I'm goin' down to Richie's for a pint, ye'll join me?' He could sense Sean wanted to talk about Alison, could feel it coming. And he wanted no more of it: going over all the same old ground again, Sean trying to find something in what Tom had said that would give him some hope of her wanting him back.

'I won't, Tom, thanks all the same.'

'I'll leave ye then, if ye're sure.' Tom pulled the back door behind him and breathed out his heaviness into the night air.

* * *

Kathleen had changed the beds, walked the dogs and washed the floors, and although the evening wasn't cold she had lit a small fire in the sitting room. It would make the place nice and welcoming for them.

Alison hadn't told her much on the phone. Just that William would be returning with her and staying at her place for a few weeks. Something in the rush of her voice had told Kathleen there was a lot more to the story.

There was no sick aunt, Kathleen was sure of it. The two of them had had some falling out and that's why he had left so suddenly. That would explain Alison's bad form before she went. Think of her, the sly little minx, going after him like that and not a word, Kathleen smiled. Well, they'd obviously made up – more than made up, if he was coming back to *this* house. Kathleen clasped her hands together, smiling. She hoped she was right, hoped Alison had at last found someone to share her life with. If anyone deserved a bit of happiness, it was Alison, she thought, unable to ignore the little voice that reminded her that it would help ease the weight of her own guilt too.

She sighed as she turned on the tap to rinse her hands, remembering how she had watched Alison turn from a vibrant, young bride into a tense and anxious mother and wife. If only Alison had known what Sean was really like – what her so-called friend Kathleen was really like. All these years Alison had spent in love with his ghost. With this person that death had elevated to near sainthood. *Sean Delaney was no saint. He was a selfish fucker, if ever there was one, who put himself and his boat above everything and everyone else. Even at the end, who else was he thinking of but himself? Well, good riddance! The world was a better place without him.* There was no point in trying to tell Alison that, though. And she never had. What would be the point? It would only make her suffer more and cost her the only friend she knew. But this William fellow, maybe he had opened her eyes, had helped her to see the real—

The ring of the telephone interrupted her thoughts. She dried her hands on the tea towel and picked up the receiver. 'Hello?'

'Alison?'

'I'm sorry, Alison is away at the moment.'

'She's away? Away where?'

'She's in Dublin, visiting an aunt. Can I take a message?'

There was silence on the other end.

'Can I say who's calling?'

But the caller had already put down the phone. As she allowed the full realisation of what had just passed to dawn on her, Kathleen slowly lowered her trembling body onto the kitchen chair, the receiver still in her hand.

'Sean Delaney? Jesus, no,' she whispered, her heart almost jumping out of her chest. 'Jesus, Mary and Joseph, no.'

* * *

Sean stood for a moment, staring at the telephone. He could nearly swear that was Kathleen on the other end – who else would Alison have in the house when she was away? *Shit! What if she had recognised his voice?* No, she couldn't have, he reassured himself, he had hardly spoken two words. It would be typical of her to mess the whole thing up on him again. *No, put her out of your mind*, he instructed, *keep your focus. Time enough to deal with Kathleen, with that whole side of things.* For now, he had to concentrate on getting to Alison, and things, it seemed, were beginning to line up in his favour. It would be much easier to meet Alison in Dublin without the eyes of Carniskey looking on, to get her on her own. They could sort everything out between them up there and he would have her well on his side before they went back down home. If he could manage that much, then the rest would be easy sailing.

He climbed the stairs to his bedroom, his heart rising with every step. Lying back on the bed, he lit a cigarette and began picturing their meeting: what he would say to her, how she would look, the feel of her in his arms again. He didn't get into bed but lay fully clothed on the quilt, waiting for morning and the early bus that would bring him to her.

* * *

Alison opened the door and flicked on the hall lights before helping William from the jeep. It was well after ten and the journey had absolutely exhausted him. They'd had to stop several times along the way so that he could get out and stretch his legs and his back. What planet was she on? The pain that such a long journey would put him through had never even crossed her mind. She had thought they'd never reach home, had prayed that William couldn't see through the veneer of her forced humour to the doubts, the trepidation that haunted her.

More than once since leaving the hospital she'd had to ask herself if it really was William's best interests she'd had at heart when she'd made her decision. Yes, *her* decision, because she had ploughed right in without really allowing William any say in the matter. But only because she knew he'd refuse, that he would put her feelings before his own and try – again – to protect her. But she didn't need protecting, she reassured herself now, as, with William settled in bed, she sat to eat the supper that Kathleen had left prepared. She had thought this through and she wouldn't have offered if she didn't believe she had the strength and courage to see it through.

It felt good to be back in the comfort of her own surroundings, sitting in front of the fire, the dogs sleeping at her feet. She felt her confidence returning. Dr Clarke had been so supportive on the phone and she had an appointment to see him tomorrow to get everything moving. And Kathleen. She knew without asking that she could count on Kathleen one hundred per cent. But she wasn't fooling herself that this was going to be easy – the journey alone had brought that home to her. It was probably going to be harder than she could ever imagine. And it would test her, test every last raw nerve in her body, she knew that too. But she would do it. They would do it, her and William, together.

* * *

Kathleen tiptoed from the bedroom. It wasn't fair, she was keeping Rob awake and he had an early start in the morning. She crossed the landing to the bathroom and sat on the side of the bath in the darkness. Maybe she had just imagined it. It could have been anybody. Maybe, because she had been thinking about him just as the phone rang … But then why hadn't he given a name or left a message? She had grown up with Sean Delaney, she knew him more than most. And God knew she had heard him say the name 'Alison' enough times to recognise the mouth it came from, the slight mispronunciation: 'Aluson'. In her heart of hearts she knew it was him and there was no point in trying to deny it. She lay a hand over her thumping heart. Was it really possible that he could have been out there somewhere all this time? That he was thinking about making his way back? Why now? Why just when Alison had finally begun to accept that he was gone and had started to find some happiness? Why, just when Kathleen herself had found someone who truly loved her, loved Jamie? She ran her tongue over her parched lips. *Oh sweet Jesus, help me*, she prayed. How would she tell Rob, poor Jamie, Alison? But she would have to: what other choice had she? She gripped the sides of the bath, her stomach heaving.

When she had told Sean she was pregnant, he had stormed from her bed and ended their passionate three-month affair with a callousness that had numbed her throughout the pregnancy. When the child was born and she wheeled him to the house one evening to visit, Sean had barely glanced in the pram in his hurry to bundle Hannah in his arms and whisk her outdoors. What a strength Alison had been to her then. Over the following few years Kathleen had hardened her heart to Sean Delaney and found a true friend in the woman she had once so envied and deceived. But as Jamie grew, Kathleen's sense of shame and injustice had grown with him until she was prepared to sacrifice even that friendship if it meant that the child could grow up knowing his father. She had no interest in Sean any more, had seen him for the selfish coward that he was, but she was damned if he was going to walk past his own child in the street without as much as a glance in his direction. And so she had told him that if he wasn't prepared to come clean with Alison, to play a part in Jamie's life, then she would tell Alison herself.

When the news broke that Sean's boat had gone down, Kathleen had been consumed with a confusing cocktail of loss and guilt and relief. In a blind effort at coping she had buried all memories of Sean Delaney, locking them down with a driving determination to be both mother and father to Jamie and to support Alison and Hannah in every way she could. For three years she listened to Alison's pain, all the time trying to ignore the echo of what Sean had inflicted on her. Their friendship deepened through those years, Kathleen secure in the knowledge that her secret was safe, buried in the depths of the sea.

No, he couldn't come back now. Look at all the lives he would tear apart. No, please God, no, hadn't he done enough of that already? She closed her eyes, took a deep breath. She could just ignore it, just put it out of her head, pretend it had never happened. She had learned to be good at that too, thanks to Sean. But what if he turned up? What if he rang Alison again tonight, tomorrow? And Rob – how could she go ahead with the wedding, while keeping a whole part of herself hidden from him? Hot bile burned her throat and she lurched for the toilet bowl.

'Kath, you all right?' Rob switched on the overhead light.

Fifteen

The image of William lying pale and lifeless on the bedroom floor woke Alison with a start. She hopped out of bed, threw on her nightshirt and peered in through William's bedroom door. He was still sleeping. She stood a moment, looking at him. His face had grown thinner, and the arm and shoulder visible over the covers had lost the taut-ness she had noticed that morning when she had secretly watched him swim. She tiptoed into the room. He stirred but did not wake. The early morning sun stealing through the drapes and touching his pillow cast a peacefulness, a certain vulnerability and aloneness about him that tugged at her. She stepped out of her nightshirt, gently pulled back the bedcovers and slipped quietly in beside him. He did not wake but his body moved to accommodate hers as she lay melting into the warm comfort of him, her hand tracing the length of his back, his hip, his buttocks. The subtle smell of her chased his sleep and he turned, pulling her gently to him.

'Good morning, sunshine.' His low, throaty whisper was laced with desire, his hand slow-tracing the curve of her back. They lay there, neither speaking, each lost in the intensity of the other's closeness and touch. His lips and tongue sought her lips, her shoulder, her breasts; her body opening to his, her moist warmth sheathing and caressing his thrust.

* * *

Sean stepped down from the bus into a glorious, sun-drenched Dublin morning. He hadn't slept at all last night and had fought to keep his eyes from closing as the bus moved from the wilds of Donegal, through fields and towns and villages, his heart racing ahead of it, his eyes seeing her face, her smile in every field and hill that rushed past the window. A small knapsack slung over his shoulder, he walked with a new energy and purpose down O'Connell Street, crossed at the Gresham Hotel and waited for the bus that would bring him to her. The ten minutes seemed like an hour. He paced the footpath, stubbed out his cigarette, lit another. He was done with waiting. He flagged a taxi and jumped into the back seat: 'Terenure, please, Rathfarnham Road.'

Stepping out onto the footpath four doors down from Alison's aunt, Sean felt suddenly exposed and vulnerable. What if she should see him? How would he approach her? What would he say? All the rehearsing he had done for this moment and now that it was here all the words and plans that had seemed so perfect in the small hours of morning seemed impossible, ridiculous. Face bent to the ground, he walked briskly down the road and turned in at the entrance to Bushy Park. Finding a secluded spot beside a grove of beech trees, he threw himself down on the grass. He needed time, needed to do this right. If he messed up now, there was no going back. He shook out another cigarette. What if he rang the aunt, he wondered, asked her to arrange a meeting with Alison – or better still to get her to speak to him first on the phone, that'd be easier than face to face. Coward, a voice boomed in his head. But what else could he do? He couldn't just walk up there and press the doorbell. What if Alison answered? The shock on its own would be enough to turn her away. He could always let her spot him on the street – by accident. That would make it easier for her. Give her a moment before she approached him, would make the decision seem hers. He watched a small girl running on the path below, her mother following behind with a pram. And then, out of nowhere, there she was! The long red hair tied loosely behind her shoulders, her hips moving in slow seduction under her light summer dress.

'Alison!' He was up and running after her without a thought of what he might say, how she might react. 'Alison, wait!'

The woman turned just as he reached his hand to touch her shoulder. The slump of his heart anchored him to the spot. 'I'm sorry,' he mumbled, 'I thought you were…'

She fixed him with a look of annoyance, turned on her heel and walked briskly away, leaving him wordless, breathless.

* * *

Alison sat in the jeep outside Kathleen's house. She closed her eyes and for the umpteenth time that day her whole insides sighed in delicious satiation as she replayed her morning with William. She savoured again the brush and flick of his tongue, the strength and span of his hands; the way his eyes – their intent deep, dark almost – held hers as he entered her, body and soul. Never in her life had she felt such complete and utter fulfilment as in that moment, a moment that seemed to span back through time – a moment that she knew would last through eternity. She bit down on her lip to quell the desire that flared once again inside her.

'Hi!' Kathleen's rap on the window jumped her back to reality. Alison opened the door and Kathleen wrapped her in a tight hug. 'Look at you!' Kathleen smiled, holding Alison apart from her and taking in the light in her face. 'Oh, you're a dark horse, Alison Delaney. Come on in, I want *all* the details!' She led a silent Alison by the hand in through the front door, hoping that, with her preoccupation with William, Alison wouldn't notice the state she was in.

Rob had insisted that she stay off work this morning and give herself a chance to recover from the bug she had contracted in the home. It was the first thing that shot out of her mouth when Rob had appeared in the bathroom last night. The first lie in a line of many, she knew, if she didn't work up the courage to come clean with him. But the more she thought about it, the harder it seemed. Telling him that she had had an affair with the husband of her best friend, that she'd had a child for him, made her a different woman to the one Rob had fallen in love with. He had always admired her forthrightness, her honesty, the way she would blast out an opinion, no matter how controversial. Rob was in love with someone altogether different to the woman he proposed to marry.

She had been sick twice again this morning, had just been coming downstairs from the bathroom when she saw Alison's car pull into the drive. She had watched Alison for a moment through the glass panel at the side of the door: watched her close her eyes, tilt her head back, a glorious smile of utter contentment lighting her whole face. How could she steal that from her? How could she shatter what Alison had waited so long to find and then break her further by confessing the truth about herself and Sean. And Jamie.

She had taken a few minutes to steady herself before opening the door. She would say nothing for the moment, she decided. First, she would talk to Rob, tell him everything, say goodbye to him, to her dreams. Then, from somewhere, she would dig up the courage to speak to Alison. She had finally admitted to herself that this wasn't just about Sean Delaney, this was about her too. Nobody had forced her into a relationship. She had taken up with Sean of her own free will, fully aware of his circumstances. When the relationship ended, she could have left it at that, could have got on with her own and Jamie's lives and left Alison and Sean to mend whatever differences had separated them. But her own spite and sense of injustice, her own pride and stubbornness had driven her back to him, and had driven him away from his wife and from both his children.

All these years she had buried her guilt about the role she had played in Sean's disappearance. Buried it under her suffocating love for Jamie – she hadn't liked it when Rob had pointed that one out; her struggle for independence, for respect; under her supposed concern for and friendship with Alison. Lies, lies, the whole lot of it lies! She had built her entire world on lies, so why was she so surprised that it was all finally about to come toppling down around her, she had scorned herself, swallowing back her self-disgust and planting yet another false smile on her face before opening the door to greet Alison.

* * *

'How far out would Uncle Sean be, Dad?' Daniel sat with Tom at the end of the pier at Killybegs.

'Och, a long way, Dan. Those big boats go way, way out there,' Tom smiled, nodding his head towards the horizon.

'Out past the bending of the globe?' Daniel's eyes were wide with wonder.

'Aye, even further sometimes.'

'Even further,' the child echoed, his eyes fixed on the horizon. 'Can he still see us?'

'I'm sure he can, son. Those boats have powerful binoculars.' The child's face and heart had fallen the morning Sean had left and he'd carried the note that Sean had left him around in his pocket ever since. Tom would catch him, checking his pocket to make sure it was still there, taking it out every now and then to scan the few short lines:

I'm off again, Daniel. Take care. You're a fine lad and you'll make a great fisherman someday.
Your friend,
Sean.

It was the only thing he had left behind. No word of goodbye to Tom or Ella, no mention of where he was going. When Tom got up that morning and found him gone, he'd presumed that Sean would be back before nightfall. It wasn't until after eight o'clock that night, when he'd peered his head around the bedroom door and found the note for Daniel, that he realised Sean was gone for good. His first reaction was relief. At least now they could get on with their lives without Sean's heavy presence around the house. And he could relax now too, about Alison, put her out of his mind.

When he enquired the next day, Tom had learned that Sean hadn't left on a boat but was seen boarding the early morning bus for Dublin. Maybe he'd arranged a pick-up there, Tom concluded, and he'd sail from the docks in Dublin. Anyway, he was gone from their lives and good luck to him, wherever he went. He genuinely hoped Sean would find peace. But at night when he lay chasing sleep Tom's mind would throw up a thousand questions – what if Sean had gone to Waterford? What if he was down there now, tormenting and harassing her? He would feel the anger of a protective father rising inside him at those moments.

'Will he come back, Dad?' The boy broke in on his thoughts.

'We'll see, son, we'll see.' Tom put his arm around Daniel and drew him close. 'Now come on, yer mother'll kill us if we're late for tea.' He hoisted the boy up on his shoulders and strolled back up the pier towards home, wondering as he went whether it mightn't be a bad idea to give Alison a ring in the evening. Sean was gone three days. If he was going to Carniskey, he'd be well there by now. That's what he would do, he decided, whistling. He'd give Alison a call after tea and then he could settle his mind once and for all.

* * *

Kathleen waved Alison off, her mind in such a spin that she could barely separate one thought from another. How in the name of God could that girl look so glowingly happy when the man she had finally come to realise she loved lay within months, maybe even weeks of death? How could she have such a peace about her? If she were Alison, she'd be railing against God, against the whole world for what it was doing to her. But instead Alison appeared more content with herself, more calm and fulfilled than Kathleen had seen her since she had first married. *Maybe it's her way of protecting herself*, Kathleen figured, closing the door and returning to the kitchen. *Maybe Alison is not allowing herself to face the reality of it because she knows from before what it's going to do to her.*

Her secret passion for Sean rose in hot accusation in her throat. She could never tell her now, not with this. Alison would need her when William went, would need someone she trusted, some solid ground to keep her standing. Maybe it hadn't been Sean on the phone, she tried to fool herself, while another part of her screamed out that of course it was him, and she knew it.

And she did know it. She knew every beat and nuance of that voice – God knows she had spent enough nights lying close to him, clinging to every word that came out of his mouth as if it were pure gold. What a fool! What she wouldn't give now to be told that she would never again hear another syllable out of him.

She would keep calm, she decided, and if Sean did make an appearance she would deny everything. He had denied her and Jamie long enough, and anyway, who would believe a word out of him at this stage after what he had done? As for Rob…she sat at the table and cradled her head in her hands.

She would either have to tell Rob or else spend the rest of her life looking over her shoulder. She wasn't prepared to live like that any longer. She was done with lies. She would tell Rob and she would beg him, if he cared about her and Jamie at all, to keep it to himself – for Alison, for Jamie and for Hannah's sake – to keep it to himself and to walk away.

* * *

The doctor was warm and receptive – and to the point. He detailed the hospice service and what they could provide for William and Alison, reassured her of his own assistance and availability, and reiterated again and again the importance of Alison taking good care of herself. He knew she was aware of what lay ahead for William but questioned whether she had given enough consideration to the impact it would have on herself. He was taken aback by her strength, her determination to follow it through, by the courage of this young woman who had already been tossed so much by life. He saw her to the door, confident that although this would test her more than she realised Alison would survive.

She left with the wheelchair the doctor had secured for her and the contact number of the hospice team who were expecting her call. Alison was to arrange a meeting at her house for later that evening, when Dr Clarke and the hospice nurse would assess William's needs and set a care plan in place. She recognised fully the absolute necessity of involving the hospice home-care team for William's professional care and comfort, but she had refused point-blank when Dr Clarke suggested that she avail of a home-care service for an hour every day. To give her a break, he'd said.

A break? William's time, their time together was short, she was under no illusion about that. She didn't want the house, their space, taken over by strangers – well-intentioned as they might be. With the help of Dr Clarke and the hospice team, and of course Kathleen, she would look after William and keep life as normal and 'hospital' free as possible. Anxious to be back to him again, she stopped in at the chemist to pick up some aromatherapy oils and candles and was quickly on her way home.

* * *

Sean had moved the table and chair under the laced curtained window and passed his days and evenings watching the street below like a marksman. The bed and breakfast accommodation was seven doors up from Alison's aunt, on the opposite side of the street, and gave him a perfect view of the comings and goings at the house with the yellow door. He sat and smoked and ate his meals behind the window, only leaving the room after darkness fell, when he could steal through the streets unnoticed. The landlady, suspicious of his behaviour, had tried to draw him out. Sean had spun her a story about how his wife had recently passed away, how he was struggling to come to terms with his loss before facing back into the world. Propelled by sympathy, the woman did all in her power to accommodate his privacy and grieving.

He felt tired. Tired and restless. Three days now and the neat, single room with the floral papered walls and low ceiling had already begun to close in on him. He hated being confined. Hated towns and cities: detested the noise, the rush, the bland similarity of the nearly day and nearly night, the way the streetlights stole the magic from the stars. He stared out blankly at the dull monotony of it all: that row of sameness across the street, the tiny gardens, neatly mown and bordered, the front doors numbered like cells – the odd one brightly painted in a stab at individuality. And the people, like machines they were. He could tell when each was due home, what time they slept and woke, what they would wear in their morning rush from door to car or bus. And still no sign of Alison. He had seen the aunt yesterday, catching the bus at midday. She'd looked hale and hearty – no sign of sickness there. Sean had considered ringing Alison at home again to see if she had returned, but he'd decided against it. He didn't want to risk Kathleen answering again. If she got to Alison before he did, if she told her what had gone on, it would finish any chance of her taking him back. Maybe he had been right when he'd thought that over last night down by the canal. Maybe he should have gone to Kathleen first, made some kind of arrangement about the boy, got her on side. But he couldn't trust her, not at this stage. There was a time when Kathleen would have done anything for him, anything. But that day was well past, he reckoned. No, it wouldn't be worth the risk. He'd bide his time for another few days and if he hadn't seen Alison by then he'd ring the aunt, see if she had gone back home to Carniskey. And he'd take it from there.

Home to Carniskey. Home. Cradling the back of his head with his clasped hands he leaned back in his chair, allowed his eyes to close. Home. An iron fist gripped his heart as the reel of every detail of that fateful night last February, when he had returned to Carniskey, clicked and spun in the darkness behind his closed lids. He was right back there once more, as if it were happening this very moment:

Ten minutes, that's all he had reckoned it would take. Ten minutes and he'd be in and out of there. The old dear would be none the wiser and he would finally have his ticket to a new life, a new home.

Home. The word echoed inside him. Nobody ever really understood the hugeness of it until it was lost, he thought, standing from the rock now, its damp coldness beginning to seep into his bones. He checked his watch by the light of the reluctant moon. 2 a.m. How long had he been sitting there – an hour, two maybe? He tugged up his jacket collar. A south-east wind rushed in from the Atlantic, wrapping itself around him in a cloak of belonging, the wet sand beneath his feet yielding to welcome him back, to claim him. He shook his head as if to shake out his thoughts, dug his hands deep into his jacket pockets, the car jack jabbing his elbow. This was no time for sentimentality; it was his one and only chance of getting his life back on track. He had come this far and he wasn't about to let any old mawkishness get in his way.

He turned from the shoreline up towards the slipway. He didn't need a torch. He knew every inch of this place, had been carved and shaped by it just like the cliffs towering above him. His sigh was laced with satisfaction, his whole sense of being heightened by the anonymity lent to him by the darkness, making him feel more creature than human, more invincible.

He swung up onto the wooden railing that led to the steep cliff path, a short cut from the harbour to the road above. Funny, he thought, head bent as he negotiated the rubble that had fallen loose from the cliff onto the pathway, funny how you almost became a place, how you can feel the force and energy of a landscape working inside you. Wherever his new life brought him, he knew he would always carry this place deep within him: the tiny harbour nestled below the watchful cliffs, its quays dotted with pots and nets awaiting their season; the mountains, their browns and purples spread out to the west; the curved coast road dotted with houses – pink, yellow, white – leading into the single street village that hibernated through the long winter and reawakened in all its colour and glory with each new summer. And everywhere, always, the thunder and taste of the sea.

The headlights of a passing car on the bend above moved like a search beam along the cliff face. He pressed himself into its darkness, the smell of coppered water and damp earth filling his nostrils and crowding his head with an avalanche of memories that threatened to turn him. Taking a deep breath, he sucked in his lips and hurried his step. He had a right to a life, the same as anyone else, and by Jesus he'd earned it. No, there would be no turning. He crossed the road and scaled the low stone wall that skirted the bungalow.

The house was in darkness. He pulled on his gloves, yanked the jack from his waistband as he stole across the lawn, the sea below roaring at his back, its salty breath whipping the cordylines that sentried the house.

The rain that had weighed the air all night began to fall now, fast and heavy as his feet moved soundlessly across the concrete yard to the back door. He eased the lip of the jack between door and frame, the long lonely howl of a dog on the neighbouring farm swallowing the sound as he shouldered the door ajar. Stepping across onto the cork mat he held his breath a moment, eased the door out behind him. Silence. Then that cursed dog again. Almost there, he reassured himself, slipping the torch from his pocket and setting the jack down gently on the counter top. Then something inside him

294

took over, something he had cursed ever since had blinded him of any sense and led him down the dark, narrow corridor to the closed door of his boyhood room, just to stand there a minute, just to remember, to feel again. A fierce tightness in his throat restored his senses and he moved quickly back to the kitchen, careful to aim the beam of the torch towards the floor. Lifting the lid of the chest freezer he dug his gloved hand down into the bottom left-hand corner. Result! He couldn't help but smile to himself. In and out in ten minutes? Cut that in half. He bent his back, unzipped his small holdall.

The sudden glare of the overhead light froze him to the spot, his heart swelling, threatening to stall. Before his brain had time to relay the message not to turn around his head had swung and his eyes had met his mother's, met the fear and disbelief echoed in her high-pitched keen that filled the room before she slumped to the floor, the hollow thud of her head meeting the door jamb returning the room to silence.

Her eyes, wide and unblinking, stared up at him. Jesus! His eyes and mouth screwed up tight, he arched his neck and held his face towards the light. Jesus, Jesus Christ! He should check for a pulse. He should try to stem the bleed from her forehead. He should call a doctor, an ambulance. He should…

He hoisted the bag on to his shoulder, stepped over her body and out into his new life.

One fist thumping the table, Sean kicked the chair from beneath him. He grabbed his jacket and cigarettes and, taking the stairs two at a time, he marched out the door, his head bent in the direction of the corner pub.

* * *

The weekend brought August and a mini heatwave. Alison wheeled William along the pier. He was quiet in himself, thoughtful. He had refused to increase his medication for the moment, wanting to remain in full control of his thoughts and feelings, to enjoy them for as long as possible before they were dimmed and distorted by drugs. But this evening Alison could see that the pain was already more than he could bear. She would talk to him about it later when they got home and then Maria, the nurse, could make the necessary changes when she called tomorrow. Alison had felt a little resentful at Maria's interference at first. Her time with William was so precious, so short, and she didn't want to share it with anyone else. But now she was grateful that there was a Maria at the other end of the phone when she needed her.

Alison parked close to the front door. As she rounded the jeep to the passenger door, Joe O'Sullivan stepped out from the side of the porch.

'Is he home yet? Is Seany back?'

'Joe…' Alison tried to keep her voice as gentle and matter of fact as possible. 'Haven't I told you often enough? Sean won't be coming back. Not today. Not ever. Now please, Joe, go home, I'm busy.'

He lunged forward and pressed his face close to the glass, his eyes dancing over William. 'Git out! Git away! This is Seany's place!' His screech was high and hurried, his clenched fists beating and shaking the glass.

'Joe!'

He ran and jumped the ditch to the next field.

'Who was…?'

'I'm sorry, William, please, don't mind him,' Alison

sighed as she helped him from the seat. 'He's not all there, poor lad. Sean made a bit of a pet of him over the years and he still expects him to come back.' But inside she was seething, silently cursing Joe for the shock and discomfort on William's face.

While William showered, Alison busied herself preparing the room. She lit the nightlights and placed them in a row along the windowsill, on the bedside lockers, and blended drops of basil and lavender with the carrier oil. Music of panpipes and water whispered from the CD player, the oil burner filling the room with a subtle scent of frankincense.

William lay on the bed in the semi-darkness, her fingers stroking and kneading, brushing his back like the wings of angels, quieting the fear and trepidation that shadowed him and easing him into a more restful night.

She gently stroked the length of his back. Even in the short time since he'd come to stay with her Alison could see a change in him, his frame more accentuated than before, as if the life were being peeled from him, layer by layer, his body undressing, preparing. Never in her life had she felt so filled with love, so sensitively aware of the strength and depth of her feelings and at the same time so acutely aware of the fragility of the body, of life itself.

When Sean had been taken from her, there had been no preparation, no parting, no body. It had all been too sudden, too removed from reality for her to know how or where to begin to cope with it. Witnessing William's life force diminish day by day, sharing this sacred time with him, she felt a deeper understanding, a new respect for life, for death, felt its whole mystery calming her, guiding her.

297

She slipped out of her robe and stretched down beside him. They lay in silent union, the nightlights flickering in the growing darkness.

* * *

Kathleen placed the two mugs on the table and scalded the teapot. Of all the times for May to arrive on one of her unexpected visits. Trouble in the ivory tower again, she guessed, as she glanced over at May nervously twisting the thick wedding band on her finger.

'How's Paul?' Might as well get straight down to the nitty gritty, Kathleen thought, no point beating round the bush with useless small talk, she had enough on her mind. May really got on her nerves at times.

Kathleen had hardly seen her since she'd got back together with Paul – too busy flashing about with their 'high society' golfing friends. Had she not realised the height they'd dropped her from when Paul had left her? They'd hardly given her the time of day. Oh, herself and Alison were good enough then. Kathleen's temper flowered as she remembered how May had spoken to Alison in the pub. And then to think that she can walk in here again without a by-your-leave when it suits her!

'Paul's super – we're off to Paris with two of his partners and their wives next week, I'm *so* looking forward to the shops!'

'That's nice for you. Who's mindin' the kids?'

'Paul's mum, she'll spoil them rotten.'

Kathleen nodded. *Had she just come here to boast? Hardly, she's plenty opportunity for that at the golf club. So what did she want?* Kathleen didn't have to wait long to find out.

'Tell me, Kathleen, is it really true about Alison, that she's taken a lover?'

Kathleen looked across at the bobbing blonde head, the plumped-up pout, the two sharp eyes spidered with mascara.

'She's the talk of the place! Do you know him? They say he's twice her age and— '

'They've little to bother them!' Kathleen snapped. *Where the hell does she get off with that accent?* she seethed. *Jesus, she was reared here with the rest of us!* 'Alison has a heart. And that's what sets her apart around this place. Yes, I have met him, May. His name is William. He's a wonderful, gentle man and a great friend to Alison. He also has cancer and only a few months to live.'

May opened her mouth to speak but closed it just as quickly, as Kathleen rose from her chair and stood leaning in to her over the table.

'Now, if that's all, I'm on my way out.' She whipped the mugs from the table and poured the tea down the sink. May turned at the door. 'Tell Alison, if there's anything I can do…'

'She's managed long and hard on her own, I think she'll survive this one without you.' Kathleen grabbed her bag and keys and led the way out the hall, knowing that a big part of the anger she directed at May was due to her own suffocating guilt. No matter what she did for Alison now, it would never be enough to purge those feelings.

* * *

Alison didn't want to admit how quickly he was slipping away from her. The wheelchair sat folded inside the hall door. How William had bucked against it when he'd seen it at first, but he had quickly put his objections to bed when Alison pointed out how much easier it would make things for her. It had given William the chance to see the beach again, and Tra na Leon, and it had allowed her to bring him back to the pier in town, back to where they'd first kissed, to remember the fireworks. And maybe, who knows, she urged herself, if this change in medication works, maybe there'll be more trips…

Maria had arrived at ten and the doctor followed quickly after. They would adjust his medication again, hopefully put an end to the frightening pain she had watched him endure the night before. While she had accepted his dying, Alison hadn't been prepared for how his suffering would tear the very heart out of her. She had taken to sleeping in his room so that she could be there, at all times, if he needed her. She knew her closeness comforted him, took away some of the loneliness, the fear. She knew too that she couldn't bear to be anywhere but next to him. Right next to him.

Exhausted, emotionally and physically, she had come to look forward to Maria's visits. Maria's time with William gave her a little space, a little time to be alone and just sit with her feelings. And Kathleen had been great. She called in each morning and evening without fail, offering to sit with William so that Alison could take a walk on the beach or cliff, to get some air, clear her head. But Alison refused. She hadn't left the house now in over a week, afraid that the very moment she stepped outside would be the moment William would look for her – or, God forbid, go from her forever.

May had called at the beginning of the week with a bouquet of flowers as extravagant as her soft words. Alison hadn't let her past the door. She had come to consider the house as her and William's sacred place and wanted no one except the doctor, the nurse and Kathleen to enter it.

She wrapped her arms tightly around herself, moved to the kitchen window. The sky blushed over the setting sun, a light breeze combing the overgrown grass in the garden. She hugged herself tighter, turned around at the soft knock on the kitchen door. His smile filled with compassion, Dr Clarke walked slowly towards her, rested his hand gently on her shoulder. Alison felt the hot tears threaten.

'That should make him much more comfortable. And don't hesitate to call me, day or night, you have my mobile number.'

Alison bit back the tears and nodded. 'Thanks, Doctor. What else can I do for him?'

'Nothing more than you're doing already. He's very lucky to have you, Alison. You should be proud of yourself.'

Sixteen

'Of course I knew what I was doing.' Kathleen rubbed the heel of her hand under her nose, across her eyes, her head bent in exhaustion, shame. She hadn't been able to meet Rob's eyes since she had opened the door to him. 'I wasn't some foolish teenager, I was a grown woman. She was my friend, Rob, and there was little Hannah. But I put all that out of my mind, fooled myself that what they didn't know wouldn't hurt them, that it was between him and me, and no one else came into it.' If it was details he came for, then she would give him every last gritty one. Nothing could make her feel worse than she did already.

His back to Kathleen, Rob stared out the kitchen window. His eyes, fixed on the football net at the end of the garden, were heavy and scorched, reminding him that he hadn't slept a wink the previous night. After she had told him, after she had burst those words out like gunfire, each one striking his heart with the accuracy of a marksman, she had begged him to leave, begged him to spare her his anger, his judgement, his disappointment.

He remembered now how he had walked from the house

in a stupor, allowing himself no feelings, no thoughts. He didn't remember the drive home. But he could still feel the burn of his anger, his jealousy, the black rage that shook his hands as he tore up the house plans and slammed his fists into the table; how that same storm of rage had stalked him, hour upon hour, shadowing his every step as he paced his apartment and fought to order his thoughts. And later, in the small hours when he lay exhausted on his bed, the dead weight of loneliness that crushed his chest.

He had been right after all. He had known something had changed in Kathleen since that night he had found her in the bathroom. The spark had gone out of her. She'd been short with Jamie, with him too – especially when he mentioned anything about the new house. He had put it down to her distress over Alison and her friend's illness, and although he didn't like himself for it, a part of him resented Alison and her timing, resented her stealing the light from Kathleen, from both of them, and he'd had to remind himself that that very selflessness in Kathleen, that ability to put her own feelings aside to help someone else, was one of the things that set her apart, and he admired and loved it so much in her.

He had known by her tone when she said they needed to talk that it was going to be something he didn't particularly want to hear. He had figured that she probably wanted to postpone the wedding for a bit out of respect for Alison and her circumstances, and although he was disappointed he was willing to go along with her. But he had never for one second considered that there might be a chance he would lose her.

'Did you love him?' His own voice sounded distant to him, foreign.

'Then?' Kathleen raised her head, took a deep breath. She had lost everything now, she may as well be honest with him, honest with herself for once. 'Yes, I loved him,' she sighed, 'and I loved that he came to me, loved that I could fix him when no one else could, stupid and pathetic as it all might sound now.'

'And now?' Rob didn't turn from the window, didn't move his eyes from the net rippling in the goal mouth. He held his breath, his fingers turning the coins in his pocket. He knew as he showered this morning that this question was the only one that mattered, knew that his whole world hung on her answer.

'Now my stomach turns when I think of him, of me, of what we … what I did.' She stretched back her neck, closed her eyes to ease their sting. Almost eight years she had spent paying for her mistake. Eight long, hard years. Shouldn't that have been enough? 'It wasn't love, or anything approaching it. I know that now.' Her tears pressed again, hot and impatient behind her closed lids. 'It wasn't love, not like you've shown me.' Her teeth pressed down on her lip, bit into it. She swallowed hard against her tears. 'You'd better go, I don't want Jamie arriving in to see…I'm so sorry, Rob.' She clasped her hand over her mouth.

He turned from the window, felt her shoulders shake beneath his hands. 'I'm not going anywhere,' he said, bending to kiss the crown of her head. Never again did he want to experience the utter desolation he had felt the previous night, the feeling that all the light and energy had been cut from his world. Whatever this Sean or the future would bring, they would face it together, because without her – without her smile, her laughter, her touch – without those eyes lit with love, meeting his, without that, there was nothing. 'You're still the woman I fell in love with.' His arms stole around her. 'The past is the past, Kath. This is about us now, you and me and Jamie. Nothing, no one else matters.'

* * *

Kathleen arrived at six o'clock, a large cardboard box of groceries in her arms.

'Kathleen, you shouldn't have.'

'I didn't. These are from Joan at the shop – with the message that if there's anything you need at any time you're just to ring and Jim will drop it up.'

'Joan?'

'There's goodness in their hearts, Alison, really.' She dropped the box on the kitchen table. 'They care about you.'

'I know. Look what I found on the doorstep this morning.' Alison motioned to a basket of freshly baked scones and homemade jam on the counter. She handed the small note to Kathleen: 'Dear Alison – Sorry for your troubles. Ye're in my prayers. Theresa Doyle.'

'Ah, God love her. You know, they'd drive you to drink around here, but there's none better when you're in a real fix.'

'How is Maryanne? Did you see her, did you tell her ...' Alison hadn't visited in over a week, not wanting to leave William's side, not wanting Maryanne to see the state she was in.

'Will you quit about Maryanne, she's fine. I was in with her this morning and I told her you had a bug and you weren't allowed to visit. Maryanne's well taken care of and you have enough on your plate. Now, sit down and I'll make us some coffee. How is he?'

Alison sighed and shook her head. She placed her elbows on the table, her hands supporting her chin. 'At least he's comfortable now and he sleeps better. But I know he hates it. Hates having trouble stringing a sentence together, being cared for. He—' She burst into uncontrollable sobs.

'Oh, come here.' Kathleen gathered her in her arms and held her tightly.

'Oh, Kathleen, I don't even know what I'm feeling! One minute I feel totally peaceful and like I'm accepting the whole thing, and the next I just go to pieces.'

'Come on, that's it, let it out,' Kathleen soothed. 'You're exhausted, on top of everything else. God knows when you last had a full night's sleep. And you love him. Of course you don't want to see him like … Oh Alison, I know, I know.' Kathleen allowed her own tears to fall, knowing that the heartbreak she had felt at almost losing Rob could only be a shadow of what Alison was going through.

Alison wept like a child until it seemed she had drained every last tear from her body.

'That's better,' Kathleen said, rubbing her back, 'you needed that. And now there's something else you need. Coffee's off,' she instructed, bending to the cupboard where she knew the Jameson was housed. She poured two generous measures.

'To love!' Kathleen raised her glass.

'Love and friendship,' Alison smiled, clinking hers. 'I don't know what I'd ever have done without you, Kathleen,' she continued, her lip trembling. 'Through Sean, now this, everything – you've always been there for me and I can never thank you enough.' Kathleen's smile was forced and fixed, the darkness of her secret pulling on her heart like an anchor, threatening to drown her.

When Hannah phoned two hours later, Kathleen had just left and Alison was sitting, preparing to write, in William's lamp-lit room. She soft-stepped into the hall.

'Not long now, Mum, I'm so excited!'

'Me too, sweetheart, I'll hardly know you!' Alison fought to match the enthusiasm in her daughter's voice. When she had taken William home, she hadn't stopped to consider that Hannah might be home before – before the end. She had discussed it with Kathleen and they had decided to take it day by day and, as the time got nearer, Kathleen had offered, if necessary, to fly to London and meet up with Hannah a few days before she was due to return, to prepare her.

'Ah, Mum, it's only been three months.'

'Sometimes it seems so much longer.'

'I knew you'd miss me!' The youthful energy in Hannah's voice brought a smile to her face and underneath everything Alison could feel an excitement budding inside her at the thought of her daughter's return.

'And I'll finally get to meet your man?'

'Oh Hannah, he's not…'

'Don't tell me you've dumped him already?'

'No, Hannah, but he'll be leaving – I told you he was just visiting.'

'Yeah well, tell him to hang on a little bit longer – tell him I've got some questions for him,' she laughed.

'What about you? Bet you'll be leaving some broken hearts behind in London!' Alison knew she couldn't keep up the jolly pretence about William much longer and she didn't want to break down on Hannah. 'Oh Han, sorry to cut you short but Kathleen's just arrived. We're heading out and I'm not even dressed. I'll give you a ring at the weekend, okay?'

'Kathleen my arse!' Hannah laughed and hung up.

* * *

'Open it!' A slow smile played on William's lips as he motioned with his head to the folder he had asked Alison to collect from the camper earlier that evening. Resting the folder on her knees, she fiddled nervously with the twine binding it.

'You know I don't like surprises,' she began, her eyes and mouth widening in disbelief as she opened back the cover and began leafing through the pages. The sketches were all dated. The first was a dark charcoal of Alison on the beach, the drift-wood held to her breast. The next captured her leaning against the tall rock, her feet in the water. There she was standing in the moon's beam, the water measuring her waist. Then in her dressing gown, head tilted to one side, lips parted, arms outstretched in movement; smiling, hunkered down in the heather; head thrown back in laughter at a candlelit table. It was all there. The story of her summer, the loneliness and pain of the first heavy charcoals lifting to lighter strokes, the light of the candle catching the birth of light and love in her eyes.

'Oh, William, I ...' Words wouldn't come.

'You like them?' he whispered

'It's like ... it's like looking at a tape of myself – from the inside.' She bent her head and brushed his lips. 'Oh, William, thank you.' She lay on the bed beside him, nestling his head to her breast.

308

'It doesn't end there. When we … when we first … made love, Alison …'

She held him, waited till his words found order.

'I knew then, felt a part of something … something bigger, much bigger than this world.' His breath was short, shallow. 'It was like I was lifted to somewhere else, somewhere beyond me … The place I'm going to, it's not so far away, it's part of here, of us.'

'I felt it too.' She kissed the top of his head, her fingers brushing his cheek.

'I don't want to leave you, Alison. I wish you … were coming with me.'

'I am, in a way. And you're not leaving me, Will. We're part of each other. Part of each of us will live in both places.'

'I … love you, Ali.'

'And I will always love you.' She closed her eyes and listened to his breathing, felt the warm pressure of his head melting into her aching heart.

* * *

Coffee in hand, Kathleen sat again at the kitchen table, unfolded the pages of the letter and, for what seemed the umpteenth time, she read:

Dear Alison,

I know you'll think I'm nothing but a gutless coward for writing this and you'd be right. If I had any decency in me I would have come to you with this, in person, years ago. I can make all kinds of excuses – I can say that

I didn't want to hurt you; that you were suffering enough; that telling you would have destroyed your memory of Sean. I can say all those things and they're all true, but I have to be brutally honest now, with you and with myself. I know I also held my tongue because of my shame. I tried to be your friend, to support you, yes because I loved you but equally to fix myself, to try to feel less of a total fraud, to ease my self-hatred. I am so sorry, Alison, for what I am about to tell you, for all the years of what you will now see as deception and false friendship. But please believe me, it was never that. I will never expect you to forgive me. All I ask is that you please try to understand and to know that my friendship and support were one hundred per cent genuine. I never intended to hurt you, but I did and I will live with the guilt and regret of that for the rest of my days.

There is no easy way of saying this, no way of softening it, so I'll just come straight out with it. Sean was Jamie's dad. The man I told you about, who already had a family of his own, it was Sean. Your Sean. I loved him, Alison – at least I thought I did and through those short months that it lasted before Jamie was conceived I tried to persuade myself that he loved me too and that somehow you and Hannah wouldn't get hurt. I woke up fairly sharply when I discovered I was pregnant. When I told him, he was out of control with rage. He loved you so much and he despised me for having put your marriage in jeopardy. I hope it will be some comfort to you to know that, after all, I was nothing to him. He never cared for me and that has been my punishment, to have that driven home so cruelly to me. It was always you. You and Hannah.

310

Remember the day *I* wheeled *Jamie* to your house shortly after he was born? *I* still loved him, *Alison*, and *I* thought that when he saw his son he would soften. *But* he never even looked at *Jamie*, just snatched *Hannah* up and left the room. *I* finally got the message loud and clear and *I* steeled myself to forget about him, to put all my energies into *Jamie*. *And I* vowed that *Sean* wasn't going to break our friendship. *I* was going to make it up to you, make everything as right as *I* could. *I* was damned if *I* was going to be broken by him.

I counted on him feeling guilty as he watched *Jamie* grow but he would pass us in the street like we were strangers. *As* time went by my resentment grew. *God, I* was so bitter! *And* that led to me making my next big mistake. *About* six weeks before *Sean* went missing *I* called him, told him that either he acknowledge *Jamie* and tell you the truth or *I* would tell you myself. *And* now you know the guilt *I* have been carrying for the last three years. *I* thought he had done it because of the pressure *I* had put him under. *I* believed *I* had taken him from you again, only this time so absolutely. *But I* should have known better. *I* should have known the real *Sean Delaney*.

I know you won't be able to stand the sight of my face after reading this but *I* want to ask you please to meet me one last time. *There* is something vital (and *I* use that word for good reason) about *Sean's* disappearance that you have to know. *I* have no real proof but *I* know *I'm* right. *I'm* not prepared to put it in a letter but it's something you need to know right now. *Please* try to put aside your anger just for an hour, that's all *I* ask. *You* need to hear this, *Alison*. *Please, I'm* begging you, just hear me out.

Kathleen.

She dropped the pages to the table, rubbed her tired eyes, checked her watch. It was 1 a.m. How many drafts had she written since Rob had finally convinced her that this was something she absolutely had to do? Rob had been lying in the back garden the previous evening when she had come back from Alison's. She had stumbled out onto the patio, near hysterical under the weight of her secrets: the scalding guilt as she had tried to console Alison, the depth of Alison's gratitude – and then meeting Joe on the way home. She had stopped to pick up milk and Joe was sitting eating an ice cream on the shop windowsill. Although the evening was warm, there was nothing unusual in seeing Joe with a hat on, that corduroy number never left the side of his head, at least until now. Her heart literally stopped as she walked up to him and saw the black knitted hat, the stitching on the tail of the dolphin motif missing. There was no mistaking that hat and she remembered so well how Alison had described it to the guards when she was detailing what Sean was wearing the night he went missing. When she'd asked Joe where he got it and he told her he'd found it on the floor of the van belonging to the man 'that stole Seany's gear', her legs had barely carried her to the car. The bastard! He *was* alive! And he had bought all his own fishing gear back, made all that pretence of sending that guy Tom from Donegal to fetch it!

Rob had pressed the brandy glass into her shaking hands, had urged her to drink, to breathe, to talk to him. She'd seen his eyes fight to check his anger as she recounted again that telephone call at Alison's, how her gut had told her it was Sean Delaney at the other end. Rob had pleaded and persuaded, convinced her that despite what Alison was going through with William, she had to be told and told now. Told everything before Sean turned up on her doorstep. Dear Rob, he had even tried to persuade her to let him go with her to Alison's right there and then. She had sobbed uncontrollably, hating herself, her guilt, knowing that the moment she had dreaded for so many years had finally arrived. She would have to tell Alison and yet she knew that she would never in a million years – not even if Sean Delaney was standing there right in front of her – be able to stand herself in front of Alison and watch her face, watch her whole body crumble as the words of her so-called 'friend' struck, stabbed and shredded her to pieces. The letter seemed her only real option, the option of a coward she despised, but she knew it would be the very most and the very best she was capable of.

She folded the pages now, slotted them into the envelope. She wasn't happy with it, knew even if she sat and rewrote it another hundred times she would never be happy with it. How could Alison, how could anyone ever understand, ever forgive what she had done? Nobody had lived in her heart then, nobody would ever know how much she had adored that man, how she would have given her very life for him.

She wiped a silent tear from her cheek, pressed her wet finger to the seal of the envelope. Although writing the letter, confessing, was the hardest and most humiliating thing she had ever had to do, it had brought her a kind of peace that she had not known since that very first night Sean Delaney had come to her bed. Nobody else might be able to see things from her point of view, to ever understand, but writing the letter she had finally allowed herself to look at who she was, who she had been then. And for the very first time she had felt a little understanding for herself, a little compassion hidden in the darkness below the shame and the guilt. Yes, what she had done was wrong. It was foolish, selfish, stupid – all those things – but she hadn't done it with any malice or ill-intent. Her crime had been falling in love with someone she shouldn't have and allowing that love to blind her to all sense and reason. Rob understood her. Rob forgave her. Maybe it was time she learned to forgive herself.

She slipped her jacket from the back of the chair, fished in the pocket for her car keys. When Alison awoke in the morning, the letter would be there in the hall, waiting for her. She took a deep breath and stepped out into the night.

* * *

Alison awoke with a start, William's arms tight around her, his body spooned to hers. The bed, the whole room was like a hothouse. Careful not to disturb his precious and hard-got sleep, she kissed his hand and, ever so gently moving his arm from around her, she slipped out of the bed and opened the window. All was so dark: so dark and quiet and still. Was that what William was heading towards – no light, no sound, just nothing? A shiver coursed her naked body and she hugged her arms about herself. She licked her lips; her mouth felt so dry. Bending to retrieve her robe from the floor, the silence was suddenly torn open by the gun-burst of gravel disturbed on the drive. A visitor, at this hour? Her mind quickly sprang back to the night of Sean's disappearance and she swallowed against the dryness in her mouth. She fought in the darkness to find the sleeve of her robe, finally forcing her arm in past the belt in her hurry from the room.

The sensor light above the front door shone on the back of Kathleen's car moving swiftly down the drive. Kathleen? She turned on the hall light and checked her watch. Almost 2 a.m. Maryanne! Oh Jesus! Kathleen had obviously been on the nightshift and…

Then her eyes fell on the fat buff envelope on the floor at her feet. Brow creased, she bent towards it, the slant of Kathleen's hand calling her name from its face.

Seventeen

There had been times when she'd had to fight to keep loving him. Fight with herself. Times she had to fight against all those feelings of having given up her life, her ambition, the promise of a career, all the other paths she could have chosen, shrinking the woman she might have become to fit his world, his moods, to fit herself into his idea of who she was, who she should be. Times, she realised now, when she'd had to deny her very self. And all that time Kathleen and him had...

Alison spooned the soup listlessly into two bowls, set them on the tray and slapped the ladle down hard on the counter top. Her eyes burned with want of sleep, with the strain of having read and re-read those words, their gentle slope cloaking the serrated blades behind them that had cut and dug and gouged her out, returning her to the fold of William's arms, opened and emptied, wordless, tearless, numb. She had rested her head on the pillows, eyes wide, as William digested each page, then silently folded the letter neatly back into its envelope, set it on the bedside locker. With only his eyes speaking, he had drawn her to him, his whole body and soul entering her so urgently, filling her with his balm. She had clung to him then, the raw, exposed depths of her greedily, hungrily gripping him as if her very sustenance depended on it.

Hours of silent, transcendent embrace had brought the dawn and sleep for William. Alison had risen then, taken the letter and, page by shredded page, had flung it in the empty fire grate and set it alight before taking the dogs and walking, numb and aimless, along the cliff top for what seemed hours. Without taking notice of her direction, she had found herself at Tra na Baid, on the edge of the cliff above that clump of rocks where Sean's boat had gone down. She could see its ghost now, heaving and dipping, hear the thump of the torn hull against the rocks. The sea was calm, sleepy, barely kissing its frothy lips to the base of the rocks. The sea had had its fill. And so had she. She slipped the wedding ring from her finger and, eyes dry, drew her hand back over her shoulder and cast the ring to the water's depths. 'It's over!' The words found their way through her tightened lips as she tossed back her head and turned for home.

She wished she hadn't burned the letter now. Wished she could read it one more time, pick out the clues that should have shown her the real Kathleen. Jesus! All the stuff she had confided in that bitch! Stuff about her and Sean: the moods, the rows, the drinking, the sex or rather the lack of it! Had they laughed about it together, laughed at her while they lay naked in Kathleen's bed?

'Alison?' William moved slowly towards her, his arms stealing around her shoulders.

'Oh, William, you shouldn't be...' She hadn't realised she was crying until the wetness of her cheek touched his. 'I was just going to take this down to...'

317

'Hush, sweetheart, I'm fine.' His voice was so soft in her ear, so beautiful. She closed her eyes, let the dam inside her finally crumble. William's hand found her hair, kneaded the back of her head, her thin frame shaking against him, every vibration reverberating through the very root of his heart. How could he leave her now, like this? Now, when every last bit of comfort and companionship had been stripped from her. How could he add his leaving her to all that? He couldn't. His fear and desperation, his wretchedness and unbounded love swelled in his chest, spilled up into his throat. Whatever it took he would muster every last bit of strength in himself, every last ounce of diminishing life, and he would fill her with it, fill her and carry her those last few steps to herself, to that place that she had all but reached. His eyes closed with his deep in-breath, his arms folding tighter around her. Alison had it in her to do it. He knew she had. And he would help her to know it too.

'Let's sit.' He pulled away gently from her, led her by the hand to the table. The sun through the patio door made a halo of her red hair, emphasising the pallor of her small face. And those eyes – the deep devastation haunting them when they met his, he felt his heart physically tighten, strain, crack.

'Talk to me, Ali.' His hands found hers across the table, his thumb instinctively seeking out and soothing the exposed, indented skin on her ring finger. Her eyes, pooled with tears, searched his.

'Why?' The whisper trembled on her lips and she bit them back.

* * *

'Look, if she hasn't made contact in the next few days, then I'll go and talk to her.' Standing behind her chair, Rob bent towards her, squeezed her shoulders and Kathleen allowed her head to rise, fall back upon the cushion of his chest.

'It's already been over a week.' Her eyes burned under their heavy lids. 'She won't come, Rob. I knew she wouldn't.' Her sigh rose from her hollowed-out depths. 'And who could blame her?'

'She'll need time, Kath, you know that. Time, and lots of it. It's a lot to take in, and especially in the state she'll be in with William. But she has to be told about Sean. And now, before he—'

'I know.' Her hand reached for his. How could he still love her? How could they start out their new life together like this? She knew it had all been too good to be true. What man would want to wait around through all this, through what was supposed to be the happiest time of his life, torn apart and flung in pieces around him? Had she not paid the price of her sin with the last eight years? Was she expected to go on paying forever? Had she not done her best to make up to Alison, to Hannah? Was her crime bigger than her, than her life? Had she become it?

'Rob?'

'Hmm?'

'Thank you.'

'For what?'

'For still loving me.'

He moved from behind her chair, took both her hands and, raising her up towards him, folded her close in his arms. 'How could I not love you, Kath? The sweetest, kindest, most loveable creature that ever walked into my life.' His hand stole down her back, rested on the cheek of

319

her bottom. 'Oh, and the sexiest too, did I mention that?' He could almost hear her smile, feel it entering him. God, how he wished he could put an end to all this for her. He held her tighter. 'You're my girl, Kath, and I will always love you, never doubt that.'

* * *

'Will, are you sure you don't want to head back?' They sat at the very end of the pier, William in his wheelchair, Alison on the bollard beside him. She'd noticed how he'd begun to shift in his seat, the shake in his hand as he secured the rug around his hip. And that sea breeze had gotten cooler as the evening wore on.

'I'm good, Ali. Just to feel that breeze, taste the salt on my lips, it's wonderful.' He had tightened the rug around his lower body to cover the tremor in his left leg and hip. He knew it wasn't wise to sit with his weight on it for so long, but Alison needed this. She needed out of that house, she needed space, air, room to think.

'Will?'

'Yes?' Her gaze was lost somewhere, out over the ocean, the breeze dancing her loose curls around the exposed arch of her neck.

'Why don't I hate Sean for this? Why is it Kathleen? I mean ... I mean, he was in it as much as her and ... ' Her words trailed away as she turned to face him.

'Is it because Kathleen is here, flesh and blood, easier maybe to direct your anger at?'

'Maybe, yeah, but I think it's something more.'

'Yeah?'

'I don't love him, William.' She turned her whole body to face him now. 'I don't care.' She took a deep breath. 'This summer. You. I never knew what real love was, Will. You showed me. You showed me what it means to be yourself. To have the space and permission to be yourself. Truly yourself. And to be loved for being that very person. I never had that with him. I thought loving someone was pleasing them, almost living for them. It's not, is it?'

William shook his head, his eyes and his silence encouraging her to go on.

'All the years I wasted, hiding in my grief – and the years before that too, hiding behind him. And now Kathleen, her letter. Oh William, what I've done to Hannah – to myself. And all for nothing!' She could feel the white of her anger begin to froth and bubble again. 'I should have left this place, I should have listened to Claire and Hannah. I should have left the whole damn lot of them. Why didn't I see? What kind of a deluded fool had I become? What kind of a moron who couldn't see that her husband had long ago left her – long before he died! Jesus, all the years I've wasted on him, all the tears and the torture, and for what? All for a lie!' She bent her head, squeezed the bridge of her nose between her forefinger and thumb. If this headache lasted much longer, her head would split open.

'It was real, Alison. All of it. Your hurt, all the heartache…'

'Real?' Her head shot up, her green eyes ablaze. 'I'll tell you what was real! I lay in bed at night waiting for him to come home. Searching inside myself for some way to reach him, to help him feel my love. I lay awake wondering if there was something wrong with me, whether I was enough.' She pushed herself up and marched to the edge of the pier, turned again to face him. 'And all that time he was in another bed. Fucking my best friend! That's what's real, William, whether I like it or not.' Her hands rested on her hips as she marched back towards him. 'Well, I'm done with the childish notion of Sean Delaney the loving husband, the childhood sweetheart, the lost love. He was nothing but a selfish, cheating coward and the bastard can rot in hell!' A laugh erupted from her then, causing her to bend in two as she reached his chair. 'I don't care any more, William. I'm free.' She threw back her head and shouted the words to the cliffs. 'I'm free!'

William's silent tears trembled under the kiss of the breeze.

* * *

Alison angled the rear-view mirror, pressed the cold pad of a thumb beneath each eye. Despite the concealer, the brush of blusher on her cheeks, she still looked exhausted, worn out. She checked her watch: 4.50 p.m. Closing her eyes, she leaned her head back on the headrest. Another ten minutes before she was due to meet Kathleen in the bar. She would rest her eyes. She was damned if she was going to let Kathleen see the agony she had put her through.

She had chosen the popular bar-cafe in town as a meeting place, knowing that it would be busy with the after-work crowd, that she would contain her anger rather than risk making a public scene. It was William who had insisted that she do this. If it had been her choice, she would have never again as much as looked at the side of the road that Kathleen Collins walked on! In the turmoil of the past week she had forgotten that part of the letter – another reason

322

why she shouldn't have been so hasty to burn it. She wished she could have read it again before meeting Kathleen now, read it and known exactly what she'd said, been more prepared. William remembered that it had referred to some information around Sean's disappearance that Kathleen wanted her to know. Now, three years later? Well, if she'd had information like that for over three years and kept it to herself, there was no forgiving her. However bad the affair was, to be that cruel as to hold something 'vital' – William was sure that was the word she had used – that would be the cruellest and most unforgiveable act imaginable. But what could it be? What could she possibly know that no one else did? It wasn't that she was intimate with Sean at the time; if anything, going by her letter, they were enemies. So he couldn't have confided anything in her, could he? Well, she'd know soon enough, she thought, opening her eyes and shaking the tiredness from her head. Her hand searched in her bag for the little pump bottle of Rescue Remedy. She opened her mouth, shot three quick bursts onto her tongue. She checked her watch again: 5 p.m. 'Okay, let's do this,' she instructed herself. She took a deep breath, pulled back her shoulders and stepped down from the jeep.

Out of nowhere a lump the size of an apple lodged in Kathleen's throat as her eyes caught Alison slip through the main door. She clasped her hands tightly under the table, her palms hot and clammy. Her tongue sought the groove in her lip. Oh Jesus! Should she smile, wave, do nothing? Alison caught her eye then, held it as she moved slowly, haughtily, across the short distance of floor towards the corner table. She looked taller than usual somehow, almost threateningly so, Kathleen thought, swallowing against the lump.

'Oh Alison, thank you for—'

'I'm not interested in any small talk.' The scrape of the chair on the tiled floor as she pulled it out to sit echoed the sharpness in her voice. She was glad to sit, for a moment she thought her legs were going to give from under her. 'Or apologies or explanations.' Her confidence rose with her anger, as she looked Kathleen square in the eye. Eyes that were circled with lack of sleep. *Well, good enough for her*, Alison remarked, her eyes moving to Kathleen's mouth, the way it twitched under her gaze, and all Alison could see was that mouth pressed to Sean's, those eyes locked on his. Her stomach twisted and she swallowed against it, took a deep breath through her nose, imagined it fanning her anger. 'You said you had something to tell me about *his* disappearance. What is it?'

* * *

William couldn't rest. He rose from his bed and made his way to the kitchen, sat at Alison's desk in the window. She'd only been gone little under an hour. Fifteen minutes to drive into town, fifteen back – the fact that she hadn't arrived back meant they must be talking and that could only be a good thing. His smile was sad as he remembered her face as she left, the lengths she had gone to to hide her nervousness from him, to be brave. He knew it was the last thing in the world she had wanted to do, and convincing her had been no easy task, but that part of Kathleen's letter had stuck in his head. Kathleen had said that what she had to tell Alison was something much bigger than the affair, something 'vital' about Sean's disappearance. Maybe this something was the last thing Alison needed to hear to finally and truly release her from the past, to allow her to cut the ties and move on, really move on. Sure, she had said that she felt 'free', that she didn't care any more, but he knew that part of that was just her own self-protection, her own way of coping with Sean's betrayal. Still, after her initial almost total collapse when the letter arrived, her strength over the past few days had really surprised him. But then, maybe it shouldn't have. Look at how she had coped with the news of his cancer and how close the end was for him. Look at how she bucked against the hospital, him, everyone, to take him back home and care for him.

The tears came again now, soft at first and then gathering their strength till his whole body shook with their force. In all his life he had never known such kindness, such love. How could he ever leave her? He rose and walked to the window, leaned his tired body against the frame. He hoped that herself and Kathleen could somehow work things out, in time. Something inside him told him they would find a way. Alison hadn't mentioned the fact that Hannah and Jamie were sister and brother and he hadn't wanted to broach the subject, had wanted it to come from her. It was the one positive that had come out of this situation and maybe, hopefully, it was the one thing that would in some way unite Alison and Kathleen again.

Maybe what Kathleen had told her had upset her, he thought now. Maybe she had gone off somewhere to be on her own, to digest it. Hoping, needing to know that she was all right, he felt his whole body straining to hear the sound of her car on the gravel outside.

* * *

'Alive?' Alison shook her head slowly, her incredulity pulling her lips into a wide smile. Kathleen had had to repeat the word three times before it seemed that Alison had finally heard and understood it.

'Like I said in the letter, I don't have any real … any concrete … it's not that I've seen him or anything, but Joe O'Sulliv—'

'Ah yes!' Alison mocked, leaning back in her chair and folding her arms across her chest. 'Joe. Sure. Now, why didn't I think to listen to Joe's good advice these past three years? What was I thinking?' She leaned forward again now, her eyes narrowed with menace. 'What *is* your problem, Kathleen? Don't you think you've caused enough damage already?'

'Alison, please! He called your house – when you were in Dublin, he rang— '

'Sean. Telephoned my house? And you know for sure it was him? What, did he announce himself?' Sarcasm sharpened her words.

'Well of course not, no, but— '

'Christ, Kathleen, listen to yourself. What the hell kind of game is this? Is it some pathetic way of trying to wheedle yourself back into my life because if it is I can tell you now there's not a hope in hell of me ever— '

'I *know* it was him!' Kathleen raised her voice, not caring now who was listening, watching. 'I'd know that voice anywhere.'

Alison looked away, couldn't bear the sight of Kathleen's pleading face, that pathetic way she had of leaning her whole self into you, giving herself to you – was it any wonder Sean had succumbed?

'Then why didn't you say something at the time? Why

now? If you were so bloody sure, why wait?' She gazed out the window as she spoke.

'I wasn't, I mean I didn't...I wasn't certain.'

'Exactly. And now, when you've caused all this shit, when you've ripped apart every last shred of memory I had of him ... ' She turned her head now, her eyes, their pain, piercing Kathleen's. 'Why are you doing this, Kathleen? What is wrong with you? Guilt got the better of you?' She snatched her bag from the floor, rose to stand. 'Rob – if he's still around – needs to get you some help.'

'Oh Alison, please listen.' Kathleen, no longer able to check her tears, rose with her, her hand reaching out to cover Alison's across the table. 'He's out there. I know. Joe knows.'

The look in Alison's eyes could have burned straight through stone as she snatched her hand from beneath Kathleen's. 'I'm done listening to your vicious nonsense. I don't know what kind of a monster you've turned into, but stay the fuck out of my life – and Hannah's.'

'Joe's got the cap he was wearing that night!' Kathleen flung the words after her before sinking back into her seat and watching the door swing closed behind Alison's poker-straight back.

At the rear of the car park Rob watched from his Volvo as Alison bent in two behind her jeep and, holding back her hair, emptied her stomach onto the grass margin.

* * *

A soft rain had begun to fall as Alison made her way blindly along the headland path at Tra na Leon. 'Joe's got the cap he was wearing that night...' Kathleen's words echoed like a dark mantra in time with her step. The image of Kathleen's mouth, her lips forming the words 'Sean is alive' seared into her head like a brand. The lips that Sean had kissed while her own had burned with his absence. She slipped off her shoes, sat on the wet grass and swung her legs out over the outcrop. The cove below was hushed, almost meditative. The rocks and the cliff face were draped with a thick, white mist: the furniture of some great god under dust sheets. Smoke and mirrors, Alison thought, her eyes fighting to penetrate the mist. Her whole life, her entire meaning, it seemed, had been based on the quicksand of illusion. Other people's truth, or lack of it. Did that mean it hadn't really existed at all? That she hadn't really existed, that her life had been a lie? William hadn't stopped reminding her over the last few days that what she had felt, had experienced, had been real, that no one could ever take that away from her. Well, wait till he heard about this.

But she understood what he meant. She knew he was right, in a way. Her truth was her truth. She had loved, she had lost and she had suffered the heartache. Maybe now she knew that she hadn't really loved, at least not in the way she believed then that she had – neither had she lost in the way she had believed, but the end result had been the same. She was real. Her feelings were real. Hannah was real. She'd hardly had time to consider her daughter in the turmoil of the last few days, and she would have to be told. Hannah and Jamie were flesh and blood, brother and sister. Hannah already doted on him, but how was the poor girl going to cope with this, with her dad...

Jamie's face rose before her now, that beautiful wide smile that lit up his eyes. The exact replica of another smile she had known and loved so well. How had she been so blind? How had she never seen it before?

And then Joe O'Sullivan barged in on her thoughts. Him relentlessly turning up at the house, mending pots, sorting nets, his persistence, his utter insistence that 'Seany' would be coming back, then his resentment of William, the way he followed them around, watching. Were those just the ravings of a simpleton, the coping mechanism of a mind too naive to comprehend the absolute finality of death? But she herself had used the same tack, tricking her own mind in the long months she had searched coves and beaches when all rational thought advised that there was no hope of finding him alive. She had kept on hoping too, kept on believing.

Alive. It just couldn't be possible. And yet when Kathleen had spoken those words it was as if something had clicked into place inside her. Some other truth, that same deep truth that had driven her relentless search when the whole village had labelled her crazy. Something inside her had always been convinced of another truth – a truth she had had to fight so long and so hard to silence.

And then out of nowhere, the memory exploded like a rocket inside her head. Tom O'Donnell, the child in his arms in her kitchen. The little finger pointing excitedly to the photos on the wall: 'Uncle Sean!' The way Tom had made for the door, insisting the child was confusing the image with another Sean, a relation, the way he sang out over the child's words. A coldness gripped her, seeming to come from the inside. She hugged her arms about her shivering shoulders, eyes locked on the shroud of mist lifting from the cliffs, the rain driving in harder now from the mountains.

* * *

'Alison?' It was Rob who answered the frantic knocking at the front door. Rob who had slipped his arm silently from around Kathleen's shoulder in the bed, anxious not to wake her when sleep had been – when it had eventually come – such a welcome break and comfort for her.

'Kathleen. I need to speak to her.'

'Alison, you're soaked through, come in.' He held the door wide. Her hair, dark with the night's rain, clung to her head, emphasising the sickly pallor of her face, its only colour the red around her swollen eyes, lending her an almost ghostly appearance.

'No, I'll wait here.' Her light summer dress clung to her shaking body like a second skin. Her feet were bare.

'Kathleen's in bed, Alison, she's sleeping, she's been terribly...'

'Rob, it's okay.' Kathleen descended the stairs behind him.

'On the phone – what did he say? On the phone that night?' Alison stepped through the door towards her.

* * *

Cursing through clenched teeth, Sean staggered from the corner pub, crossed Portobello Bridge and headed left down along the canal. Minding his own business, he had drunk alone at the bar all night. The whiskey hadn't lifted his depression; if anything, it had deepened it, the buzz and chatter in the pub around him only serving to reinforce the isolation and loneliness that had driven him from his room on Rathfarnham Road.

Why was it him that had been thrown out and barred? That cocky young fucker had been asking for it all night. Sean had seen him, staring, whispering to his friends, throwing that big thick head of his back, each laugh getting louder, egging Sean on. But he hadn't risen to the bait. He'd held steady. Until he felt the fucker's pint drench his T-shirt. 'Terribly sorry.' It was the way he'd raised his eyebrows when he said it, that mocking half-smirk on his face. *Well, he wouldn't be laughing now, not through that burst lip!*

He rubbed a hand across his swollen knuckles. *Damn*, he cursed, weaving his way towards the canal bench. The last thing he wanted was to draw attention to himself. And now he'd gone and lost the sanctuary of that pub in the evenings, too. Elbows on his knees, he bent forward, his head hanging between his legs. He flexed the fingers of his throbbing hand, shook it as if to shake out the pain.

He knew he'd crack up if he had to spend one more night cooped up in the room – and not a hint or a sign of Alison. He felt the hot bile of impatience rise up through his middle. Resting his back against the bench now, he reached into his pocket for his cigarettes and a flame of hot pain shot from his hand right up to his elbow. He closed his eyes, cursing his own stupidity as he remembered his quick exit from Scotland after a similar but much uglier brawl. *Maybe tonight was a sign. Maybe there was no point in hanging around here much longer either. Fuck it!* He'd spent long enough considering other people and their feelings; it was time to stand up and be counted, time to claim back what was rightfully his. No more of this waiting around, he would find out once and for all if Alison was still in Dublin. And if she wasn't, if she had already returned to Waterford like he suspected, then it was back to Donegal for him. Tom owed him. All that good fishing gear he'd got – for nothing! Plus, he already knew Alison and she seemed to get on well enough with him. He'd get Tom to go back down to Carniskey, break the news to Alison and set his going back home to her in motion. Why hadn't he thought of it sooner? He raised himself up slowly on unsteady legs, took a few minutes to reorient himself, then started out in the direction of Alison's aunt's house.

* * *

When Rob dropped Alison home, William, by then out of his mind with worry, had insisted she have a hot shower and a brandy. She did as he bid, but not before she had frantically searched out the telephone number of Tom O'Donnell in Killybegs. The call had been answered by whom she presumed to be Tom's wife Ella and, Tom not being home, Alison had pressed the woman as to whether they had a friend or knew of the whereabouts of a Sean Delaney from the south-east. 'Certainly not,' had come the curt reply before the call was abruptly ended.

She lay now, the soft warmth of her curled into William's arms. 'How can someone do that, Will? Just walk out of their own life, just walk away from everything, from everyone?'

She had been silent for so long now he had thought that she was sleeping. His hand stroked her still-damp hair. What could he tell her? What comfort could he offer? 'Who can say.' His voice was low, laboured. 'Which of us ever truly knows what's in another person's head, their heart.'

'But wouldn't it have to be the cruellest mind, the most selfish heart? To do that to people who love you. To just walk away, leave all that devastation.'

'Maybe they think they're not being cruel.' He could only

offer his own thoughts. 'Maybe it's the complete opposite...'
He broke for a moment, recovered the rhythm of his breathing.
'They might think that what they're doing is an act of kind-
ness...best for everyone.'

'Like suicide?'

'Yeah,' he paused, 'like suicide.'

He silently cursed his tongue, its distorted and leaden
feel in his mouth, how his brain had to chase words that
circled like butterflies in his head. 'It's a dangerous place,
the mind...when you sink so low, in your own estimation.'

She was quiet then for a moment, remembering those
times, back in the early raw stages of her grief, when she had
considered ending it all, thinking that Hannah, Maryanne,
everyone would be better off in a world without her. Hope
had kept her going then. Hope that she would one day find
him. Hope that somehow he would return and all would be
right again. A cold fist tightened around her heart. What if
he did return, now? What if all those years of praying and
hoping and longing were to be finally answered? She moved
closer to William.

'Do you really believe – I mean, Joe and the cap and
everything?' It was the detail of the cap's motif that had
almost convinced her. Almost. But then Joe was clever.
Cleverer than most. So his mind might not have developed in the way that was considered 'normal', but Joe had
developed other skills, other kinds of knowing and coping
that were foreign to most. He had the greatest knack of
creating his own reality despite the world's protestations
that things were not so. Joe was a true survivor and he
held fast to what mattered to him, to his own truth, no
matter what was flung in his path. We could all learn a lot
from Joe, she thought, picturing him helping himself to

the cap from Tom's van, patiently picking out the stitching from the dolphin's tail until it resembled exactly the one he remembered so fondly.

'How would you…feel if it was…if he was…'

'Angry, mostly. And a bit sad.' She turned her face up to look into his. 'I know I would never even want to begin to understand him, never mind thinking of forgiveness.' Her smile was slow, sad. 'It's over, me and him. Whatever that was, whatever we had. It's in the past.' They fell into silence again, each wrestling with their own thoughts.

'Maybe – if it is true – maybe he'll have changed.' He felt selfish, provoking her, teasing her out, but he had to know. Had to know before he went that she was strong enough, that this wasn't going to defeat her.

'It wouldn't matter. He just doesn't matter. I've changed too, William, and I'm never going back to the person I was then. Never. I'm no longer Alison Delaney.' Rising up on her elbow, she kissed him softly on the lips, her naked breast brushing his chest, sending a tongue of fire coursing through him.

'Thank you.' She kissed him again.

'For what?'

'For showing me myself. Opening me to myself, my strength, the woman I'd denied for so long.'

'Don't thank me, you did that yourself.'

'I could never have done it without your guidance, without your love.' She closed her lids to stop her tears from falling. 'I'll miss you, William. I'll miss your love, so much.'

He pressed her head to his chest, held her to him with every last ounce of strength left to him. 'You'll be fine. You're a survivor…Poised…ready to take on the world.' He could feel his heart almost physically tear open, every fibre of him wishing, wanting to stay, just even for a few more short months, to watch her, to witness her bloom.

* * *

Sean rested his elbow on the window ledge at the back of the bus, shaded his eyes with his still swollen and blackened hand. His head throbbed from the want of sleep.

He had hardly rested at all in the past week, had taken to walking, tormented, through the streets, the face of Alison's old aunt constantly before him: the terror in her widened eyes, in the tight clench of her mouth as she watched him from the upstairs window, the phone pressed to her ear, her hand shaking. He had never meant to frighten or harm anyone, never meant to kick in that door, but neither the aunt nor Alison had answered, though he'd rung the doorbell what seemed like a hundred times. And tried the windows. He'd barely had time to scale the back garden wall before the squad car pulled into the drive. Stupid fools announcing themselves with that siren! Still, Jesus, if they'd caught him! He'd been a fool to stay on for the rest of the week. It was only his imagination he knew now, only stupid wishful thinking that had persuaded him he'd caught a glimpse of Alison through the window of a bus heading for town last Tuesday. The stupid ramblings of a tormented fool! He'd let some senseless notion of being near her run away with him, sitting like a dumb statue behind that window, wasting time. Much as he'd been tempted he hadn't gone near the aunt's house again for fear of the guards keeping watch. He palmed his cap, pulled it down lower on his forehead. He had been lucky, he knew, but that kind of luck didn't last forever. He closed his eyes and, as they had all the past week, his own mother's eyes returned to haunt him now, widened with that same fear, that same disbelief that he'd seen Alison's aunt.

His mind shot back to February, to his frenzied newspaper searches for reports on the attack in Waterford. It had got enough column inches for him to be satisfied that his mother was still alive, was relatively unharmed. But the reporters had got it all wrong. It hadn't been an attack. He had never intended to harm her. He had known where she kept the money, had known she had no use for it. He had known it would be enough to buy him that fake passport, a ticket to a new life, a new identity; enough to end the anonymous half-life he had endured since leaving Carniskey; to put down roots, to start again. In that split second when he had turned his head and their eyes had met he knew beyond doubt that his mother had recognised him and that look on her face, her anguished wail that had filled the whole room, had haunted him day and night ever since. He slammed his head back against the headrest now, jerked his mind back to the present. What was done was done, he told himself. There was no changing the past. There was only now. Now and the future. He had control over that and he would use it. He would use it and put things right again, with his mother, with Alison.

His sigh was long, laced with darkness. When Tom had shown him that paper with Alison's ad, it was as if the gods had intervened and granted him a second chance. He would buy the gear from Alison with the money he had taken and put the guilt of his mother, of everything he had done in the past, behind him. He would be free to start again. But Tom had changed all that when he'd come back from Carniskey, with his talk of the place, of Alison, of how she had searched for him, mourned him. He had never thought of returning to Carniskey, had never even considered it a possibility. But, listening to Tom, he had felt the years burn away, felt like he was back in those teenage days when she would leave at the end of the summer and the whole place would scream with her absence. All the guilt and the loss and the longing that he had kept buried for three whole years erupted inside him. That was when he knew that there was no starting again. Carniskey was his home and back there, with Alison, was the only place he would ever belong.

The bus trundled along the quay. He stared out the window, his thoughts wandering back to the first night he had gone to Kathleen's bed. He had convinced himself that it was a one-off drunken mistake to be cast to the back of his mind. But it wasn't that simple. Nothing was ever that simple. Kathleen asked no questions, expected nothing for herself. He could come and go as he pleased, unannounced, no explanations. He had found a place where he could unleash the darkness, the anger and frustration inside him – the parts that he fought to keep hidden from Alison and Hannah. Soon he had sought Kathleen like a drug. His long hours on the sea had provided a perfect excuse and Alison never questioned where he had been so late and so often. Self-loathing swelled in his throat as he pictured her face that last evening as he drove away: her hurt, her frustration, how near she was to breaking. He knew then that he had lost her. Knew that once Kathleen opened her mouth there would be no going back. And that had decided him. He would rather be gone, absolutely, than spend the rest of his days near her, wanting her, knowing that it was his own selfishness and stupidity that had driven her from him.

He whistled a sigh through his tight lips, his fingers

massaging the knuckles of his right hand. Three years now and Katheen hadn't talked. And Alison, Alison was still waiting. Tom would help him, he knew he would – hadn't he offered as much that night when he'd shown him the ad? The best plan was for Tom to go to Carniskey on his behalf, talk to Kathleen first and make some kind of arrangement about the boy – the money was there, waiting – and in return Kathleen would promise to keep their past a secret. Tom could then go to Alison, prepare her, lessen the shock and make Sean's return all the easier for everyone. A half-smile pulled at his lips as he closed his eyes, settled back into his seat. The bus swung onto the main Galway road.

Eighteen

Tom did a double-take as he sat at the bar at Richie's to order his drink. Where in the name of God had he sprung from? Sean Delaney sat at a small table in the corner, his head, as usual, bent over his drink. Tom pretended not to see him and turned his head in towards the bar to collect his thoughts. It was weeks now since Sean had done his disappearing act and Tom hadn't been sorry to see the back of him. He had intended giving Alison a ring when he'd heard Sean had left by bus, but he'd mulled it over and decided against it. If Sean had gone down to Alison, there was little he could do about it. And anyway, if that was the case, Tom was probably the last person she would want to hear from. Imagine what she would think of him, knowing all that time that Sean was alive and not telling her? She'd think one of them was as bad as the other. And maybe she'd be right. No, he had decided to let it lie. Sean was gone and it was no longer any of his affair.

But now here he was again and Tom could sense trouble all around him. He watched him in the mirror behind the bar. His face when he lifted it was thundered with thought.

Tom picked up his whiskey glass and drained it in one gulp before nodding to the barman for a refill.

'How long's he been in?' he asked the bartender.

'Came in just after five, been at it heavy since.'

'For four hours? Should ye still be servin' him?'

'Not my call, Tom.' The barman nodded sideways towards the owner, who sat playing cards with a few of the regulars.

Keeping one eye on the mirror, Tom finished his drink. He tried to ignore the anger that welled up in him every time he caught a glimpse of Sean's sullen face. He no longer felt sorry for him – at least not in the way he had when Sean had first told him his story. Tom understood more about it now. And he had heard Alison's side. What the hell was he doing back here? What if little Daniel saw him? He didn't want the child hurt all over again. He noticed the bruising on Sean's right hand when he raised the glass to his lips. He sighed. No doubt he had left some other heartache behind him, wherever he'd been.

Sean lifted his head, fixed his eyes on the back of Tom's head. So, that was the way it was to be now, Sean brooded, drink and exhaustion weighing his head. He had seen Tom come in. Seen him look away and pretend not to notice him. I could have had a good friend there, he thought, if I'd kept my mouth shut. He had never before spoken to anyone about Alison. Or about the Sean Delaney that had left Carniskey. *And that's the way I should have kept it*, he cursed into his drink. But there had been something about Tom that had drawn him out. He felt he could trust him with his secret. And look where it had gotten him! Now that he knew the shadows in him, Tom wouldn't even look his way. He should have known the man would grow to despise him, just as he despised himself. Anyone in his life that

340

he had ever gotten close to he had destroyed: Alison and Hannah; his own mother; Kathleen and the child; poor old Joe O'Sullivan; Tom and the young lad, Daniel.

He pushed the empty glass away from him. It had been a wrong move, coming back to Killybegs. He should have known he'd no longer be welcome here. Tom had had his fill of him and he couldn't blame him. He caught up his knapsack and swayed towards the door. Tom studied his every move in the mirror. Their eyes met in the glass and when Tom looked away Sean turned to leave. Keeping his eye on his retreating back, Tom saw the moment that he changed his mind and stopped, hand on the door, before turning to stagger back towards the bar.

'Tom,' he dropped his knapsack to the floor, threw his arm around Tom's shoulder. 'I ju-just came back to say th-th-thanks – you were good to me once.'

'Don't mention it, Sean.' Tom sipped his drink, avoided meeting his eye.

'I will mention it! A good friend is hard to find, am I right?'

'Ye are indeed.' Tom coughed into his fist. Heads were turning to look in their direction.

'How's the lad? Di-did he get my letter?'

'He's good, Sean, aye, he did.' Tom finished his drink and made to stand. 'Well, I'm for home. Good luck, Sean.'

'You'll let me buy ya a drink for Christ sake!'

'Thanks all the same.' Tom nodded his goodnight to the barman and stepped out through the door, pulling it shut behind him. He sighed his relief into the cool air. There was a darkness, a malevolent energy around Sean that made him shiver.

'No time for Se-Sean Delaney now, big man!'

Tom turned to face him, his anger rising. 'Look, Sean, I've done what I can for ye. It's time ye moved on – there's nothin' around here for ye now.'

'There's nothin' anywhere for me! Why's that, Tom, huh? Why's that?'

Tom took a deep breath, turned to walk away.

'I tried to find her…Alison. They told me sh-she was up in Dublin.'

'Who told ye?' Jaw set, Tom turned, retraced his steps.

'I rang the house.'

'Ye did what?' He caught him by the collar, half-lifting him off the ground. 'Didn't I tell ye to leave her alone?' he whispered through clenched teeth. 'She's happy. Happy without ye!'

'Sh-sh-she's not happy! What would you know about her?' Sean sneered. 'She's waitin' for me.'

'Not any more, sonny!' Tom loosened his grip on Sean's collar, pushed him away. 'She's with someone else. I saw them. Ye're in the past. Ye're forgotten. As far as she's concerned, ye're a dead man.'

'Someone else?' Sean's anger had softened to a whisper of disbelief.

'Yes. Someone else.' A part of Tom pitied the hurt and incredulity on Sean's face. 'I didn't want to tell ye before … it's probably for the best.'

'For the best, is it? And what the fuck would you know about it?' He spat on the ground at Tom's feet and shuffled away in the direction of the pier.

Sean threw his knapsack down against the storm wall and sat with it cushioned against his lower back. He lit a cigarette. Someone else? Never. Not Alison. He threw his head back, his eyes, his whole face, tightening as he remembered the night he had rang the house and some fellow had answered the phone. A hot jealousy surged inside him. Someone else. In my bed? In my house – with my wife! He leapt to his feet and kicked the knapsack again and again in quicker and harder succession. The money he'd sent for his gear – Tom's gear now – she'd be spending it on him! His mother's savings, his own father's death money – on him! On her fancy man? He paced unsteadily to the edge of the pier and back again, back and forth till he'd walked some of the whiskey from his head and planned his next move.

* * *

Tom turned again onto his left side, cursed under his breath as he pushed the bedclothes down from his shoulders. He'd thought he was done with sleepless nights. He half-heard a shuffle at the kitchen door but was so caught up in his thoughts that he didn't respond until he heard the car engine spit to life below the window. By the time he had jumped from the bed it had screeched its reverse and he watched from the bedroom window as it disappeared at speed down the hill and into the night.

He ran down the stairs in his bare feet and switched on the kitchen light. Sean Delaney's knapsack lay thrown inside the open back door. He closed the door and sat at the table, his fingers pulling at his chin. The lad was full of drink. And temper. He'd never manage a car. Let him off, was Tom's first thought. Let him kill himself. It would be no one's responsibility but his own. How had Sean turned from the quiet, withdrawn lad that had first come to stay with them into that dark, hate-fuelled man he'd encountered tonight? A heavy guilt pressed down on his chest. If only he had left him alone and not drawn him out. If he hadn't shown him the ad, hadn't helped to bring Alison alive in his mind and his heart again, it would probably never have come to this. There was no denying his culpability, his downright stupidity. He should ring the guards. It was his responsibility. What if Sean hit someone else, some other poor innocent on the road? Could he live with the guilt of that?

He rose from the table, took the phone in his hand. If the guards caught Sean, then the whole story would come out. And Alison would have to be told. He paced the kitchen, looked up at the clock. Almost midnight. Maybe he should give it another fifteen minutes, give Sean a chance to change his mind, to come back. But a lot could happen in fifteen minutes. He lifted the phone and dialled the Garda station.

* * *

Sean raced along the narrow, winding road, the feel of the wheel in his hands and the power of the engine's roar fuelling him on. Four hours, five at tops, should do it. He'd leave the car down behind the caravan park and make his way up through the fields to the house. No one would see him, there'd be no one about at that hour. He still had his key to the back door. Alison would be sleeping. *Sleeping with him in your bed*. The thought fanned the fire raging inside him. He pressed the accelerator harder to the floor. He imagined her face when he stood by the bed and called her name. At first she would think she was dreaming. But then he'd call louder, stretch out his hand and touch her face. Then she'd know. Then there'd be no doubting! He sneered at the thought of the shock on her face, of the fear in the eyes of the other bastard lying beside her. Who did she think she was – the child shipped off to England so she could play the merry widow? Her and her fancy man living it up on the money that *he* had slaved for! Oh, he'd soon put an end to her dance! He threw his head back, his triumphant laugh drowning out the radio.

The sharp bend rushed at him through the darkness. He jerked the wheel, the blood draining from his face and legs, his heart bursting against his chest as the car spun across to the opposite ditch and then righted itself before ploughing head-on into the high stone wall.

The twig-snap of his neck was lost in the thunder of the engine's combustion. Orange flames licked and leaped like hungry savages, engulfing the car and lighting the darkness, the rabbits in the adjoining field darting to the black safety of their burrows.

* * *

Joe O'Sullivan screamed out in his sleep. His elderly mother rushed to his room, where she held and comforted him through the night, his deep sobs racking his body.

Alison woke with a start, her eyes wide, heart pounding, her body turning, arms stretching out, searching for him. The light of the moon through the uncurtained window bathed his peaceful face. Relief then as her fingers found his warm arm, stroked its downy hair, her lips bending in benediction to his eyes, his cheeks, his lips, her whole being desperately longing to fill him up, to course her life-force, her determination, her strength, the force and the fierceness of her love right through him.

* * *

Tom stowed the knapsack in the cabin of his boat, secured the lock and set about sorting the nets for mending. Ella would be along soon with the young lad. He'd wait until Daniel was gone back home for tea before heading out to dump the bag in the ocean. Two guards had called to the house before daylight. They'd found the car, burned out, forty miles south. The driver's remains, propelled on impact onto the mangled bonnet, were charred beyond recognition but still – though it would be no easy task – they reckoned that the dental remains and a belt buckle that must have come loose before the 'sole occupant' was thrown through the windscreen would give forensics something to go on. Meanwhile a search and enquiry would be conducted in the surrounding area to establish if anyone was missing, if anyone had noticed anyone acting suspiciously around the area in the past few days.

'I'm sorry I can't tell ye more. If I think of anything ...' Tom couldn't wait till the two young officers left the house. He knew Ella had seen the knapsack under the stairs, knew she had been about to confront him just as the guards had knocked on the door.

'You've been a great help, Tom, we'll keep you informed.'

'You'd better move that bag before Daniel gets up.' The guards gone, Ella had continued cooking the breakfast without once meeting his eyes. Her words rushed at him. 'A woman phoned last night, asking if he was here. I told her nothing, Tom, because I knew nothing.'

346

'I wasn't…' When Tom opened his mouth to speak, she turned towards him, raised her hand. 'No, I want you to listen to me now. I've stayed quiet on this long enough but no more. No more.' She turned her attention back to the grill, her voice clear and firm over her shoulder. 'After that awful night when Daniel went missing I never wanted to see that man again. God rest him now, but I never wanted to see him or hear a word from him again. But whatever he told you, it … it changed you, Tom. It changed us – didn't you see that? Didn't you care? Did you never for one second stop to consider what it was like for me, watching you go into yourself, pretending to be asleep beside you while you tossed and turned in the bed all night? And never one word of explanation. Did it never cross your mind what that was like for me, your wife?' She forked the sausages onto a plate, slipped it beneath the dying grill. 'He's gone now and I don't want to know his business. But I do want to know what's happened to us.'

When he made to move towards her, she sidestepped him, turning at the kitchen door to finally meet his eyes. 'I'm calling Daniel down and I don't want him to know any of this. I don't know what kind of tangle you've gotten yourself into but you can't just bury what you know – from the guards, from that woman. Surely she deserves better than that. And surely Tom, after all these years, so do I.' She turned sharply from him, called up the stairs to the child.

Tom leaned back against the cabin now. Ella, Ella, Ella. God, the disappointment in her eyes when she'd looked at him this morning. She hadn't spoken another word to him at breakfast and who could blame her? What the hell kind of mess had he gotten himself into? And all for what? Sean Delaney. It was a terrible end for the young lad, but at least he'd have peace now – something that Sean hadn't had in years. He folded an arm across his chest, his fingers drumming his chin as he shook out the nets with the toe of his boot. Peace. What he wouldn't give for a bit of peace, to have all this stuff out of his head and gone. Gone! Ella was right. Of course she was right – the girl *should* know, she *should* be told. But how in the name of God was he going to go about it! How was he going to put her through all that for a second time? How was he going to look into that trusting face and tell her that all the time he had listened to the story of her loss he had known that Sean was alive and well and living in his very own house?

He rubbed a hand over his eyes. Sean was gone now. Definitely gone. It was over. Surely that should be an end to it. The guards were no fools. And there were plenty around here more than well able to talk. It would only be a matter of time before Sean was identified and then it would be the guards' job to tell Alison, not his. She need never know of his involvement – wasn't the end all that really mattered anyway? And if he apologised to Ella, did his best to make it up to her, surely the whole thing need never be raised again.

'Dad, are we goin' out?' Daniel raced down the quay and climbed the ladder down to the boat like a monkey. Ella turned without speaking and walked briskly towards home.

* * *

Leaning on the sink, Alison gazed out at a watery sun half-heartedly shining on the sea beyond. She arched her aching neck, tensed and released her shoulder muscles. She hadn't had more than a few hours' sleep since all this

Sean business had broken. And William ... the doctor had been again yesterday, adjusted his medication. It would be another twenty-four hours at least before he would feel the benefits – if there were any. All of this had been a terrible strain on him, he could well have done without it. Why couldn't Kathleen have waited to drop her bombshell until after he was ...? She tried to blank out the thought of his going, and yet she knew she must face it. Dr Clarke had hinted yesterday, as subtly as he could, that time was getting short and that she needed to prepare herself. He had gone to the trouble of arranging a home help to come in for a few hours each day to give her a break. She knew he was just looking out for her, probably saw the strain of all that was going on screaming out of her and put it down to the weight of caring for William. And while she really did appreciate his kindness, a part of her resented what she saw as yet another intrusion. She didn't want a break, she wanted to spend every last waking minute they had together. Waking minute. William slept so much these days, his body slowly accustoming itself to that final eternal sleep. But she had, at William's insistence, accepted the offer. She had to get on with life, he had reminded her, prepare for Hannah's return, visit with Maryanne, look to her own future.

She rubbed an index finger along her wet cheek. Please let him stay to meet Hannah, she prayed. She wanted Hannah to know him, to know his goodness, his wisdom, to know that there are such people in the world and never to settle for less. She wanted her girl to understand just how much she had loved him.

Alison spun around, jerked from her thoughts. She hadn't heard Joe come in through the back door and the sight of him filled her heart with pity. He stood in the open doorway, shoulders stooped forward, his face red and blotched by tears, his eyes wide with childlike sorrow, searching hers. She stepped towards him and folded him in her arms. 'Oh, it's all right, Joe, hush now, hush.' He clung to her, fresh sobs heaving his frame. Some stupid fool in the village must have taunted him, she guessed, remembering other times when he would come to Sean, convulsed by the sting of some idiot's tongue. 'Come on,' she took his hand and led him to a chair, 'sit here and I'll make us some tea. We'll have a chat, like the old days, yeah? And maybe later you could help me in the garden.'

They worked side by side in their own silent worlds, Alison only stopping to check on a sleeping William. Within half an hour they had dug a new patch of garden along the bottom of the stone ditch beyond the kitchen window. The smell and the feel of the fresh earth in her hands comforted Alison, its heavy warm texture seeming to soak the loneliness from her.

Just after midday she walked Joe to the mouth of the drive. 'Will you come another day, Joe, and we could sort out that shed? There are things of Sean's there that I know he'd like you to have.' She stood a moment watching him disappear down over the hill. Poor Joe. What or who, she wondered, had hurt him so deeply? He had hardly spoken a word to her as he bent over the spade in the garden, seeming almost to fold his sadness into the newly turned soil. But she knew that just as he had done with Sean, Joe would tell her what had happened in his own good time. The midday sun now warm on her shoulders, she turned to stroll back up the driveway. A half-smile played on her lips. Joe had come to her. After all the times she had railed against him, all the times she had lost her patience with him, putting her own frustrations above his pain, Joe had still trusted her enough to seek her safety. She knew he didn't trust lightly, knew he had learned long and hard not to. And she felt his trust strengthening her now, somehow easing the dread of what she knew lay ahead of her.

She stopped and leaned her arms on the weathered railing, gazed out over the sea. Coming back or not, she knew now that Sean no longer had a part in her life. If it were true, if he had been out there somewhere all this time – no matter what William said about him maybe thinking it was an act of kindness – to do what he had done to herself and Hannah, to walk away and leave them so broken, that she knew he could never repair. If only he had told her, if only he had come clean about the affair – she had loved him so much back then she knew she would have found a way of understanding, of forgiving. But not now. Not after all those years of so cruelly destroying her. Whatever love she had felt for him once was gone. And so was the woman he had left behind. And in an odd way she had something to thank him for. All the destruction Sean had left in his wake had eventually provided a clearing, a space where she could begin to grow again. All the pain she had experienced had been part of her transformation, part of her self-realisation. When she looked back now at the woman she had been in those years before his disappearance – how she had given away her power, her heart, her whole sense of herself to try to please someone else, to try to fix someone else's broken-ness – she could see the utter futility of it. It was a mistake she would never repeat. From here on, she would please herself, be true to herself, live for herself.

Since Kathleen had told her about that phone call, about Joe and the cap – since the seed had been planted that Sean might well be alive – she had felt something, slowly, ever so slowly, shift inside her.

Yes, what Kathleen had done was wrong. It was so wrong as to be almost unforgiveable. Almost. She tried again now to imagine what it must have been like for Kathleen: carrying her terrible secret, the weight of her guilt as she witnessed Alison's grief and all that time struggling to make a decent life for herself and Jamie – which, despite everything, she had managed single-handedly to do. Alison had always admired, even envied Kathleen for that. Envied her strength, her independence, her optimism, how she'd always manage to plough through whatever obstacle was put in her way, always clutching tight to the hope, to the knowledge that one day she would get where she wanted to be. And finally, with Rob, she had got there. Only to have it all tarnished again by the past. By Sean Delaney.

Sean Delaney: whether dead or alive, he had managed – was still managing – to control and manipulate their lives. She felt the hot burn of anger spread like a stain in the centre of her chest. Perhaps William had been right. Perhaps she had been directing all her anger and blame at Kathleen because, like William said, she was there, in flesh and blood, she was convenient. But maybe she was a convenient target in another way, too. Maybe, by blaming Kathleen, she didn't have to face up to the cold fact that Sean had betrayed her, had made a lie of their love, their lives together – the cold fact that he had left her by choice and not through some random, tragic accident.

She eased herself from the railing, continued her slow stroll up the driveway. With all that had been going on in the last few weeks she hadn't allowed herself – had perhaps been too angry to allow herself – to acknowledge how painfully she missed Kathleen: missed her friendship, her warmth, the support she had come to depend on so much. No matter what, Kathleen had always been there for her in every possible way. Without her friendship, Alison could never have survived those first raw months, those first years, after Sean. She saw that now – now that she was without her. Kathleen had been her lifeline. And surely that should counter her anger, her hurt – in at least some small way, in time? Sighing, she stepped up to the front door, reached for the handle.

Did she really want to end up – having come this far, this painfully – with a heart full of bitterness and resentment? Did she really want to allow Sean Delaney to continue to dictate her life? That's what it would amount to, she knew that. She had almost tasted freedom, had got within inches of knowing what it was like to be captain of her own life, and she wanted it. She would settle for nothing less. Holding onto anger and resentment would be like fastening a whole new set of chains around her heart and she wasn't going to allow that to happen. She was in control now and it was going to stay that way. It was her life, her call. She, not Kathleen or Sean or the past, would decide how her life would move from here on and learning to forgive, she knew, would be a first and vital step. Of course it wasn't going to happen overnight, she wasn't foolish enough to think that, she reminded herself, stepping back inside the hall door, but just deciding, just being willing to think about it, to consider it, was enough for now. The rest, she knew, would follow.

William lay in the same deep sleep, his body covered by a single white sheet. The hum of the electric fan at his feet sung to the silence that filled the room.

'I've started a new garden.' She sat beside him, took his hand and pressed it to her lips. 'Joe helped me. We're pals again,' she smiled, stroking her hand along the curve of his brow, his cheek, his chin. 'I had an email from Hannah. She's so excited about coming home. Hard to believe it's the same girl who couldn't wait to get out of the place a few months ago. I can't wait for you to meet her, Will. I know you two will get on.'

He lay there with no sign of hearing her, of being aware of her presence. She sat on for a long while in silence, just looking at him, watching the slight rise of the sheet over his chest with each shallow breath. 'But you don't have to hold on, Will. For me, for Hannah. Whenever you're ready, you just go.' She kissed his cheek. The words came, low and sad, pouring in a whisper from her lips – that beautiful song her father had so often sang to her as a child when she was afraid of the thunder or some dark presence she imagined loomed in the wardrobe or under the bed:

Angels are keeping you safe in your bed
White winged angels over your head…

The fading light through the window fell on her bowed head. Curled on the rocking chair beside the bed, her hand in his, Alison read to him from her book. When darkness fell, she placed lighted candles along the open-curtained windowsill. Through the night, chapter by chapter, she read to him from her pages.

'It's our story, William. A story of opening to love and to loss. To truth. But more than anything, Will, it's a story of love. True love. Love that doesn't end. Our love.'

She felt the gentle pressure of his hand squeezing hers and her tears began their slow, hot meander down her cheeks.

'I knew you'd like it,' she whispered, swallowing back

the lump of loss swelling in her throat. 'I love you, William Hayden. More than I ever knew I could love.'

His eyes flickered and were open, filled with an indescribable brightness and light. He looked at her, into her. A smile lit and lifted his whole face, washing away all the traces of pain and suffering, returning to her the William she had met that very first morning.

* * *

Although she had hardly slept and was just about falling on her feet, Alison had to get out. She needed to be alone. Away where she could close her eyes, listen to the silence and let reality settle into her. Susan, the home-help organised by Dr Clarke, was sitting with William. The woman had been a godsend, she knew now, holding the door open as the two dogs bounded into the back of the jeep, glad of some sign of normality.

The sun bouncing off the windscreen pained her eyes. This must be one of the brightest days of the whole summer, she smiled sadly to herself. It was as if the sky and the sun, the very heavens themselves, were putting on their best, preparing for William's arrival. She parked at the bottom of the track to Tra na Leon. She needed to walk, needed to feel the ground beneath her, let the salty breeze wash over her. Her feet felt heavy as she trudged the steep path. She stopped halfway and gazed out beyond the beach, out over the still water, its calmness entering her like a deep peace.

Life would go on. No matter how devastating the circumstances, life would always go on. That she had learned. And so too would William. She loved him so completely and he had returned that love. And that was life. That was the essence, not how long it lasted. In her heart William, their love, would live forever. And she could feel him now, all around her. Could see him in the kiss of the surf at the feet of the rocks below; in the deepest yellows of the wild gorse; his eyes smiling and winking in the myriad silver lights dancing the ocean's back.

* * *

'Damn,' Tom cursed, righting the gear stick and inching forward into the tight parking space. He still wasn't used to the rental the garage had loaned him while his insurance claim was being processed – and that didn't look like it was going to be any time soon. Still, at least he had something to get around in, he sighed, slipping off his seat belt. He clasped a hand to the back of his neck, stretched it backwards, the months of broken sleep beginning to tell on him.

He had decided to break the journey in Galway, stay there overnight. He was looking forward to the time alone, with no one asking questions about the break-in, the car, if there was any word from the guards. And then the few cute ones who casually dropped his ex-lodger and his whereabouts into the conversation. Oh, they knew the story all right, not much would pass them by.

He had told Ella he was going to Wexford to look at a boat, but she hadn't even made a reply, had barely looked in his direction when he'd left the house after breakfast. Never, through their seven years together, had there ever been as much as a hint of a secret between them and Tom felt a sharp stab of guilt each and every time he sidestepped her questions. Day after day the tension in the house had grown like a stone wall between them. Much as he'd wanted to, he hadn't been able to bring himself to tell her the full story about Sean, knowing too well that his part in it would change her love for him forever. He had told her that Sean was separated, that he had asked him to buy the fishing gear from his ex-wife on his behalf, tried to make it seem simple, straightforward. 'So he paid out good money for his own gear and then handed it over to you, for nothing?' The tone of Ella's voice had cut through him. Who did he think he was fooling? He was never any good at lies, never one for secrecy. She had asked him, calmly, to go to the guards, and for the first-ever time since they'd met he had raised his voice to her, told her to give him a bit of room to breathe. She had given him that, and more, and it was clear from her silence thereafter that Ella had had her fill of his secrecy, his moods. He knew it wouldn't take a whole lot more to break them.

Last night, in the small hours, he had finally made up his mind. He would travel down to see Alison and tell her the truth about Sean. The girl deserved to know the real story, the whole of it. It didn't matter what course she'd decide to take when she learned what Tom's role had been in the whole affair. What mattered was that she knew about Sean's genuine love and remorse. And his death. Whatever would follow would follow. Tom needed a peace restored to his life and he knew he could never have that until Alison was told the full story.

Nineteen

Kathleen waved the boys off, closed the front door and leaned back against it, her whole body joining in her smile. She pictured Rob's face again at the breakfast table, the way his jaw had literally dropped as if its hinge had suddenly snapped. No quick, silly quip, no stupid impersonation – her Rob stuck for words? It had to be a first.

'Dad?' Jamie had addressed him between spoonfuls of cereal, letting the word drop as naturally as if it had ripened for that very moment. 'Do you think we'd have room for a basketball net at the new house?'

Kathleen's hands had frozen in mid-air at the sink, her head turning as if in slow motion. Jamie hadn't even lifted his head, just filled his mouth and dug the spoon back into his bowl. 'If I want to make the school team next year,' he continued after he'd swallowed, 'I'll need to get in some practice.'

'Sure,' Rob nodded, recovering. 'Tell you what, why don't we head up there now, choose the right spot?'

'Cool,' a beaming Jamie had met Kathleen's eye.

She walked back into the kitchen now, her whole being

liberated, a feeling of absolute invincibility she had never experienced before coursing through her. This was her. This was her life, her family, and nothing could ever steal it from her. There were no secrets any more, no need to hide out, to prove herself. Rob knew everything, *everything*, about her and he loved her. He loved her for exactly who she was, nothing more, nothing less. If Sean Delaney were to appear in the kitchen before her right this minute, it wouldn't knock a whit out of her. All that was finished. Over. She didn't want or need him and she would have no problem in telling him exactly that. If he ever did return, if Alison were to decide that she wanted him back in her life, then good luck to her, but Sean would never again be a part of her life, or Jamie's. Jamie certainly didn't need him, she smiled, gathering her bag and her keys for work. He had the best father any child could wish for in Rob. Jamie was one lucky boy.

She stopped in front of the hall mirror to check her make-up. Even if she plastered it on with a trowel, she thought, it still wouldn't hide the evidence of the sleepless nights, the terrible angst of the past weeks. Alison's face popped into her head again now, as it did so often, day and night. That awful, wild desperation in her eyes the night she had called, soaked through, to the door. How was she doing now? And William? She hadn't heard a word since but she knew Susan Murphy was going up there, helping out. Alison had made it crystal clear that she wanted nothing more to do with her and as long as she felt like that there was no point in her trying to shift things, it would only make Alison more entrenched. She could only put her faith in time. If and whenever Alison was ready to talk, she would more than gladly welcome her with open arms. And Hannah. Her heart tightened. Hannah was due home and Jamie did nothing but talk about seeing her, even suggesting they should go to the airport with Alison to meet her. Poor Jamie. If only he knew. And one day, she hoped, he would. One day Jamie and Hannah could be what they really were to one another, brother and sister. No sins of the past should be allowed to carry on and destroy the next generation. Alison would see that in time, she knew she would. And they would find a way, all of them, she knew that too, deep inside her. Hadn't finding Rob proved that life always had a way of working out? She leaned in closer to the mirror. Yes, she did look tired. Tired but happy, she nodded. All she could do now was keep trusting, keep positive and be grateful for every day that she woke with that wonderful, indescribable feeling that loving, being loved, by another wraps you in.

She locked the front door and stepped down into the bright morning sunshine. She had started walking the fifteen minutes to and from work as part of her trimming and toning regime for her big day and now she couldn't imagine starting the day any other way. The fresh air, the time alone, the very act of walking cleared her head and left her energised and positive and ready to tackle the day.

Alison would no doubt be in at some point during the day to see Maryanne, she thought, turning in the direction of the town. Poor old Maryanne, she'd gone even further into herself, it seemed, this past week, had even begun refusing her meals in the last few days, and coaxing only seemed to make her more determined not to touch a bite. Kathleen didn't want to agree with Nurse Hassett's opinion that Maryanne was giving up completely, was wanting to be gone; her theory was that withdrawing from food was withdrawing from the last and only social activity that

Maryanne took part in. Pure nonsense! Kathleen spat now in defiance. Maryanne probably just had a bit of a bug, was maybe feeling a little bit down in herself. She must remember to remind her again today – several times – that tonight Hannah would be back home with them. Wouldn't that raise anyone's spirits? She veered off the main road and began the short hill climb to the home. Maybe Alison had already visited. Part of her secretly hoped so, she hated that awful awkwardness between them now, the turning of heads, the frantic digging in handbags. Still, what could she do? Nothing. She was the villain.

Well, maybe not nothing, she thought, nodding her head in decision. From today, she could stop turning her head in shame, stop ducking into corridors and rooms every time she saw Alison approach. From today, she would stand her ground, act normally and leave Alison in no doubt that she was there and willing to talk whenever and no matter how long it took.

* * *

Hannah zipped up the second, smaller suitcase and stood it beside the empty wardrobe. All that was left to do was to pack her in-flight bag and she was ready to go. She was so thrilled that Claire was travelling with her, it would make leaving so much easier and she could just picture Mum's face when Claire stepped through the Arrivals gate with her – it was by far the coolest present she could bring home to her. Home! Hannah could almost feel the salt water tighten her face, feel the pull and yield of the waves under her surf board. She could hardly wait!

She checked her watch: 8.15 a.m. Harry would be here in less than an hour. He was taking her back to the London Eye for one last outing together. Butterflies stirred in her stomach. She would miss Harry most of all. Miss the way she could talk to him just like to one of her girlfriends. Miss the way he was always interested in what she had to say, what she thought about things, as if she were special, different – but in a good way.

There were no boys like Harry back home, just idiots like Peter O'Neill who were only interested in themselves and how far they could get with you. Harry wasn't like that – but oh my could he kiss, slow and gentle, like your lips were covered in his favourite chocolate. Claire said he was well brought up. A real gentleman, she said, and the only kind of boy that Hannah should consider good enough for her.

She fingered the soft cotton of the dress spread out on the bed. She hoped Harry would like it. Claire had helped her to pick it out, but she had paid for the whole outfit herself – even the shoes – although Claire had tried to insist. Mum would be proud of her, she smiled. It had felt so good handing over her own money, money she had earned. It made her feel proud, less like a kid. It was a feeling she wanted to hold on to and the first thing she would do when she got home was to find herself a part-time job before the savings she had made from working at Claire's gallery ran out.

Well, not the very first thing, she smiled, gathering her towels and padding across the hall to the bathroom. The first thing she had to do was to convince Mum to allow Harry to come for a visit during his mid-term from college. Herself and Harry had already planned it all out and Harry said, that way, today wouldn't really be a goodbye. Still, that didn't stop her missing him already, even before she had left.

How had Mum coped after Dad, she wondered again now, turning on the shower and stepping out of her bathrobe. No matter how much she thought about it she just couldn't imagine what it had been like for her. To know that you were never, ever going to see the person you loved again. She could never cope with that. During her first few weeks in London she had missed Mum more than she ever thought possible and she had worried about her back home on her own. Grandad had said at the time that there weren't many people as strong as Mum and she could see now what he had meant.

She stepped under the jet of water. She couldn't really imagine Mum with a boyfriend. How had that happened? When Aoife told her first she'd thought it was gross – a boyfriend at Mum's age? But then, as Claire had pointed out, she was older than Mum and Hannah found nothing gross about her dating. Even Grandad had 'a companion', as he liked to call her. And Mum deserved a bit of happiness, just like everyone else. Plus, Hannah smiled to herself, tilting her head back under the hot stream, Mum having someone of her own would definitely work in Hannah's favour when it came to persuading her to let Harry visit.

* * *

Although Hannah's flight wasn't due in until nine that night, a girlish giddiness had driven Alison from her bed before seven that morning to hang the banners and balloons for her daughter's homecoming. She had helped William to take what little breakfast his diminished appetite would allow and when a deep sleep had stolen him from her again she had walked the dogs and completed her shopping before midday, allowing an hour for an afternoon visit with Maryanne. But almost two hours later she found herself still at her side. Maryanne had refused to leave her bed today and there seemed such an unbearable sadness in her lost eyes that Alison couldn't find it in herself to leave before she had spoken to the doctor and tried to figure out what was troubling her.

As Maryanne dosed in and out of sleep, Alison's mind wandered again to William, remembering Barry O'Driscoll's reaction three days ago when she had dropped the sketches William had given her into his shop in Cuan Roan to have them framed. Remarking on their ethereal, other-worldly quality, he had studied them closely, all the time trying to fathom why they seemed so familiar to him. His wife, Addy, had joined him behind the counter, her eyes agog as she detailed the similarity in style to the two treasured sketches she had inherited from her father, sketches by an R. W. Hayden, a young Dublin artist that she remembered her father being so taken by when she was a teenager. Addy had almost collapsed with excitement when Alison's finger had pointed to William's signature. Never mentioning that William was actually living at her house, they had arranged to meet again next week when Alison would collect her framed sketches and have an opportunity to see William's earlier work.

Then that telephone call yesterday from Nigel Collins, William's solicitor. It was typical of William not to have told her himself. Typical of his endearing humility and grace that he would not want to be seen as a benefactor and yet would want her to know, before he was gone, that she would at least be financially secure and not have that worry. The generous lump sum that he was leaving her was shock enough, but the solicitor had been more ebullient about the back catalogue of work – valuable work, he had called it – that William had bequeathed her. And that was why she had spent the previous night and the whole of that morning trying frantically to contact Claire.

'Ah yes, R.W. or William Hayden – disappeared off the face of the planet more than thirty years ago.' Claire had known immediately who Alison was talking about.

'After his fiancée left him?' Alison had nodded, pressing her lips together.

'The ghostly Helene,' Claire sighed. 'The bulk of his first – and last, as it happened – exhibition were studies of her. The whole lot sold out in just two days. She took a great talent with her when she decided to walk, but you know that yourself, you've obviously read up on— '

'No,' Alison shook her head.

'No? Then how do you— '

'He told me.' And Alison recounted the whole story to silence at the other end of the phone.

An hour later, Claire called back and, without preamble, launched straight in: 'Robert William Hayden, born Dublin, Ireland, 10th April 1955. Studied architecture at University College Dublin before moving to Paris in 1976 where— '

'He taught English while studying art at night. That's him,' Alison smiled through her tears.

'And he? You? You mean … oh my God!' Alison held the receiver away from her ear, Claire's excited shriek filling the whole room. 'Alison, do you realise what those sketches are worth?'

'They're priceless to me, Claire. I'll never part with them.'

'But you can't just sit on them, Alison, you don't realise— '

'I would be willing to lend them out – to a certain trusted gallery owner?' Alison realised their worth only too well. When she'd been unable to reach Claire she had scanned the internet in open-mouthed disbelief.

'Oh, Alison! You can't imagine – oh my God, what a coup! This is going to fix me on the map – dead centre! Oh Alison, how can I ever thank you…'

'No, Claire, I want to thank you. Without your help, without you caring for Hannah, this summer would never have happened for me. God knows what state we'd be in by now. This is just your own generosity looping back on you.' Alison's heart swelled. At last she was able to give something back, something worthwhile, and in Alison's experience there was no better feeling. And she could truly understand now that all Claire had done, all she had given them over the years, hadn't been charity. It had all been given in the spirit of generosity, of love. To Alison, William had been the embodiment of that very spirit and she would do her best to ensure that, after he was gone, through his work, William's spirit, his enormous talent, would continue to be felt and appreciated in the world.

'Alison?' The staff nurse smiled at her from the door. Alison rose from her chair beside the bed, walked towards her.

'I'm afraid the doctor's out on a house call, it'll be at least another hour before he'll get to see you.'

Alison checked her watch. Almost two thirty. She would have to leave for the airport at seven at the very latest. She still had to shower and change and grab something to eat and she wanted to be able to spend as much time as possible with William. Late evening was his best time now, when he was most alert, and she didn't want to waste a precious second of the time they had left together.

'I can't really wait around any longer.' She didn't want to have to leave William again before the airport trip. There was something about him at breakfast this morning, something in his eyes – she couldn't describe it, but it was as if some knowing inside her felt him being pulled farther away from her. 'Could I maybe just call, have a chat with him on the phone?'

'You could try, but there's no guaranteeing when he'll be in his office – there'll be his rounds and … if you were here, you'd definitely get to have a word.'

'Right. Okay, I'll need to get home to William – and Hannah's coming tonight.' She drummed her lips with her fingers. 'If I say I'll be back at four?' Surely fifteen minutes would be enough to spend with the doctor, then she'd only be away from William for about half an hour, she reckoned.

'Perfect, he'll be here till at least five and he knows you're anxious to see him, so take your time.' Her smile was almost too kind, as she squeezed Alison's upper arm. 'We'll try Maryanne with a little dinner in the meantime.'

'Thanks,' Alison smiled, backing away towards the bed, the warning burn of tears for some reason stinging the back of her eyes. 'I'll head off, promise me you'll try to eat some dinner.' She kissed Maryanne on the forehead, collected her bag from the chair. 'I'll see you again in a little while.'

* * *

Unable to sleep, Tom had left the hotel early to continue his journey south. His heart felt even heavier this morning, the battling voices in his head refusing to be stilled. Was he making the right decision? His head assured him that confessing to Alison was the only and honest thing to do. But his heart refused to be persuaded. Was he telling Alison for her own good, or was he just using the girl to quiet his own conscience? What had she to gain from learning that Sean had been alive these past three years? Surely telling her only amounted to taking Sean from her for a second time. He pictured her smile, her enthusiasm about the house, about her daughter returning; the way she had skipped down the drive to meet that man, leaned her head in towards his shoulder. The same way Ella had once leaned into him: trusting him, loving him, filling him with a warmth and comfort, with that deep stillness that comes only from being truly accepted, truly understood. With more than half of his journey south behind him, Tom felt the binds of indecision begin to loosen and fall away from his chest, his whole body suffused with an urgent longing to be back in the shelter of Ella's trust. Only by sharing his story with Ella, with the guards, with Alison, only by speaking out the guilt, the gnawing culpability that plagued him, would he finally be able to find the peace he had been chasing, finally find his own truth.

Alison's truth, she believed, was that her husband had been lost at sea. Three whole years she had struggled to make that truth a part of her. When Tom had lowered that knapsack to the ocean's depths, he had denied her the right to her whole truth, denied her the right to know, to heal, to get on with her life. It was high time that was given back to her. And this time she would be left with no uncertainties, no doubts. Sean's body was lying in a morgue waiting to be claimed and the only thing that stood between that man and a decent burial, the only obstacle to Alison finally being able to lay her husband and her past to rest, was him. He would go directly to the guards, face whatever consequences were to come and confess the one thing that could set him free to return to his life and to Ella: the truth. He sighed out his relief as he circled the roundabout, pointed the car north.

* * *

'Thank you, Doctor.' Stepping out into the corridor, Alison closed the office door behind her and sneaked a look at her watch. It was just after 5 p.m. Still gripping the door handle, she closed her eyes to steady herself. Her head felt light, almost dizzy, her stomach angry and gnawing. No wonder, she hadn't had a chance to eat since her hurried breakfast at seven. William's colour had really worried her when she got home to him earlier and, although he had rallied and tried his best to join in her excitement about Hannah's arrival, the weariness in his eyes, in his whole face, had given him away. He was sleeping heavily again before she left, but she was conscious of every moment she was away from him. She thanked her lucky stars again for Susan, for William's insistence that she accept the offer of home help – where would she have been without her?

When she'd returned to the home at four, she'd had to wait a further thirty long toe-tapping minutes before the doctor was able to see her, and after all that she was really none the wiser. Maryanne's condition hadn't altered 'medically', he'd assured her, and when Alison raised her concerns about Maryanne not eating, about how removed she seemed, his only response was, 'Well, I'm afraid we

369

can't force her. We can only continue to tempt her …
little portions, see how she responds.' And he had left it
there, hanging, his eyebrows raised above his glasses as
he glanced from the file on his desk to Alison, as if questioning her, as if challenging her to … to what? She didn't
know. And what more did he know – or care, for that
matter, she cursed to herself, digging in her shoulder bag
for her car keys, her hurried footsteps echoing along the
empty corridor.

'Shit!' The word came out louder than she had meant it
to, as the strap of her bag snapped, its contents spilling and
clattering to the polished floor. 'Shit! Shit! Shit!' she hissed
through clenched teeth, her frustration boiling as she
squatted to the floor, her hands reaching in what seemed
ten different directions at once to stem the roll of lipstick,
loose coins, William's tablets she had collected earlier from
the chemist and all the other useless paraphernalia she
burdened her shoulder with each day.

'Alison?' The soft voice had the effect of almost turning
her to stone. Her hands hovered a moment in mid-air
before – refusing to lift her head in reply – she returned to
refilling her bag.

'Let me help you with …' The creak of a knee as Kathleen
squatted down beside her.

'I'm fine,' Alison barked. She could feel the heat of Kathleen's body beside her, that so familiar fresh-washed smell
of her uniform somehow managing to enter her, squeeze
her heart.

'I know, but just …' Both their hands reached for the car
keys at the same time, Alison snatching hers away as if it had
been scalded before turning her eyes to meet Kathleen's.

'I said I'm *fine*, okay?' Her eyes burned into Kathleen's,

their deep green an ocean of tears she was trying to keep in check.

'Maryanne took a small bit of chicken and veg at dinner,' Kathleen risked, holding her ground. 'I think it's the thought of Hannah coming that…oh Alison…'

Alison turned her head, tried desperately to turn her whole attention to gathering up the contents of her bag, unable any longer to hold the tears that coursed her cheeks now. The warm grip of Kathleen's hand on her shoulder caused her whole upper body to shake as she hunkered back, covering her face with her hands.

'Aw, don't worry about Maryanne, she'll be fine, honestly. She's just got a bit down in herself, that's all. Come on now, you should be concentrating on Hannah and— '

'It's not Maryanne, it's … ' Her words caught on her breath. She drew her fingers down and across her cheeks, under her nose.

'William?' Kathleen pressed a tissue into her hand. Eyes closed, Alison nodded, scrunching the tissue tight in her fist.

'Not good?' Kathleen encouraged, her hand moving again to Alison's shoulder.

'This afternoon…there was something about…a change, I can't explain … ' She opened her eyes, arched back her neck and swallowed against her tears. 'Susan says she'll sit with him while I go to the airport but…'

'But you don't want to leave him?'

'No, but Hannah…I can't not be there.'

'I could always— '

'No!' The word was as sharp as a blade, slicing them apart. Alison pulled away, gathered her bag and made to stand.

'Alison, please!' Kathleen rose with her, held out the

comb and the hair slide, the little blue pocket diary she had gathered from the floor. 'I'm not asking for friendship. Please, just let me do this one thing for you, for William.'

Her lips clamped and her head held high, Alison straightened her back, shook back her hair and made towards the door. Sean in *her* bed, a voice in her head reminded her. Sean entering her, getting her pregnant when he had feigned sleep in his own bed at home so often when she tried to get close to him.

'It's a long drive to Cork – and your mind won't be on the road,' Kathleen persisted, coming up behind her. 'I'm finished here in another half an hour, I could be on the road by six.'

Alison stopped, bowed her head, resting her chin on her clenched right hand. Every last piece of her strained to be with William, needed to be with him, knew she *should* be with him. Much as she had fought against it, the stark reality was there, written so plainly on the lifeless grey of his face, the leaving in his eyes.

'Hannah wouldn't know what to think,' Kathleen started, braver now, standing before her, searching out her eyes, 'if you met her at the airport in that state! She might think you didn't want her home at all. Come on, let me collect her. Let me do this one thing. You get yourself a rest, spend some time with William – you'll be in much better form for her then, when I drop her off.'

'But she would think I was … I couldn't not be there for her again.'

'Again? And when haven't you been there for her? For Hannah, for Maryanne. Come on, Alison – you've given them your life! Time to cut yourself a bit of slack.'

Alison shook her head, checked her watch. Almost five fifteen.

'No point in wasting time standing here,' Kathleen urged. 'I'll tell Hannah that Maryanne's been poorly with a bug and you had to stay with her. She'll understand.'

Alison relaxed her shoulders, let out the sigh that seemed to have been holding them there, tight. Would Hannah really care if her mother wasn't the first face she saw when she came through Arrivals? Her heart would probably burst with joy at the sight of Kathleen ... and maybe it would be good for Hannah to spend a few hours with Kathleen, to remind her of how close they'd been, how good Kathleen had always been to her, maybe it would help to cushion the blow when she learned the truth about Jamie, about her – their – dad. Hannah would still be home to her before midnight – and this way she'd be rested and less stressed herself. Better able to show Hannah the strong, in-control mother she had promised herself she would be, that she could be. That she was. 'Well, I suppose ...'

'Go on,' Kathleen placed an encouraging hand to the small of her back, 'get yourself home. I'll finish up here, get ready for the road.' The tight bud of hope in Kathleen's chest unfurled a little, feathering her with its warmth. 'What time's the flight due in?'

'Nine. I'll text you the flight number.' Alison moved towards the door, then turning: 'It would be a real treat for Hannah if Jamie went along.'

A wave of hot pleasure gathered and broke around Kathleen's heart. 'The hounds of hell wouldn't keep him away,' she beamed.

'Thanks,' Alison half-smiled, bending her head towards the door.

Arriving back home within minutes, she thanked Susan, threw the post onto the hall table and skipped straight to the

373

bedroom. William lay in a deep sleep. She wouldn't disturb him. She would shower first and then make something for them both to eat. She kissed him softly on the lips, slipped silently from the room.

* * *

The sweet, subtle smell of her called him back – that heady redolence of warm, freshly rained-upon earth that she always seemed to carry about her. He opened his eyes slowly against the evening sun, the soft hum of the shower drifting to his ears. She was home. And she had been to him. He touched a finger to his lips, could still almost taste her there, the soft warmth of her, the promise.

'Alison,' he mouthed her name, conjuring her image: the flaming coils of red hair loose around her girlish face, picking out the fire, the light in her eyes; that little dotted pathway of freckles across her nose, her cheeks; the full, ripe lips that seemed always to mould and cling to the pressure of his kiss; the white delicacy of her exposed neck; her body, long and lean, the outward span of her hips, taut, lustful; the pressure of her naked breasts against his chest, skin soft as the softest velvet; the warm, dark comfort of her secret places. His whole body ached for her – her beauty, her comfort, her love.

He imagined her smile now, the shyness of it when they'd first met, how she had seemed almost embarrassed to share it; and then, in these last months, her wild abandon as she threw back her head, lost herself to laughter. The sorrow in her; the joy. All those contradictions: the young girl, the mother; the loner, the confidante; the fear in her, the utter determination;

her vulnerability and her steely strength; the fierce pride and almost crippling insecurity. All those tiny things that made up the whole, the individual, the spirit – the woman that summer had seen emerge. Emerge and redeem him.

Eyes wide, he fixed on her now, his laboured breath whispering her name as he fought to chase the darkness, the emptiness, everything in him straining towards her, willing her to come to him, to lie beside him, to hold his hand. To release him.

* * *

Alison straightened the neck of her new shirt, smoothed its ruffled hem at her hips. She towelled and spritzed her hair and stood back from the mirror, head held to one side as she turned from left to right, appraising her reflection. She wanted to look good for Hannah, wanted to look as young and alive and full of optimism as she felt deep inside.

She grabbed her post from the hall table and, crossing to the kitchen, flicked on the cooker switch and ran her thumb under the seal of the brown envelope. The solicitor's compliment slip was paper-clipped to the document detailing William's catalogue of work. She folded the pages neatly back into the envelope. She didn't want to even think about it for now. She would put it away safely until…

She closed her eyes for a moment, took a deep breath. No more tears today, she instructed, reaching for the second envelope. Her heart skipped, recognising her own handwriting on its face. Could it be? She took another deep breath, held it, her hands trembling as they tore at the envelope.

She bit down on her lip in utter disbelief, her heart racing, her eyes wide, flying back and forth across the page. She read it through a second, a third time in case she had got it wrong. But the wording was short and to the point. They had enjoyed the chapters she had submitted and would be interested in reading the remainder of the manuscript with a view to offering her a contract. What? A contract? An actual contract for her manuscript – for her and William's story?

'Okay, steady,' she instructed aloud. It was nothing definite. Not yet. But a *real* publisher had read her first three chapters and wanted to see more. Alison let out a loud, 'Yes!' She clutched the letter to her breast, a rich warmth coursing her veins. This was it! She could feel it. She gazed out the window, cupped a hand over her wide smile. A triumphant sun burst through the bank of cloud, silvering the sea with its dazzling brilliance. From its perch high in the whitethorn tree, a lone blackbird nodded towards her.

This was her new beginning.

'William! William!' Her heart full to bursting, she raced down the hall.